ʜUNGER . . .

"I am glad she is in the cage," Katherine said. She admired Stephen's fearlessness. These wolves were his kindred spirits: comfortable in solitude, sleekly beautiful, with a potentially dangerous side.

"Come hither," Stephen coaxed, offering her a slice of meat. "Feed Vixen and you will have a friend for life."

Katherine knelt by the side of the cage. Stephen crouched beside her . . . As Stephen had promised, Vixen was soon licking her fingers through the square slats.

"It seems so unfair that she is caged," Katherine said softly.

"A moment ago you were grateful for it."

"That is because she was unknown to me. Now she is not. Europa says they mate for life. All of God's creatures that know such loyalty should be free as the wind."

Still kneeling, Stephen reached out and stroked Katherine's cheek. She shut her eyes, and a burst of light, like a shooting star, filled the darkness that ensued. In her mind's eye she kissed his chafed lips, inhaled the musky scent of leather that clung to him. And when her arms coiled around his well-muscled shoulders, she surrendered to his arms like a lamb curled against the chest of a lion . . .

LADY AND THE WOLF

JULIE BEARD

DIAMOND BOOKS, NEW YORK

This book is a Diamond original edition,
and has never been previously published.

LADY AND THE WOLF

A Diamond Book / published by arrangement with
the author

PRINTING HISTORY
Diamond edition / July 1994

ISBN: 0-7865-0015-8

Diamond Books are published by The Berkley Publishing Group,
200 Madison Avenue, New York, NY 10016.
DIAMOND and the "D" design
are trademarks belonging to Charter Communications, Inc.

PRINTED IN THE UNITED STATES OF AMERICA

10 9 8 7 6 5 4 3 2 1

To my husband, Dale,
and Audrey Kraft Limber,
for never doubting I could do it

ACKNOWLEDGMENTS

Special thanks to Elsa Cook, whose skillful critiques added so much to this story.

Much gratitude to my editors, Hillary Cige and Beth DiPentima, and to my agent, Evan Fogelman, whose support and encouragement helped make a dream come true.

Thanks to my parents for their generosity and for sharing their love of the written word.

Love and thanks to all the special women who have supported me along the way, particularly Carm Utz and the St. Louis chapter of RWA, and my dear friends in the Chicago North RWA critique group.

LADY AND THE WOLF

PROLOGUE

✠

England, 1349

Katherine bolted up the winding stairwell of Shelby Manor two steps at a time. She would not cry. There were no more tears to shed. How could she grieve for half her father's household? Nay, half the world.

Georgie groaned from his chamber. At the heartrending sound, Katherine stumbled and spilled some of the potion steaming from the silver tankard she clutched in one hand. The hot liquid burned her pale fingers, but she barely blinked. The pain was nothing compared to what her brother endured.

After regaining her balance, she brushed away a damp tendril of red-gold hair from her forehead and raced on to his chamber. Her brother's page sat at the far end of the hall in wide-eyed terror, squatting against the wall.

He looked up at her and then averted his eyes in shame. "Forgive me, milady. I cannot go to him. I fear for my life."

"Georgie would understand." She smiled with compassion. "He loves you, Jeremy. He does not want you to die in his service."

The boy's shoulders relaxed, and he managed to meet her gaze with a nod.

Katherine understood his fear, the same fear that kept her parents from Georgie's chamber. The Pestilence felled victims so quickly, so agonizingly that it sundered the bonds between pages and knights, parents and children.

But not even the threat of death will allow me to desert Georgie, Katherine thought, wiping the tears before they could fall from her eyes. He had been her North Star, her champion, and her mentor. One look from his golden eyes told her all she needed to know: that her world was intact, orderly, and filled with infinite love. Every girl should have such a guardian angel.

Knowing that bright nova would soon shoot across the heavens and disappear, Katherine took a deep breath and threw open the oak door. Six white tapers flickered in the rush of air, the only movement in the still, darkened room. The stench of imminent death hit Katherine fully, like a blast from Hell. Hot. Smothering. Through a closed window, the setting sun cast a single beam of light on the stone slab floor at the end of Georgie's bed. The golden shaft illuminated her brother's coiled form, swathed in linens. She placed the steaming goblet on the ledge and then threw open the window, gasping for air. In the distance, funeral pyres lit the sky. The dead fueled the flames; there were too many to bury.

S'Blood! she thought. *This is real. Georgie, dear, beloved Georgie is dying!* She turned back to examine what now seemed more like a torture chamber than sleeping quarters. Georgie's soft down bed might as well have been a rack stretching his body to the breaking point. Gasping for another breath, she turned to find him staring at her. His eyes were yellow with fever, his lips an unnatural white. His lithe body, once as beautiful as some mythical god, now curled with pain.

"Do not let them burn me when I die," he whispered. "I dream at night that I hear the dead screaming from the flames. Do not let them burn me, Kate."

"Never," she whispered savagely and started forward.

"Do not come near me!" he shouted, and doubled over in pain.

Katherine's leather-bound feet shuffled over cool, flat stones. Ignoring the pounding of her heart, which deafened all other sound, she reached forward and pulled back the blanket that hid Georgie's illness. Only then did she see the evidence that condemned her brother to death—black circles painted his flesh, the mark of the Black Death.

"Dear God, Georgie, you have the Pestilence." Her words gurgled hoarsely over trembling lips. " 'Tis the Death. Don't turn me away now. I will not let you die alone."

Georgie's face compressed in sorrow, and tears fell down his temples. His mouth twisted with unuttered words. He did not have to speak. She knew what he was thinking. He was ashamed, embarrassed by this weakness, by his own mortality. And that, more than his physical pain, drove her mad with the urge to console him. What could she say to ease the humiliation that this wretched death wrought? It left him no dignity, no easy parting from this scathing world. She knelt at his side.

Georgie reached for her hand without looking at her. When he found it, he pressed her palm to his chest like a precious jewel. "You shouldn't have come, Kate, but I thank God you did," he said in a wheezing voice. "I thank God you did."

With cool, delicate fingers she stroked his feverish brow.

"Only you had the courage to come, Kate."

She squeezed his hand. "Without you this life is not worth the living. The Death can take me as well."

"Do not speak so. I will die, but you must live."

Katherine took in a deep breath and closed her eyes, leaning her head back. Did she even want to survive this scourge, already a year old? She feared it would go on forever. Survivors could only anticipate when their time would come. If she knew what caused the Death, how it spread, then she could save herself. But no one knew. Some said it passed through the eyes, but she did not believe it. Katherine had been eye to eye with many who had later succumbed, and still she lived. Others said it passed through the breath. She exhaled and blinked at the dust floating in the fading beam of light. No cause, no cure—only violent deaths. In a year, it had already killed off nearly a third of their world. *The dead are the lucky ones,* she thought.

Katherine retrieved a bowl of water from the washstand. She moistened a cloth and stroked Georgie's hot forehead. He was not only her brother, but her best friend, and comfort was familiar between them. He was twenty-one, her senior by three years, but no wiser, they both knew, and certainly she was the stronger of the two.

The girl with spun-gold hair went to the window ledge and retrieved her tankard. Like a good witch with promises of magic, she brought her potion to Georgie. "This is from the crone in the village, brother. Please drink it. Ignore the wretched smell. She says she's cured a dozen people with it."

Georgie waved her off. "No, sister, your concoctions will not work. But there is something you can do for me."

Katherine put down the tankard without argument. "What is it? I'll do anything you ask."

He licked perspiration from his upper lip and tried to lift himself up on his elbows.

"Pray for me, Kate," he said at last, with fervency. "If you pray for me, I know I will go to Heaven. If you do not, I fear I will burn in Hell."

"Nay, you could never—"

Georgie raised a shaking hand to silence her. Like a mad prophet, he whispered his next words with a faraway look. "I have dreamt terrible visions of fire. Only you can send my soul to Heaven. Do not ask me how I know, but it is true. Only you . . . only the pure at heart can appease the rage of God. If you survive this deadly plague, go to a convent and pray for me, pray for the world."

"A convent," Kate whispered. She tried to imagine the beauty of ripe orchards enclosed within the stone walls of some ancient sisterhood, nuns praying serenely, noble women reading of ancient civilizations, free to study in the confines of their cloistered world. She wondered if such holy places still existed in this chaotic world. What did it matter? Her fate was not her own to decide.

"Father will not hear of it, Georgie. He has other plans. He wants me to marry."

"To hell with Father!" Georgie's face grimaced as a spasm of pain jolted through his body; Katherine held his hand until the worst passed, but he never fully recovered, and the light in his golden eyes began to fade.

Gasping for air, he continued. "Father . . . Father wants you to marry the richest . . . anyone with power to . . . to keep other barons . . . off our land. Too few vassals . . . fend them off." He blinked and swallowed hard. "Blackmoor . . ."

Katherine waited for him to continue. She had heard Georgie curse Blackmoor before and waited for the oaths now.

"Father would betroth you to Blackmoor's son . . . if, if he could. Don't do it. He is . . . is rotten to the soul. He is a murderer with no regard for . . . for chivalry."

"Hush, Georgie, it does not matter now."

"Nay, hear me, Kate." He smiled a desperate, sweet smile. "You are too good for some beast to . . . to mount you in the night and lord . . . over . . . your lands by day."

His words conjured a chilling image, and Katherine listened soberly.

"Go to a convent. The fate of my soul depends on it."

They were silent for a moment. The sun had set. Only the tapers illuminated the chamber with pulsing light; their wax fell like teardrops, and Georgie began to weep. Tears washed over his quivering lips. "I am afraid, Kate. Pray for me. Please pray for my soul."

"Oh yes, dear brother, I will," she whispered, her voice mellowed by deep love. Katherine gently wrapped her arms around him and lowered her head to his chest, weeping. Her tangled hair fell down around him like a shroud. Georgie had always been the one who promised to protect her from the world's sorrow, but now that sorrow welled in her throat like bile and choked her.

When their tears were spent, he said, "Then you will pray for me?"

"Aye, brother!" Words whispered emphatically. Resolve burned like embers in her eyes. "I swear it on the blood of the Christ. I will get you to Heaven."

Georgie sighed his relief and sank deeper onto damp linens. But then his head snapped in her direction, his eyes bulging. "Kate?"

"Shhh, Georgie," she pleaded. "Say a prayer. We must begin to pray for your soul."

Georgie did not hear her. He fell into a fever. "A convent, Kate!" he later cried out. They were his last words. The fever gripped him through the night. He moaned intermittently in his unconscious state. Katherine uttered her prayers even before his soul had passed over, and so the litany began. Her life's devotion. Recognizing the importance of her promise, she realized she could not let her father marry her to anyone. The aching loneliness inside, her natural passion and love, would find no relief. Somehow she would have to convince the baron to send her to a convent. She would be the bride of Christ. It had to be. For Georgie's sake.

The next morning Georgie died. Katherine dragged his body from the manor into the field, where she placed him in a shallow grave. Her face, swollen and red from crying, showed no expression. Numb grief was her mask. Having fashioned a crucifix with two branches, she pushed it into the soft, black earth and prayed for Georgie's soul.

CHAPTER ONE

✠

In the winter of 1350, snow fell on Yorkshire like the final, cruel blow of a broadsword. And no one felt it more keenly than Katherine. Rolling fields covered in white surrounded Shelby Manor, enforcing an involuntary solitude not unlike that of the Pestilence, which had come to an apparent end. It had been a year since Katherine buried Georgie.

Daily she recovered from her loss, a transformation reflected in her looking glass—green eyes once dulled with grief again glistened with hope; golden brows once knitted in sorrow now softened with acceptance. The Great Mortality had left its permanent mark, though. She was much the wiser, and that wisdom added compelling depth to her heart-shaped face. Rage against fate gave the once tame Katherine, with her burnished gold hair, the air of a lioness, a wild creature who had yet to learn the magnitude of her own power.

Throughout the period of mourning that followed Georgie's death, Katherine had begged her father to send her to a convent. But in the end, Lord Gilbert had done as Georgie had predicted—he promised his daughter to Stephen Bartingham, the Earl of Blackmoor's second son. In return, the earl promised to protect Gilbert's lands which were threatened by a neighboring baron. Despite protestations of the most profound and stubborn nature, Katherine knew she had no choice but to do as her father bid. Praying all the while for reprieve, she set off in late March to fulfill her odious duty under the watch of Sir Harold, a drunken sot much loved and trusted by the baron.

During the journey, Katherine was humbled by her ignorance of the world outside her father's barony. She knew that even King Edward had lost a child to the Death; bowing to the calamity, Edward, the paragon of chivalry, signed a treaty with France during the Pestilence's reign of terror, forestalling the Plantagenet claim to France. But she had not known how efficiently the disease had combed through the entire country, leaving survivors reckless and uncaring about the future.

Katherine and her escorts rode through one abandoned village after another, overwhelmed by the devastation. In surrounding fields, lonely crows guarded frozen fields of rotten crops. Skeletons of cattle too numerous to feed a shrunken world lay scattered like the runes of wise women, thrown haphazardly, portents of a bleak future.

"Such desolation, Sir Harold. It brings a terrible chill to my blood."

Her escort reined in beside her. " 'Tis a sorry sight, indeed."

Reaching for comfort, Katherine pulled out her rosary while Sir Harold consoled himself with another wineskin pulled from a seemingly endless hoard packed in his saddle pouches.

Swinging his head back, he took a gulp, swallowed, and belched. Katherine feared that if they were attacked along the way, Sir Harold would be too drunk to protect her. Still, they made it safely to shelter on the first night, but the next day brought a late spring snowstorm worse than any downfall winter had offered. It was a bitter blow to a countryside that was just beginning to thaw. By nightfall, they were suffering a blizzard and were still far from Lindlay Manor, where they were to meet the earl's escort.

When the last wisps of gray light succumbed to darkness, Katherine pointed to a tiny village that was no more than a plaster and timber inn, a stable, and a hut or two. "The

Cock and Boar Inn," read a decrepit shingle. Though her father would have preferred her to chance the blizzard than to lower herself to such crude lodging, she thought of the blessed Virgin, who had fared well enough in a stable, and so, with no words of protest belching from the drunken Sir Harold, she led them to shelter.

It seemed strange that so many horses were tied outside the inn, but this gave Katherine no pause. She was propelled by the enticing aroma of roasting mutton and the comforting sight of smoke billowing from the chimney. When she dismounted, weary from the saddle, her knees buckled. She regained her balance and pushed past Sir Harold.

"Take the horses yonder to the stable, and I will go in with our lady," Sir Harold ordered their two young servants. In a drunken lurch, he fell from his saddle into a snowbank.

"Cursed be to bloody hell!" he cried, futilely attempting to free his ankle from its stirrup. "Help!"

Katherine looked at him with disgust, blinking to ward off the huge snowflakes that pelted her. *How could father send me with such an irresponsible guard?* she thought, ignoring the fact that Sir Harold was one of the few knights still alive who owed fealty to the baron.

"Sir Harold, you shame the honor of my father. You will not escort me into any public place in such a state. And I will not freeze out here waiting for your sobriety to return."

"But . . . ," he muttered, his arms flailing at the stirrup.

She turned to the two servants her father had sent. Though both were tall and strong, one of them was a half-wit, a fact that added to her concern. "Joseph, carry Sir Harold to the stable with the horses. When he has regained his senses, send him to me and not a moment before. I will see what shelter there is to be had."

Katherine started for the inn. "And when you return to Shelby Manor, do not tell Lord Gilbert of Sir Harold's behavior. Father will give him the whip if he learns of this."

Joseph threw Sir Harold over his shoulder like a sack of goose down while the half-wit took the horses. Raising the latch, Katherine threw her weight against the inn's heavy oak door and stumbled in with a rush of wind at her back. Snow billowed under her cloak. Quickly, she shut the door and leaned against it wearily as she surveyed the large room and its dark beamed ceiling.

A hush fell over the crowd. A veritable sea of rosy faces, dirty for the most part, turned in her direction. People stared at her unabashedly, lowly peasants every one of them. The air was thick with smoke and the pungent odor of unwashed bodies. Against the far wall a fire roared, and next to it sat a large-handed minstrel who ended his ballad on a sour note to regard her with curiosity.

The walls were recessed in several arched indentations, giving a semblance of privacy to some patrons, but otherwise the room was strewn with long tables and benches crowded with townspeople and travelers who, like herself, were stranded for the night. No one seemed to move except for the serving wenches who passed back and forth to a counter where they filled pitchers of ale and mead from wooden casks and barrels.

"There is a blizzard," Katherine announced to the hushed room, awkwardly trying to explain her appearance. But of course they knew this, and she felt blood rush to her cheeks, already red from the wind. Adding to her embarrassment was the uneasy realization that these churls did not acknowledge her social position. Two years ago, her arrival at such a place would have sent the room into a flurry of activity while the villeins anxiously made a lady of her bearing welcome. But after the Pestilence, the lower classes were bold and embittered. They had outwitted certain death and no longer feared nobility.

Determined to restore her dignity, Katherine added more imperiously, "My escorts are in the stables. I should like food for them."

No one spoke. They merely stared at her with dull hostility or drunken apathy. Except for one angelic, sooty-faced little girl who danced forward and took her hand, oblivious of the difference in their social standing.

"Yer cloak, milady," she said in a rough accent.

"Thank you," Katherine murmured, shrugging off her snow-covered mantle and handing the luxurious garment to the child.

"Where . . . ," Katherine began with chattering teeth, "where is the innkeeper? I would like rooms for the night."

A ripple of laughter washed over the crowd.

"There are no rooms, " a surly voice replied.

Katherine squinted in the torchlight, seeking the one who had answered. But none of the downtrodden faces matched the deep voice.

"Are you the innkeeper?"

"There is no innkeeper," answered the same impertinent scoundrel. "The poor sot is dead. Like the others."

Katherine would not be deterred. "Then I will pay whomever well for whatever chambers are left. It will be well worth your while."

"Aye, by the grace of the angels, if you are the payment, then 'twill indeed be well worth my while."

Lecherous laughter filled the room, and Katherine swallowed hard, fighting a desire to melt into the shadows. She would not be put down by an ignorant debaucher. She pressed a protective hand to her breasts, which rose and fell in snatched breaths beneath the square cut of her kirtle. Everyone awaited her response to the mysterious, brazen speaker.

"Show yourself," she demanded, covering her eyes above the brow as she searched the room.

"Hither, milady."

Wood scraped on stone, and Katherine's eyes followed her ears to a man standing against the far wall. Even through the smoky haze his eyes bore shamelessly into hers. She had not expected to find such a lowborn cad, for his manner was too bold, his speech too perfect. But he was a member of the lower class if clothing could peg a man. He wore a tattered, filthy tunic, muddied breeches, and torn hose that barely contained his well-muscled calves. And even in that sorry state, he was a handsome sight, she noted with some discomfort, for a proper lady did not admire a peasant.

She arched her brows. "Your audacity is beyond sufferance. Surely you have a room set aside for those of nobler bearing."

"Nay." The man worked his way across the room, watching her without blinking it seemed. When he stopped near her, it was too close. He held her gaze with implacable, proud blue eyes. "I may be a scoundrel and a rogue, but I do not lie, and on that I'd lay my life."

He looked the part of a rogue, with his tousled brown hair and his cocky stride, but his face was refined, smooth, pleasing to the eye. A bit out of character.

He finished his tankard of ale with one swig and set it on the nearby serving counter. A young peasant girl filled it, smiling at him all the while.

"Verily, milady," he said, winking at the girl, "we will all sleep together tonight."

Katherine blinked in surprise. She had been so long without company that any dialogue would likely have taken her aback, but a conversation of this saucy nature left her speechless.

The bold peasant continued. "We are stranded just as you are, but you are welcome to sleep with us. Or me." He flashed a cunning grin. "Or you may travel onward. The choice is yours."

Before Katherine could reply, the minstrel resumed his song, and several couples, already bored by the confrontation, began to dance in the center of the room.

"Here. Drink this," the stranger said, offering his own tankard. " 'Twill warm your bones."

Katherine's translucent skin flushed again, this time with indignation. He obviously thought he'd ply her with spirits just in case his fermented charm did not succeed in wooing her to his bed. She pushed away his proffered hand. "Nay, I could not possibly indulge. And your lack of respect is not in the least appreciated."

She shivered anew when a blast of air seeped through the cracks in the door, but the only area not crowded with people was the counter. She crept to its corner, standing as far from the roguish man as possible. "I would rather freeze than sleep with the likes of you. But the servants will not want to travel on." Feeling all too weary, she pulled off her gloves and rubbed the tension from her forehead. "Whatever will I do?" she mumbled to herself.

The stranger did not offer any more advice, which was just as well since she would not have taken it. There was something incongruous, something wholly suspicious about him. And he might have been winsome, even attractive, with his ruddy, strong face and his intriguing eyes, but it was ruined, all of it, by his lips. They were too wide, too wandering against the square line of his jaw, too poised with sensuality. She could never trust a promise spoken from such lips, even if it were true he never lied.

And just when she had decided this, he indulged in engaging laughter, his entire demeanor awash with tenderness and charm, his eyes brightening with a look that would have convinced her the world was round. She turned away, for she knew he was not to be trusted. Georgie would have chastised this one in an instant.

"I am not a thief, maiden," he said, his laughter fading to a teasing grin. "You needn't scowl at me so furiously. Now, tell me, what the devil is a lady doing alone on such a hazardous night?"

Katherine bristled at his patronizing tone. "I am not alone. My escort is . . . tending the horses." She did not want this man to know of her irresponsible escort, and was glad she'd sent Harold to the stable.

"You may be stranded for days," he warned, motioning the serving girl for a cup of mead. "Drink this, it will be more to your liking than the ale, methinks."

Katherine eyed the drink warily. She had never indulged in the mead and ale her father had offered her when she was growing up. But this had been heated, and steam rose enticingly from the goblet. She took it, as much to warm her hands as her belly.

"Might I know your name, milady?"

"I am Katherine, daughter of Lord Seymour Gilbert, baron of Shelby Manor." She took a sip of the warm mead and immediately felt the knot in her stomach melt. "I am traveling to Blackmoor Castle, where I will be betrothed."

The stranger choked on a mouthful of ale, regarding her with astonishment. He laughed loudly and slapped his thigh, irony crinkling the edges of his eyes. When he calmed somewhat, he raised his tankard in a silent toast. "God shows his small mercies when they're needed most."

"Do you know my father?" Why else such thunderous recognition? If this man was a servant of one of the baron's peers, he might wish to assist her where Sir Harold had fallen slack. Or did he know Georgie? The thought that they might share the love of her brother made her smile with hope.

"Um . . . ," he muttered with great thought, regarding her and then turning his focus back to his ale. "Aye. You could say that I know your father. We are . . . closely tied."

"Did you know my brother?" She smiled openly.

But here the stranger scowled, staring hard into his ale. "Aye, I did know your brother. But not well."

Katherine frowned at him. "I have not seen you before in the service of any barons my father knows. What is your name?"

He pulled forward two stools. When they were both seated, he crossed his arms and cleared his throat. "My friends who know me well call me the Wolf."

She smiled at his indulgent self-appraisal. "And those who do not know you?"

"The Lamb."

This time Katherine raised her goblet in wordless acknowledgment. An intelligent rogue. Already the mead was softening her spirit.

"But you may call me Guy, milady."

A short, young, bearded fellow came bustling through the dancers and bowed low before Katherine with the air of a trained squire.

"Milady," he murmured politely and turned to Guy. "Milord, your gipon and cote-hardie are nearly dry, though your boots are still wet. It should not be long before—"

"That will be all, Geoffrey," Guy interrupted him, waving him away impatiently.

Geoffrey's obedient expression fell to despondency. "Is there something amiss, milord?"

"No, Geoffrey. Everything is in order. That will be all."

The squat man bowed and backed away, staring strangely at them.

"He's just another poor squire who lost his master during the Pestilence," Guy said in answer to Katherine's questioning frown. When she remained unconvinced, he added, "Gone mad, poor fellow. He calls me 'lord' because he cannot bear his own freedom and must pretend that I am his lord and master. 'Tis a pity what madness the Death has brought."

"So you are one of the opportunists!" Katherine said, comprehension finally dawning. She was not so much repelled by his greed as she was contented with her own great understanding of human nature. "You were in service to a nobleman and his family. When they died from the Pestilence, you took his house and even his servants, pretending to nobility yourself."

Guy stared at her slack-jawed. "Where did a girl of your innocence learn so much of the world?"

Katherine took a languid, deliberate sip of mead, tossing back her head as she swallowed. "I know far more than I care to admit to one of your gender." Under the influence of drink, her mood suddenly darkened. "I've seen more than a woman of eighteen years needs to see." She forced an image from her mind: her last glimpse of Georgie, his glassy, frozen eyes staring up at her as she refilled his grave with moist dirt. Katherine threw her head back and took a long draft of mead.

"Indeed." His response was uncommonly gentle. Holding out his hand, he led her to the table where she had first seen him. "Even worldly-wise women do hunger now and again, do they not?" he offered, pulling back a bench and sliding in. He motioned for her to join him and called to a serving wench for food.

"I do not think it proper that we should sit side by side," she said, her voice trailing off as another wench brought out a leg of mutton, peas porridge, two trenchers, and two knives.

"You may stand then, milady," Guy replied, thrusting his knife into the meat, tearing away a hearty chunk.

She stared hard at this bold man, a twinkle of reluctant appreciation moistening her eyes. He was confident, she'd say that much for him. And then her eyes wandered to the juicy meat waiting for the taking.

"Well, since I have not eaten in a very long time . . . ," she reasoned and sat next to him. But her excuses were cut short when the door burst open. Sir Harold staggered in amid a whirl of snow, still obviously inebriated. He kicked the door shut and weaved his way toward her after tossing his empty wineskin to the counter for replenishment.

"Sir Harold!" Katherine exclaimed. Her embarrassment about his condition was quickly replaced with fear that he would report her own conduct to her father. "He will not like seeing me in your company," she whispered to Guy.

"That is your escort?" Guy asked incredulously. "Your father should be placed in the stocks for letting such a one tend to your welfare."

It was true, she realized. From the beginning, she had been too intent on proving her self-sufficiency to admit that her father had not shown the greatest forethought.

"The horses are abed, young Kate," Harold said too loudly, rocking in place before their table.

"Sir Harold, " she said, no longer fearing his disapproval, emboldened by the presence of her new champion, "my instructions were that you should remain in the stable until you had regained your . . . composure."

"Oh, I am not drunk," he said, shaking his head so vehemently he momentarily lost his balance.

"I see." Katherine decided not to argue the point. "Sir Harold, this good man says there are no rooms to be had. The horses may be abed, but it means only that they will fare better than us."

Harold turned the upper portion of his body, taking in the sight of several weary revelers who were already sleeping on the floor. Then he twisted around and leaned in for a closer look at Guy.

"Your father won't like this at all, milady. You were supposed to be in the comfort of Lindlay Manor tonight. Not in the company of peasants," Harold said, glancing at Guy with a sneer, "and the like."

"There is always the stable," Guy suggested. Still intent on his meal, he tore a chunk from the stale trencher bread and sopped up the mutton juice. "There, you can have a loft to yourself, and you will not have committed any impropriety."

"There's a thought," Harold said, slapping his hands together gleefully. "I will prepare bedding for you."

Harold staggered toward the door, retrieving his refilled wineskin.

Katherine let out a shuddering sigh of resignation. She could not fight the forces of nature and make the blizzard disappear. And if she was here for the night, she could at least find some pleasure in it. If the stables were acceptable to Sir Harold, she would not give another thought to propriety. In truth, she was already beginning to enjoy herself. The extraordinary circumstances that had brought together such an odd mixture of people acted as a euphoric drug, heightening the sense of time and aliveness. The dancers skipped about with a gaiety that verged on delirium; the minstrel strummed and sang as Katherine was sure he had never done before. She felt a tingling inside, sensing herself that this night was somehow different, special, never to be lived again in quite the way it was unfolding. She had not felt even the hint of such excitement in the months following Georgie's death.

And mutton had never tasted so good! If that was due to her indulgence in mead, she would have to indulge more often, she concluded, wondering why she had refused the heady drink in the past. Just a foolish bent toward discipline. God, she wanted to live! She longed to rip off her veil and shout to the heavens that she was alive. She had survived. *Forgive me, Georgie, but I am so happy to be alive*. How lucky. She was so very lucky.

"How long has it been since you've eaten, milady?"

Katherine paused. Her hand clutched a piece of mutton poised in midair. She found Guy staring at her askance and realized she was inhaling her meal.

"I have not eaten since yesterday, though it seems like it has been a year. When my brother died, I lost my appetite for many things. Though somehow it seems to have returned tonight."

"One time, dear lady," Guy said in a low voice, the heat of his breath reaching, just barely, the inner recesses of her ear, "there was a mighty feast in the Great Hall of Lord Richmond, my master. King Edward honored Richmond's castle with his presence that night as he traveled home after a hunt . . ."

The rich tones of Guy's voice kneaded her spirit and softened her reticence further still. His voice seemed to drown out all other sounds, and her eyes focused on the minute details of his face: bold eyebrows announcing deep-set blue eyes that sparked with intelligence far beyond his social status; a short scar carved down one sculpted cheekbone, bespeaking his courage in fight, his ability to wear well the wounds of time.

" . . . and so when Lord Richmond went to bed, I hung back and helped myself to the feast. On my way to the servants' bower, I stopped in the garde-robe to let my urine, and there did I see King Edward, royally seated and none-too-pleased to have company at that indelicate moment."

Katherine paused, waiting to be shocked further. When Guy signaled the end of his risqué story with a smile, she let out a peal of laughter that brought great warmth to his hard eyes. When she could laugh no more, she shook her head in protest, begging him to cease.

They pushed away their trenchers and fell into amiable silence. Katherine surveyed the room and saw it with new eyes. She smiled longingly at the familiarity these common folk shared with one another. Forever under her father's rule and soon to be under a husband's, she would never know what it was like to live only for herself. She envied the contented faces of the tarts and peasant girls who lolled in the arms of their lovers. In any case, her fate was already cast. Her life would be devoted to prayer. If not in a convent, then in her husband's house. And though she could never allow herself to love any man, she did envy the freedom these tarts had to do as they pleased. She wished she were that free. Not to couple with a man, for that was no better than the beasts of the forest, but to have the chance . . .

"You seem pensive, milady," Guy said softly. He placed his elbows on the table and rested his chin on folded hands.

She was startled and pleased by his perceptive observation. Her lips smiled, though her eyes remained heavy with thought. "I was merely thinking that soon I will be tied to a husband I can never love, or even respect, never to be a carefree lass like some of these."

He turned his body toward her, and she felt his attention engulf her, pressing against the emotional wall she hid behind. It was not merely his physical presence, which was powerful, but his keen intuition, which she felt nudging into her innermost thoughts.

"Nay, Katherine, you must not judge it so. Give him a chance. You may love him with all your heart."

She drank the tenderness from his eyes, which intoxicated her heart and mind so she no longer knew or cared where she was or who witnessed her frank attraction to this man who, though lowly born, was so full of depth and wit.

"I will never love him."

"By why not, lass? Your life is just beginning. I see the longing for love in your eyes."

She touched the rosary pouch hanging at her waist and smiled with melancholy. "I promised my brother I would pray for his soul. God will not hear those prayers from one who is tainted with earthly desire. Besides, the man I will betroth is someone I can never respect. My brother knew him and said he killed a man in no honorable way."

A spark of anger torched the shadows that veiled Guy's eyes. "Do not judge a man until you know what fate has befallen him."

She would have argued, but her speech had grown heavy, and she lost all desire to explain herself. Her senses were taking over. Her skin pulsed with warmth. She inhaled the musky scent of leather wafting from Guy's bronze skin, the smell of a man who has ridden his steed hard in the blistering sun. Her eyes disobediently found their way back to his lips. *Strange how first impressions change,* she thought. She had mistrusted those lips, but now she was drawn to them. And just as she admitted this to herself, Guy leaned forward. With the grace of a knight, he loomed over her, his chiseled features larger than life, then those seductive lips brushed hers, softly, reverently.

Katherine shivered and shut her eyes. His full lips took hers in exquisite fashion—warm, kneading. Her own response made a mockery of all she had just professed. She could not pull away. Would God forgive her this one indulgence?

Guy withdrew, his delicious breath fanning her cheeks, and he brushed her full lips with his thumb.

"There," he murmured, "now you do not have to go to your rogue's bed in total, dreaded innocence. And surely God will forgive you that one little sin. Come, milady, in this forgotten inn where no one will remember, let us dance to our youth. Then, and only then, will I deliver you unto the night, unto the husband you may never love."

Katherine glanced at the crowd. It was true they would never remember her. They were all too drunk to notice if a young woman and her ruddy, brash escort indulged in a flirtatious dance on a snowy spring eve. And so she let Guy lead her to the center of the room where the other merrymakers danced their jig.

She did not know the steps but the dance was informal. It was wild and loose, and soon she felt like a falcon set free. Guy pulled her close, scooping a strong arm around her waist, and Katherine fell into the strength of his embrace. Her flushed cheeks rubbed against the soft, worn material of his tunic. His broad shoulder muscles rippled like the smooth, massive flanks of a destrier. His collarbone, carelessly exposed beneath his ill-fitting tunic, glistened with perspiration. And like an artist, she longed to reach out and caress her model, to study the mystery and art of the human form. The vibrant sounds of the lute struck her ears, and in an instant she was transformed. Guy led her with ease and grace in a raucous little dance—where her feet flew and landed, she knew not, but the muses were her guide, and she threw her head back with abandoned laughter, her reddish curls whirling behind her. The folds of her royal blue cotehardie obediently followed suit, the long gown melding into the graceful movement of their legs.

Their eyes locked through the torchlight haze, and for the rest of the dance she swirled and skipped, heedless of all else. Distant clapping drowned all sounds, and soon that was vanquished beneath the loud beating of her own heart.

For Katherine, the excitement she felt in Guy's arms was all new. She'd never experienced such closeness with another, such passionate joy. Was passion the right word? It could not be love, for she would never give her heart to a man. She might have to give all else—control, possessions, rights—but not her heart. But this that she was feeling, call it anything but love, this was extraordinary.

She delighted in the way he beheld her in the torchlight. With hypnotic eyes, he drew her closer. When her desire exploded in ripples of nervous laughter, his eyes crinkled with delight, and his mouth parted in a smug, but loving, half smile. With each tilt of her head, each coy toss of her hair, she entranced him as he entranced her.

The music came to a sudden halt, applause bursting anew, and their twirling dance crescendoed and died with the last vibrations of the lute. They stood panting for breath in unison, Katherine tossing back her damp hair, save for the strands that clung adamantly to the pulsing nape of her neck. The music resumed, a slower melody, and the dancers began to disperse, but Katherine would not budge, stubbornly holding his embrace. Would God strike her dead for her wantonness?

Guy drew her closer, kissing her with an intensity that startled her. A wave of heat crashed over her, and she thought their bodies might meld together for a blissful eternity.

"God's Wounds, but you please me," he muttered against her lips, but then withdrew, leaving a cruel rush of cold air against her tender skin. "But I am not behaving honorably. You are betrothed, and I, a lowly peasant, cannot even think of having you, despoiling your honor."

He was making fun of her. She could see the laughter in his eyes, the sarcastic twist to his mouth, as if he were playing some game for which she did not know the rules.

"Perhaps you do not care so much for what is proper. Perhaps you merely do not desire me." Her tone was full of hurt, and hot humiliation flooded her cheeks. It was all so foolish—arguing with such a common man—all because she had been too impetuous and bold.

Guy's face hardened. "Then you would prefer I take you in some dishonorable way?"

Katherine uttered an incomprehensible gasp, pulling indignantly from the vestiges of his embrace. A moment ago, she would have danced into his bed, impossible as that scenario would have been to her only a day before that. Now she had regained her senses, blaming this temporary lapse on the mead.

"Fie on you!" She turned coldly and marched to the table, nearly tripping over several lovers prone on the floor. When he followed, she turned to him with a brittle smile that hid her vulnerability. "I should thank you, really. Your flippant rejection of my affection reminds me of what men are truly made. Fearing a life unknown with a man I can only disdain, I momentarily thought I wanted some . . . some bit of life I had never known. But I was wrong. Dancing, like lovemaking, is for beasts and hedonists. Not for ladies. I will pray all the harder to be forgiven for this unpardonable lapse."

She turned away with tears burning her eyes, for she was a lady and still she wanted him . . . or at least wanted him to want her. As Katherine had dreamt of in secret, she longed to dance, to be free, to be loved with the passion and chivalry she had heard about in gleemen's tales. But she had sacrificed her fantasies with her promise to Georgie.

"Katherine," Guy said. He came up behind her and rested his hands on her shoulders, but she spun around and regarded him as she would an enemy.

"Get you hence! I have been too forward, and you do not deserve to witness my embarrassment. You understand nothing of what I will face in the days to come. Nor do you care. So like a man. Where is Sir Harold?" She took a step toward the door, but Guy grasped her arms with both his hands.

"Come hither," he demanded, firmly pulling her into the privacy of an archway. A torch fluttered near their heads, casting a pulsing glow on his features. "By God's Bones, when you have lived twenty and nine years as I have, you may understand what thoughts drive me now, though I doubt it if you do all your thinking with that hot head of yours. But until then, do not compare me to those whelps you call men."

His impatience vanished and consternation creased his brow. He pulled her tightly into his arms. "How can you not know how desirable you are? Katherine, we may never have this chance again. Know me as I am now, without your preconceptions, without the titles and formalities—"

"Titles?" she mumbled in a small voice, distracted by his sweet breath. His lips were so close.

"You might have hated me for what you've heard. But fate has been kind to me at last."

His lips found hers, and Katherine writhed with pleasure—traitorous pleasure.

Pushing futilely against the strength of his arms, she choked, gasping for air. "Let me go. My vow . . . I've made a vow to my brother. And I'm betrothed to Sir Stephen."

"Sir Stephen," she heard her words echoed, and turning her head, she saw Geoffrey, Guy's bewildered squire, waiting patiently at their side.

"Sir Stephen," Geoffrey repeated, addressing Guy, "forgive my untimeliness, milord, but I would beg permission to bed the horses. This storm only worsens. We cannot go out tonight. I am sure Gilbert's girl is safely ensconced somewhere."

Guy sighed wearily. All tension vanished from his body, and he regarded Geoffrey with resigned hostility. "Very well, Geoffrey. And do not worry about Lord Gilbert's daughter." He tilted his head in her direction. "She is indeed safe."

Geoffrey looked to her with sudden comprehension. He bowed deeply and turned away.

Katherine's passion was quickly squelched, making room for the wave of anger that would soon break.

"Perhaps I should have told you immediately," he said contritely. "I am Stephen Bartingham."

Katherine felt a wall crash down between them, crumbling what little trust she had felt. She pulled away as if he were fire scorching her skin. Her head began to pound. She realized with mortification what this meant. Guy was her betrothed. And she had proven herself to be a faithless creature no better than a tart.

He had proven himself deceitful, no better than a viper.

"Don't you see, Katherine," he said, his voice calm, insisting on reason, "it happened so accidentally, but so perfectly. When I discovered who you were, I saw a chance for you to know me without your preconceptions. The Stephen you knew was already condemned in your eyes, without trial."

"But . . . you tricked me. Those stories about your childhood. You let me call you Guy. You disguised yourself as a peasant." She shook her head, searching his face for something she could believe.

"The stories were all true except for different circumstances," he insisted. "As for my clothing, this tunic is borrowed. My own gipon is drying by the fire. And my friends do call me Guy."

Katherine laughed bitterly. "Nay, Sir Stephen, your friends call you the Wolf. As I shall to my dying day."

She turned and stalked with wounded pride to the door.

"Remember this night, Katherine," he called to her as she retrieved her mantle. "One day you will remember that you wanted me unadorned, with no title other than 'peasant' or 'rogue.' "

Katherine shuddered at her own naïveté and then flung open the door to the raging snowstorm.

CHAPTER TWO

✠

Stephen thought his frostbitten bones had endured the worst that nature could offer, but then he had not ridden for three days with the churlish humor and icy frowns of a young woman whose pride he had wounded. So he contented himself with Katherine's silent presence, smiling when she unwittingly let down her guard. If compassion would not melt her hardened sentiments, he hoped that age and experience would eventually soften her around the edges. Experience had tempered some of his rage against the world's injustices, teaching him the need for comfort on a cold, dark night.

Katherine was like him in so many ways, he realized, as they cantered down the snow-covered road to Blackmoor. With an eye well versed in the pleasures of feminine beauty, he studied her arched back, her chin thrust defiantly forward, her stubborn pride, and her steely sense of purpose draped in velvet. Beneath the quick flutter of her long eyelashes, in the depths of her bottomless cat-green eyes, he saw intelligence that would be both her salvation and her curse. The world did not suffer bright women gladly.

Stephen's way of thinking was different. His spirit quickened to the smart retort of an intelligent woman. To Stephen, Katherine's wit stirred thoughts of his own and something more base in nature—an instant longing. He dropped back, rode at a distance from her, and reined in his rough longing behind a placid countenance. He resolved to approach her gently now, for soon the treachery they would encounter at Blackmoor Castle would call for a unity uncommon in those yet to be wed, and the subtleties of courtship would be lost. In an effort to counter his brother's political maneuvers within the family, they would no doubt marry soon after their arrival. Stephen was loath to pluck the bloom so quickly from the vine, but such was the fate of marriages arranged solely for politics.

"What the devil?" Geoffrey muttered. He squinted against the glaring sun and pointed at the distant figures of Katherine and Sir Harold. "Milord, look yonder."

"What is she about now?" Stephen wondered. He rode several yards farther and gave his reins a yank. He rose in his stirrups for a better look. Curiosity turned to irritation. Katherine had dismounted, and fetching bread from Sir Harold's saddle pouch, she offered it to four beggars on the side of the road. Their gnarled hands clawed at the hem of her mantle; their weather-beaten faces twisted with grief, embellished for her benefit. "By the Mass, they won't let her go until they've taken her last farthing. She should have ridden past them, the devil take the willful girl."

Stephen put a quick heel to the side of his stallion and galloped forward until he reached the four rustics who clamored around Katherine.

"Get you back!" he commanded. The wind whistled past his reddened ears, twisting locks of hair against his unflinching expression. "Leave the lady be, I tell you."

"No!" Katherine exclaimed, clutching the loaf of bread to her breasts as if Stephen had demanded it for himself. "How can you be so cruel? These people are starving."

"Katherine, you behave as if you've been locked in your father's manor all your life." Stephen dismounted and strode forward. With a cry, the beggars scattered beneath the shadow of his towering presence.

"A woman does not mingle with beggars," he bellowed. "If you wanted to give them something, you should have instructed Sir Harold to do your bidding."

"They asked me for a bit of kindness and a crust of bread," Katherine said, rebelliousness now added to the list of other hot emotions sparking from her eyes. "I suppose if Christ our Lord were traveling to the Holy Land, you would turn him away with your anger."

Unable to stifle a grin, Stephen turned and feigned a cough so as not to reward her churlishness with humor. Recovering his stern and dour expression, he turned back to her and took a step forward so that she might feel the full force of his masculine presence.

"Katherine, I am not angry at these churls for begging. I'm angry at you for giving to them with no thought to your safety. You've been thoughtless and irresponsible. They could have been robbers or murderers."

Her face registered a haughty victory, and immediately he regretted his choice of words.

"Sir Stephen, I am not intimidated by the presence of murderers." This last word she stressed with utmost skill while the confused peasants stared accusingly at Stephen and then anxiously at the coveted loaf of bread clutched in Katherine's arms. "Was it not you who said 'Do not judge a man until you know what fate has befallen him'? These people are guilty of no crime but poverty. I would ease their burden if it's in my power."

Stephen thought a moment before he spoke, a habit he had cultivated to balance his dauntless nature. In that moment, while Katherine self-righteously tore the bread in equal parts, gently giving each shivering beggar his share, he found himself admiring her beauty. It had never been more obvious than in this moment when she was engaged in an act of genuine charity. The muscles in his broad chest tightened around his heart, and he let out a long, low-pitched sigh. This woman would have the power to create heartache. Far from over, his troubles had just begun.

He turned from his holy temptress and pulled himself up into his saddle. From this vantage, he watched her careful ministering. No doubt she thought the battle won, but it took many battles to win a war. Besides, his tactics had changed over the years. He did not want to fight for love. He would let it come to him in its own sweet time. That is if Katherine had the wit to see his goodness, and with sudden, quiet cynicism, he doubted she would. Perhaps she was too young to look beyond circumstances and tarnished reputations. Drawing his mantle close, he spurred his horse forward, looking back only to see that she had safely remounted and followed.

He rode on ahead of Lord Gilbert's servants, but alone, letting Geoffrey lead the way. Anticipating their arrival at his family estate, his mood grew dark. What evil machinations was his brother plotting? When he'd left England for Brittany a year ago, all was well. Trusting in the law of primogeniture, his brother knew he'd inherit the estate. Marlow had been at peace, as much as his cruel demeanor would allow. Now the peace was broken, and Stephen had been called home with great urgency. Soon he heard Katherine's horse galloping near, and he put his troublesome thoughts temporarily to rest.

Joining him at his steady pace, she stared ahead with a prim gaze. "I did not want this marriage."

The raw truth in her voice drew his gaze to Katherine's profile. Though merely a baron's daughter, she held herself like a queen.

She graced him with a thoughtful glance. "If it's any consolation, I did not wish to marry at all."

"Then I will not take it too much to heart." He bowed as best he could in his saddle.

"Do not mock me," she said, squaring off in confrontation. "Did you know that this match dashed every dream I had?"

"Nay, I did not."

"Aye, milord. It was my dearest wish to spend the rest of my days in a convent, in meditation and prayer. I was to remain chaste and pure. Now this marriage will change that forever."

"If all goes well." He turned his gaze back to the road just in time to dodge a low branch covered in snow. The limb

caught on his shoulder and dumped icy crystals down his
back and on his head. Brushing them off with an exasperated
sigh, he added, "Dear lady, if you wish to remain chaste and
pure in our marriage, then you may do so. No one will observe
our wedding night. But I pray you do not be so distant on a
cold day like this. This is an arranged marriage. Though I
hoped for love, I cannot expect it, but surely some truce can
be arranged. If even King Edward and King Philip managed
to keep peace while the Death wreaked its misery, can we
not be civil in its aftermath?"

She looked at him in pleasant surprise, but then her features
clouded over, and she shook her head in disgust. "So you
confess this is nothing more than an arranged marriage. No
false words of courtship from you, scoundrel."

Stephen blinked slowly, then cut the space between them
with a sardonic grin. "If a scoundrel I be, then a scoundrel's
wife you'll soon become."

"Not by choice."

"Nay, in this world 'tis not a woman's choice." He spoke
evenly, distracted by the stunning breadth of a hawk's wings
soaring overhead. "But you will love me one day, Katherine.
Aye, I do believe it, and that will be by choice."

She let out a loud, bitter laugh, her voice breaking against
the alder trees that sheltered them on either side of the road.
"Churl! But you are full of yourself. What gives you confidence, milord? Is it manly boasting, or is it a gypsy fortune-
teller who keeps you warm at night?"

"Faith," he answered without pause. His eyes met hers,
blue and green melding like the colors of the sea. She felt
it. He knew deep down she'd felt the gist of his intent. Faith.
A word he could not explain with the mind, only the heart.
Katherine looked at him in consternation, then lowered her
head and rode silently for the next half mile.

"My brother was full of chivalry," she said, breaking the
silence just as the sun broke through an overcast sky. Bright
rays bounced off the hilt of Stephen's sword and struck
Katherine's eyes, illuminating her fierce determination. "To

Georgie there was no higher duty than love. For surely if a man loves, he cannot be a cheat, a liar, or a murderer. He would never kill but on the field of battle. He would never fight but to save his honor or that of someone he protected, and then it would only be a fair fight with squires and witnesses on hand. If we do not follow the laws of chivalry, then we are but heathens living and dying for no reason at all."

Stephen's lips parted in a crooked smile, as if he had just bitten rue and somehow found the bitter taste pleasing. His eyes smoldered with gray. "This thing called chivalry, this honor you worship as your god on earth, 'tis much overrated, milady."

Her hands tightened around her reins. He was sorry to frighten her, to reinforce her notions that he was a common murderer, but she would soon face greater fears at Blackmoor Castle. Best to prepare her now.

"You think I ripped the life from an innocent man? Is that the deed for which you condemn me, wife-to-be?"

Katherine frowned, thinking before she spoke. "Georgie said you slew a man in the shadows of an alley. Not for a just cause, but because of the darkness in your soul which you cannot contain."

Stephen felt old wounds bleed afresh, scars he had thought healed, in his heart and mind. How long would that deed haunt him? God's Wounds, certainly he did not care. And yet his breath came raggedly from his lungs. He wanted to explain, but he would not. He would rather burn in Hell than explain himself to this woman.

"You have no choice but to trust me. As my wife I expect you to judge me on fact, not on rumor. The man I killed, Lord Roby, was no man of honor. My reasons for killing him are between me and God above."

They rode on, their silence disturbed only by the snorts of their mounts and the creaking of saddles.

"Since I was second born, my parents never pressured me to marry." Stephen voiced his reflections in a low baritone.

He had been so long fighting in Brittany, ignoring the King's truce, that it was an effort to speak fluently of anything other than longbowmen and battering rams. "I had once harbored hope that my marriage would be blessed with love, and so I resisted a permanent union until the time arrived when I would find a woman to my liking. I was young, in no hurry. S'Blood, I cared naught for lands and dowries! Lady, you know that to be true. Now my father is very ill, and other dark clouds hang mysteriously over Blackmoor. For that reason, my father bade me urgently marry. Though I obey, I know a true union will not form until there is trust. The woman who shares my bed and my grave, who bears my name, must believe in me as others do not. Despite all of fate's crafty blows along the way. That will be better than the woman who gave me birth."

He turned to find the bold beauty staring at him, and if he were any judge of thought, she found him both repellent and fascinating. *She does not frighten easily,* he thought. *Then let her be the one to see my soul.*

"You're a woman with a man's courage, Katherine, but you're not so bold as to be foolish. Say the word and I will take you back to your father's barony. Is that your wish, lass?"

His heart pounded within his chest, and he was startled to realize he wanted her to say no. He wanted her to want him.

She blinked and looked at the intriguing path ahead. Some new determination sparked from her bright eyes. He smiled, content to let his question die. Tossing back his head with pride, he felt something that in younger days he might have called hope. Gracing her with an open smile, Stephen put a heel to his stallion's flanks and quickened his pace.

"Blackmoor Castle ahead!" Geoffrey cried over his shoulder. He pointed to the horizon.

"Blackmoor! At last." Stephen rose in his stirrups for a better view of the sprawling fortress. He couldn't behold it without excitement. Four towers, each painted a different

color—blue, red, white, and green—pierced the sky. It was
his home. The place where he had jousted and beaten many
an older knight; where he had fought side by side with his
father against those greedy for Blackmoor's rich lands; where
he had lain with his first maiden in the stables; where he
had beaten his older brother, over and over again, at chess.
This was home. Whatever wicked schemes lurked within the
fortress, he would overcome them.

The closer they drew, the more magnificent was the presence of the sprawling bastion. Unlike older Norman castles,
Blackmoor didn't contain a single keep towering over inner
and outer baileys. A Plantagenet structure, it was built to keep
transgressors at bay with a large outer wall connecting the
four towers. To Stephen, as a child, that inner sanctum had
been the world. He had spent his days in the brewery, cajoling
the brewer for a sip of ale. Even at the age of five, he knew the
giddy effect of that strong-smelling drink. When the earl's son
was turned away without a drop, he napped in the mountains
of hay at the stables. There the earl kept his mighty destriers,
ridden in battle, and the gentler palfreys that pulled the litters
for Stephen's mother, the countess, and her ladies-in-waiting.
At dawn he visited the armory, where the clanking sound of a
hammer on an anvil always drew his curiosity. The indulgent
armorer let Stephen hammer his own shield, and he owed
his great strength, in part, to those lessons from the brawny
craftsman. From the orchards, young Stephen plucked and ate
apples and pears as he pleased, until his belly ached. Those
memories were as vibrant as if they'd happened yesterday.
All the events of his youth occurred within the castle walls.
The armory, the stable, the Great Hall, and the earl's inner
chambers were attached at various places to the outer wall,
and just within it, so that the castle was really a circle of
connected functions, completely self-sufficient under siege.
A haven.

Stephen's pace naturally quickened in his eagerness to
reach the familiarity of home, and Katherine spurred her
horse, matching him stride for stride.

"Sir Stephen!" Her voice was filled with awe. "You should have prepared me for this. Blackmoor is like nothing I've ever seen. I had heard tales of its magnificence, but none did it justice."

Stephen turned in his saddle and saw her trepidation. He smiled, hoping to bathe her countenance with comfort. At his smile, she returned one of her own, dazzling and evocative, and he felt a jolt of pure desire. If they had been within the warmth of the Great Hall, he could have unclasped her mantle and once again appreciated the luscious curves of her neck. He might have caressed that porcelain skin, and if she had not been so frightened he would have stopped her now and planted kisses on her heart-shaped lips, puckered with vulnerability. To warm them. Nay, to consume them.

S'Blood, he could not pretend nobility. An aching need rose up in him too long unquenched. He wanted her as a man wanted a woman, and there was no use acting noble about it. He glanced again at the young vixen who suddenly appeared to him more like a goddess. A tress of golden hair fell from beneath her hood, framing her face, a glistening accent to her feminine silhouette—her pert nose, her long, willowy lashes, her melting smile. *By my troth,* he thought, pulling his gaze at last from those luscious details of womanhood, *may she want me soon or I will overwhelm the damsel like some bull in heat.* Feeling very much like the man in his prime that he was, reveling in his fierce existence, he spurred his horse. *Such is the power of a woman.*

He touched her arm, urging her to join him, and they lurched into a full gallop. Katherine's unexpected laughter broke the air like tinkling chimes. Stephen grinned, savoring the graceful, audacious thrusts her head made in unison with her chestnut mare. But when the shadows of Blackmoor Castle darkened the muddy snow on the road, Stephen reined in his stallion. Katherine, too, slowed her pace. A sense of foreboding replaced Stephen's joy, and he knew she sensed it as well. From the steward's message, Stephen had surmised his father would die soon. The earl's steward, Sir Ramsey, concluded his missive with a plea for Stephen's return. Stephen had sensed foul play. Especially after receiving a message from the earl himself, calling Stephen home.

"I am sorry about your father's health," Katherine said.

Her words gently intruded on his thoughts, and he swung his head about to regard her, wondering if she had read his mind. Such a skill would be a mixed blessing in a wife.

"I am sorry, too," he replied. "I love him well. But the seasons of time are unforgiving. The Reaper will have his due."

They rode on, Stephen tensing with a mixture of eagerness and dread. The darkening sky was clear. The castle towers grew more distinct, throbbing red in the waning rays of the sun, silhouetted against an endless line of black trees on the horizon.

Geoffrey and Harold rode ahead, announcing their arrival. When Stephen and Katherine drew up their horses in front of the lowered drawbridge, a cluster of knights and ladies quickly gathered beneath the portcullis to welcome Stephen and to glimpse his bride-to-be.

"Sir Stephen." The castle steward rushed forward and clasped Stephen's hands warmly in his. Relief smoothed the deep worry lines etched above the steward's brow. "You've made a timely arrival, and I'm heartily glad of it."

" 'Tis good to be back, Ramsey," Stephen replied. He nodded acknowledgment to his old friend, and then watched in admiration as Ramsey dispatched orders for the kitchen and the stables. *Organized as usual,* Stephen thought. He could always count on his father's loyal steward.

Stephen's smile faded when he spied Marlow standing at the far edge of the drawbridge, isolated from the others. *What foul thoughts fill his mind tonight?* Stephen knew his brother was loath to leave his warm chamber, and he doubted Marlow had stirred just to greet him. Marlow raised his torch, and in the golden light he scrutinized Katherine. Stephen frowned with displeasure. His brother was as handsome as ever. A

long fur cape rippled over his large frame; his sensual lips
and smooth brows were grimly set. Constance, his embittered,
ill-used wife, stepped from behind Marlow and peered at
Katherine with suspicious eyes, as she would watch one who
had come to take her place.

Stephen adjusted himself in the saddle, getting ready for a
return to the political intrigue so common in powerful, noble
families. A chill of foreboding filled him, and he reached
out to take Katherine's hand. "I will not let anyone harm
you."

Katherine did not recoil as he had half expected, but rather
clutched his hand in return. "Who is that man there? The one
who waits like a vulture?"

"My brother, Lord Marlow, the next Earl of Blackmoor.
Now you see why I was so anxious to return. I do not trust
my father's welfare to him."

"The next earl?" Katherine shook her head. She withdrew
her hand and clutched the reins tightly. "Fate does not seem
fair, or even wise, in matters of inheritance."

Stephen looked hard at Katherine. Could she have guessed
Marlow's true nature so quickly and accurately? The evil in
his brother was slippery in nature. Marlow had never committed any act so heinous that he could be condemned without
question. It was more his general character that damned him:
his greed for power that was already, undeniably his; his
blatant disrespect for his wife; his cruelty to peasants, animals, women—anyone weaker than himself, with no right of
defense.

Taking Katherine's reins, Stephen led the way through
the gatehouse. At their approach, the gawkers dispersed.
Constance and her servants started for the inner chambers
while Marlow led the arrivals to the stables. Once inside, he
leaned against a stall while several hands bustled in care of
the weary horses.

"Well, Stephen," he said, crossing his arms in a hostile
gesture, "I see not even an unexpected snowstorm could keep
you from father's deathbed."

"Your joy at my arrival is overwhelming, Marlow," Stephen said dryly. After dismounting, he reached up and gripped Katherine's waist. He was struck with the urge to pull her into his arms, to feel the natural warmth of her body against his, to smell the sweet scent of her hair, washed with rose water. Resisting the temptation, Stephen lowered her to the ground, and their bodies touched for one tantalizing moment. He held her gaze, and though her eyes were wary with trepidation, an intimate spark passed between them that warmed his veins like sweet malmsey. He wanted to be alone with her. Perhaps Blackmoor would bring them together, not tear them apart as it had so many others.

"I envy my brother such a pretty one," Marlow said, spoiling the moment. "Better than the shrew I bed out of duty." He took a step forward, and his malignant demeanor wedged them apart.

"You play with words, Marlow." Stephen smiled coldly. Turning to Katherine, he touched her arm, drawing her away from his older brother. "Perhaps if Constance received half the attention you bestow on other women, the attention that is her due, then she would carry your child longer than a few moons."

"Bastard," Marlow growled, pulling back a fist, but a shout of glee from the stable entrance stopped the blow before it was launched.

"Guy!" cried Europa, clapping her pudgy hands in front of her old, rosy cheeks. Stephen turned and grinned broadly at the voluminous woman who had been his nursemaid and, through his growing years, more of a mother than his own had been. The woman waddled toward him and enveloped him in a fleshy embrace.

"The Lord in Heaven has blessed me again, Guy. Will you look at how well you be? And this one!" Europa's eyes flew open at the sight of Katherine. "A fairer one I've never seen. A perfect wife she'll be. A perfect wife!"

With her pronouncement ringing in his ears, Stephen watched with satisfaction as the serving woman pulled

Katherine into a smothering hug, pressing the young woman's cheek against her ample bosom. When freed again, Katherine shook her head in bewilderment.

Stephen laughed, and his weariness fell away like manacles. "Katherine, you shall know this woman well soon enough. She is Europa. She raised me and loved me, and I'd trust her with my life."

Marlow sniffed, showing his repugnance at the affectionate scene being played before him. "You always were one to waste yourself on servants and tarts, Stephen." He started away, but turned back with an imperious frown. "I expect you and Katherine at the evening meal tomorrow. Only then can you see Father. We will visit him together. Do not disturb him before then. He is weary tonight."

Europa shook her head in despair as Marlow retreated. "That one's been planting his seeds while you were gone, Sir Guy, and I do not mean children. I would see your father as soon as you can. He's been asking for you, and Marlow likes not a bit of it."

Stephen nodded and turned his attention to Katherine. "You have formally met my beloved brother. What say you now?"

"It was no pleasure. I can not lie," she murmured, trembling from the encounter.

"I will not let him harm you," Stephen assured her and tucked his finger under her chin, forcing her to meet his solemn gaze. "Europa will take you to your chamber, where you may sup in privacy. Tomorrow you will meet the rest of my family in the Great Hall."

Katherine looked hesitantly at Europa and then at the darkness beyond the stable entrance. Even beneath a veil, her hair glistened like a halo in the soft, orange glow of the torchlight.

"I will see you tomorrow then?" she said in a small voice.

"Aye, lady." He sensed she was afraid to be alone, and he longed to comfort her, but it was too soon. If he touched her, she would recoil. Tonight she would sleep with her mistrust.

"Go to bed, Katherine," he said abruptly. "You will feel better in the morning."

She started to go, but paused. Turning, she regarded him with a mixture of curiosity and coyness. "Milord?" she said.

"Milady?" *God, you are beautiful*. He blinked slowly and sucked in a draft of cold air.

With a feminine twist of her wrist, she brushed aside a tendril of hair that shadowed her forehead in the torchlight. "Milord, how did you know that I am not feeling well?"

"Instinct," he replied. The word reverberated in his chest. "I sense your feelings by intuition, if you will."

He ran his tongue over his bottom lip, wondering how much she understood, how much of him she could fathom and learn to love. "Instinct. 'Tis the sister of faith."

A flash of understanding sparked in her eyes. Then a wave of fear or guilt, Stephen could not discern which, wrinkled her brow and stole the pink hue from her cheeks. Katherine clutched the pouch at her waist, feeling for her rosary, and once she found it, she turned to go, taking Europa's outstretched hand. Together the women lowered their heads and braved the frigid air that whirled through the courtyard.

Stephen watched them go, sighing with bemusement. *God's Wounds, she is perceptive,* he thought with a glimmer of contentment. *But like a caged bird, her spirit has not yet soared. She protects it in a gilded cage.*

Thank the saints above, she hadn't been seduced by Marlow's noble airs and looks, or been deceived by his dark soul. Stephen shook his head, wondering how so many others had been taken in. Their mother doted on him, and the barons praised him as a just and ambitious peer. Even their father, though somewhat cool to Marlow, had no real quarrel with him.

With his father in mind, Stephen gave a last few orders to the stable hands and jogged across the bailey and through the gate to the earl's inner courtyard. He entered the Great Hall, stomped his feet, and shook himself free from his snowy mantle. The warm air from the Hall was a welcome contrast to the cold he'd endured. He inhaled the familiar scent of rushes scattered on the floor and freshly baked bread consumed at a recent meal. Both warmed his heart with memories of his youth. He wove his way across the room, around the trestle tables to the long hallway that ran the length of the feasting room. It led down to the solar, the earl's private chamber, at the opposite end of the giant edifice. A servant guarding his father's door bowed low, and Stephen waved him aside.

When he pushed open the door to his father's chamber, a waft of incense struck his nostrils, flooding him with thoughts of the castle chapel, where the incense burned daily. A priest softly chanted Latin incantations at the earl's bedside. Two female servants hovered in the corner next to the physician, an old man who dozed more often than not. Now and then he awoke to the sound of his own snoring. And then there was Sir Ramsey, pacing anxiously. He smiled brightly when he saw Stephen approach.

"Guy," he called out in a restrained whisper. Swiftly, he crossed the room and embraced Stephen with a slap on the back. "Again, I must tell you what a welcome sight you are. I knew if I came here I would eventually get a chance to speak with you alone, without eavesdroppers."

With a nod, Stephen motioned for the others in the room to leave. They rose in silence and left without a murmur. He turned to the trustworthy, practical steward, who was his senior by ten years. "How fares Earl James?" he said in a whisper.

The steward blinked against despair and gave a helpless shrug. "I am no judge, Stephen. Only God knows a man's fate. But if his pain-racked body is a sign, then the earl's time is short. His blood has been let so many times he's nary a drop left."

"Then we must expect the worst." Sadness filled Stephen's eyes. Pain gripped his chest as real as that which his father now endured. He covered his heart with one broad hand. "This is a sad homecoming for me. Perhaps I stayed away too long, but I did not think the earl wanted me near. Especially after the scandal that followed Lord Roby's death. Now my hesitation seems a waste of precious time. Life is too short, Ramsey."

He studied his father's pale face, his emaciated body, his thinning tufts of gray hair. Turning to Ramsey, he said, "But my father's health is not all that bothers you, is it? Tell me what happened."

Ramsey laughed hollowly. "It's that devil Marlow. God forgive me for calling your dear father's progeny such a name, but 'tis true. He is conniving with two of the castellan's strongest and most nefarious men. I am told Marlow sends Cramer and Bothwell on secret errands. Odious schemes are afoot. Those henchmen are stirring up discontent among the knights who swore fealty to your father. It is rumored they mean to strike up their own army. To what end, I know not. I sent for you when your uncle arrived. That was more than I could take."

"My uncle! Robert has returned?" Stephen was incredulous.

"Aye, he arrived a month ago. His presence has been a travail for the earl, and his condition has only worsened."

Rage rose up in Stephen and pressed against the back of his eyes, pounding in his head. Why was Robert here after so much time and animosity? Robert was the earl's younger brother, banished years ago from the castle for reasons never divulged to Stephen. He remembered so clearly the autumn morning when Robert left the castle for the last time. He could not forget the look of stoic pain in his father's face as he lingered before the fire in the Great Hall, refusing to see his brother off. Stephen recalled his mother's anguish. She stood stiffly and watched Robert's departure from the battlements. Later that night, her cries of sorrow echoed from her chamber. Lord Roby had said . . . Stephen pushed the thought from his head, refusing to see for the hundredth time his dagger piercing Roby's belly, the scarlet rush of blood staining his hands. That was the past. *Let it go.*

"I'd wager Robert and Marlow are plotting something," Ramsey said.

Stephen shook his head. "It makes little sense. This will all be Marlow's soon enough. He need not plot to claim his due, and he does not need to share it with Uncle Robert. Something has happened. Maybe Father knows. Whatever it is, surely that is what has sucked the life from him."

Ramsey placed a reassuring hand on Stephen's shoulder. "My first allegiance is to James, but you can count on me. I will do what I can as long as it does not go against the earl's commands."

"You look weary. I will stay with the earl awhile. Go get you some rest." Stephen's eyes narrowed. "And keep Marlow away from my woman."

The steward laughed ruefully. " 'Twill be a pleasure."

When the door closed behind Ramsey, Stephen turned to his sleeping father, his pale figure covered with soft ermine hides. Kneeling by the bed, Stephen grasped the earl's hand. Even though James was fifty, a ripe age, he seemed too young to die. Stephen had always thought him immortal. Seeing his father's sallow cheeks and the faint pulse of a vein in his neck, Stephen realized how wrong he had been, and a fear of loss as he'd never known gripped him. Until now, James had been so strong, but Stephen knew the sickness dwelled in his father's heart, not in his body.

Time passed slowly. Outside, the bailey grew still, save for the shouts of several knights. *Returning from their war games, weary and content,* Stephen thought. The solar's warm fire, the muted sounds of laughter, and a minstrel's song floating down the hall stirred a sense of familiarity and peace within Stephen. For a moment, sighing raggedly, he forgot his sorrow.

In the silence that followed, the earl's eyes blinked open. He looked at his son, puzzled, and then shuddered with relief. "I knew you . . . you would make it back in time, my son. You . . . always were indefatigable." His dry lips parted with an appreciative smile. "Your mother never understood your ways, but I . . . I always knew the man who dwelled within despite your reputation." His voice was weak, like the wind of a distant storm.

Stephen winced. How many times had he wanted to explain to his father the circumstances of Lord Roby's death? But it would have been easier to sever his sword arm than to inflict his father with the painful truth.

"Did you find Gilbert's girl?"

Stephen nodded. "Aye, Father. She pleases me greatly." Her porcelain face came to mind and disturbed him in an uncanny way. He would never forget the tender gaze she bestowed on him when asking about the earl's health. "Her beauty is astounding. She has wit, intelligence, and great courage. She will make an extraordinary wife."

"As Rosalind was. Your mother was also beautiful. Stephen," he said solemnly, clutching his son's hands, "I have been so blind . . . if you only knew."

"It does not matter, Father. Do not let us dwell on regrets. Time is so short."

"Nay, hear me," the earl replied adamantly. "I misjudged you. I thought you a murderer who had not the courage to confess your deed. Truly, I did. Even though I secretly held you dearest in my heart, I believed you had gone astray and shamed me, casting shadows on a name I'd spent a lifetime building. I damned you for blackening the name of Bartingham."

Stephen's face hardened. He would not let the earl know how much those doubts hurt him.

"I was wrong, my son." James's voice grew weaker, and perspiration beaded on his upper lip, his temples. "We must make repair while there is still time. I can confide in you now that I know the truth beyond question. You must make the betrothal official and marry immediately. Katherine must get quick with child. We will clear your name of the rumors. We will tell the King—"

A sudden, cold whoosh of air momentarily squelched the flame burning in the torch stand; a long shadow darkened

the earl's wary features. Like a hound smelling fox, Stephen
tensed. He turned and saw Marlow looming in the doorway.
Marlow shut the door and leaned against it, his expression
hidden in the shadows. Like a hound, the darker side of
Stephen's nature longed to tear at Marlow's throat.

The earl squinted at his eldest son, then clutched Stephen's
arm and pulled him close. "We will discuss this later," he
whispered, "when we can speak in private. Pick your best
men, Stephen, for tomorrow we will send a missive to the
King. It must get there safely."

The dying man looked back at Marlow, squeezed his eyes
shut, and sank into a fitful slumber.

"It will all come out soon enough, Marlow," Stephen said
laconically, still regarding his sleeping father. Then his eyes
coldly met his brother's. "Whatever it is that has changed
this household, turning blood against blood. It will all come
out in good time."

Marlow walked to the bedside opposite his brother and sat,
his face a blank parchment save for the dash of his lips and
the fallen ink spots of his eyes. "Aye, it will indeed come
out. Unless he dies first."

It was the simplicity of Marlow's statement that turned
Stephen's blood cold. The death that Marlow alluded to
would not be by natural causes. Or was Stephen, too,
becoming riddled with suspicion and doubt? He could not
think Marlow would harm their father. Why would he? There
was no reason and too much to lose from such a course of
action. Already Marlow was heir. It was just a matter of time
before their father's natural death made him lord and master
of the earldom.

Still, Stephen's heart beat with new urgency. A gruesome
image forced its way into his mind's eye. He could see his
father's lifeblood dripping between the bony fingers of the
Reaper.

"Father will not die until he is ready, because that is the
kind of man he is." Stephen rose and marched to the door.
He opened it for Marlow. "If he should die during the night, I

will know it was not by the Reaper's hand. Tread cautiously, brother."

Marlow rose and casually straightened his silk gipon. He sauntered past his brother and stopped in the hall. Laughing with irony, he said, "You forget, Stephen, that you are the murderer. I am but the jackal."

"He will be well guarded, Marlow. I promise you that."

"Sleep in his bed if you wish. I have nothing to fear. Or to hide."

"We shall see."

When Marlow departed, Stephen shut the door and returned to his father's bedside. He felt hollow deep within. As he kneeled again at the bed, a numbing, bitter wind whistled through his heart. He had lost a brother. Not tonight. Long ago, and it cut deeply. But no tears. No, not for the wicked.

CHAPTER THREE

✠

"Milady! Up with you now. The cocks will soon be crowing, and Sir Guy desires yer presence."

Europa's muffled voice hummed through the door and woke Katherine just before dawn. The morning air was bitterly cold, and she shivered beneath her warm fur covers.

"Sir Guy would break the fast with you, milady. You must come quickly before he sets out on his business."

Katherine groaned and stretched a ripple of pain from her saddle-sore body. Her sweet dreams quickly vanished, replaced by hard reality. She had dreamt she was safely ensconced in a convent, a noble boarder, praying for Georgie's soul. But upon waking, she remembered she lived at Blackmoor Castle, with a man she barely knew and trusted less and a family who made him seem like an angel in comparison.

She reached for the rosary under her pillow.

"Hail Mary, full of grace . . ." The prayers for Georgie sprang from her tongue in an unconscious effort.

"Milady! Sir Guy can not wait long. You must dress."

"Come in, Europa," Katherine called out with resignation. She was loath to start the day, but start it she must.

The spirited old nursemaid bustled in, wrapped in a blanket for extra warmth. Katherine had to admit she was happy to see her. She yawned and rubbed her sleep-filled eyes. "Is it Sir Guy's practice to roust women from their beds so early on a cold morning?"

"Now do not let yer feathers ruffle, milady," Europa said with a chuckle. "He has something on his mind, to be sure, or he would not stir you so. Let me dress you now. You look as natural as a peach just as you be."

Katherine forced her legs over the bedside. "I daresay he can look at whatever sight I may be if he wants to waken me thus."

Europa let out a throaty laugh. Her large melon-shaped breasts jiggled under her linen gown. "There's the way, young lady. You'll be off on a good start if you show him yer spirit from the beginning." Europa cracked the ice in the washbowl with her knuckles.

Quickly, Katherine washed her face and changed into a kirtle, which hugged her lithe body from shoulder to ankle. She relaxed when the woven burgundy flax warmed her skin and the goose bumps vanished.

Europa's fingers, though bent and swollen with rheumatism, nimbly buttoned Katherine's sleeves from the elbows to the wrists. The old woman was much more efficient than Katherine's handmaid, Agnes, had been. And for a brief moment Katherine felt a glimmer of hope that those she'd loved and lost to the Pestilence would be replaced by others equally loving. Europa paused in her rapid motions to catch a wheezing breath. She glanced at Katherine with a look so full of warmth Katherine couldn't help but smile.

"Please stay with me, Europa. I confess I am frightened by the dark mood in this castle. You are the only one who has greeted me kindly."

Europa patted her cheeks with both hands and kissed her forehead. "Not to fret, child. All will be well. Sir Guy will see to that. Won't be but another minute now, milady."

Resuming her work, Europa held out a velvet cote-hardie, which Katherine shrugged into. Europa's quick hands fixed the buttons down the front. The thick burgundy gown was snug from the low collar down to the waist; from there the luxurious velvet skirted out over the kirtle in regal folds. Europa swept Katherine's hair away from her face, knotting

the thick skein in back. A few errant tendrils returned to
Katherine's temples, framing her oval face. Europa draped
a thin, white veil over the maiden's red-gold tresses. An
amethyst fillet, stunning in its thin elegance, kept the veil
in place. The band rested lightly on Katherine's forehead,
as if to rein in her headstrong ways. Though woolen hose
would have been more graceful, Katherine favored her leather shoes. The floor was simply too cold to bear.

"Such a beauty!" Europa announced. The old woman
fetched her taper and held it high as she led Katherine down
the darkened hall to a room that adjoined the earl's solar.

Before the carved oak door, Katherine paused and thanked
Europa with glistening eyes. She gave the old woman a quick
hug and entered the room alone.

Katherine was taken aback by what she saw. Before her
at the fire, lost in thought, unaware of her presence, stood
the man she professed to dread, the roguish knight, bearing
the crest of Blackmoor on his surcoat. Stephen had discarded
his yeoman's garb, but for all his formal dress and titles, he
still could have been mistaken for that winsome peasant at the
inn. Locks of hair hanging down his neck had been tugged
at by an impatient hand, some gesture of frustration, and
thus the tousled brown mane hinted at the wilderness in
his soul. His ironic bent, which she had glimpsed that first
night, consumed him now, tinged with sadness. His serious
demeanor seemed to deepen the scar on his right cheek, and
she shivered at the chord of empathy his current state struck
in her. He was such a man, and all the more so for the dark
humor that had obviously consumed him upon his return to
Blackmoor. His complexities, his inconsistencies, aroused
in her a desire to know him better, a desire to assuage his
sorrow.

With a hesitant step, Katherine moved forward and cleared
her throat.

Stephen's head pivoted and his distant eyes brightened.
"Katherine!"

He stepped from the shadows, and she was surprised to see

that beneath his black-and-red surcoat he wore a shirt of mail. Hundreds of tiny metal loops wove across his thick chest; silver glinted in the golden flare of the firelight. The flash caught in her eyes, and she smiled, momentarily mesmerized by the beauty of the armor and the grace of the man who wore it. The moment passed, and a gloomy mood overtook her when she reflected on his purpose for dressing so. Did he need such protection in his own home?

"Are you planning a fight, milord?" she queried. "Will you don your coif and helm, too?"

He glanced down at his chest, and his lips curved in a sardonic half smile. "Indeed. This is not so much protection as it is a show, lady. I will parade through the village today and must display my armor and crests. The villeins and burghers expect strength from the sons of their liege lord. It reminds them that they are protected from any other lord who might choose to overtake them on a whim." His eyes narrowed, and the muscles in his jaws flexed with tension. "Besides, you never know when a dagger will jut from the shadows of Blackmoor Castle."

His voice was hard. His obvious lack of sleep had roughened the edges of his civility. Something must have happened overnight.

"For a moment I mistook you for that charming and errant peasant who greeted me at the inn." She tilted her head, aware that in some small way she longed to engage him as she had the first night they'd met. "There is a callousness about you today, milord. Did you not sleep well?"

"Nay, there is no time for sleep. I'm sorry to disturb you so early, lady, but this room is surely warmer than yours. I have kept a fire burning all night through. My father's room is next to this, and I kept vigil. But now Ramsey is once more with the old man."

Katherine nodded, and her eyes settled on a tray of manchet and fruit resting on the table near the fire.

Catching her glance, Stephen waved his hand at the food. "Please eat," he said, then led her to a leather chair and watched her nibble on the thick bread. After a moment of silence, he moved behind her, leaned forward, and gripped the carved arms of her chair. "I warned you of many things, but I fear I did not adequately prepare you for the treachery that was waiting in this household."

His warm breath greeted her ear like a caress, and she shut her eyes against unexpected pleasure. "Treachery?" She forced herself to speak. "I do not understand. Has something happened that I should know about?"

When he did not immediately answer, she turned to him with real concern. "What is it, milord? What has happened?"

Stephen stepped in front of her. Katherine looked up in his shadow.

"Aye," he said gruffly. "Already, 'tis time I must tell you more than you should have to bear."

He took her chin in a callused hand and tilted her head back. Her heart beat like the wings of a moth hovering near fire. Would he have been so bold yesterday? She thought not. From this angle, his eyes bore into hers, searching.

Like a branding iron, his fingers etched a hot trail on her cheeks that left her spellbound. She hated herself for feeling pleasure when his caress should have brought pain. *He wants me to forget my oath to Georgie,* she reminded herself, but she did not pull away.

"Come with me, milady." With a quick snap of his hand, he reached for his mantle draped on a nearby chair and eased the fur-lined cape over her shoulders. "Let me show you Blackmoor from on high. There, we can be sure we will not be overheard."

Stephen led the way through a maze of corridors to the south tower. He glanced up at the dark, winding staircase encircled by a wall of cold, gray stones. When their eyes had adjusted to the lack of light, he bolted up the stairs two at a time, waiting at each landing until she joined him. When they reached the top, Stephen threw open the door to the battlements. A stone curtain, eight feet thick, encircled the entire castle. This wall, connected at four different points with towers, each with its own circular staircase, allowed castle guards to observe the approach of friends and enemies from afar. Katherine pulled Stephen's cloak around her shoulders and stepped out into the frigid air.

Dawn was breaking. Purple and yellow rays rose from the ground like a vibrant fan, soon melting into softer hues of pink and blue. Down below, hungry horses neighed in their stalls. The faint trill of doves and pigeons floated from the dovecote. From this high vantage, Katherine could see the farrier at the far end of the bailey hammering horseshoes, and the miller delivering grain to the kitchen door. They were tiny figures to Katherine's eyes, and she thrilled at the feeling of power that came from this omniscient view. It was the same feeling she had had eavesdropping on her brother and his friends as a child. She used to hide in an apple tree, until she grew too large and was spotted by the boys. From that secret place, she had learned words not spoken in a girl's presence, and she realized then that it was a man's world, much of it forbidden to her sex. Like God, she could observe the boys' private lives. Unlike God, she could not affect them. And, much to her frustration, she could never join them.

Stephen shut the door behind and waved to a guard who stood watch on the high wall several thousand feet across the bailey. Recognizing Sir Stephen, the youth bowed and turned back to his duty, studying the horizon. Stephen took Katherine's arm and escorted her at an easy pace. With a note of pride in his voice, he described some of the battles that had raged along the wall-walk.

"It is here that I first learned to aim at the enemy's heart, Katherine," he said, pointing to the jagged line of battlements through which defending knights had aimed their arrows in sieges past. The wind whistled through the crenellations. Stephen fairly bellowed to be heard. "My aim improved considerably when, from down below, a flaming arrow sailed over this rampart, striking me soundly when I was but ten and six. Not only did the arrow's point leave a lasting scar on my neck, the flames caught in my hair and left me bald for a month."

Katherine, who had walked ahead, paused and turned back, askance. "Your head was on fire?"

Stephen chuckled and leaned against the edge of the parapet, which came to his midsection. He regarded her with inviting eyes. "Aye, 'tis a life of danger and heartache I've led, Kate. I lost my hair."

Why was he so full of charm when she least expected it? "Then your misfortune served you well, milord. When your fleece grew back, it was with force and beauty. Now it longs to be combed." She reached up and brushed her fingertips through his hair, wondering what, other than his irresistible beauty at this moment, compelled her to be so bold. The wind, so powerful at the top of the castle, immediately displaced the locks she had straightened. She brushed his hair again with warm fingers that trailed his temple, and Stephen groaned, shutting his eyes.

"Aye, the return of my shaggy mane was my fortune, indeed," he murmured.

Pleased by his pleasure, she withdrew her hand and smiled. He groaned again, this time in complaint. His eyes flew open and pierced her with vibrant scrutiny.

"Do not stop, lady. Or do you fear me still? I think not so much as before."

She gave him an enigmatic smile. "I fear for my future. Aye, I do not trust you to be sure, Stephen. But after meeting your brother, I do not know who I should watch more guardedly."

Stephen turned and leaned over the edge of the curtain. "This land that you see stretching out to the horizon, that will all belong to the next Earl of Blackmoor."

"Your brother," Katherine offered.

"Aye, Marlow. Katherine," he said, and with a resoluteness that bespoke his masculine strength, his self-confidence, he reached out to pull her closer. He tugged at her waist with willful hands until their clothing enmeshed. She felt the give and take of his breath beneath his chain mail. Her trembling hands found his hauberk, the rough mail cold and hard against her fingertips.

"Katherine, my brother is not to be trusted. Whether you like me, love me, or loathe me, we must be unified should anything come to pass. If Marlow takes over, we will need all our forces. Do not listen to him, Katherine. Do not let him poison you with tales of my past."

"He can surely tell me no worse than I have already heard," she said, pushing away from his close grip. "How can I forget you slew a man out of dark passion? It was no joust *à outrance*, no honorable fight to the death. I can not align myself so soon with a man I don't trust, even if you are the better of two evils."

Stephen's eyes flickered as if a dagger tip had pierced his callused skin. "You have already listened to stories that bear no truth."

"How can I be sure if you yourself will not tell me what the truth is? Why did you slay Lord Roby?"

"The circumstances can not be repeated without dishonoring another. 'Twas a fair fight. That is all I will say."

"I do believe in my heart, Sir Stephen, that if you are innocent, no words of man will ever harm you."

"If you judge a man by action and not by words, then you are right. As my actions will prove my innocence."

"Georgie said—"

He took a step toward her. "Georgie did not know me, though he may have thought he did."

Stephen's massive frame was a shield against the gusty wind. She was aware of every inch of the man—how much taller he loomed over her, how wide and sure his stance was on the narrow wall-walk, how hot his weathered cheeks would feel on hers if their lips would join in longing reunion. Aching for that warmth, she pushed him away. Tears of guilt blurred her vision.

"Ho, my lord!" A faint voice interrupted them from the far end of the castle bailey.

Katherine blinked back salty tears and focused down below. There a man stood next to the mews, tiny in the distance, a small peregrine perched on his arm.

" 'Tis Jasper, the falconer." Stephen gave the man a big wave. "He has a peregrine ready for the lure. He wants to show off the bird."

A page came running from the nearest tower, clutching a leather glove and a lure pouch. He bowed low before Stephen and gasped for air. "I came as quickly as I could, milord. Jasper says the peregrine is ready for a fly. Here is a glove, milord. Put it on and hold the lure tight, then give her a whistle."

Stephen smoothed over the lad's blond hair with a hand. "Do you think me a beginner, boy?"

The lad flushed with embarrassment. "Nay, milord, I just repeated Jasper's instructions. Forgive me, milord."

Stephen chuckled, a kind look illuminating his handsome features. "By dale and down, you'll make a good falconer one day, boy." He accepted the pouch and glove.

Warmed by Stephen's compassion, Katherine smiled. She looked over the wall, eagerly awaiting the bird's ascent. "At Shelby Manor, we lost our merlins after the Pestilence killed our falconer. It had been years since we had any peregrines, though. I envy you that."

Stephen fitted the glove and pulled the raw meat lure out of the pouch, gripping it within the glove. "Jasper has raised a gyrfalcon, which Father planned to give to the King. 'Tis the largest bird I've seen. Its wings span four feet, white as goose down. Be sure to visit the mews for a look."

"Aye, I will." She settled in comfortably next to Stephen.

From afar, Jasper waved one arm, signaling his readiness. Stephen raised the lure in the air and let out a high-pitched whistle. For a moment, there was no reaction, until the wind carried the sound back to the bird. Then the peregrine alighted, soaring from the falconer's arm. With great flapping wings, it climbed the air with the speed of a longbow.

The bird is free, Katherine thought. Her heart lurched with empathy. Blinking fast in the harsh wind, Katherine studied the bird's every movement. She imagined she was the falcon, conquering the wind, soaring without hindrance. As the bird approached, its talons stretched wide in anticipation of the spoils. Though this creature possessed stunning grace, it was a hunter and ready for the kill. In a matter of seconds, the falcon reached the top of the battlements. Wings spanning three feet ripped through the air.

A sharp cry screeched from the bird's throat as it hovered overhead, as if contemplating the options: fly back to the wild, or sate its appetite with its master's offering.

"Fly free," Katherine whispered, overwhelmed with a bittersweet feeling.

The falcon bolted forward, and for a moment Katherine thought it would claim freedom. That was always a risk when a young bird's leash was loosed from its jesses for the first time. But it did not vanish. The peregrine made a wide circle, gaining altitude, and then dove fast at Stephen's lure. His fist was encompassed with flapping wings; the lure on his falconer's glove jolted with each thrust of the bird's beak.

Katherine gasped and stepped back. She let out a shuddering breath, moved by what she had witnessed. "Utterly stunning."

"Aye, you are," Stephen replied in a deep voice.

She tore her eyes from the feeding bird and found Stephen regarding her with unabashed desire. Somehow the moment had ripped away their facades; this was the real man, a man of honesty staring at her soul, oblivious to the bird that clutched his leather glove, pecking with greed at the lure.

"My God, you are beautiful." Stephen spoke as if he'd just discovered a cask of gold. "If you expect me to ignore that, you will be disappointed."

She could not match his stare and so averted her eyes back to the peregrine. The bird looked up from the raw meat and paused, cocking its head sideways, as if it, too, had suddenly realized Katherine's beauty.

Katherine waved them both off and withdrew, pressing her back against the stone wall. She had to escape, to be alone.

"No more, Stephen. Please, I must get back to my chamber."

With his free hand, Stephen reached out and grasped her wrist as swiftly as the peregrine had snatched the lure. "I want you, Katherine." His brows furrowed with intensity. "Not just for this marriage, not just to please my father. I want you as a man wants a woman. I'll hold off as long as I can, but I can't predict when the bough will break."

Still resisting his grip, her body taut, she nodded stiffly in recognition. She saw his desire, and that wanting was something she felt, too. Try as she might to be the innocent one, innocent enough to pray her brother's way into Heaven, she felt a connection with Stephen that could not be denied. Later she could pretend it didn't exist, but on this cold spring day truth rang out like a mournful choir in the wind, and she had to hide. His hand was a vise around her arm, but finally she tugged free. What did he want from her? A protestation of love? She couldn't give it.

"You expect too much," she whispered in a ragged voice.

Stephen sighed with frustration. Shifting his stance, he turned and studied the bird. "Perhaps so." The normally rich timbre of his baritone voice sounded dull and flat. "I do not mean to frighten you. Perhaps we should talk business, which is why I brought you up here."

"But of course," Katherine said. She gave him a brittle smile. "That is my only reason for being here. To secure some matter of business. Aren't all marriages for that purpose?" She spoke more harshly than she'd intended. All she wanted to do was hide her sudden feeling of vulnerability. But like a gosling who'd lost her way, the farther she went astray the louder she honked.

He ignored her provocation. "My father is gravely ill and will soon die. My brother is conniving and maneuvering some ill-advised plan which I have yet to unearth. Bear with me. Do not trust Marlow in any way. I have made arrangements for your safety in any event. Your father had no lands to give me, save for a token field."

Katherine turned to him with sudden embarrassment. "I am sorry for that."

"S'Blood, I do not want you for your lands, woman. I thought you knew I was different from other men. We promised your father protection in exchange for this match. I mention it only because you need more security. I am giving you Downing-Cross, a small estate run by tenants. Should anything happen to me, it is yours to keep."

"What could possibly happen to you?"

Done with its meal, the bird took off. The dark mood that consumed Stephen earlier returned. He grasped Katherine's hand. "Hopefully, nothing, but we must both be on guard."

The door to the tower creaked open, and Geoffrey rushed forward. "Milord, Sir Ramsey awaits you down below."

"In a moment, Geoffrey. I'll escort Katherine back to her chamber."

A lone wolf howled in the distance. Its forlorn cry pierced the silence of Katherine's chamber, and she looked up from her needlework with a start. Following her early morning rendezvous with Stephen, she felt uncharacteristically skittish. Again the chilling howl jarred the silence of her chamber, and Katherine placed her stitching down next to Europa. She rose from the comfort of the crackling fire and went to the window to glimpse her companion in despair, the creature who cried out against solitude, but there was nothing to be seen except sheets of snow and sheep, a flock of off-white specks on the landscape, and the village below.

" 'Tis just a wolf crying for her mate, love. Do not let it bother you," Europa said in her robust, cheery manner, her eyes fastened all the while on her needle.

"We rarely saw wolves at Shelby Manor." Katherine pressed her hands against the cold, soldered window; her breath clouded her vision, and she wiped the glass with her fist. "They've always frightened me, I daresay. They're so

haunting and sad. How strange that this one should cry for
all to hear in the middle of the day."

She shrugged beneath the weight of melancholy. It was
only her first full day with her new family, and already she
felt keenly out of place. Stephen had gone out on business.
So it was Europa who had given her a complete tour of
the grounds, from the dovecote to the kitchens. Aside from
her visit to the mews to look at the magnificent gyrfalcon,
Katherine had been most impressed by the size of the men's
and women's quarters. There was a hierarchy of life here
in the castle; whole families dwelled within the confines
of the bailey, all employed to serve the earl and countess.
Katherine tried to imagine how busy it must have been before
the Pestilence.

She would have to meet Stephen's family at the evening
meal, and as the hour drew near, she made nervous trips to
the window, hoping to see Stephen's horse approaching from
the distance.

The sun lowered steadily, casting golden beams of afternoon light on snow that glistened without a jot of warmth.

"They mate for life, you know." Europa's voice, gravelly
and warm at the same time, rattled Katherine's ruminations.

"What's that?" Katherine pressed her nose against the
frosty glass.

"The wolves, I said. They mate for life. Just like humans.
Their love runs deep. And if their mate is killed, poor things,
they sometimes die themselves."

"No!" Katherine exclaimed in disbelief, turning slowly
as Europa's words registered. "How can that be? You are
too romantic, Europa. How can beasts know anything of
promises and faith?"

"I speak truthfully, my lamb. The poachers have told me
'tis so. They know the ways of God's creatures. The animals
act on instinct."

Instinct. Faith. Now she knew where Stephen learned his
nobler notions. Or did he merely mimic the words to impress
Katherine? When he drew her close on the castle wall-walk,

she had glimpsed the depth of his entrancing eyes, like deep
pools of frosty blue in a freshwater cave. Wisdom and spirit,
defiance and daring—it was all there. She felt faint even now
remembering the strength she had beheld beneath his strong,
carved brows. That iron will bespoke integrity, and though
she had no proof of it, she would take that on instinct. But
faith was a different matter. Remembering how ragged the
scar on his cheek looked up close, she was reminded of
his battles, his fights. She could not forget he had killed
Lord Roby. Perhaps Stephen was no better than his mal-
feasant brother. Baffled, Katherine sighed and turned back
to the narrow window, and there, in a nearby field, stood a
gray wolf.

The animal looked around in seeming bewilderment, and
then threw its head back with a high-pitched howl. The
creature's neck pointed straight up to an indifferent sky, with
rigid muscles as it sung its poignant dirge. The animal ceased
its howl, waited for something, then loped off through several
feet of snow.

Katherine shivered. "The poor creature must be lost. Or
perhaps its mate died, Europa. You see, its loyalty led to
heartache."

"Love does not always end so cruelly, milady."

"I suppose not," Katherine said distantly, pushing away
from the window. She could not waste her sympathies on
every sad creature she encountered, and she could not indulge
in romantic notions of eternal love and mating for life. A few
nights ago, when her head was spinning from the effects of
mead, she might have thought otherwise, but her life had to
be devoted to more than frivolous love. She had made a
vow to her brother, and she would keep it. Even if Stephen
claimed her body, and as a husband he would, he could not
claim her heart. Ever.

Katherine realized it had been an hour since she'd prayed
for Georgie, and she felt a pang of guilt. "Dear Father,
forgive us our sins," she muttered, resuming her litany. The
sun slowly retreated back to the earth; an orange glow pulsed

at the horizon. Europa lit three more tapers while Katherine prayed at the window. Soon she grew fidgety. She couldn't put Europa's words out of her mind. Katherine rejoined the older woman at the fire and resumed her stitching.

"Europa, let us not indulge in foolhardy notions about mating for life. You know as well as I that any man or lass with half a mind will find another when their mate dies, if not before. It's all a matter of survival and, too often, even greed. I for one will marry only because I must. And that would not have come to pass in this dreadful way, shuffled off without warning, if it had not been for my father's eagerness to raise himself up a notch." She shook her head disdainfully.

Europa glanced up from her work and smiled; a twinkle of light reflecting from the fire played gently on her wrinkled face. "Is that why you have been to the window twenty times today? Because you do not care for any man?"

Katherine blushed at the truth. "Is my lack of devotion so apparent?" She sighed. "I swore to my brother I would dedicate my life to prayer. After only one day in this household, I'm already looking to Sir Stephen for comfort. It frightens me that he should be my only anchor. My brother condemned him as a murderer. I trusted Georgie's opinion implicitly." She let her stitching fall to her lap, and she turned to Europa. "I feared for my own safety when I met Sir Stephen, but now I don't know. He doesn't act like a murderer. Underneath his sometimes gruff exterior, I see a tenderness not often found in a man." She threw her hands up and pressed them with frustration against her face.

Europa laughed gently and patted her knee. "There, there. It will all come clear soon enough. In less trying times, Guy would be a gentle man all the time, but times are hard. You must be on yer guard. As for you, when you marry, you must be loyal above all else. Treachery is all around us."

Katherine gave her a knowing look, one eyebrow raised in acknowledgment. "Stephen said as much this morning."

She recalled the bitter twist of his mouth when he spoke of his brother's malevolence. And then Georgie came to mind, an image of his racked body, spotted with black circles, the mark of the Black Death. She looked sadly at Europa and said in a shallow voice, "What if you are torn between two loyalties?"

"When you marry, you must side with your husband."

Katherine rose in frustration and paced the stone floor. "If only it were that simple."

Europa hoisted herself from her chair and stopped Katherine in her tracks. Pressing loving hands against the girl's shoulders, the old woman gave her as stern a look as she could muster. "I have known Guy since he was a babe, Katherine. I suckled him at my own breasts. Believe me when I say he's no murderer. Oh, the times and dark ways of his brother try him now, but by my troth, only Guy will look at the sun without blinking when all is out and out."

Katherine was struck by the old woman's loyalty. She trusted Europa, and the nursemaid's obvious love for Stephen intrigued her. He was certainly an enigma. She had to confess that until his deception at the inn had been revealed, she had liked him. She had liked him very much.

A rapping on the door came so softly it might have been a mouse scurrying through the rushes.

"Enter!" boomed Europa's voice.

Constance, Marlow's wife, stepped in with an air of arrogance that did not fit her downtrodden appearance. *She means to claim her territory,* Katherine thought.

Constance's eyes widened when she spotted the nursemaid. "I had not thought to find you here, Europa," she said with a touch of disapproval. "You certainly look after Stephen's interests; I must say that much for you."

The stiff-backed matron glided forward but stopped with interest when she saw the women's stitching on their chairs. Eyeing the work critically, she said, "I've come to see if Katherine would care to join me with our embroidery. After all, she will soon be part of the family. Her children will one day appreciate a tapestry showing the history of their forefathers."

She looked up at Katherine like a falcon that had spotted a lure. "What say you?"

Katherine cleared her throat and turned to Europa, inwardly pleading for reprieve. Realizing the rudeness of her hesitation, she quickly agreed with a faint smile.

Constance's dull eyes lit briefly with genuine pleasure, and Katherine was happy she had had the good grace to acquiesce.

"Lead the way, Lady Constance." Katherine squeezed Europa's shoulders as she departed, hoping to draw some strength, for she suspected she would need it. She followed Constance down the hall to a small withdrawing room equipped with a bed, chairs, and a large tapestry frame. Several torch stands positioned around the tapestry illuminated a pattern of burnished bronzes and golds that depicted a long-ago battle scene. Pulling a stool forward, Katherine sat down and admired the enormity of the project and the skill of the Bartingham women who must have worked on the piece for decades. Running her hand along the linen, she wondered who had stitched the blood spilling from one wounded knight.

"This scarlet is so striking," she said. Curiosity displaced her caution, and she turned to Constance with a fascinated look. "Who is this fallen warrior?"

Constance, already seated and thrusting her needle to and fro, glanced up with a dark glare. "That is Sir Hugh of Blackmoor, great-great-uncle to the earl. According to written history, he died nobly defending the castle." She returned her focus to her needle with a wry smile. "But hearsay tells it otherwise. He was second born and wanted the castle for himself. He died at his elder brother's sword point."

Katherine shook her head, wondering at the foolishness of men and their battles. "So much blood is let for land that no one can ever truly own, Lady Constance. We are all but yeomen tilling God's soil, borrowing His pastures. When we die, we leave it behind. It goes back to God. It is never ours to claim. Why do men not realize their ownership is nothing more than foolish posturing?"

Constance eyed Katherine coldly. "Do you think so?"

Katherine could not pull her hands away from the striking artwork. She caressed the stitches as she spoke. "The devastation of the Pestilence was wretched, but that was God's will. War is another matter. That is man's doing."

Katherine sank back into her chair with a sigh. "Yet I must confess when I was young, I longed to be an earl."

"You mean an earl's wife?"

"Nay," Katherine said, looking up with a brash smile as she began to stitch. "An earl. It's silly, I know. Now I think it was a blessing to come from humbler origins. After all, no one will try to kill me for lands I do not possess."

They worked in silence. Soon the cold settled in Katherine's hands, and she slowed her pace to steady her increasingly awkward and numb fingers. She stole a few glances at the woman who would soon be her relative. Constance must have been attractive when she was younger. Her features were well formed, but her mouth was tight, drawn down at the corners. Her eyes were brown, passionless. Any beauty or spirit she might have once possessed had long since been trampled. All that remained was the ghost of a woman, save for an intermittent glimmer of rage, or bitterness, Katherine could not tell which.

Constance looked up suddenly. Returning Katherine's scrutinizing gaze, she said, "You are very beautiful." Her voice was filled with sorrow. "I have never been pretty. But I brought lands to this marriage."

"I think that if a woman brings lands to a marriage, she should have some say in their distribution, wouldn't you agree?"

Constance stopped the incessant motion of her hands and stared suspiciously at her companion. "No good will come from such thoughts, Katherine," she warned, shaking her head ominously. "Marlow would be furious if he heard you say that."

"The devil take Marlow," Katherine answered as her temper flared. "You are not his slave. You are a woman with your own mind and will. Marlow can not read our thoughts, Constance. Even if he could, he does not have reign over them."

Constance's hands flew to her ears, as if she were fearful that Katherine's rebellious ideas would poison her beaten spirit.

"You foolish little snippet," Constance hissed. "Harbor those notions and I'll see you cut down to size in time enough. Do you think you are so special that men will do your every bidding? Not even Stephen is fool enough for a woman's wiles to be ruled by one. You will see."

"Can you not be loyal even unto yourself? Would you not claim the dignity due you if someone offered a way to retrieve it?"

"I am loyal to the only one that counts, foolish girl."

Katherine stared at the embittered woman with amazement. Constance had placed her unquestioning loyalty in the wrong hands. Katherine was still uncertain if Stephen deserved her trust, but she had no doubt her first loyalty would always be to herself.

Constance thrust out her chin with indignation. "Marlow will soon be lord of this castle, and I will assume my rightful position at his side if no one else gets in my way."

Katherine bristled at her implication. How could she even think Katherine would want to take her place next to Marlow?

"Dignity," Constance continued in scoffing tones. "What do you know of dignity? You were shuffled off from your father's barony without a second thought, sold to a murderer because he bore the name of an earl. You will have it no better than I, Katherine, and soon, when the bloom has wilted from the stem, the thorns of faded love will prick your hands as they have pricked mine."

Humiliation coursed through Katherine, warming her cool cheeks with hot blood. It had been painful enough to judge her own lot as less than dignified, but to have someone else voice it, name her ill-used, was too much to bear. Blindly, she pushed back her chair and rose to leave, but she halted when Constance cried out in pain.

"I have stabbed myself!" Constance clutched a bloody finger, her brows twisted in frustration. "See what you made me do? It will be days before I can use this finger to stitch."

"Are you badly hurt?" Katherine hurried around the tapestry to Constance's side. "May I get something for you?"

Constance shook her head, recoiling from Katherine's touch. "Leave me alone. You have no right to touch me. You have no right to be here."

Katherine breathed in sharply as if she had been slapped hard on the cheek. "I will not do anything to harm you. And I will leave you be if that is what you wish." A distant wave of melancholy flooded through her as she realized the extent to which her presence was unwelcome. It would be a long, lonely life here, indeed, but it would do not good to let Constance see her hurt. Checking an impulse to run from the room, Katherine regained her composure and returned to her chair.

"You know nothing of what your life will be like when you marry Stephen," Constance rambled angrily, wrapping a cloth around her finger.

"That is true," Katherine admitted.

"I have not yet delivered a living child." She spoke bitterly, emotion gurgling in her throat. "What do you know of that? Nothing. Nothing."

"I am sorry."

Constance laughed derisively. "I would like to believe that. Oh, how I would like to believe that."

"How can you believe otherwise?" Katherine replied incredulously.

"If I do not bear a son, then your heirs will inherit this land."

Katherine shook her head in bewilderment. It seemed that not only would she marry Stephen, she would wed the family's animosity as well.

Constance brushed back a tress of hair that had fallen down her temple, sable strands streaked with gray. "For years my womb shriveled daily. Every month it twisted with barren grief and cried a flood of red tears, an unnatural flow, staining me with an unwanted sign of my childless state. And when God blessed me with a spark of life, I could not hold the child within for more than three or four months. I could count my miscarriages like beads on a rosary." Constance continued in quieter tones, her bitterness once again hidden behind a flat expression. "But now I am pregnant again. Four moons have come and gone, and still I cling to hope this babe will survive."

She molded her hands over her belly, and for the first time Katherine noticed the swell of pregnancy.

"Nothing must get in the way of this birth. If I do not bear a son soon, Marlow will be done with me."

"Surely you do not mean . . ." Katherine's words drifted away. The distant cry of a falcon and the coaxing voice of the falconer rose and faded on the wind. Divorce would be impossible, but if Marlow were as ruthless as Stephen claimed, he could find other ways to rid himself of a barren wife.

Constance handed her needle to her serving woman and rose, smoothing the crushed satin of her cote-hardie. She looked at Katherine, not unkindly, and said in a whisper, "Until I do bear a son, I am certain you will remain childless. If you were to have a boy-child, Katherine, the chances of it surviving are . . . very grim. What with so much illness rampant these days. One never knows when the Pestilence will surge again."

She whisked out of the room, leaving Katherine in stunned silence.

CHAPTER FOUR

✠

A somber mood hovered over the Great Hall when Katherine approached Stephen's family during the evening meal. The Bartinghams sat at a long table raised on a dais at the end of the Hall. From that height, the lady of the castle could see that her guests were well served, and the lord could watch for any traitorous dagger waiting idly beneath a table. The countess sat imperiously in the center, seemingly oblivious to her husband's absence, observing the festivities.

Pages served their lords and ladies, who shared trenchers and imbibed liberally from the earl's best stocks of mead and ale. Hounds waited patiently for bones beneath the tables, and knights waited impatiently for time alone with the countess's ladies-in-waiting. The gales of laughter, common during any other evening meal, were subdued. Several knights, fulfilling the forty days of service owed in fealty to the Earl of Blackmoor, sat at long trestle tables and benches arranged in a U-shape around the Great Hall. Several basked in the pulsing glow of the fire, weary after a day's practice at the quintain.

In the shadow-cloaked entrance, from behind drawn curtains, Katherine peeked at the festivities with great trepidation and clutched Europa's hand for comfort. In a soothing voice, the nursemaid rattled off a list of people Katherine would meet. She tried to listen, but her mind was consumed with thoughts of Stephen. She had waited in her chamber until the very last moment, hoping he would return, but he had not, and she had taken the insult far more personally than she cared to admit.

Finally arousing her natural grace and an inner strength forged on far more tragic circumstances than social embarrassment, Katherine released Europa's hand and swept into the room. Her confident smile and sure steps masked her inner turmoil. The knights who quietly traded stories around the trestle tables greeted her with appreciative stares. Sensing their admiration, Katherine blushed with new confidence. When she reached the dais, she curtsied in a manner befitting her station. "Lady Rosalind, may I be so bold as to present myself? I am Katherine, Lord Gilbert's daughter."

The countess pulled her eyes away from the ornately dressed nobleman at her side, and in an encompassing glance measured Katherine with merciless acumen. "So you are, my dear."

With downcast eyes, Katherine curtsied to the floor and waited until the countess lifted her chin with one ruby-studded finger. "Come, come, my dear, with the woman who will soon be your mother-in-law you needn't be so formal."

Rising, Katherine studied the countess with awe. The elder woman was strikingly beautiful despite the wrinkles that fanned out from the corners of her eyes. With her diminutive frame cloaked in black velvet and red silk, she looked like an exotic flower that still clung to the vine well past the first frost. A black lace veil covered her raven hair, and the rigid folds of a wimple protected her neck. Her flashing eyes and expressive eyebrows bespoke a brilliant wit, biting at times Katherine had no doubt. But the most dramatic of all the countess's physical attributes was a widow's peak that formed a slick raven-colored V against her pale forehead. Her berry-stained lips drew attention away from the lines of age that knitted her mouth. Katherine suspected the illusion of youth was very important to this strong-willed woman.

"Welcome, my dear," Countess Rosalind said, studiously polite. "Of course you may present yourself, if you will forgive my son's rudeness. He should not have left you alone on your first day, and I regret I was not able to meet you sooner. I have been preoccupied. If I had known Stephen was still away, I would have sent Ramsey to escort you here. I hope you have rested well from your arduous journey."

"Indeed," Katherine replied. "Your hospitality is most generous."

"In that case, may I present you to the Earl and Countess of Montbury?"

Katherine curtsied again, feeling like a doll on display, disdaining the lecherous grin on the old man's face.

"Lovely, my dear," Montbury said, and rubbed his tongue over toothless gums. "Lovely."

As Katherine modestly nodded her head, she felt Rosalind's eyes on her, narrowed in scorn.

"My son has chosen well, Katherine. You are lovely, indeed." Rosalind spoke so evenly Katherine could not assess her sincerity. "And I welcome you to the family. Let us just hope you can keep his interest longer than the rest of England's ladies have."

Katherine felt the wind vanish from her lungs, and she struggled to keep dismay from her expressive face. The earl laughed appreciatively, exchanging a knowing look with Countess Rosalind, heedless of the jab he received from his wife's elbow.

Katherine's smile faded as a wave of insecurity engulfed her. With a subtle jibe, the countess had swept away the small bit of trust Katherine had developed with Stephen and replaced that trust with a painful reminder of his worldly past. She raised her eyes, swimming with vulnerability, and focused on her future mother-in-law. Why had she purposefully raised a painful subject? Did she take pleasure in taunting others? Blinking away the hurt, Katherine managed a thin smile. She had no one to blame for her dismay but herself. If she would just remember that this was an arranged match and nothing more, then she would be invulnerable to the emotions associated with marriage—love, frustration, sometimes even hatred.

Next the countess introduced Katherine to Stephen's uncle, Robert, and to John, Stephen's distant cousin. In a daze, she graciously greeted them all, then could remember none of her polite banter. She sat in the spot reserved for her and studiously avoided Marlow's insinuating eyes which followed her every move. And, thankfully, Constance would not even look at her.

For all her reticence, Katherine was famished and indulged in the richly spiced brewet and the delicious beef marrow fritters presented as the first course. She listened distantly to the boasting of Uncle Robert, a man both handsome and charming. For a time she even enjoyed herself, but then the men concluded their debate over speculation of a peasants' revolt, a constant source of fear among the nobility. The upstart cousin, John, sat down drunkenly after nearly picking a fight with Marlow over who would win the next jousting match. The trenchers were pushed aside, and with them the activity that had distracted Katherine from her solitude. She sadly clutched a goblet of mead and pressed it to her lips, forcing herself to drink. The taste merely reminded her of the night she'd danced with Stephen. Why wasn't he here? She thought they had come to some small understanding. He did not have to want her as a wife, and she certainly did not want him as a husband, but to cast her aside before introducing her to his family was humiliating. She sat next to an empty seat where her betrothed should have been presenting his beloved to a happy family.

She laughed to herself, amused at her own flights of fancy. She did not want that kind of devotion and love. She wanted time alone to pray. She should not forget her vow to Georgie. With prayer in mind, Katherine wiped her hands with a warm cloth offered by a page and rose to leave, but noise at the Great Hall's entrance caught her attention, and she turned to satisfy her curiosity.

The loud banging stilled the drunken shouts, which were now less respectful of the earl's illness and more convivial, after the spilling of much mead. The door at the far end of the Hall was flung open, and all heads turned. A wind-bitten traveler, hidden beneath a dark cloak, stood poised in the door-way. He stepped forward, followed by a band of peasants—a fat, toothless woman, a one-armed boy, an old beggarman, and a stocky farmer—all shivering and awestricken by the luxury of the Hall and the wealth of its inhabitants. Behind them stood three others of higher bearing who carried instruments, obviously minstrels.

"Could you not have waited for me?" bellowed the traveler, tossing back his hood.

It was Stephen! Katherine's pulse quickened at the sound of his voice. Her irritation and anger faded at the sight of his imposing presence. Even from a distance, righteous indigna-tion gave added strength to the strong line of his jaw. Anger stiffened his spine, and he seemed to loom over the others. His arrival was like a fresh wind on the moors, carrying the hint of a brooding storm. Stepping forward with wide strides, Stephen surveyed the room. His cutting gaze took in all who feasted.

Katherine's gaze tenuously met his, and she shivered, cer-tain his stormy eyes held some secret message meant for her alone. Forgetting her anger at his absence, she felt honored to have his attention. His eyes flickered past her and on to the others. He would not fail to shock her this night, she realized with eager curiosity. Her prayers forgotten, she took another sip of mead and resolved to enjoy the fall of the dice. Something had changed in him. Every day they spent together, the landscape shifted, his demeanor revealed more depth, his raw inner strength displayed deeper hues of emotion.

"I have ridden all day on business of the castle, and you did not leave food for me?" A servant rushed forward and caught Stephen's cloak just as he unclasped it and tossed it to the floor. "And I have brought guests."

Stephen motioned for the cowering, numb peasants to step forward, and they did so reluctantly. Their chafed and rough-hewn faces poignantly showed their discomfort.

"Stephen," the countess said, collecting herself at last. "Send your guests to the kitchen and come join us. The Earl and Countess of Montbury are with us."

Stephen gave Katherine a comical, questioning look. *Should I behave myself?* he seemed to ask her, and she smiled openly, invigorated by his devilish carefree attitude. News that outsiders would witness his presentation only added fuel to his scheming, she could tell by the heightened gleam in his eyes. He'd never looked so dashing as he did now.

"My lord earl," he said with an edge of mockery, and bowed before Montbury, "I am most honored."

"What is the meaning of this?" Marlow said. He rose from the table, wiped his mouth, and regarded his brother with contempt.

Stephen shrugged ironically. "I wonder the same. Such somberness here. Do we bear sad faces for the benefit of our guests?" His voice rose to a roar as he made a sweeping gesture across the room. "If you truly loved Father, you would have music and dancing. That is what he brought to this castle. You would laugh with the love of him if love were in your hearts."

"That is quite enough, Stephen," the countess said. "I'm surprised you remember what your father liked. You've been away so long. Until, of course, he lay down on his deathbed."

Her bitter words echoed through the hall.

"One never forgets the bonds of blood. Even if it means the ruination of one's name," Stephen replied in a frigid voice, his meaning lost on the countess. "Let us celebrate life and all its wonderful ironies. Play, minstrels."

With fingers still numb from the cold, the musicians struck up an incongruously merry ballad, and several knights, the most drunk, began clapping.

Anxiously, Katherine rose from her seat. She wanted to be near Stephen at this moment, to lend her support in any way she could. It was so clear he stood alone in this room except for Sir Ramsey, who watched him with obvious loyalty. Before

Katherine reached Stephen's side, Marlow marched toward his brother and stopped inches away.

"You are despicable. How dare you return with your blackened name and show such disrespect to our father?"

"And what of your disrespect, Marlow?" Stephen replied, confident and poised despite his growing anger. He pointed to the peasants. "I found these poor peasants futilely chiseling at the frozen ground. They wanted to bury their dead, but the ground was as solid as granite. When I asked them why they did not build fires to thaw the earth, they said there were no trees they might fell and burn. The Earl of Blackmoor, they said, forbids them to go into his woods. When I asked them why they do not buy wood with the money from their crops, they said the earl has levied a new tax against them. For what purpose, they do not know. Nor do I."

Stephen poured a goblet of mead and swilled a portion. Marlow pulled him close by the arm.

"This is not the place to discuss estate policy. Father had his reasons."

"Father had nothing to do with it," Stephen countered. The muscles in his jaw pulsed wildly; his blue eyes were colder than the deadliest winter frost. "This is your doing, Marlow, and do you know what it will have brought you? In the summer, when they can travel easily enough, your workers will leave for service in a different barony."

"They can't!"

"They can and they will if you treat them so harshly. The Pestilence made them bold. They have seen lords felled by the Scythe of the Reaper as easily as serfs. They will no longer cower under your threats. You must make it worth their while to tend your crops."

"You have grown weak, Stephen. I will not compromise my duty to the realm to placate a few animals."

Stephen sneered. "You are an idiot. A contemptuous idiot." He turned to the others. "Feed my guests. Would you make the King wait so long unattended?"

No one moved. Even the servants were frozen in place, unsure where their loyalties should lie. Finally, Katherine broke the tension. She returned to her place and with trembling hands retrieved her half-filled trencher. Ignoring Rosalind's scathing look and Lady Constance's gasp of astonishment, Katherine handed the dish of food to the oldest peasant, who bowed awkwardly and took the trencher with an embarrassed nod.

"Bless ye, milady."

As she stepped away, Katherine felt Stephen's focus on her as surely as if it were a caress.

Softened by her kindness, Stephen motioned to Ramsey, who called for servants to escort the peasants to the kitchen for a full meal. The other guests in the Hall broke into nervous laughter and talk—the moment of confrontation had passed. Marlow returned to the head table, temporarily mollified, exchanging glances with the countess, who then returned her attention to her guests.

Katherine let out a sigh of relief and then started in pleasant surprise when Stephen tugged at her tippet sleeves.

"Come hither," he commanded, and pulled her into the shadows of a corridor that ran the length of the Great Hall.

"Why? Why did you take my side when you do not trust me any more than Marlow?" He squinted at her as if she were a new species discovered, and she felt her breasts grow warm beneath her heavy velvet kirtle.

"Why?" he repeated. This time it was a whisper, his words a gentle entreaty nestling against her hair. His hand gripped her elbow, sparking a lightning bolt of warmth.

" 'Twas not such a valiant deed, milord."

"I disagree," he countered. "Are you always so bold? One day in this household and you have already raised the ire of Rosalind. Did you not consider that taking my side would bring condemnation from those more powerful than I?"

Katherine tossed her hair aside with a bold gesture. "Nay, husband-to-be, it takes more than disapproval to dissuade me from action once my mind is set."

Stephen's face brightened with a slow, winning grin. As if to reward her, his hand slipped around her waist, a strong grip that claimed and protected her. "It seems I've bargained for more than the naive little vixen who met me at an inn not so long ago."

"Indeed." Her eyes flashed indignantly. "You thought me nothing more than a nimble-minded female? Now you know better, but my prize is still a scoundrel in disguise."

A frown marred his handsome visage, and he pulled his hand away, squaring off for battle, but her arrogant demeanor cracked with an impish grin and genuine laughter, the first she had uttered in a month.

"Who does the deceiving now, Kate? Methinks it is you. You must learn to humor a wayward rogue."

Katherine smiled, riding the current between them. She enjoyed the vying of their wits. But it ended quickly when he frowned with concern.

"I must check on my father and speak with the physician. When I return, you and I will have a moment alone. I did not intend to thrust you into this den of vipers. Believe me, it will not always be like this."

Watching him disappear beneath the arch, she did believe him, though she didn't know why.

The musicians began to play a pensive ballad, and a young tenor broke into a high, quavery melody. Katherine returned to the dais feeling more distanced from her new family than before. Marlow stared after Stephen with a sullen expression, exchanging whispers with Uncle Robert. The countess and her guests turned their attention to the minstrels. Something was amiss. Katherine could feel it in the pit of her stomach. She realized how curious it was that no one in the family had been tending to the earl during the meal. As if to confirm her suspicions that all was not well, Marlow rose suddenly. He glanced anxiously at his mother, who was too absorbed in the music to notice. He bowed to the table and had started making his way across the Hall when a distant voice stilled him in his tracks.

"I told you never to leave him unattended!" Stephen shouted down the corridor. His booming voice echoed from the earl's solar. "What manner of priest are you that you can not keep vigil? Where is the physician? Guards! Fetch the physician."

In a moment Stephen returned and stood at the far end of the Hall. "Ramsey, find the physician and send him to my father. I do not want him left alone."

As Ramsey barked his orders and men-at-arms scurried about, Stephen stood alone, drawn back in the archway like a bear ready to attack. Anger embellished every feature—his wide lips were thin strips, his eyes flashed like torches, his brows furrowed. Katherine saw his fear, his love and concern for his father, and some new horror. She did not know what had happened, but she felt Stephen's pain as if it were her own. If his anger were directed at her, she would surely run.

Stephen reached Marlow in three quick strides. Breathing heavily, he slammed his hands to Marlow's chest and pulled him close, ripping his finely embroidered gipon.

"You bloody bastard!" Stephen raged. "I warned you to keep your bloody hands off him. What did you do? Bribe the physician? Or is it your own dark potion that keeps him from waking?"

"What is it, Stephen?" the countess demanded. "Is James . . . ? Is the earl . . . ?"

"He is alive," Stephen said, still raking his dark gaze over Marlow, "but unconscious. I fear he will never stir again."

Countess Rosalind stifled a cry; pressing a hand over her mouth, she hurried toward the solar. Robert followed her, as did several servants.

Marlow flung his brother's hands from his chest, sniffing indignantly. His gaze swept around the room to survey who had witnessed this challenge to his honor.

"I know not of what you speak, Stephen," Marlow said smoothly. "I have been here supping with the others."

Sir Ramsey had returned and stood poised near the two men, ready to intervene if necessary. The other knights in the room shrank from the confrontation. There were those whose hearts favored Marlow and others who held allegiance to Stephen—never overtly, of course, for they all fought under the same banner. None of them wanted to come between their lords, who stood tensed like dogs ready to tear each other apart.

"You did not touch him?" Stephen said, his voice incredulous.

"Don't be a fool," Marlow whispered. "Even if all the black things you think of me are true, I would not kill my own father. Would you?"

Stephen frowned, resisting the lure of Marlow's obvious taunt. His brother was half a head taller than him, but Stephen's passion and rage more than balanced the difference in their physical statures. Marlow had the advantage of age and position, but he did not have Stephen's character, and that was the persistent thorn in the older man's side.

"Get you hence, Stephen, before I have my men put you in the tower. I'd cut off my own hand before I'd hurt Father."

"Liar," Stephen shouted, and his anger once again boiled to the surface. He pulled his dagger from its scabbard, metal singing. Stephen swung the point around to his brother's neck. The sharp tip pricked Marlow's skin and blood bubbled. A chorus of gasps rose around the Hall.

"No, Stephen!" called Ramsey, taking a step forward.

Katherine clutched the table, her mind reeling. Stephen had not denied he'd killed a man. He could slay his brother now, and then she would be proven right about him. He would be a coldhearted murderer. For once, she hoped she was wrong.

"It would serve you well if Father never regained consciousness, wouldn't it, Marlow?"

"On the contrary," he replied with sarcasm chiseling his handsome features, " 'twould be tragic were he never to wake."

Stephen pulled away slowly and threw his blade to the ground. Just when it seemed he had contained his anger, he drew back his fist and smashed it into Marlow's astonished face. Marlow fell back as his brother leapt astride his prone figure.

"I should have killed you long ago, you bastard," Stephen said. "You do not deserve to bear our father's noble name."

The intensity of his voice sent a chill down Katherine's spine. She had never seen such animosity between brothers. It sickened her, and she longed to feel Georgie's embrace.

Everyone stood still, uncertain whether to intercede or run. Ramsey motioned his men to keep their distance. At last, Marlow kicked his brother away, taking the advantage. He pulled Stephen up by the collar and thrust him brutally against a marble pillar.

Katherine started forward, but Ramsey stopped her.

"Ramsey," Marlow shouted between gasps, spitting out blood. "Get this scoundrel into the tower. This murderer . . . this heathen who calls himself family has returned to overthrow us."

But the steward merely stood his ground, his arms outstretched in front of Katherine and several knights who had retrieved their swords, ready for the worst.

"Why do you hesitate? I command you." Marlow turned over his shoulder to see the mutinous look in Ramsey's eyes. "Traitor! I'll have you in the stocks when Father dies, Ramsey. I promise you. Is there no one who will come to his master's defense?"

"You are not master yet, Marlow," Stephen countered, pushing them both away from the pillar with the force of a bull.

"Hear me now, Marlow. You are not now the Earl of Blackmoor. Nor will you be until he dies. Even then it will take a lifetime to replace a man whose honor is without blemish. You may call me knave if you wish, but God above knows who bears that title. The one who would take another's life because he has something to hide. The one who must steal to gain stature in the world."

Stephen straightened his collar, wiping blood from a cut above his brow. He calmly went to Katherine and proffered his arm. "Let us pray that Father regains consciousness soon. For if he dies without waking, I will slay the one responsible for his death."

Katherine rested her hand on Stephen's and walked numbly from the room. She felt a riot of amazed and hostile stares penetrating her back as they exited through the archway. Neither spoke as they proceeded down the hall and up the winding stairs.

Stopping outside her chamber, Katherine leaned against the door and sighed with a shudder. As much as she was disturbed by the confrontation and upset by the violence, she was more concerned about Stephen's state of mind. His father might have been poisoned.

"Do you think your brother is capable of such a thing?" she whispered.

Stephen smiled jadedly. "Unfortunately, I am certain of it. He is smooth. He covers his tracks. Proving it is another matter."

Stephen rested one arm against the door frame.

"I am ashamed to call him my brother," he said. "We were both raised under the same roof. How can we be so different in character? It burns my heart that our mother is so blind to his true nature."

Katherine blinked slowly, listening to every word. A combination of torchlight and compassion twinkled in her eyes like cut emeralds.

"Poor father. A man spends his whole life building his land and propagating his lineage, and to what end? It is all so dependent on the next generation. For despite it all, Katherine, time sweeps away man's crumbled monuments like so much dust in a charnel house. Father will not live long, even if he survives this . . . this drugged sleep. So it is up to Marlow and me to carry on his legacy, his life."

Katherine found herself spellbound by the melody of his deep voice, husky with emotion. She listened, and heard his sadness, but comprehension came on a deeper level. Somehow he awoke in her an empathy she had not felt since the death of her brother. She longed to caress away the concern that cut a jagged line in Stephen's forehead, to run her hand over the day's growth of beard that gave him an earthy appeal.

"You are so innocent," he whispered in amazement, and did the very thing she had only dared to contemplate. He reached forward and cupped a warm cheek in his hand, gently kneading the tension that settled there.

At his touch, Katherine uttered a short gasp and shut her eyes. Her breasts rose and fell with each short-winded breath. All she could hear was the distant shuffle of leather shoes on stone as minions scurried through the castle, and the muffled pulse of her own hammering heart.

Stephen then cupped both her cheeks in his hands, as if he contained a precious handful of clear, pure water. "Look at me," he demanded.

Her eyes fluttered open and focused on his chest. She did not want to meet his gaze. Then he would surely know that she wanted him to hold her. He would see the tenderness she had never expected or wanted to feel. She reached out and placed her palms on the crest that adorned his broad chest. She longed to lay her head against that strength, for whether he was evil or good, he was a man of strong will, a man to warm her against the icy winds of fate, a knight who would hold high his shining sword.

"I recognized your beauty the first night I saw you, Kate, but I did not know until now how innocent you are. It is so obvious here at Blackmoor where deceit and treachery abound. I'll not forget you stood by me tonight."

Finally, Katherine forced herself to look into his eyes. They were so intent, so searching that she shivered with a sudden chill. She shook her head, fighting a sense of shame. "I am not innocent." *I desire you.* "I am unfaithful to my vow."

Stephen frowned and then smiled with a confident, entreating gleam in his eyes. He lowered his head and their lips met. He brushed his lips against hers, grazing her mouth ever so slightly. It was a tender introduction to a promise of ecstasy.

"Stephen . . . Guy," she whispered, confused by her emotions. She pushed away in a meager gesture of restraint.

"What vow have you broken?"

"I promised to be chaste, to pray for my brother, but in my heart . . ."

He brushed his fingers through her hair, and shivers coursed down her neck. For so long she had ignored the longing that rumbled in the depths of her soul, the natural passion that came with womanhood. Now that it had erupted at his hot touch, could she abandon her longing for the rest of her days? Her moist lips parted in a sensuous moan of consternation and delight.

Stephen chuckled and encircled her waist with strong, muscular arms. She tilted her face up to his. In sheer delight, she wrapped her arms around his neck, marveling at the sense of freedom she felt surrendering to his embrace. He was not nearly so ominous as he had appeared moments ago in the Great Hall.

"I love the touch of your lips," he whispered. His mouth sought hers as if by some prearranged appointment, some pact coordinated by destiny. Katherine groaned and grasped the back of his head with both her hands. His bronze, weathered cheeks smelled of an autumn camp fire, the brush of leather from a worn saddle, the faint remnants of perspiration—all the elements that made him a man, a man of the world, a man she wanted with a need she had not even known she possessed.

His tongue slipped between her lips and spoke to her in a wordless language that was new to her. Following his lead, she let her tongue meet his in a timid greeting. Soon timidity melted beneath his slow, burning kiss.

Katherine began to tremble, sensing the profound connection discovered accidentally through physical contact. As much as she longed to let her newfound passion quench its desire, she was too disturbed by the emotions that came with it. This was no man to toy with. This was a man who would see her heart, claim it, and never let go.

Such is the power and danger of passion, she thought, withdrawing from his kiss. She stroked his cheeks and solemnly studied his imperfect nose, slightly askew from a lance's blow. His high cheeks were smooth beneath her touch, save for the scar she stroked as if she had the power to heal some long-ago wound. At last she knew why lovemaking was so feared and so desired at the same time. Sensing she stood at the precipice of great love, she quaked within. She had never meant to lose her way, to stand at the boundary of self-control, eager to leap into an abyss of sexual and soulful union.

"I have never known anyone so intimately," she whispered, fear fluttering in the depths of her eyes like a butterfly unfurling from its cocoon. "You toy with me, Sir Stephen."

"Nay," he murmured sensually.

"You strip me of my guard with no thought to my innocence. If you take me carelessly, you will steal the very heart of me. How many women went before me? And after our political marriage is sworn by the priest, how many will follow?"

"Nay, dearest," he entreated, and kissed her eyelids, her forehead, her cheeks. "Do not be afraid."

He kissed her again, slipping his tongue briefly between her parted lips for a final taste of the honey he was sure awaited him there, and then withdrew.

Recovering from the jolt of warmth that ensued, Katherine shook her head in disbelief. He had disarmed her with a mere kiss. She inched along the stone wall, retreating until his arm blocked her path.

"Why do you run from me, Kate? Why are you afraid?"

"I am not afraid," she said defensively, and then tore her gaze from his haunting face. Risking all the trust they had built so quickly, she voiced her fears. "Would you have killed your brother, Stephen? Are you capable of that?"

His blue eyes hardened and glistened with frost. "If he killed Father, then I would have slain Marlow. But that is a matter of duty. Surely you would not judge me harshly for doing my duty. Do not let imagined sins burden your thoughts, Katherine. I did nothing more than wound my brother's bloated pride. Did you not fight with your own brother?"

"Never," she said with a touch of self-righteousness. "I would tell the world that we loved one another freely, without rancor or jealousy."

"I can only wish you held me in such high esteem." He ran one finger across her satin lips and looked at her wistfully. "Ah, sweet Kate, have we met too late? Is the armor encasing our hearts made of metal forged in too hot a fire?"

Stephen blinked with sadness in his eyes. "Time will tell. For now, I must tend to my father's needs. Tomorrow I will show you Blackmoor, the part that I have known and loved. Even though it will never be ours, I want to share that with you. Till then, sleep with angels."

He touched her cheek and turned away. Katherine waited until his footsteps grew faint. Shaking still from the passion of his kiss, she entered her chamber. A taper burned at the bedside. The yellow glow illuminated a form fast asleep beneath the covers. Katherine gasped and slammed the door in her fright.

"Milady!" a young maidservant cried out. She sat up with a look of guilt and jumped out of bed. "Beggin' yer pardon, milady, I did not mean to sleep. I was sent to undress ye and warm yer bed."

"Well, the bed has certainly been warmed." Katherine caught her breath and stared at the rumpled covers. She wanted to be alone, but the slip of a girl looked at her with an appealingly open and simple face. Katherine liked her instantly.

"What is your name?" Katherine asked with eager affection.

"Rosemary, milady." The girl pushed aside the long strands of tangled chestnut hair that had fallen in her eyes.

Katherine nodded and pointed to a trunk in the corner. "Rosemary, I have a robe there. Will you fetch it for me?"

"Aye, milady." Rosemary grinned and made a dash for the trunk.

Katherine ambled to the window, her thoughts in turmoil. She scanned the dark landscape, searching for the wolf she had seen earlier, but it was nowhere in sight at this late hour. She lowered her head in disappointment. She felt a kinship to the animal. They were both lonely, lost in a strange setting, fearing the future, yet anxious for it to come. Katherine raised her head and noticed the moon, perfectly round, casting a blue light on the ground, illuminating an unknown path.

"I shall not need a bed-warmer in the future, Rosemary," Katherine said and turned to the waiting girl. Smiling, she added, "But tonight, I am cold."

Rosemary's head bobbed up and down, and her face lit up brightly. "I keep a warm bed, milady. I have the blood of a horse!"

Katherine undressed and pulled on her robe, unwilling to sleep naked with a stranger. Rosemary brushed her hair and followed her to bed. Without speaking, the maid crawled in beside Katherine, and soon the heat from their bodies penetrated even the southernmost regions of the down covers.

Katherine fell asleep quickly, but her dreams were fraught with despair. She dreamt of thunderous blue clouds that threatened a storm. Beneath the churning clouds a woman ran crying over the moors. The poor creature was in love. Then Katherine entered the dream, dressed in a bloody white gown. She was about to be married, but not to the man she loved. At the altar, Katherine's betrothed turned to her, but it was not who she had expected. It was someone else, someone horrible. And just when she was about to see the face . . .

"Dear God in Heaven!" Katherine bolted upright and gasped for air. The cold night weighed heavily on her chest, pressing her down, smothering her.

"Milady? What is it? Did you dream?" Through the darkness, Rosemary stared at her in bewilderment.

From outside, carried on a piercing wind, came the reply—the spine-tingling howl of a wolf.

CHAPTER FIVE

✠

For the three days following her nightmare, Katherine did not stir from her chamber. She rebuffed Stephen, the countess, and even Europa when they came to see if she was sick. For all her boldness of spirit, she could not keep pace with the changes that were occurring. She was exhausted. She had never given herself time to rest from her journey to Blackmoor, and an irritating cough beset her. That was due, in part, to the castle itself—so much larger and draftier than Shelby Manor.

Mostly she was assailed by loneliness and a longing for home. Days after her tumultuous welcome, when she realized she was here to stay, Katherine was overwhelmed with sadness. Her heart ached for all she had left behind. No more the comforting talks with her mother before an evening fire; no more the haunting and familiar clang of church bells from the abbey near her father's manor; no more the secret, wild rides over the moors on her brother's steed, with a full moon lighting her path. She would be a wife now.

Her churlish humor had nothing to do with Stephen's kiss, she reassured herself. Her brush with intimacy meant nothing in the scheme of things. It had been pleasurable, of course, but she had never aspired to pleasure. Like Georgie, her life was devoted to nobler causes. She clutched her rosary throughout her three-day respite, hoping her prayers would compensate for the desire Stephen had stirred in her. Nay, the lust! She would call it by its true name. Lust had no place in her life.

A promise was a promise, and she had sworn to see Georgie into Heaven. Human desire could only hinder that cause.

The intoxicating warmth of Stephen's kiss had made her light-headed, as if she had drunk the finest claret, altering her perceptions in a new way that was as profound as it was pleasurable. Leaning her feverish forehead against the cold windowpane, Katherine stared out at the snow-filled bailey, where several knights shouted orders to their pages. She blinked in the desolate morning light, and in her mind's eye she saw Stephen's haunting, rakish face. She couldn't quite trust him, nor could she turn from him. Before she had met him, she was carefree. Now she was full of care and indecision. Even while she blamed Stephen for her chaotic emotions, she longed for his touch, and her loneliness increased. Tears of frustration rimmed her eyes, but she quickly regained her composure when she heard a fist pounding on her door.

"Katherine! Open this door and let me see you."

It was Stephen, and from the sound of anger in his voice, Katherine knew her days of solitude were over.

"Katherine, why are you hiding? Are you ill?"

His voice jarred the solemn air, and she turned sharply from her place at the window, staring wide-eyed at the spacious room that separated them. Surely he would abide by the rules of propriety and honor her privacy.

"Katherine!" The tone of his voice was sharper now. Apparently, Europa was at his side, for she anxiously chattered away in the background.

Katherine clutched the ledge of the window, uncertain whether to answer or to pretend she slept. She could not let him see her in her present state. Her hair was a tangled mess, dark circles shadowed her eyes, and her robe was wrinkled, hanging loosely at the edges of her shoulders. Then she cursed her frivolous concerns, for when had she ever cared what a man thought of her appearance? If only Europa would tell him to leave. Katherine did not know why reticence had overcome her. She only knew she didn't want to see Stephen.

"Katherine, if you do not answer, I shall storm this room with my guards in tow. Answer me. What is wrong?"

"Nay, milord. 'Tis nothing. Go away," she called out, rushing to her bed. She climbed beneath the covers and pulled them tightly around her neck. "I am but a trifling ill. I have a cough. In a day or two I shall be well." She coughed loudly for his benefit.

His voice rumbled in the hall, punctuated by an occasional, indecipherable exclamation from Europa. Then silence.

Finally, he said, "Katherine, Europa says you have not eaten since the night before last. The physician can be spared from my father's side long enough to examine you."

"I do not need a physician," she said irritably. In truth, she didn't know what she needed.

"Very well. As you wish, Katherine," Stephen said after a moment.

The rattling of the door latch ceased. He'd given up after all. She relaxed, but only for a moment. Without warning, Stephen kicked the door open and rushed inside. Katherine shrieked in astonishment and outrage. The door swung back against its hinges, revealing a worried and bemused Europa standing in the hall. The nursemaid shut the door, leaving them to argue in privacy.

Katherine gasped at the sight of Stephen. He looked like a dashing highwayman come to take his pleasure after loading his horse with the castle's booty. His broad chest bulged beneath a billowy shirt cast open at his neck. Dark tendrils of hair curled up in a manly fashion through the V-necked collar. How did a nobleman acquire so much brawn, she wondered breathlessly. But then he was not a man to rest on titles. He was a knight who worked as willingly and as hard as a common soldier. And what anger! His eyes seared her to the spot. He strode forward and stopped at the foot of her bed.

"What is the matter? You look dreadful." Anger and the faintest hint of fear exuded from him like a powerful blast.

"That is a despicable thing to say to one in my state."

"And what state is that, pray tell?"

She turned away sheepishly, burrowing into her pillow, watching him from the corner of her eye. He looked damnably handsome for one who had come to scold her. Sunlight caught his dark, shiny hair. Breeches, a deep burgundy nearly the color of blood, tightly gripped his hips and muscular legs. Their reddish hue mirrored the shade of his ruddy, high cheeks. And those lips—widely set, always poised with bittersweetness.

"Go away" was all she could manage to say.

His anger waned, and his face turned ashen. " 'Tis not the Death, I pray?" His hoarse whisper sounded like a prayer. "You are not sick with the Pestilence?"

"Nay, 'tis not the Death," Katherine answered rancorously. "Do I look so dreadful as to have the Death? Or do you mean that I am so wayward in nature that I alone could lure the wretched disease back into the realm?"

Her sharp words took him aback. "Nay . . . nay, it is only that you look so pale, and I have seen so many fall these two years passing."

She did not doubt the depth of pain that clouded his eyes, and she regretted her harsh retort.

"Do not fear, Sir Stephen. I will not succumb to any disease in the near future, God willing."

Stephen ran a hand through his tousled hair, sighing, then, remembering his anger, he turned to her with piercing eyes.

"What is amiss here? Are you ill, or is this pretense? If you are sickly, I will not have you lying here suffering alone. I want Europa by your side and a careful examination by the physician."

"Do you intend to hold sway over my every waking moment when we are married?" she rejoined. "Where is the laughing, charming man I met in the inn?"

"I do not laugh when the woman I am about to betroth is ill. Now, let me have a look." Stephen eased down at the edge of her bed.

Katherine held her breath a moment in disbelief. His nearness was unexpected and her reaction unwelcome. She felt a sudden desire to tuck her hand through the opening in his shirt and explore the rippling muscles that flexed his bronzed skin. Ashamed, she recoiled in horror and scrambled out of bed.

"Milord, you are too bold." She pulled the blanket to her thinly covered breasts, backing away toward the window. "Do you intend to have your way with a sick woman?"

"S'Blood!" he cursed. He stepped forward and grasped Katherine by one arm, tilting her head into the light from the window with the other. His hand on her cheek was rough and tender at once. "Just as I thought. Too much spunk for a sickly lass. You've lied to me. You aren't ill at all. You've been crying."

"I pray you, milord, when you're finished scrutinizing the salt on my cheeks, why not examine my teeth? Then you'll know for certain what sort of beast you got in the trade."

His grip stiffened around her wrist, and just as she was about to cry out in pain, he dropped his hands to his sides. A bitter look briefly creased his brow, and then concern softened his features. She tried to maintain her defensive glare, but it was impossible beneath his tender look of solicitation.

Still clutching the covers to her breasts, she turned to face the window and tears welled in her eyes. Her confusion about the man she would soon marry was matched only by her confusion about her own feelings.

"Yes, I have been crying, Stephen. What do you expect? You force me to break my promise to my brother and then try to appease me with tender words when this is nothing more than a loveless match."

Stephen stood behind her, staring out the window as he spoke. "I have misjudged you. I thought you were opening to me."

"Oh, I was," she whispered, taking in a sniffling breath. "That is precisely the matter."

She felt his nearness, a gentle shadow looming over her shoulder, entreating, protecting. The desire for something more threatened to cut loose between them like wild horses.

"I know you not, Stephen Bartingham." Wiping a tear that had fallen down one cheek, she turned to him with a frank expression. "You may care naught for the nuances of my humor, nor that I must know you before we . . . become as one." She faltered with embarrassment, and then whispered, "I have my honor and like it not that you shake it from me as easily as dust from a hearth rug."

Stephen sank into a chair and stretched out his lean legs. He stroked his clean-shaven chin and studied her.

"Katherine, honor can not be shaken like dust. It is in a person's heart, like nobility—true nobility. Were I to take you here on this bed today without sanctity of marriage, you would still retain your honor."

She looked at him with astonishment. "You blaspheme! I am nothing without my honor, and a woman is shamed to be taken in such a way. How can you think otherwise?"

He laughed jadedly. "How can I think otherwise? It is easy." He entwined his fingers and settled his hands on his even stomach. "I have seen much of the world, Katherine. I have seen valor in the living and the dying, and I tell you when a woman gives herself in love she knows no higher honor."

The air was still and close; heat flushed through Katherine's petite frame. Weakened by hunger, she wondered if after her fabrications, fate had not contrived to plague her with some genuine illness.

"Do not speak of love." She waved him away and weakly made her way to the bed.

"So that is it," Stephen said with a smug smile.

"Nay, it is nothing," she hurried on, regretting the turn of conversation. "I just do not care to dwell on trifling fancies of the heart."

"The heart is no trifling matter, Katherine."

"Nay!" She turned to him like a caged animal. Her pink cheeks flamed red, and her velvet brows gathered in consternation. "I will hear no more of it. You have made me desire you in a way I never wanted to. You have shaken my vow to Georgie. You have invaded my thoughts and my mind. I dream of you, and when you are near, I want your touch. I have even taken up your cause against your family. And still, all I know about you is that you murdered a man, your father is dying, and your brother is more wicked than you. You have told me nothing more, and you expect me to fall before you in some thoughtless fit of passion. I have more pride than that, Stephen. I would rather wither here in my chamber than to fall the way of so many hapless, fawning girls before me."

Stephen rose and went to her, pulling her up as easily as a willow leaf. He held her by both arms, staring fixedly into her eyes.

"What has frightened you so, Katherine?" His voice came hoarsely. "I do not understand you at all. You would choose proud, lonely solitude instead of affection and love."

Katherine's breath grew shallow and her heart beat urgently. "You do not mean what you say. Do not speak of love."

The muscles in his square jaw rippled wildly, and anger flashed in his eyes. "Am I so appalling? I have not beaten you. I am not a toothless, pockmarked fool. Why do you not shout with joy that you will marry a man who would honor and love you as a wife?"

"Because you may not always," she answered in a bitter whisper. "Because you are mortal. I loved my brother, Georgie, and I loved Agnes, but they are gone. Dead with the Pestilence. What did my love fetch me but grief and tears?"

Though her lips were set like stone slivers, tears fell down her cheeks, her eyes luminescent with remembered horror.

"Where were you when I laid my brother's body in his grave because no one else would touch him, when even my parents would have left him to rot rather than risk their own lives?" Her voice was a dagger scraping the space between them.

"Where were you?" she screeched with a strangled cry. Her face contorted with grief; blood flooded the veins bulging at her temples and neck. Her arms struck out aimlessly and sent a pewter mug flying across the room.

Stephen did not flinch. He took her verbal blows with quiet strength.

"Where were you, Stephen? What could you have done? And what would you do if the Pestilence returned? Would you die as my brother died? Would you leave me alone, all alone with my love?"

She squelched the shaking sobs that waved to the surface, unwilling to give in yet again to stinging sentiment. "I felt so alone," she whispered harshly and pressed both palms to her eyes. "I do not want to be alone ever again."

"Katherine," Stephen said.

He stroked her hair, and something in his voice, some knowing compassion, broke the dike creaking inside her. She burst out in fresh tears and fell into his arms.

A long time passed in this way, her small body shaking against his while all the hurt, fear, and anger poured out in an inglorious fit of tears. Finally, her shaking gasps subsided to sniffles. Her body was spent and relaxed, free from another stage of grief. Stephen held most of her weight, and she felt as if her tears had somehow melded their bodies together. It was such a perfect fit. The wind howled outside, begging entrance, and the window latch rattled its denial. Oh, what contentment! To feel the fire, to know the cold was at bay, to nestle in the arms of another, arms as strong as a sword forged in the hottest fire, yet as soft as worn leather. No chain mail to separate the syncopated beating of their hearts. She heard the muted thudding of his heart against her ear. Her left arm was flung over his shoulder, and her right arm clutched his waist. He stroked her cheek over and over until her breathing returned to normal. She did not know how long they stood thus. Soon the heat of the fire diminished, and the flames gave way to hissing embers. It was a truer heat, more intense than flames, but the logs needed stoking to thrive.

She withdrew from the haven of his arms to keep the fire alive. She knelt at the hearth and fumbled with a heavy log.

Her mind was still cleansed and dazed by her tears, and the log slipped from her lax fingers.

Stephen gently pulled her up and deftly thrust the log into the fire with one hand.

"I'm sorry," she mumbled, smiling at his tender solicitation. "I thought I was done crying. For two years the tears poured forth like an ocean, and I thought I was finished with such tiresome displays of emotion."

"At least you can still weep, lass. When you no longer have the heart to do that, you may as well be dead like the others."

She nodded in agreement, grateful for his view of what she considered a terrible predisposition to tears. He made her vulnerability sound like an admirable trait.

"You see, I did not speak out of turn," she said a moment later. She brushed her fingertips across her tear-laden eyelashes and looked up at him with mischief. "You've seduced me into your arms once again, even as I cursed my oaths against your character."

"Hmmm. Indeed, 'tis true." Stephen stepped back and bowed grandly. "I beg your forgiveness, milady."

"Very well, you are forgiven," she said magnanimously, casting him an exaggerated look of arrogance over her shoulder. She flopped back onto the bed. Her eyes caught his, and the fire burning between them flared with new life. "I warn you I shall be wary from this point forward."

Stephen frowned. He leaned against the hearth and studied her, his arms crossed. New flames glowed against the backs of his legs, giving his towering stature added height. At last he smiled, a slow grin that promised trouble. "Very well, milady. I assure you, you have no need to be wary. I pushed too hard, I see that now. The next time I touch you, it will be your doing, your wanting, your asking. Nay, your commanding."

He taunted her with a cunning grin, his eyes placid. The knight had put forth his challenge. She nodded her acceptance.

CHAPTER SIX

✠

In the days that followed her confrontation with Stephen, Katherine regained much of her spirit and heartiness. When she shared moments of laughter with him, their exchanges were laden with words unspoken. Like a latent bud that unfurls at last with quick determination, the understanding between them had become a sturdy blossom, a rare specimen of beauty in the otherwise dark castle. Yet she held back, still tormented by her obligation to Georgie, still haunted by his warning about Stephen. She continued to protect her innermost thoughts, the tenderness that coiled fearfully within, that prize Stephen seemed to long for the most.

Stephen, however, had little time to dwell on the changes in Katherine. He was consumed with affairs of the estate. Along with Ramsey, he poured over the reeve's records, taxes, expenditures, and the yield from the previous summer's crops from all of Blackmoor's fiefs. Stephen suspected that the figures would reveal some meddling or incongruity, but everything balanced to his satisfaction. If Marlow's furtive dealings stemmed from the finances, the books did not show it.

Earl James still lay in a deep slumber. No amount of leeching, no poultices, no prayers seemed to free him from the cage of his unconscious. But his heart still beat steadily, and Stephen clung to the hope that he would recover. He could not bear the thought of letting his father go. When Earl James died, Marlow, the vulture, would pick his bones clean.

Stephen made sure that when he was not at his father's side the earl was well guarded by Ramsey and his men.

Tension in the castle was almost palpable. Especially at meals. Stephen kept his civility when dealing with his brother, yet he brooked no fools or treachery. He was a hard man to those who betrayed him and did not put on a false show of affection. Katherine found that comforting.

Even though she had settled into a daily routine by the end of her first week, she still felt oppressed by the gloomy mood of the castle. So when Europa came in one morning to announce a short journey with Sir Guy, Katherine dressed quickly, eager to be gone.

"We are traveling to Downing-Cross, Katherine. That is my wedding gift to you," Stephen called to her as she hurried from the inner chambers to the castle stable. His horse pranced impatiently, hooves crunching the crusty remains of the late snowfall that still refused to melt. Stephen steadied his stallion with a tug of the reins and chuckled at Katherine's mad dash toward the saddled mare that awaited her. "At last you show some eagerness for my company."

At his smug remark, Katherine slowed her pace and cast him a haughty frown. "Think not that I was dashing into your arms, Sir Stephen."

"Nay, I'd not have you even if you did, milady. We have agreed. The next time we embrace it will be at your command. You will not be allowed to stumble into my bed without a truce. I'll not be accused of lechery again."

"Lechery, indeed. No doubt 'tis not a new charge against you. Georgie had much to say about the faded posies in your past." Katherine spoke with an air of superiority as she surveyed the dappled gray mare saddled and ready for her. She did not look at him to see if her sword had found its mark. She knew from the boisterous sarcasm in his voice that he was well armed against her verbal thrusts and parries.

"Come, Kate, do you not long for a virile man to warm your bones? Admit it, thorny rose, you did dream of me last night."

"I do recall some nightmare, now that you remind me. But a man to warm my bones?" Even though he embarrassed her in front of the stable hands, she smiled at his audacity. "Not for all the King's gold. I'd not command such dishonorable behavior since we are not yet married. If I had my way about it, there would be no marriage at all."

"Aye, there's the way of it then. You are a hard woman, Kate."

She ignored his chiding remark and stepped into the foot mantle offered by a stable hand, who then cupped his hands for her to mount. Comfortably seated in her saddle, she was at last on Stephen's level.

"What are you about now, milord?" She couldn't contain a grudging smile or mask the attraction she felt. After all, he looked so dashing in his billowing mantle and velvet gipon. His high cheeks, rugged and burned by the wind, exuded nobility. He was obviously determined to enjoy himself this day no matter what daggers and arrows she hurled at him. "Why are you so good-natured this morning, Stephen? Are we off on some adventure?"

He did not answer, but his eyes, briefly flickering with sensuality, spoke volumes. He studied her face, and then his gaze lowered. She was confident his searching eyes would be disappointed. He would find no voluptuous signs of femininity, for she was wrapped in her cape like a cocoon. But then he was a man who seemed to view life with an inner vision. He was like a riddle, a labyrinth she could not walk away from, and she would not be content until she found her way through to the other side. She grasped the clasp that secured the mantle at her neck. Content that it would hold tight during their journey, her hand lingered a moment at her breasts. Her heart throbbed beneath her gloved fingers. The more he stared at her with his wanton display of appreciation, the louder her heart beat.

She detested the vulnerability she often felt in his presence. It was as if he could see into her soul. In a flash of inspiration, she dashed her heels against the belly of her mount and lowered her head when the animal bolted forward.

"What ho!" Stephen cried as she streaked past him.

"I'll race you, Stephen," she called back triumphantly, pleased that she'd taken him off-guard.

"You do not know where we're going," he shouted, loosening the reins on his eager steed.

They galloped side by side with great clamoring past the barbican, over the drawbridge, and out to the main road, where he easily took the lead. Realizing her defeat, she slowed her pace. Stephen reached out and pulled her horse short, and then reined in his own. Seemingly enraptured with her bold game, he let out a booming laugh, his face alive and gay. A golden ray of light sparkled in his mirthful eyes.

"I'll not chase after a woman, Kate, so if ever you want me, make sure your mount is but a slow nag."

Katherine smiled at him with a sidelong glance. A rush of boundless joy and affection filled her heart, and her eyelashes fluttered in a coy dance.

"You're full of jest and insinuation today, Stephen. What have I done to deserve this ribald exchange? Why will you not be content with my reticence? Must you goad me into confrontation at every turn?"

"You've been peevish all week, and I mean to put an end to it." He nudged his mount into a trot and filled his lungs with a deep breath of air. When he exhaled, white plumes billowed from his lips.

"Nay, I have not been peevish. I've been to the Great Hall every evening since you forced your way into my chamber."

"True. And while you're full of polite smiles for my family, you're a stranger to me. 'Tis the thanks I get for cajoling you back to life. If it hadn't been for me, you might have starved in your chamber. I deserve better, Kate. 'Tis true, and you know it."

It was true. He deserved a wife who would love and honor him, and she could allow herself to do neither. At the very least she could be pleasant company.

"There has been much on my mind. Forgive my selfish behavior."

"I don't want your apologies, Kate. You've done nothing wrong. I just want your willing hand in marriage."

They reached the crest of a hill and paused to appreciate the stark beauty of the rolling hills that stretched to the horizon. Katherine swallowed the strangling emotions that clutched her throat when the subject of marriage arose.

"You have my hand," she said without conviction. "It was given you by my father."

"Aye, but I want it from you."

She turned her head in his direction. Half-moons of tears cradled her eyes. Did he know how much she wanted to kiss him when he spoke so plainly? Certainly he did not know how much their growing affection tore at her heart.

"Neither my hand nor my heart are mine to give." Katherine nudged her mare forward, and Stephen followed. Her mantle snagged on a tree branch when they passed a copse of rowans. Three ravens stirred from their leafless haven, cawed in complaint, and swooped overhead with wide, black wings. She glanced up and sighed with melancholy. The haunting birds added to her gloomy thoughts of Georgie. Her vow of chaste prayer had been made freely in the Pestilence's darkest hour, but now it seemed like a millstone around her neck.

Stephen did not press her further, and Katherine was grateful.

They arrived at Downing-Cross two hours later. Katherine was hungry, saddle-weary, and overjoyed when she spotted the old, square manor house and the plume of black smoke billowing from its chimney. The grounds were empty, and indeed, as Stephen explained, many of the peasants who had once tilled the soil had succumbed to the Pestilence. Small fields surrounding the stone fortress had not been harvested, and brittle barley stalks bowed in icy deference to the snow. An orchard near the manor filled with skeleton trees remained unpruned. The fief had not been abandoned entirely. An older couple scurried from the house, their heads bobbing in welcome.

As they approached, Stephen dismounted and eased Katherine from her saddle. When her hair fell across his face, he breathed in deeply. "Rose water," he murmured in her ear. "Such a sweet scent. You fill all my senses, Kate."

She shivered and lingered a moment in his gentle grip. The warmth of his firm chest against hers was soothing, and she was loath to pull away.

"Sir Guy," the old man called, drawing near.

Stephen turned with a loving smile. "John! Elizabeth!"

"By Beelzebub, yer a welcomed sight, Sir Guy," the nimble man said. He scuffled through the snow without a cape or hood, heedless of the cold that turned his aged cheeks a bright pink. Gray hair hung over his forehead like the strands of an exhausted broom, and a full beard flowed to his chest.

Stephen embraced the old man and his hearty wife, then stood back and appraised them. His affectionate glance encompassed their shrunken figures. "I knew you would be here. There was never a time in all my childhood that John and Elizabeth weren't waiting for me with a sweet cake and a word of encouragement. I have brought the woman I will betroth, Katherine Gilbert. That is if she will deign to have me," he added for her benefit.

Katherine ignored his sarcasm and nodded her head, clasping Elizabeth's outstretched hands. She instantly felt welcomed by the older couple. "I'm so happy to meet you," she said.

"We were never more than servants to the master, milady," Elizabeth said, "but Sir Guy treated us as equals. He is still like a son to us, and we welcome you with open hearts."

"Yer father is a fine man, milady," John said, ushering them into the warmth of the house while a minion from the stable tended their horses. They paused in the manor's Great Hall.

Katherine looked up in surprise. "How do you know my father?" She shrugged from her mantle and hurried to the fire burning in the large hearth.

"Lord Gilbert often did business with my master, Sir Charles." John's jovial face grew solemn. "Until the Death took him. Sir Charles, Lady Mallory, and their daughters all fell in a week. It was a wretched time, Stephen. There was naught we could do to save them."

"We tried, that we did," Elizabeth said. She took her husband's hand in consolation. "Do not think on it now, John. Let us forget the sadness. Sir Guy has returned."

John nodded his gray head and forced a nearly toothless smile back on his worn face. "Aye, the past is past."

"You were not to blame for their deaths," Stephen reassured the old man, resting a hand on his back. "Now that they are gone, you can begin a new life if you wish. You are master of your own fate now, John."

The older man scowled and shook his head. "Nay, but for a time, until your brother takes a fancy to the land. Or until the Church discovers some hidden covenant. They can have it. It suits not a man to serve others all his life and then find there's no one else to serve but himself."

"The land is yours as long as it pleases Katherine. If our marriage comes to pass, it will be her wedding gift," Stephen said. "She will need a retreat if I am felled by my brother."

Katherine looked at him in astonishment. Could things be that bad between Stephen and Marlow?

"It is a gracious gift," she said with forced lightness, "but I have no need of Downing-Cross now."

"Not yet," he said, and turned to the old man. "Much has changed, John. You'd not recognize Blackmoor for all the secrecy and deception lurking there now."

"My boy fares well, though?" John replied with concern. "He has done well for you?"

Stephen smiled and patted his shoulder. "Your son is healthy and strong. We're glad to have Giles in our service."

"Enough of yer worries now. You both sound like two old crows," Elizabeth admonished, shooing them toward the kitchen. "Let us get by the fire and quench our thirsts."

She ushered them to the trestle table near the ovens, where they sat comfortably on benches. Pitchers of ale and mead, waiting for consumption, perspired in the heat of a fire that glowed several feet away.

Katherine sat next to Stephen. An easy feeling flowed between them, and she felt as much at home as she did in her own kitchen at Shelby Manor. There, she would sit and listen to the chattering of the scullions until her mother scolded her and chased her from the kitchen.

Presently, the fire sizzled with the dripping juice of a plump goose. Freshly baked manchet was sliced and set out with cheese. They all helped themselves as they talked.

"I see Geoffrey made it safely to warn you of our arrival. Or did your tea leaves tell you we were coming, Elizabeth?" Stephen said.

She laughed and rose, stoking the fire beneath the bread ovens. "Geoffrey arrived long ago. I am not a witch with powers to read the future, Sir Guy. I only work with my herbs."

"Hush, woman," John said quietly, glacing furtively at Stephen. "Don't speak of such things."

"You need not fear me, John. I know Elizabeth is not a witch. She's a healer," Stephen assured the old man.

"You might accept it, Sir Guy," John said, frowning still. "There are those who'd condemn the woman for her concoctions. Some have burned at the stake for witchcraft. The Church sends more to Hell than Heaven these days, and any woman who relies on her own wits rather than the local priest asks for trouble."

"The Church would not punish a good woman," Katherine argued. "It's not the way of our Lord. Christ forgave Mary Magdalene. Surely he would not judge a natural healer."

"It's not Christ we're talking about, Kate," Stephen replied, spreading a thick slab of goat's butter on a chunk of bread and popping it whole into his mouth. He chewed while the others waited for his next words. Swallowing, he added, "It's the vicars of Christ you need fear."

"Surely you do not question the piety of those who devote themselves to a holy calling," Katherine said, suddenly fearful that he had no faith in God or Church. She had sinned enough by failing to enter a convent, but to marry an infidel would surely condemn Georgie to Hell.

Stephen took a long draft of ale and set his tankard down heavily. "I do not spurn faith, Katherine, but I have seen sights that you have not. These jaded eyes have witnessed reality while you dream, in your pure heart, of holy ideals."

He poured himself another serving of ale. "Just before the Pestilence paralyzed the world, I traveled through southern France. I stopped in a small town where the Fraticelli kept a hospice for the poor. They were the Franciscans, the Spirituals who renounced earthly goods to be more like Christ. Poor sots, if they only knew what wrath their poverty would inspire from the Pope in Avignon."

A distant look of horror filled Stephen's eyes. Katherine felt his anguish, and she longed to wrap her arms around him with loving tenderness.

"One rainy day in autumn, when most roads were blanketed with leaves, I headed back to Calais. I was crossing through the village on my horse when I saw a stake thrust through a pile of wood. Upon orders of the Inquisition, a young monk was dragged to the stake—he couldn't have been more than twenty, though it was hard to tell his age. His limbs had been stretched on the rack. They were twisted in unnatural positions, one arm disjointed from the socket. They had to drag him, for he couldn't walk. His feet had been slowly roasted over an open flame. They were as red as boiled meat, blistered and oozing. His skin had been pricked with hot sticks. He looked like a leper. They tied him to the stake and started the fire."

Katherine winced. "What had he done?" she whispered.

"He preached that Christ lived in absolute poverty. That is heresy, you see, at least in the eyes of the Inquisition. Since the Pope lives in splendor, it is a heresy to deny that Christ had lawful ownership of possessions, to say that He lived in poverty."

"Bloody, unholy bastards," John muttered in a choked voice.

"By then the rain had begun to pelt us all, but not enough to quench the fire that raged beneath the monk. He died in excruciating pain."

Stephen had been staring at the fire, temples perspiring, but he broke his gaze and sighed with exasperation. "Because the Pope wants to live in riches, a monk who believed in Christ's simplicity was burned to death. Such is the justice of the Inquisition."

A heavy silence descended on them all. John tapped his knife against his pewter tankard in a hypnotic rhythm. The faint clinking lulled Katherine deeper and deeper into an abyss of sadness, but before she succumbed to despair, she braced her hands on the table and stared defiantly at Stephen. "How can they commit such horrors with the Pope's approval? How can they condemn others to death so easily? As if we have not seen enough death already. Such cruelty will never come to our land. We would never stand for it."

"Fate has been good thus far," Stephen said. "The Inquisition has not ventured to England. Even so, the Church itself conducts its own trials, mostly by overly ambitious bishops who would gather more lands to their estates. I suppose there are a few who genuinely loathe heresy and witchcraft, but such things are found only when they are sought. Never you fear, Elizabeth, you keep your medicines, but do not go bragging about."

She shook her head solemnly. "Aye, 'tis good advice, Sir Guy. I did not know such cruelty existed."

"Oh, it exists," Stephen said, finishing off his ale. "It exists."

They ate awhile with heavy hearts, until Elizabeth steered the conversation to a lighter subject.

"How fares Giles, Sir Stephen? Does he ask after his mother now and then?"

"I'd best say aye for his sake," Stephen answered with a wink. He turned to Katherine. "Giles came into my service when he was a boy. Sir Ramsey took him under wing and has made him into an excellent chief messenger. I'd trust any deed to Giles. You should be proud of him, both of you," he said, turning back to John and Elizabeth.

"Soon you will be busy with your own sons, Stephen," John said, his eyes gleaming.

Katherine felt Stephen's sudden focus on her. At the mention of children, a powerful stillness settled over him. Of course he wanted sons, she realized, and when they married she would be expected to bear them. She had been too intent on her oath to Georgie to contemplate a family, but the notion stirred a deep need in her to love and give to others. And yet she could not forget Constance's veiled threat.

"Children would be a welcome blessing to any home, Stephen," Katherine said. "But not at Blackmoor. Lady Constance has said as much to me."

"Do not fear her, Kate." He grasped her delicate fingers in one massive hand. "A child would please the earl as much as it would me."

He examined the pink creases in her palm like a fascinated gypsy. Was motherhood the fate this gypsy divined?

"That is if you would willingly bear a rogue's son," he added with a sly grin.

His voice, as intoxicating as the golden mead she sipped, was gilded with friendly mockery. She faced him with nothing but appreciation for his wit, for the inner strength that exuded from him here in friendly territory. What a man he was! Such earnestness swimming in the deep, azure pools that regarded her with unabashed intimacy. Still, he jested and teased her about her reluctance. He would keep her dancing on the thorny brambles of her own insecurity as long as she let him badger her on the subject of marriage. Withdrawing her hand from his, Katherine leveled Stephen with a confident glare.

"Bear a rogue's son, milord? Perhaps. I do not yet know what I'd willingly do, but I can hardly decide with you taunting me at every turn. Go softly, milord, and we shall see."

Stephen let out a low chuckle. Elizabeth smiled with appreciation for Katherine as she poured Stephen another tankard of ale.

"Outspoken, she is," John enthused. "I knew you'd settle for nothing less, Sir Guy."

"My lord, Sir Stephen thinks to embarrass me into some protestation of devotion," she said. "Methinks love is not a battlefield with the prize going to the victor. It is a maze, a wonderful garden of twisting hedges protecting the sweetest flower growing at the center."

The mead and ale had softened everyone's spirit, and Katherine's companions merely nodded at the wisdom of her words. But the vision of Constance filled her mind's eye, and a sense of foreboding churned within. Perhaps there was some way to help Constance, to make her an ally.

A combination of hope and firelight flickered with a topaz cast in Katherine's green eyes. She reached out and grasped Elizabeth's arm. "Do you have herbs that will quicken a child in the womb?" she inquired.

Stephen turned to her with an expression of surprise.

Elizabeth made no apparent judgment. "Aye, milady, I have a recipe as old as time itself. I will gladly give it to you before you leave."

Katherine smiled contentedly. "Thank you."

"There's the spirit, now," John gushed. He looked back and forth between the young couple. "With a little luck you'll spawn a healthy one like our Giles in no time. And then another and another. Soon the world will be alive again. Oh, glorious day!"

Katherine could endure Stephen's frank stare no longer. She took a quick sip of mead. "Is Geoffrey here?" she inquired, changing the subject. "I have not seen him."

"Out back at the cage, he is," John said. " 'Tis—"

"Nay, John, do not explain. I'll show her." Stephen wiped his mouth with a backhand, a devilish glint in his eyes. "She thinks me a wolf. She may yet change her mind."

He rose and motioned toward the rear door. "Come, Katherine, I will show you something that fascinated me as a child. Whenever I come to Downing-Cross, I always visit John's cage."

Elizabeth called for their mantles. The young boy who had tended the horses carried them like a heavy stack of kindling, and Elizabeth brushed a hand affectionately through his hair. "Young Callum here has no parents, poor lad. His mum and pa were stricken with the Death. We found Callum and his sister begging by the side of a road and took them in."

"God be with him," Katherine said, and compassion deepened the timbre of her honey-smooth voice.

"You two go on by yerselves," Elizabeth said. "I'll tend to the goose, and John, you'd best stay put. Just because it's spring, you think you can carry on without a cloak in this unnatural cold. If you do, you'll catch a chill again."

Stephen and Katherine donned their cloaks and wove down a path of trampled snow past rectangular garden plots, around the dovecote and the geese pen. The honking cry of geese cracked the still air like a clarion.

"What a beautiful, glorious day," Katherine exclaimed and clapped her hands together with unexpected glee. Nature aroused an incomparable sense of joy in her.

The sun shone like a dollop of butter in a clear, blue sky. Friendly rays beat down on her fresh cheeks and pert nose and warmed her despite a cutting wind that swirled tempestuously. Katherine was so entranced by the brilliant sun that she stumbled and fell into a drift of crusty snow. She sat up with a look of astonishment, her hair splayed every which way, dusted with white.

"Did you push me?" she said.

Stephen looked down at her as if she were a child. "Nay, and you know I did not. But I'll tell you this. I will think twice about dancing with you if you stumble over your own shadow."

An abandoned peal of laughter spilled from Katherine's lips. Stephen joined her, laughing until he gasped for air. In the sunlight, his teeth glistened white.

"Come, my graceful swan." He extended his hand. When she grasped his thick wrist, he gave a yank, but her wet cheveril gloves slipped over his hand, and she fell again. With giddy laughter, she lay back in the snowbank, surrendering to the forces of gravity.

"It is nature's way of telling me I'm less of a danger lying prone," she uttered through broken gasps for air. Her laughter mellowed to a deep giggle, and she shaded her eyes with her hand, looking up at Stephen's lean figure. His arms akimbo, his legs set wide, he regarded her with bold familiarity.

"It suits you well." His words cut through the air with sudden intimacy. A gaggle of geese honked and flapped about when a dog gave them chase.

"Lying on my back, you mean?"

"Did I speak so boldly?" he queried, all innocence.

Katherine sat up and brushed the back of her snowy cloak. She felt suddenly coy, and somehow womanly. "It must have been the geese I heard. I misconstrued their cries for words. I thought you admired my unseemly state of repose."

"I did." Stephen's eyes pierced through her even while he squinted against the sun. "I do." He extended his hand again, and she accepted it, this time gripping firmly. With one easy tug she was back on the worn path, barely touching his lean body.

Looking up into his loving face, his head blocking the sun, she wondered how long she could stand so close to him and still not fear her reaction to him, still trust that he would keep his word. It was all she could do to resist brushing her cheek against the faint growth of a beard that shadowed his square jaw, to keep her lips from his.

Stephen leaned forward and brushed his cold nose against hers. Inhaling her essence, he groaned with frustration.

"It will not work, Katherine." Stephen turned abruptly and marched along a stone wall that bordered the path. "I will not break my word to you. No matter how you tempt me, nay, test me! I will not succumb. You must dust the snow off your own back for I will not touch you until you demand it. And demand it you will."

Katherine shook her head with dismay and followed reluctantly. How self-centered! He assumed she wanted his touch. How arrogant! How accurate. The realization sent a chill rippling down her arms. *Dear God,* she prayed silently, *steel my heart against these irrational feelings.*

They stopped when they reached the top of a slope. At the bottom of the incline, Geoffrey stood near a large wooden-slatted cage.

"Milord," he hailed.

"Geoffrey. How are they?"

Katherine followed Stephen, but halted abruptly when she realized what the cage contained. Gray wolves. Stephen casually joined Geoffrey, but Katherine could not move. She gasped and pressed her fingertips to her lips, struck with awe at the creatures' magnificence. Five wolves shared the long cage. She had never seen so many this closely. Their clean, thick fur kept them amply warm, and several panted in the sunlight, their teeth white and jagged. Two arguing over a piece of meat from Geoffrey viciously snarled and snapped at each other, but after a moment's observation Katherine realized they were quite tame. Swallowing back her fear, she inched forward until one of the wolves spied her and began to howl.

"That sound . . . ," Katherine murmured. The doleful wail did not frighten her. She was drawn to it, as if the creature had spun a golden strand around her heart. She stopped a few feet away. A blank expression masked the haunting feelings that moiled within her. A cool memory of pain blew through her soul, and Katherine hugged herself as the wind whipped her hair freely about.

The creature threw her head back, revealing a pearly-white breast, and emitted another howl.

"Hush now, Vixen. You have startled her, Katherine," Stephen said. He glanced up with a reassuring look. "See, she is afraid of you, so you needn't fear her."

"I have seen that one before," Katherine said. "She was howling outside Blackmoor Castle several days ago. I thought she was wild."

"Nay, she is one of John's 'children.' Vixen, he calls her."

"Not the original Vixen," Geoffrey explained, clucking like a proud uncle to the silver beast. "But one of her daughters. She is harmless, milady."

"Still, I am glad she is in the cage," Katherine said. She admired Stephen's fearlessness. These wolves were his kindred spirits. Like the wolf, he was comfortable in solitude, sleekly beautiful, with a potentially dangerous side. Suddenly she remembered Georgie's warning that he was a murderer.

"Come hither," Stephen coaxed, offering her a slice of raw meat Geoffrey had brought from the kitchen. "Feed Vixen and you will have a friend for life."

Katherine forced her feet forward and knelt by the side of the cage. Stephen crouched beside her. Warmth and encouragement emanated from the bold knight.

As she had done so many times before when facing a challenge, she did the deed, not consulting her fear or hesitation, knowing that once it was done she would be the better for it. As Stephen had promised, Vixen was soon licking her fingers through the square slats.

"It seems so unfair that she is caged," Katherine said softly.

"A moment ago you were grateful for it," Stephen countered, rubbing the nose of a smaller he-wolf.

"That is because she was unknown to me. Now she is not. Europa says they mate for life. All of God's creatures that know such loyalty should be free as the wind."

Stephen did not answer at first. Still kneeling, he reached out and stroked Katherine's cheek. "Were you born with this tenderness, lady? Or did you learn it? And will it never go away?"

"I know not" came her weak reply. Her thoughts scrambled, and she was aware of nothing but his touch.

She shut her eyes in languid repose. A burst of light, like a shooting star, filled the darkness that ensued. With one touch, she was transported to a distant world of dreams and hope, hunger and satisfaction. In her mind's eye she kissed his chafed lips with a boldness she had yet to reveal; she inhaled the musky scent of leather that clung to him long after their hard ride. And when her arms coiled around his well-muscled shoulders, she surrendered to his arms like a lamb curled against the chest of a lion.

Then the image vanished, but a longing remained that beat urgently in the depths of her body and soul, a cursed feeling that made her vulnerable to him. She pushed his hand away.

"Your promise, milord. You've forgotten your promise."

"When will you learn to trust me, Kate?"

She pulled away and stood as stiffly as a wimple-bound nun. Wishing she had remembered her rosary, Katherine fumbled for something to do with her hands. When was the last time she had prayed for Georgie's soul? It had been two days. Filled with shame, she let out a tortured sigh. "Perhaps I will trust you, Stephen, when I learn to trust myself."

CHAPTER SEVEN

✠

They lingered awhile at the cage, until the sky clouded over and a chill wind whipped across the fields. Then the men went out to survey the land, and Katherine joined Elizabeth inside.

With an eager smile, Elizabeth reminded Katherine of her request for herbs. Katherine willingly followed the old woman up several flights of stairs to a drying room. When Elizabeth opened the wooden door, a dozen herbal scents wafted into their faces with a rush of hot air. The sweet smell of fennel and dried berries flooded the room, and Katherine breathed in deeply.

"How rich and comforting, Elizabeth," she said as she surveyed the chamber. Her leather shoes slid effortlessly over the worn floorboards. Dried flowers hung from the ceiling in colorful bouquets of lavender, rust, and gold. Wooden shelves loaded with small casks lined the stone walls. Open barrels in the center of the room spilled over with dried fruits, berries, and garden-grown spices.

"You have seasonings enough for a lifetime," Katherine said with marvel and reached into an open cask of dill. She crumbled the evergreen-colored plant in her fingers.

"This place is my pride and joy." Elizabeth paced a small circle around the room and gazed lovingly at her hoard of herbs and spices, tilled with patience and skill. A hazy light sifting through a high window brightened her contented features. "Earlier this year, every barrel brimmed over with my harvest. But it takes so much spice to season dried beef in the winter, as you know, milady. Sometimes my store goes quickly. With the Death, I tried every remedy I could devise, every combination of roots and herbs to concoct a cure, but none worked."

"Nay, that would have taken a miracle," Katherine said with a melancholy sigh. Then, with a flicker of hope in her eyes, she added, "You do have something for a woman who can not carry a child to term?"

"Aye," Elizabeth whispered. The web of wrinkles deepened around her eyes, and her drawn cheeks seemed more pronounced in the dreamy blend of shadow and light. To Katherine, she was like the earth mother offering healing. Were it not for her loving demeanor, Elizabeth's careworn visage and gray hair, drawn into a stern bun, might have been mistaken for a crone's. Such was the depth and strength of her spirit. In her milky gray eyes, wisdom and a hint of dark secrets glistened like enticing jewels.

In Elizabeth's presence, Katherine felt the reawakening of a spirituality that harkened back to her childhood, to that time in life when children are still attached more to God than to the earth, when magical happenings are an everyday occurrence. With great clarity, she recalled an encounter at the age of five. Little Katherine happened upon a gypsy in a meadow near Shelby Manor one spring morning. Wrinkled like a dried plum, with raiments swathed around her balding head, the gypsy beckoned to her with slurred speech. Katherine thought the old hag had indulged in too much mead. But something in the old woman's eyes drew her—some wisdom, some unspoken vision. Without fear, Katherine took her outstretched hand, a veritable claw. She sat peacefully in tall grass while the gypsy sobered from her bout with drink. Without so much as a word spoken, the child saw power and beauty in the old woman. Kate wanted the moment to last forever, but unexpectedly the gypsy's hand grew limp, her wild eyes grew dull and still. With a gurgling breath, she died. She hadn't been drunk at all. Katherine did not say good-bye, had not even bothered to learn the gypsy's name. She stood up with sudden understanding and ran as fast as she could from her sense of loss, from the realization that she had done nothing to help the old woman save for holding her hand.

Remembering that poignant moment, Katherine felt renewed determination to act. "I need this potion, Elizabeth. Something to help a woman carry a child to term."

"I do have something, milady, a mix of herbs taught me by my mother. I will gather just the right combination of dried Yarrow and lady's mantle."

A solemn mood overtook the older woman. Her nimble hands dipped into a wooden box of dried plants, and then another. She slowly sprinkled leaves in a bowl. Elizabeth began to speak as she worked.

"Dear Goddess of the Earth," she whispered, "Mother of Nature, bring me yer healing and grant goodly progeny to the receiver of these gifts. I pray that yer wonders shall heal the sick."

Moved by the strange incantation, Katherine shivered with a sudden chill. As if she had forgotten Katherine's presence, the motion startled Elizabeth, and she looked up.

"Do not mind me, milady. 'Tis but words I learned from my mother."

"You say you are not a witch," Katherine said in a hushed whisper, "yet you pray to a pagan goddess. I do not understand."

Elizabeth covered the bowl with a rough cloth and handed it to her. "Nay, I am not a witch, but there is much to the pagan practices. There lies the wisdom of the ages, despite the condemnation of the Church. All that is of life comes from the sweet earth."

She smiled and touched Katherine's cheek with a gentle pat. "There, there, lady, do not be afraid. Trust what Mother Earth has given us. Steep some of these herbs in boiling water and then drink it. Do this every day until the child quickens. I'm sure it will help."

Working swiftly from many years practice, Elizabeth reached into another box and pulled out dried flowers, leaves, and twigs, and wrapped them up in a separate cloth.

"Once yer with child, if you feel sick, then steep this—black horehound mixed with a little meadowsweet."

Katherine took the herbs and pressed her smooth cheek to Elizabeth's wizened one.

"Thank you, dear friend. This fills me with such hope. Your concoction may help matters more than you can ever imagine."

Elizabeth brushed away a strand of red-gold hair that had fallen in the hollow of Katherine's cheek. "You are so eager to bear him a child." She smiled with satisfaction. "I see that you care very much for Stephen, and with good reason."

"Oh—" Katherine opened her lips to speak, realizing the misunderstanding, unsure how to rectify it. "It's not . . . I'm not . . . The brew is not for me. It is for Constance. If I can help her to keep the child in her womb, perhaps she will not hate me so."

Elizabeth nodded her acceptance of this explanation, but doubt lingered in her eyes. Katherine hesitated, then admitted her deepest thoughts with a soulful smile.

"Aye, Elizabeth, I do care for Stephen, though I do not know why."

This confession, quietly uttered, rustled like a soft breeze through the dried plants hanging overhead and vanished. He would never know how much she cared if she did not tell him, and she feared what such knowledge would lead to.

Elizabeth drew in a sharp breath, understanding so much in her intuitive way. "He does not know?"

Katherine shook her head, her heart suddenly pounding in her chest. "Nay, Elizabeth, nor shall he until I understand it all myself."

"Love is not to be understood, milady. It is a precious gift to be accepted with grace and joy."

Katherine looked at her skeptically. "You speak so glibly of something incomprehensible to me. I wanted to hate him, and yet I see nothing but his nobility and tenderness." She closed her eyes. "Oh, sweet Father above, I swore upon my brother's deathbed to live my life in meditation, but when I'm in Stephen's presence, I barely remember the words of our Lord's prayer."

Her eyes snapped open, full of confusion. "Stephen expects my blind faith and will not tell me why he killed Lord Roby. Georgie said he was a scoundrel, and yet—"

"And yet you do not believe it."

Katherine's eyes softened. She shook her head and sighed. "Nay, I do not. I believed everything my brother told me . . . except this."

"Then you are learning to trust yer own wisdom. 'Tis the first step toward love."

Elizabeth's simple truths pounded in Katherine's head, snatched her breath, and sent bolts of lightning through her veins. Her knees weakened with giddy joy, and she began to tremble. Fear, hope, dread, and ecstasy parried in her mind, each fighting for dominance. Her fragile relationship with Stephen verged on love. She finally admitted it to herself, and she quaked in the depths of her soul.

"I do not love Stephen," she said without conviction. "I do care what he thinks of me, but that is not the same as love."

Elizabeth smiled patiently. "The longing in your voice mocks your words."

Soft light filtered through the shutters and pierced the dusty air. Katherine stood in a daze, momentarily entranced. Shutting her eyes, she whispered, "I shall never be able to open to a man, not with my heart. If I were to love a man, it might be someone like Stephen, but it would not do to become besotted with one's own husband."

"Goodness, milady, if not in love with yer husband, then who? A lover taken on the side?"

Katherine's eyes flew open. "I would never do that, Elizabeth. But once a husband plucks the sweet flower from the vine, he'll cast it aside to wither without succor.

Besides, a husband is just as mortal as all the other loved ones we've mourned. I've had enough tears for a lifetime."

Elizabeth crossed herself and wrapped her arms around Katherine, pulling her close. "Milady, do not speak so hopelessly. You are young. Life is long." The older woman drew back and looked pleadingly into Katherine's misty eyes. "Love is not to be expected in marriage, but it can be hoped for. Give yer heart a chance to speak. Love is the only thing left us now, for these are bitter times. Without love we are nothing. Nothing."

Katherine smiled when confronted with the woman's relentless cheer.

"Very well, Elizabeth." She nodded reluctantly. "I will not cast love out forever. Indeed, if it is as important as you say, it can catch me dancing through the woods, dodging Cupid's arrows."

Elizabeth clapped her hands together with satisfaction. "Love has its ways. Mark my words!"

By the time the men returned to the house, the sun dangled low in the sky, and red fingers of light clawed across dark clouds.

His mood expansive and relaxed, Stephen entered the kitchen and slapped John good-naturedly on the back. He winked at Katherine and nonchalantly announced that they would be staying at Downing-Cross overnight. They had planned to reach Blackmoor by nightfall, but that would require an immediate departure, and no one wanted that, least of all Elizabeth, who'd spent the whole day preparing her goose and frumenty.

Katherine objected briefly. Even though she enjoyed being away from the tense atmosphere at Blackmoor and felt at home with John and Elizabeth, she was concerned that her new family would judge her harshly for being too free before her marriage.

Stephen reassured her that they were probably unaware of her absence, and that John was known and trusted by his family. He could vouch for Katherine's honor if it came to that, and this he said with a wink to John, who then clucked his tongue disapprovingly. Katherine was easily persuaded, as was Geoffrey. The fire spewed the juicy aroma of a perfectly basted bird. Soon they were all quiet, feasting on the perfection of Elizabeth's cooking.

On one matter Katherine had misjudged Stephen utterly, she concluded as she watched a multitude of emotions animate his features: humor, indignation, tenderness, passion—equally directed at all his dinner companions. She had once thought Stephen to turn the poor away. She smiled to herself, remembering their journey to Blackmoor, when she had stopped to feed the beggars. How cold and arrogant he had seemed that day. But tonight she saw him in a different light. He loved these people, and without his guard raised he was a divinely attractive man.

After Elizabeth had cast out the trenchers for the geese, Katherine rose and announced that she was ready to retire. Elizabeth showed her to an upstairs room that had been a small bower in years gone by. Now it was empty, save for a large feather mattress thrown on the floor before a blazing fire and a wooden chair. Katherine borrowed one of Lady Mallory's old robes. Callum's eleven-year-old sister helped her undress and then scurried off for the night. Katherine carefully placed her kirtle and cote-hardie on the chair and then donned the robe. Wrapping herself in a thick wool blanket, she sat cross-legged on the mattress and warmed herself in front of the fire, contemplating the day's events.

Without love we are nothing. Elizabeth's words haunted her. That notion sounded romantic, but what did it mean? This she pondered as she fell into a gentle trance, watching the fire. Blue flames licked at the burning logs, almost shy in their approach, yet persistent. The larger, yellow flames shot up in the air, so bold, like Stephen's fearless nature. Together blue and yellow mingled, different yet both achieving the same end—an inferno.

"Will you be comfortable here?"

Katherine turned with a gasp and pressed a hand to her heart.

Stephen leaned casually against the door frame and smiled. He had not meant to startle her, and the look of innocence that shimmered in her firelit eyes, her surprise and then pleasure, was enough to wrench his heart with longing. She was such a portrait of feminine pastels that he wanted to sketch the image permanently in his mind. Hair hung down her back in creamy waves flecked with gold, and her velvety cheeks were flushed pink in the heat of the fire.

She broke the silence at last. "I am quite content, Guy."

His heart skipped a beat hearing her address him casually. "I like when you call me that."

Katherine smiled. "It pleases me to please you, milord."

"You do it so well." His voice was husky, intimate.

Katherine blinked her eyes in slow motion, unable to focus precisely on the masculine force that exuded from him. Amber firelight shimmered against his neck, illuminating chiseled sinews that curved down to his shoulders. Dressed much as he had been the first night, when they met at the inn, he was an unkempt rogue who regarded her with blatant desire. A sense of shame finally overcame her own longing, and she cast her eyes downward.

Her reticence compelled him. He had wanted women before, but never had he wanted to claim a woman's soul. Her pureness drove him wild with the urge to show her the comfort of a man's embrace.

"Do not fear me, Kate, I have only come to warm my bones by your fire."

"Nay, I am not afraid," she protested too quickly. She smiled at her deception and turned her face up to him with a mischievous look. "Come then, Stephen, come join me by the fire. If your learned theory is correct, my honor will not tarnish with you upon my bed as long as I hold love in my heart. At least that is what you said when you forced your way into my chamber. Do you remember?"

He smiled with deep satisfaction and sauntered to the edge of her mattress. "Aye, but that would be much more than I had hoped for—love in your heart. I will settle for time alone without a scolding or a beating."

"You cannot think me so hard."

"Nay," he replied. "Harder." An ill-chosen word, he thought wryly, aware that his masculine nature had already risen to this intimate occasion.

She turned back to the fire without remarking on his play on words, ignorant of their implication. He had no doubt she was a virgin. If not physically, then in her heart. For even if she had given away the prize that can only be given once, it was clear she had given no one her heart, and that was the prize he cherished most.

"It's a precious thing, a fire." He lowered himself to the mattress beside her and held his scarred hands toward the flames. "When I was but four or five, my mother would call me and Marlow into her chamber. She had favored Marlow ever since he nearly died from a childhood fever. As she nursed him day and night, an impenetrable bond formed between them. Even so, she let me into their secret world now and then. We would sit at her feet before the fire while she told us tales of Merlin and Arthur and Guinevere. Of course, I fancied myself Arthur and Marlow was Mordred."

" 'Tis an apt comparison. I sense none of your nobility in your brother."

Her tenderly spoken words worked magic in his chest, and a lump formed in his throat.

"A man with a sword, Kate, can conquer a city and burn it to the ground. But a woman with love in her heart can raise a nation from the ashes. Never underestimate your power."

He leaned back on the mattress, bracing himself on one arm, and tugged at her shoulder, forcing her to recline beside him. Stroking her cheek, he whispered, "Do you have faith in me yet, Kate?"

Like freshly fallen dew, tremulousness quivered on a flower that blossomed in the depths of her eyes.

"I do have faith," she whispered, her eyes still bound to his. She blinked, and her gaze fell to his lips, moist and smooth. She groaned softly, and a frown rippled across her brow, breaking the love spell. "I do have faith. But you have not answered all my questions."

"Ask them, love. I will answer if I can."

Katherine hesitated.

"What is it, Katherine?" he said gently, his fingers again stroking her cheek.

She felt like a traitor to the one who had shown her the most kindness, the man she longed to embrace, but she could not ignore her doubts. Unlike Constance, she would be true to herself. "I must know why you killed Lord Roby. *I must know*. Was it some fit of dark passion as Georgie said? Or was it a noble match with witnesses and pages in attendance?"

Stephen sat up slowly and cast a steely look at the fire.

"We were alone. In the shadows of a tavern in London. There were no witnesses. 'Twas no chivalrous display for honor's sake, if that is what you were hoping for, but it was a fair fight. I was the better swordsman, and so he fell. Would you condemn me for that?"

He turned to her and flinched, for Katherine regarded him as she often did Marlow—with a dark frown and a cold mask to hide her condemnation. God's Wounds, but he could not lose her now, not to her false assumptions, not when they had come so far.

"I am not my brother, Katherine."

"Nay," she said sadly, "I could never mistake you for Marlow." *Yet I am falling in love with the very man my brother warned me against.*

She shivered and rose. Hugging herself like one of the orphans she had seen on her way to Blackmoor Castle, she stepped closer to the hearth for warmth. "I am not abiding by any of Georgie's last wishes. He had such a high standard of honor. I promised him, I swore I would pray eternally for his soul, but then I had not known you, Stephen."

She turned to him with accusing eyes. She hated herself for feeling so much comfort in his presence. Even now he drew her inexorably into his spell.

"Katherine," he whispered intensely, "there is nothing I can say to assure you about my past. Only in your heart can you judge my true nature. But I want you to under-stand—I thought I was doing the right thing when I killed Roby."

She nodded her head, and then impetuously swooped down beside him, taking his hand. "I want to believe you, Guy," she whispered earnestly. "It is so important to me that you be a man of chivalry, a man of honor. I do not want to live like Constance. I can not live with the devil."

Stephen's heart constricted with sorrow. "Oh, woman," he groaned, "did I cause you this absurd fear?"

He enveloped her in an embrace and kissed the corner of her satin lips with exquisite tenderness. "I will not treat you as Marlow treats Constance. You will never live like my brother's wife," he muttered against her cheek. "I will always cherish you."

Katherine had frozen beneath his kiss and then thawed as a strange warmth tingled through her body.

"Yes, my love. Sweet love," he murmured, sensing the awakening of her desire. His lips meandered along the grace-ful curves of her throat until she arched her head back with a groan of acceptance. Yellow and blue flames burned brighter, licking higher. He had finally kindled in her the torch that blazed in his chest.

Katherine recoiled from the inferno. With both hands, she pushed against his broad chest. Panting for air, she stared at him with a mixture of doubt and wonder, and then she giggled like a child. Even while tears formed in her eyes, she laughed in a strained timbre, pressing the back of one hand against her mouth.

"I am on fire," she whispered. "What have you done to me?"

Then her laughter turned to genuine tears. "I am frightened of what I feel for you," she whimpered. "Oh, help me, Stephen, but I am afraid."

"Nay, dear lady. Do not fear. I swear I will never hurt you."

"After the Death, I thought the numbness inside me would never fade. I thought my life was over. You make my heart feel again. I am alive. Mine is no longer a heart of stone." She drew her knees up to her chest and wrapped her arms around them, rocking back and forth as she softly wept.

Tears burned in Stephen's eyes as well, but he dared not touch her. He knew the depth of her pain.

Finally, she grew silent. She sniffled, ran her hands over her eyes, brushed a finger under her nose, and then, looking up like a petulant child, said, "Yet I must know. Why did you slay Lord Roby? Do not expect me to forget him just because I am weak with desire."

"S'Blood," he muttered. Exasperated, Stephen shook his head with a helpless laugh. "I can not discuss this, Katherine."

"If you trusted me, you would tell me."

"Nay, it is more complicated than that."

"Yet you want my trust?" Her voice rose in indignation. "I suppose you want me to accept your past without question."

"Aye, woman, I do," he answered, the tone of his voice as cold as a steel sword cast out overnight. "That is the least you can give me. My family may doubt my character, but is it too much to ask the woman I will marry to believe in me?"

"Churl! But you are stubborn," she cried, her eyes afire with anger. "I am so sick of trusting the whims of men."

She bolted upright, leaving her blanket in a crumpled heap. Like a sheep surrounded by wolves, she pivoted one way and then the other. For a moment, Stephen thought she would run from the room, but then she turned on him like a banshee on an Irish moor. Defiance blazed in her eyes, and he realized with great appreciation for this ultimate specimen of feminine beauty that the girl had turned into a woman before his very eyes. He half expected her to break into a heart-wrenching ululation.

"Why should I trust you blindly?" she cried. "Faith, milord, give me one good reason why you can not tell me what happened."

Stephen's eyes, smoldering with hatred, turned to the mellowing flames that coiled round the burning logs. "I killed Lord Roby because he defiled the honor of a woman."

Katherine hesitated, waiting for more. "Whose honor, Stephen?"

"My mother's. Countess Rosalind."

"Oh. I see." Her hard stance melted, and she unfolded her crossed arms. "What did Roby say?"

"If I were to divulge that, Katherine, I would be equally guilty of defaming her name."

"Then what Lord Roby said was false."

Stephen blinked several times in quick succession, a shadow of doubt flitting through his eyes. He rose on stiff legs and went to the window. "Aye, 'twas false."

Katherine took small steps toward him, her approach slowed by a million thoughts, most of them remorseful. When she reached him, she placed a hesitant hand on his arm, forcing him to look at her.

"All this time, I doubted your character because of that deed," she said with a frown. "I listened to what my dear beloved Georgie thought of you, and I took his opinion for my own. Now I regret it."

Her admission suddenly made Stephen feel petty. "Do not blame yourself, Kate." He twirled a lock of her hair round one finger and then released it. "You asked me to tell you what happened, and I stubbornly refused. Of course you wanted to know."

She shook her head. "That does not matter." She began to pace slowly, twisting her hands as if unraveling the knotted skein of events. "Whether you told me what happened or not, I formed my own opinion about your nature. I did so the first night we met. Then I did everything I could to ignore my own instincts. I replaced them with my brother's opinion."

Stephen quelled a slowly building urge to whoop with joy. This was the realization he had been waiting for Katherine to make. Now she could trust him. Now she could have faith in him as no one else ever had. This beautiful, gracious creature had finally seen his goodness; the very realization cracked open a door inside him. Years of anger and doubt poured out of his heart, and he realized how much effort he had spent pretending he didn't care what others thought of him.

A glimmer of blue shone in his watery eyes, and though he blinked furiously to hide his feelings, she stretched out her hand to him.

"Nay, Kate." He turned away. "I'll not have your pity."

Stephen wiped his eyes with a growl, willing away unmanly sentiment. He snatched a quick breath when he felt her hands encircle his torso. His body jolted stiff when she leaned her head against his back. For her sake, he knew he should fling her compassionate gesture aside. As much as he longed for consolation, this was not the time. The pulsing in his groin was evidence of that. But he did not cast her aside, and his hunger for her only grew as her hands caressed his belly in a gesture naively meant to be consoling. One too many stones had been chiseled from the wall that divided them for that. He filled his chest with the scent of her—heather and spice and rose water. Lord, she was close. So close.

Certain the last barriers to their sexual union had finally crumbled, Stephen gave in to his powerful hunger. He twisted around until he loomed over her. Scooping an arm around the small of her back, he pulled her against his chest and hips. Barely hearing her gasp of surprise, he lowered his lips. She did not struggle as he kissed her, but a tiny groan eked from her chest. He knew that sound. It rumbled unexpressed within his own shaking body. *For when pleasure is too intense,* he thought, *it cuts like a knife.* His tongue dipped into the sweet moisture of her mouth, dancing, exploring, and for a timeless second it seemed they exchanged souls with the give-and-take of each breath.

She tasted as sweet as she smelled. Oh, he wanted all of her! He placed a hand on her throat and caressed her creamy skin. His fingers inched lower, desperate for the pear-shaped mounds thinly veiled beneath her robe.

Katherine gasped against his mouth when he cupped a breast in his warm hand. With a groan he opened her robe to expose the delightful fruit. Stephen knelt and consumed his prize, drawing her nipple into his mouth, his tongue swirling, inhaling, until she clutched him closer, desperate, small hands pulling his head nearer.

"Oh, Stephen," she groaned.

Finally, she pulled back, unkempt, with her hair tangled from the passionate sway of her head. She drew her robe back over her swollen nipple and stared at him numbly, breathing heavily, forcing the desire away.

"We came too close," she whispered. Moisture glazed her eyes with a poignant sheen. "Too close."

"Nay, not close enough." Though he wanted to shout the words, he only managed a mutter when he saw her open expression close like a flower at sunset.

She covered her face with shaking hands. "Why am I doing this?" she mumbled into her hands. "I know it is wrong."

Stephen rose but did not follow her lost steps around the empty bower. "Nay, Kate, you are listening to your own heart. How can that be wrong?"

She pulled her hands down in an angry gesture. "Because another's soul hangs in the balance. Because I'm breaking a vow. If I break a vow to my brother, how will you ever be able to trust a vow I make to you? Especially a marriage vow?"

Stephen kicked a log resting on the hearth and crossed the room in impatient strides. "What you are saying makes our marriage impossible! How can making love to your betrothed, to the man who will be your husband, be wrong? Would you prefer I take a mistress when we marry? How long will you cling to this vow? Till death do us part? Do not forget you did agree to this match."

"In a manner of speaking. It was not exactly my idea, as you recall."

"Will you marry me only in name and expect me to honor your idiotic promise to someone who is dead?"

"Yes," she hissed, turning on him with flaming eyes.

"Kate . . ." He stared at her with disbelief, unbearable frustration. And then he fell to his knees before her, snatching and holding her hand, although she tried to recoil.

"Kate, dear Kate. I thought all it would take was for you to see my honesty, my honor. But even that means nothing to you, does it? You condemned this marriage long before I met you. Please change your mind now and end this war of wills."

Katherine's lips began to quiver, and she turned her head to one side, unwilling to share her vulnerability.

When she did not answer, he flung her hand from his and hoisted himself up like an old man. "Cursed be your oath to your brother. Your misplaced sense of duty will be a wedge between us evermore," he said with despair, running a weary hand through his hair.

"If all you want is my body, you could always take me without my consent," she said with accusing eyes. "That is what you're after, isn't it?"

Every muscle in his body went rigid. He wanted to slap her for that crude remark. But she was clearly goading him. He'd not give her the satisfaction.

"Yes, of course, your bed is all I'm after," he said, and added sarcastically, "but remember, I still have my honor. I never steal, not even a woman's virtue, and I never force myself on a woman who doesn't beg for me—as you soon will, dear lady. Mark my words. As you soon will."

As he stalked from the room, she took a step after him and cried out in frustration, "Why must you force this issue? Is it so important?"

Stephen shrugged and snorted an ironic laugh. "Clearly not. I thought it was. But I was mistaken."

He gave her a curt bow and left her to contemplate his bitter assessment.

CHAPTER EIGHT

✠

During their return to Blackmoor the next morning, Katherine and Stephen shared an uneasy silence. They said farewell to John and Elizabeth in good humor, both hiding the discord that had marred an otherwise perfect visit. After their departure, Stephen engaged Katherine in light banter, but there was an undercurrent churning the waters between them. It was as if every word, every gesture on his part were designed to elicit a set response. Though this was nothing so overt as blatant seduction, she knew from the amused gleam in his eyes that the cat would not rest until he'd battered his captive mouse into submission.

Despite the tension between them, Katherine felt exceedingly alive and full of hope as her mare pranced the well-worn path home. The respite from Blackmoor Castle had refreshed her, and she was actually eager to return. With the herbs from Elizabeth, she had hope of befriending Constance. Katherine was determined to conquer her enemies with love, the only weapon her ideals of chivalry would countenance. Her pulse quickened when she saw the towers soar through the pink morning mist.

Once they had passed through the gatehouse, Stephen went quickly about his business. He strode directly to the solar to check on his father.

Europa bustled Katherine into her chamber, leading her to a wooden tub filled with hot, delightful water.

"Europa, you know exactly what I need before I even ask

for it," Katherine said. She groaned and hugged herself as she slipped naked into the steaming bath.

" 'Tis my duty, my lamb." She bent down and pinched Katherine on the cheek. "The earl is no better but, thank the Savior in Heaven, no worse. No one missed you but me. And I am much too wise to ask what you were about with that rogue of a man."

Remembering how close she had come to losing her self-control, Katherine blanched, but then forced an easy smile. "Nothing and everything, you dear woman."

"Oh?" Europa stretched the word with suggestive meaning.

"Europa, I never thought relationships with men could be so complex. If I could only feel nothing for Stephen, I'd be so much better off."

"There, there," Europa said with a lusty laugh. "I'm sorry I brought it up. Whatever happened betwixt you is not the concern of an old woman. Yer love for the man is plain to see. Yer pink cheeks and swollen lips tell a story of their own."

"Europa!" Katherine cried. She blushed and sank lower in the tub until her chin touched the water.

The robust woman cut loose with laughter so deep the wooden tub vibrated. When the laughter faded, she wiped tears from her eyes and muttered, "There, there. Now, by my troth, not another word. So what plans have you for today?"

Katherine had already plotted her benevolent scheme and dispatched her orders in businesslike fashion, eager to change the subject. "Tell Rosemary to lay out my blue kirtle. I shall join Lady Constance as soon as I am dressed."

Europa nodded compliantly. "As you wish, milady. Though I didn't think you would be striking up such a fast friendship with Lady Constance."

"I haven't yet, Europa." Katherine spoke confidently. "I haven't yet."

When Katherine entered the tapestry chamber a half hour later, she felt refreshed and invigorated. Her velvet kirtle kept her warm against the chilly air, her long tippet sleeves buttoned down to her wrists, with a rich, golden surcoat hanging loosely over that. She wore no wimple, as she seldom did, and her finely chiseled collarbone stood out above the low, square neckline. A simple veil and circlet modestly covered her hair, and yet the golden strands hung loosely, hinting at the wildness she had only the night before glimpsed within herself.

"Good day, Lady Constance." She shut the door and smiled boldly at several women who kept Constance company, each working on a section of the tapestry. She recognized them from the Great Hall. They waited on the countess.

"Katherine, what a surprise." Constance peered at her from across the room. Her face was pinched in a wimple that tightly swathed her neck. Her dress was a dull gray.

"The tapestry has been in my thoughts ever since we worked on it," Katherine said, "and I can not seem to get the colors out of my mind. So I would join you again today."

She circled around the others, who stared quizzically at her, and took the chair brought forward by Constance's serving woman.

An awkward silence filled the room. A fire roared from the hearth, and distant shouts from the castle guards stirred the stillness as a group of merchants passed through the portcullis.

Katherine did not feel welcome, but that was to be expected, she concluded, waiting adamantly until the other women resumed their chatter, though she was tempted to excuse herself or to make some silly, idle conversation. When the other women were once again absorbed in their own laughter and talk, Katherine turned to Constance.

"I would speak with you alone. I have a gift for you."

The older woman looked up suspiciously, stitching all the while. At last she tipped her head toward the window.

"Have you seen the view from this side of the castle, Katherine?"

Together they rose. Constance motioned for the others to

continue while she went to the small privacy afforded by the arched window.

When Katherine joined her, Constance turned with a dour expression. "Do you wish to chastise me for our last conversation?"

Even while she pitied the embittered woman, Katherine admitted Constance was intimidating, and she struggled to hold her resolve.

"Nay, I do not wish to chastise you. I want to give you a gift." She pulled a pouch from the folds of her gown. "It is an herbal concoction to help you carry a child to term."

Constance studied her a moment and then looked out the window, eyes blinking. She turned abruptly and said to the others, "Ladies, look in on the countess now. She is probably weary in her vigil and would welcome company."

The women did as they were told. When the door closed behind them, there was a rush of unintelligible whispers, scurrying footsteps, and then silence.

"I hope I am not too forward, Lady Constance. I only wish to help you. I mean you no harm . . ."

Katherine's hurried words died quickly. Her entreaties were met with stony silence. More softly, she added in a tone of defeat, "You should take a small handful steeped in boiling water every day until the child quickens. If you grow ill, I have black horehound for you."

She turned to go, but Constance stopped her.

"Wait, Katherine." Still she stared out the window. "Why have you done this?"

"I see the pain you endure, Constance." She rejoined the older woman by the window. "At times I feel another's sorrow as if it were my own. It is a curse and a blessing I inherited from my mother. You want a child dearly, I see that. I want you to be happy. Even if you hate me forever, I can not stand to see you suffer. Not if you will soon be a member of my family."

Constance glanced at her with tears welling in her eyes. "Is that all? The only reason?"

Shrugging, Katherine added, "I must confess I did want to prove to you that I mean no harm. I like it not that you think me capable of usurping your rights. It is not my way."

Constance smiled. "Nay, I can see I was mistaken."

Just when Katherine felt some camaraderie, coldness swept over Constance, and she grabbed the pouch with clawing fingers. "How do I know what this contains?"

"It was made by Elizabeth at Downing-Cross. She would not have blended any potion that would harm you."

"Elizabeth . . . they say she is a witch."

"Nay, it is not so. She is a kindly woman. I saw her mix the herbs myself."

Constance nodded her head and returned the pouch to Katherine. She wandered over to the tapestry and roved lovingly with one hand over the thousands of stitches. "Perhaps you are right. When I first came to Blackmoor from my home in London, Elizabeth traveled over with Lady Mallory. She gave me some tea to settle my nerves. She showed me more affection in that one day than Rosalind gave me for the next fifteen years."

"I liked her very much. She said . . ." Katherine hesitated.

"What?" Constance gave Katherine her full focus, raising her proud chin against the stiff folds of her wimple. "What were you about to say?"

"Oh, it seems inappropriate now, but she said something that impressed me terribly." As she joined her at the tapestry, Katherine's eyes raked the vibrant blue-and-red stitching. "She said we are nothing without love."

A low, cynical laugh emanated from Constance. "I do not even remember what love is. I knew it once, when I lived with my family. Now all that I know is determination, ambition, distraction, obsession. Like Rosalind, I failed to find happiness somewhere along the way. Unlike my mother-in-law, I have no sons to live for."

Katherine held out the pouch. "Then take this, please. It is worth a try."

Constance gave her a pitying look. "You are so naive.

Though I do not trust you, I hope I will not be witness to your fall from grace, your disillusionment when you discover how brief and unfair life is."

Katherine felt a surge of anger wash over her. This woman would deny the existence of love with cynical words and warnings. "Do not speak to me of such things. My life will be different."

"Why?" Constance retorted, a vicious gleam in her eyes. "What will be different? Do you know this love of which you speak?"

Katherine wanted to say yes, but in truth she couldn't. She had known desire, but it would hardly do to confess the awakening of her passion. "Nay, I can not speak as an authority on love."

"Is it Stephen who will save you? Has he convinced you of his honor and how faithful he will be when you are wed?"

"Aye, he . . . Nay, he has not said as much." Katherine's cheeks grew hot with embarrassment. She did not know anything at all about what sort of husband Stephen would make.

"Marlow spoke sweetly to me before we married, Katherine. He has been a bastard ever since."

Katherine's jaw dropped in shock, and Constance threw back her head and laughed.

"You are surprised? I'm not the fool I may seem. I just can not reveal all that I know. It is too dangerous. And if you repeat my words to my husband, I will say you are a liar. Or worse."

This was not going as Katherine had planned. Instead of winning Constance over, she felt as if she were being shown the world through a shattered, dirty glass. She tossed the pouch onto a chair and started for the door.

"Do not go." Constance's voice was suddenly pleading, almost desperate. "I have frightened you, and I did not mean to. It has been so long since I have spoken frankly to one of my gender, Katherine. My bitterness is not a pretty sight. Just as I have never been. But I do not want to hurt you more than you will be hurt by life itself."

Katherine turned to her and smiled halfheartedly. "I am unscathed, Constance, but Stephen was right. I sometimes act as if I've never ventured beyond the walls of Shelby Manor. I do not know as much of life as perhaps I should, but I do not want to learn what you have known. No matter what you say, my life will be different."

Constance nodded skeptically. "Perhaps you are right. Never forget yourself, no matter how much is taken from you. I lost myself long ago. I joined my fate with a man who knows only ambition. If love is everything, then I am nothing."

"Only because you have deemed it so, Constance. I would like to be friends with you."

"I don't believe you."

Again, the glazed look descended over Constance's face. They were at another impasse. Katherine turned to go, leaving the herb pouch on the chair.

At dusk Stephen paced the wall-walk like a nobleman who did not trust his own guards to keep the castle safe from attack. He watched the horizon with angry eyes and stalked from tower to tower with stiff strides, hands clutched behind his back. Black-and-red pennons, thrust into an amber sky from each of four towers, snapped in a fitful wind, the same wind that twisted his shoulder length hair beneath his fallen hood.

From atop the battlements, he could see in every direction. In the distance, an entourage traveled toward the castle from the moorlands road. Earlier, when the clarions blew to announce the approach of strangers, Stephen had assured the castellan he would see if it was friend or foe. At first the visitors were indiscernible, the size of ants, but as they drew closer to Blackmoor at a steady pace, Stephen was able to count their numbers—fifteen in all. Some were obviously mercenaries and knights. There was a jongleur, a minstrel, and a herald, a woman and a nobleman. Though they carried the French flag, their weapons were sheathed, and Stephen had given orders to let them in. The porter was to lower the drawbridge after he confirmed their peaceful intent.

Satisfied that all was well, Stephen might have rejoined the crowd making merry in the Great Hall. Instead, he chose to pace alone, to sort his thoughts.

God in Heaven, came his silent, surly prayer, how did he and Katherine get into a battle of wills? That was not at all what he had intended. He had planned to give her time—time to realize how noble and good he was, time to learn to love him as he had known in an instant he could love her. But his plans had been foiled, stopped short by her inane logic. He very much feared that if they stayed this course, this contest to see who would accept the other's verdict on their union, all would be lost very quickly.

"What a stubborn woman," he growled, shaking his head. His stride lengthened as he tried to place his spurred heels on the horizontal cracks in the wall-walk. He ignored a half dozen guards who stood at the towers, grinning in amusement at his childish task.

At last he stopped, his attention suddenly drawn to the horizon. It was stunning! His heart wrenched with a longing for Katherine, and at the very same moment he wanted to weep at the beauty of nature. That was what his craving for Katherine Gilbert did to him. It hurt. It hurt his heart, his mind; it cracked open his imagination, his connection with so many things: God, nature, life. It was too painful. He didn't want to feel so much, and yet he couldn't control his feelings. He wanted her, he longed to make love to her, to cherish her, but he didn't want to expose himself so completely.

"Dear God," he muttered, his chest aching, "thank you for this beautiful sight."

The sun glowed in the distance like a garnet drapped in purple silk. Fuchsia clouds swathed the red bulb like a taunting lover rustling bed sheets in a twilight invitation.

"Devil take the woman," he grumbled as his high-flying mood crashed seconds later. It was her fault that he could not even look at a sunset without stiffness in his groin. Frustration had driven him to these ramparts. Frustration was driving him mad. And he was still very worried about his father, for the earl had not stirred from his drugged slumber. But as if he were a callow youth, the greatest number of his thoughts centered on Katherine. He was so entranced he did not even hear Sir Ramsey step onto the wall-walk from the nearest tower.

"Good God!" Stephen cried and swung around when the steward touched his shoulder.

The shorter man, brushing a hand over his gray speckled beard, gave Stephen a knowing smile. "Forgive me, Guy. You are distracted. Perhaps your mind is still at Downing-Cross."

"Indeed." Stephen's eyes narrowed with a silent warning to tread carefully, but the steward merely smiled all the broader, a spurt of amusement whistling between a gap in his front teeth. "Go on, Ramsey. Let me have it. Accuse me of debauching whilst my father hovers near death. At least you would then have the courage to say what others merely think."

When Stephen folded his arms and leaned against the parapet, Ramsey did likewise. "Nay, milord, I did not think it, therefore I will not say it. Katherine will soon be your wife. Naturally, you are taking the time to win her over. 'Tis a luxury too seldom taken by noblemen. I trust you succeeded at your mission."

Stephen barked out an ironic laugh that ended in a snarl. "God's Teeth, would that I had. I've not met a woman more stubborn in my life. She looks sweet enough, with honey tresses and that supple little form of hers tucked into soft gowns. In truth, she's a ripe berry waiting in a patch of thorns. I would not care, Ramsey, what she thought or felt if I did not know that we might share something rarely found in arranged marriages."

Ramsey twisted round, shifting his view from the horizon to the bailey. Below, Marlow greeted the arrivals while stable hands dispatched their sluggish horses. " 'Tis not like you to fret over a damsel. Tell her you love her and have at it."

Stephen turned to his friend with a lopsided grin. "Have at it? That's the easy part. Speaking of love is a different matter altogether."

Ramsey's eyes danced with excitement. "But that's what a woman wants, Stephen. She may take your seed in a fit of passion, but what she really wants is to know she's loved. That's the very heart of it. Without that, you'll have a battle on your hands till she sees you into your grave."

Stephen shifted weight from one foot to the other. "Nay, Ramsey, it is not as simple as that."

"Aye, 'tis milord. Did you tell her you love her?"

Stephen shook his head, unable to disprove Ramsey's theory. "I did not."

"And yet you want to bed her?"

"Foolish question, my friend."

"Ah, you're the fool, if you ask me. You've known her but a short time, but you love her. Why not tell her?"

Stephen smacked his lips at a sour taste that filled his mouth. "You are mistaken about my feelings for Katherine."

"I know you, Stephen. I see that lost look in your eyes. You've never met a woman like Katherine before. She is pure in heart."

"Damn her for her noble heart!" Stephen shouted, pounding the parapet. "The damned woman will not bury a brother because of a deathbed vow. And she will not bed me until his soul flies off to Heaven."

Ramsey's face crumbled with dismay. "Oh, Stephen. You above all should know the importance of a vow. Only she can put such a promise to rest, in her own way, in her own time. I'd bet my best gelding there's only one thing that will relinquish her from her vow."

Pride glued his eyes to the horizon, but Stephen's curiosity was piqued. By now the sun was gone. Only an afterglow remained. He shivered with a new chill. "You've snagged me, Ramsey. Go on then and share your great wisdom."

"The only thing that will free her of a vow made from

love is another vow of love. 'Tis plain to see. You must tell her you love her."

Stephen squinted against the gathering darkness, but it wasn't the lack of light that screwed his face into a distorted mass. It was a sinking feeling. A feeling of drowning. *I love you.* Even thinking the words made him gasp for air. Why was it so difficult?

"Nay, Ramsey, I won't tell her those words."

"But milord . . ." Ramsey cajoled him.

"Ramsey, in all the times my father told my mother he loved her, not once did she say 'I love you' in return. I am not as strong as my father. I could not bear silence in return."

Stephen turned with relief when a page burst through the nearest tower door, dispelling the tension. The boy ran forward with torch in hand and fell to one knee.

"Sir Stephen, Lord Marlow bade me tell you that he has accepted on your behalf a challenge by the French nobleman who just arrived through Blackmoor's gate. There is to be joust *à plaisance* tomorrow. Lord Marlow said you should prepare."

"A joust of peace," Stephen murmured, stroking his square chin. His troubled expression brightened at this news. He glanced down at the stables, where the last of the Frenchman's entourage tended to their mounts.

"So I am to joust with a wandering knight eager to make a name for himself in the romances. I am to be a player in the tales of heroism and love penned by his traveling minstrel." Stephen eyed Ramsey speculatively, a plan forming in his mind.

"Aye, milord," the page replied. "Lord Marlow says Seigneur Etienne Darbonnet is traveling in search of the Black Prince, to settle a score between them with a joust of war. But the seigneur would like to practice with you, milord, with blunted lances, of course."

"Do not accept on your brother's word, Stephen," Ramsey warned. "I'd not be surprised if Marlow is setting you up for a mean blow."

"Nay, Ramsey, I will speak with our visitor before this challenge. If he is what he claims to be, I'll take him on for the sport of it. This may be just what I needed, after all."

"What are you up to now, milord?"

"Maybe our wandering knight has brought minstrels who will write a chanson about my courageous victory. One so sweet and noble it will ply the heart of even the sternest maiden."

A conspiratorial grin parted Ramsey's closely cropped beard. "I see your scheme, and 'tis a good one."

"I may not put much stock in words, but there's more than one way to win a woman's heart, Ramsey."

At least so he prayed.

CHAPTER NINE

✠

"Enter!" Stephen bellowed.

Katherine paused only a moment. A voice of reason told her she should not enter his chamber alone, but then what could happen? The joust would begin shortly. Even if Stephen did choose to test her virtue one more time, he wouldn't do so if it meant delaying his challenger, Seigneur Darbonnet.

She swept into the chamber, gently closing the door behind her. It wasn't until she had moved forward a half dozen paces that she looked up to greet him. She gasped and paused, her hands flying to her open mouth. Stephen stood across the room, resplendent and masculine in what she could only conclude was the very state in which God must have first found Adam and Eve—stark naked.

Her round green eyes widened against her fair complexion and then narrowed in scorn. No doubt he had planned this ill-timed rendezvous, but in the split second before she could conjure a curse, her eyes roved from his delighted grin down the robust curves of his chest, moving quickly past the flat plain of his belly to . . .

"Oh my," she muttered. Saving her curses for another day, she turned and made a mad dash for the door.

"Geoffrey!" Stephen commanded, flinging his hand in the direction of the fleeing maiden.

Before Katherine could make her escape, the stocky squire leapt the distance between his lord and the door, blocking Katherine's exit.

"You needn't blush, milady," the younger man said in an

irritatingly innocent manner. "Sir Stephen is dressing for the joust *à plaisance*. Watch closely and you'll learn a thing or two about the proper preparations for combat."

"I thank you, no." Katherine spoke to the door, unwilling to watch Stephen while he dressed and reluctant to prove herself faint of heart with another hasty attempt to escape. Willing away the raspberry blotches on her cheeks, she stood as nonchalantly as possible with her back to Stephen.

Geoffrey returned to the rug cast down before the hearth and continued the ritual begun moments before Katherine's entrance.

"Here you are then, milord, put on your leggings. Hold steady, Sir Stephen, grip my shoulder. One foot then the other. That's the way, milord."

"I'm not a child, Geoffrey," Stephen barked.

"On with the mail chausses, milord."

Still hovering at the door, her back facing the knight and his squire, Katherine did not need to see firsthand what her vivid imagination all too eagerly painted in her mind's eye. As Geoffrey tended his lord, Katherine envisioned herself carrying out the squire's intimate duties. It was *she*, not Geoffrey, who lifted the flexible mail armor that would protect Stephen's legs and calves. *She* raised the shimmering mail, thousands of tiny metal loops rustling in her hands, over his rock-solid thighs. A faint groan of pleasure crawled from her throat, and she swallowed it quickly. Distrusting her own desire, she reached for the door latch.

"Do not leave yet, dear lady," Stephen said with an imperious tone. "I've summoned you for a purpose."

With a confounded sigh, Katherine slowly turned and cast about for something safe on which to affix her gaze. She settled on Stephen's sword, resting on a bedside table. "Your timing is impeccable, Stephen. I would not have come if I'd thought it was an invitation to watch you dress. Or is that, like a joust, considered a spectator sport?"

He laughed loudly, rich bellows ringing through the chamber. "Nay, now, do not ascribe malicious intent to my request, maiden. We're running a bit behind today."

Her eyes daringly wandered to his just in time to catch him throw a meaningful glare at Geoffrey, who tugged a shirt over Stephen's torso. "It seems my squire chose this morning to begin some ill-advised courtship."

Geoffrey turned red but did not argue.

"In any event," he continued, his clever eyes alighting on Katherine, "it worked out perfectly. You wanted to get to know me better before we bed one another, *n'est-ce pas?*"

"S'Blood," Katherine cursed, ignoring Geoffrey's eyebrows, which shot up nearly to his hairline it seemed. "You are an ill-mannered rogue."

By now Geoffrey was tugging on Stephen's gambeson, a quilted coat, pulling it around his hips, followed by a mail shirt. Katherine gaped at the sight of his taut buttocks ensconced in the seat of his leggings. Like a finely bred horse, Stephen was a work of God's art.

"Milady? Katherine?"

Only belatedly did she hear Stephen call her name. With chagrin, she forced her gaze from his hindquarters to his twinkling eyes.

"Do you find something of interest?" His lips rippled with sarcasm.

"Nothing of particular interest, milord."

"Indeed." Doubt shimmered in his damnably entreating voice.

"What is it you called me for, Stephen?"

"As I'm sure you've heard by now, I've been challenged to a joust by a French nobleman seeking adventures. I expect you to wear my colors. And I would hope to wear your wimple on my lance."

He paused when Geoffrey lowered a coif over his neatly combed hair. Stephen tugged at the mail hood until the open circle fit snugly around his face. Once it was adjusted, he sat down on a stool and leaned forward, resting his arms on his thighs. "I trust you won't disappoint me. Unless, of course, you harbor some hidden anger."

"Not so hidden, milord," came her dour reply. She glanced at his surcoat spread without a wrinkle on the bed. The surcoat was made of four panels, alternating black and red silk. Each panel was adorned with an emblem—King Edward's leopard on one; a wolf, Stephen's own heraldic emblem, on another; and the Bartingham's coat of arms spread across the back, encompassing two panels.

Next to the surcoat lay a silk cape in matching colors and crests designed for a lady. Instead of a hood, the collar rose up a foot in the air in a wide arc, stiffened by whalebone shafts. Nestled above the collar on the down bed lay a crown of oyster shells and peacock feathers.

"Surely you jest," Katherine said with a spurt of laughter. "You can't expect me to wear this absurd costume! I'd look like the queen of the faeries."

"Nay, you'd look like Guinevere. It was made for the very first round table my father sponsored. All the jousters dressed like knights in King Arthur's court. I assure you this is a most favored costume."

"One can only wonder who wore it before me," Katherine said archly. She picked up the gleaming crown and stroked an iridescent blue feather.

"None of my past amours, if that is what you mean. Only the women in this family have had the honor of wearing that gown. Blast it, Geoffrey, will you hurry it along?"

"Coming, milord, coming." Weary from lifting so many heavy garments, the squire wiped a trickle of perspiration from his temple. Stephen donned a leather cuirass over his chain mail, the final piece before his plates of armor and the adorning surcoat. The protective hide fit snugly over Stephen's massive chest, and suddenly he looked like an arrogant, brave knight. The scent of leather wafted through the room, exuded from the time-worn animal skin. Katherine inhaled the foreign, masculine smell, her gaze again compelled to Stephen's chest.

She felt him watching her watch him, and her insides grew warm and fuzzy and a little frightened. He had discovered her secret—she wanted him as much as he wanted her. To her surprise, his eyes, rather than mocking her, blinked like twin stars in the sky, distant, beckoning.

"Katherine . . ." He held out a coaxing hand, and without thinking she took a step forward. But a fanfare of trumpets blasted through the silence, and she halted.

It seemed as if the entire castle suddenly burst into a frenzy of celebration and anticipation.

"The joust will begin soon," Stephen said, turning to the open window, where the sounds of horses neighing and cart wheels churning echoed from below.

The castle's inhabitants started to make their way to the lists outside the curtain. Children shrieked and laughed, dogs barked and snarled, howling when they followed too closely to the clomping hooves of destriers. Applause erupted when a jongleur shouted the last verse of a romance for the ladies who strolled through the portcullis. Katherine smiled at the sounds of merriment, but then shivered when a herald called spectators to take their places for the joust. She looked at Stephen with solemn eyes, worrying for him as she had always worried when Georgie accepted a challenge from a knight he did not know.

"I must get dressed," Katherine said. She dropped the crown to the bed and scurried toward the door.

"You'll at least wear a wimple," Stephen called to her.

With a hand on the door frame, she turned back to consider his request. She detested wimples. The tight cloth restricted and irritated her neck. And she didn't fancy giving encouragement to this arrogant knight any more than she looked forward to giving him her virtue.

"I'll see you at the lists," she said, making a swift exit but no promise.

At twelve-thirty, she joined Rosalind and Constance in the stands built for spectators. Katherine marveled at the pomp so quickly organized for the joust. Three risers were constructed in front of the lists. Over the risers a vermilion canopy wafted in a crisp breeze. Katherine shivered and hugged herself within the folds of her gray mantle. Though she had refused to wear Stephen's colorful costume, she wore a pale red gown and wimple in deference to his wishes.

"*Allons!* Let the tournament begin!" shouted the French visitor's herald, while his minstrel strolled along the lists singing a romantic tale of Darbonnet's previous feats.

Stephen was the first to approach the spectators. He marched in wide strides, negotiating each step with care in his cumbersome armor. With his helm tucked under one arm, and Geoffrey at his side, he knelt before the women, his knee sinking into the soft sand and straw cast for the occasion over the ice that still lingered from the late spring snow.

"Miladies," he said, "I pray for your applause and goodwill should my opponent prove too worthy."

"I've never worried about you on the lists, my son," Rosalind said with boredom. Across the gathering crowd, she spotted Marlow conversing with Stephen's opponent and rose to join them.

"Katherine, may I have a word with you alone?" Stephen motioned with a nod of his head, his chain mail clinking against his armored breastplate. Geoffrey extended a hand and helped his master rise.

"You wore a wimple," he observed when Katherine joined him a stone's throw from the canopy. "And I thought you'd spite me yet."

"Aye, and I shall. I wore a wimple, but I fear 'tis too cold to part with today. You must strike your opponent with a naked lance." She reddened at her poor choice of words, remembering how Stephen had looked but an hour ago when she entered his chamber.

"Am I so repugnant to you still, Kate, that you must thwart my every wish?"

Ignoring him, Katherine focused on a jongleur who whipped across the lists in a series of back flips, bells on his polka-dotted hood tinkling with every turn. A crowd of peasants, standing around the fence that enclosed the jousting area, broke into applause.

"Admit it, Kate, you are mad with desire for me." Stephen touched her shoulder and forced her to look at him. Mirth churned in his azure eyes. His windburned cheeks twitched with humor.

How she hated this game he played.

"Be done with your mockery, Stephen. You'll bed me soon enough when the priest anoints our union. Leave me alone until then."

"Nay, I'll not bed you even on our wedding night. Not until you beg for it. I'll be no act of duty, no act of charity. You're risking a precious thing, the feelings you know you feel for me. I pray God you do not dash them on that rock you call your heart."

"*Pardonnez-moi,* am I interrupting?"

Stephen and Katherine turned and discovered Seigneur Etienne Darbonnet, clearly amused by their row. He pulled a white helm from his head and tucked it under an arm. Curly red hair framed his dashing features. Katherine thought she'd never seen a knight dressed quite so elegantly for a joust. His surcoat was made of cream and blue velvet patches. He rode a white steed with black stockings; its trappings, made of blue-and-white paneled silk, covered the animal like a mantle fit for a king. Like its master's, the armor protecting the horse's head exploded with a bouquet of white feathers at its peak.

"If I have come at an inappropriate moment, say the word, and I will make my retreat. Do you wish me to go, Sir Stephen?"

"*Mais non,*" Stephen replied in his opponent's native tongue. "May I introduce you to Katherine Gilbert."

Katherine nodded when the armored knight bent to kiss her gloved hand. "*Enchanté, demoiselle.*"

The Frenchman was at least five years younger than Stephen, if Katherine judged accurately. His deep chocolate eyes melted in the hot gaze he bestowed on her; his full lips puckered in obvious appreciation of her beauty.

"I see you have not yet given the good Sir Stephen your favor. May I claim your allegiance in this joust, *demoiselle?*"

"Impossible," Katherine replied, and from the corner of her eye she glimpsed a smug smile dash across Stephen's face. "But I thank you for your flattering request."

"What a shame." The charming Frenchman started to don his helm, but paused, his eyes lighting brightly. "I just thought of a way to console my broken heart. We have yet to name the prize. What say you, Bartingham? If I win the joust, I will sup tonight with this fair lady. And to sweeten the prize, we will not only share a trencher and goblet, which is customary, we will also feed each other . . . by hand."

Katherine's eyes widened with alarm. She could only imagine how this lecherous knight would take advantage of such intimacy.

"Nay, Stephen, I think it would be better—"

"A grand idea!" Stephen interrupted her. His eyes narrowed with a demonic glint. "I'm sure Katherine would prefer your company to mine, Darbonnet. She can barely tolerate me, it seems."

The French nobleman emitted a sultry chuckle, eyeing her as if he were about to bed her. He turned to Stephen with a frown. "But what of your prize, Bartingham?"

"I have the honor of eating with Katherine every evening, *mon ami.* We shall think of another prize for me. Come along and I'll tell you what I have in mind."

Darbonnet nudged his destrier, and they proceeded to the lists, but Katherine called Stephen back for one last admonition.

"If you lose this match, I will never forgive you."

"Ah, but Kate," he said cheerily, chucking her chin with the cold maindefer encasing his fingers in metal, "I never lose a battle."

He started away, but turned back with a devilish grin. "Almost never."

With a low groan of contempt, Katherine returned to the stands, where a half dozen other ladies from the castle had joined Lady Constance. Still ill at ease from her last encounter with Marlow's wife, Katherine kept to herself, refusing to enjoy the festivities. But soon her discomfort gave way to the infectious excitement that brimmed over in the crowd. With gleeful expressions, the women behind her watched their knights, many of whom would joust after Stephen and Darbonnet's challenge. Some of the women waved their sleeves at their lovers and threw ribbons at them as they passed by. Others tittered with laughter when a minstrel approached, singing a song he had hastily written for the occasion, praising the English women for their exceptional beauty.

But Katherine's enjoyment fizzled when, in the distance, she watched Stephen approach a member of Darbonnet's entourage, a female member who could be described as nothing other than a tart. Though she did not bear a prostitute's badge as required by law, Katherine had no doubt the young woman had earned that title in deed. She hung on the arms of two French mercenary knights, all a rough-and-tumble lot. She had blond hair with curls that rioted around her voluptuous lips and come-hither eyes. At Stephen's approach, she swaggered up to him, hips swaying, with a smile that nearly split her painted cheeks from ear to ear. Katherine couldn't hear what she said, but it took little insight to discern her intent. The woman pulled a kerchief from the depths of her bosom and swished the yellow silk back and forth beneath Stephen's nose. Stephen passed the kerchief to his squire, who ran off and tied it around his master's first lance. Gushing with gratitude, the tart planted on Stephen's lips a kiss that would have been appropriate only if her champion had been on his deathbed and she were attempting to revive him.

"By the Mass!" Katherine uttered, heedless of the attention she drew to herself. The other ladies followed her gaze, and several gasped at the sight of Stephen's brazen exchange.

Some turned to Katherine with pitying looks; others sneered at her. Furious, Katherine could watch no more and turned away from the humiliating scene, only to find Constance gazing directly at her.

" 'Tis not what you think," Katherine said, sounding foolish even to herself. Katherine hated that Constance was a witness to her embarrassment so soon after she had tried to convince the embittered woman that Stephen would be a better husband than Marlow. " 'Tis no doubt some whimsy of my lord's. Nothing more."

"Most certainly," Constance said, her tone flat, her shallow eyes giving away no emotion. Then, unexpectedly, she gave Katherine's hand a compassionate squeeze.

The gesture left Katherine speechless, and she smiled with gratitude when Constance cried out, "Look yonder," distracting the other ladies, who still gaped at Stephen and the tart. Constance pointed to the jongleur, who now juggled five gourds at once.

Grateful that the others had looked elsewhere, Katherine returned her attention to her tormentor. Despite her embarrassment, she studied Stephen with admiration as he mounted his destrier. His silver armor gleamed and winked in the midday sun. Behind him, a row of pennons fluttered in all their glory—blue and white, red and black, triangles split with crosses, leopards, lances, emblems of honor, emblems of war.

Though Seigneur Darbonnet was dressed with more dazzle—a plume of white feathers cocked high out the top of his helm and a rich velvet surcoat dangling down his legs—it was Stephen who cut the better figure. What was it about him that made Katherine brush aside her anger, her pride? Was it his uncompromisingly strong physique? The way his broad shoulders seemed to rebel against the confines of his armor? Or was it his nature? Indeed, his noble character.

"Oh, Stephen," she whispered, casting him a loving gaze she knew he could not see. Too late she wished she had given him her wimple. It did nothing but strangle her, dampen her spirit, when the simple act of giving it away would have made his spirit soar. But damn his pride, his games! His flirtation with another woman was designed only to raise her ire. It was his way of manipulating her into his bed, and that would be no act of love; it would be an act of conquest. Love was not about conquering.

In any event, she wished she had given him her favor, if for no other reason than to inspire his victory. Katherine grew queasy at the thought of how the ladies mocking her now would titter with delight at the sight of Seigneur Darbonnet popping succulent morsels into her mouth at the evening meal, his fingers lingering on her lips.

"Fight on, Sir Stephen!" she shouted, content when he turned toward her, somehow having heard her cheer through the armor encasing his head. He nodded ever so slightly.

"Bully on! Go! Go to! Knock the whelp on his arse!" Shouts of encouragement burst from the crowd when the knights began their charge. Sunlight glittered off the armored foreheads of their horses as the steeds bolted forth, heads bobbing, nostrils snorting, hooves spewing sand and straw. Both knights leaned forward as they dashed along the lists. But in the final few seconds before impact, they sat upright, a technique that aided their thrust but left them virtually blind, each unable to see his opponent through the narrow slit in his visor. Katherine prayed that in those final seconds Stephen would not lose his mark.

He did not, but his opponent had better luck. Though their lances met coronal to coronal, it was Stephen's lance that shattered on impact. Katherine groaned. It was a good start for Darbonnet; the Frenchman's direct hit counted as three broken spears on his score sheet.

Only when the jousters fell back and prepared to make a second go at it did Katherine realize that she felt faint. For though jousting was a noble sport, and the jousts *à plaisance* were meant to harm no one, it was not uncommon for a helm to go flying on impact, the jouster suffering a sometimes fatal head wound.

The second run down the lists was even more exciting than the first, for the crowd was now in an uproar, and the jousters seemed infected with their spectators' enthusiasm. The smudged and sooty faces of peasants from Blackmoor village were contorted with fierce pride as they urged their master on. The knights serving fealty to Blackmoor stood tense on the sidelines, many wishing they could have a crack at the Frenchman, for though there was a temporary truce between the nations in the wake of the Pestilence, England and France were still at war. The victor of this challenge could claim a symbolic victory for his country.

For Katherine, the tension was unbearable. She slipped away from the stands, behind a row of knights. Stephen would not notice her absence; he could barely see his opponent through his visor. She would watch the match from the challenger's end, at a comfortable distance. Besides, if Stephen won, she wanted to make sure the buxom young woman cheering him on would not enjoy a victor's kiss.

The horses drummed forward, and Stephen's lance hit Darbonnet's shield with a splintering crack. "Ooohhh," the crowd groaned in unison. But Katherine did not join the chorus. She was distracted by a cloaked figure meddling with Darbonnet's remaining lance. When his head fell back, she recognized him as one of Marlow's henchmen. When the seigneur's squire came to retrieve the lance, they shook hands, and Marlow's man slipped away.

Katherine's heart began to beat faster. Her mouth grew dry as she imagined evil plots. Why would Marlow's man aid Darbonnet? Though the squire made an effort to hide the lance tip in the frosty grass, the glint of steel could not be ignored from where she stood. This lance bore no coronal with three wooden stubs on the end. This was a tip of sharpened metal.

"Milord!" she shouted without thinking, but her voice was lost in the crowd. "Sir Stephen!"

Katherine pressed through the throng of villeins and peasants who hugged the palisades bordering the lists.

"Watch yerself, dearie," a plowman muttered when she nearly fell into his thick arms.

"Eh, by Beelzebub, it's good Sir Guy's betrothed!" a pockmarked woman cried out.

Katherine ignored the ruckus her shoves provoked and stepped on the lowest rung of the fence, rising above the crowd.

"My lord Stephen!" she cried out in a shriek so piercing virtually every face in sight turned in her direction.

Stephen paused just as he was about to take up his final lance. Seeing Katherine, he pulled off his helm.

Suddenly worried about the attention she'd drawn to herself, Katherine ripped the wimple from her chin and waved it in the air with a coy flick of her wrist. "Milord! You'll not fight another joust without a favor from me, will you?" Wanting to hide the seriousness of her ploy, she batted her lashes for the benefit of the audience. A few drunken merchants elbowed each other's ribs, guffawing over the sight of what they considered another oversexed noblewoman hiding behind fancies and lace.

"They're all alike, devil take them. All alike," one of the men said, a belch burbling through his blackened teeth.

Stephen dug a prick-spur into the belly of his warhorse and cantered to the fence. A slow, triumphant smile creased his cheeks. "Katherine?"

"Milord, you were quite right. You deserve my allegiance. How selfish of me to think otherwise. I beg you, please do me the honor of donning your final lance with my wimple."

"I see you've come to your senses, lady." Rather than accept her gift, he paused to gloat over her turnabout.

Katherine gritted her teeth and cocked one eyebrow. "Just take the blessed favor before I throw it at you, noble knight."

"Now, there's the Kate I know and love." Stephen clucked his tongue and reached for the satin garment, but then he paused, hand poised in midair. "Why the change of heart? Are you up to some mischief I'll soon regret?"

"Just take the bloody wimple!"

"Why, Katherine," Stephen said with mock horror. "What shocking language."

He leaned forward, but before he could snatch the wimple from her hands, she tugged on it, pulling him forward. Flinging a hand around his neck as if to kiss him, she whispered in his ear, "Your opponent has a steel-tipped lance. He means to kill you."

Stephen wrapped an arm around her while he stole a glance at his opponent waiting for the final round. Just as Katherine had warned, Darbonnet's squire stood next to his master equipped with a lance that could easily kill him no matter how slight the blow. He turned to her, his lips but inches away, and smiled, teeth flashing, regarding her with new appreciation.

"And I thought you called me over here because jealousy had gotten the best of you, Kate," he whispered.

Katherine basked in his loving gaze. "Nay, milord, I am not the jealous sort."

"Such a pity. 'Twill make courting all the harder."

"Sir Stephen," Darbonnet said, drawing his horse up to the fence. "I see you have made progress with Demoiselle Katherine. She has given you her favor. I trust this will not change the outcome when I win this final bout. She will still be my prize."

Stephen forestalled Katherine's sarcastic reply with a gentle touch to her shoulder. Nudging her back, he said, "Of course, Darbonnet, but I would not be so certain of the outcome. Though your score is still higher than mine, we have each won a round. I'd say we're well matched. The last joust could easily go to me, good sir."

"Indeed," Darbonnet said, bowing his head deferentially.

"What is of more concern to me is your lance."

Katherine admired the way Stephen contained himself. His smooth voice gave no hint of anger or betrayal.

"One of your squires must be sleeping while on duty. The

lance your men have chosen is for a joust *à outrance*. A good hit with that weapon might end my days too early, though such a fate might please at least one stubborn damsel I know."

Katherine helped him salve over the embarrassing confrontation. "Aye, I'd not weep a tear for you. I merely gave you my wimple out of sympathy since it's clear you're outmatched."

The seigneur's eyes twinkled with delight, Katherine's flattery having hit the mark.

"Your lance, Seigneur," Stephen insisted.

The French nobleman looked at the squire who held his weapon. After squinting in the sun, his eyes widened with astonishment. "*Merde!*" he cursed. "*Mais, je regret.* What a terrible mistake. I'll have my man flogged for this."

Stephen waited patiently while his opponent made a show of remorse. Katherine thought it was an act, but she couldn't be sure. It was possible Marlow had set the Frenchman up.

"I hope you will forgive me, Sir Stephen, and trust that I knew nothing of this."

Stephen's eyes hardened, but then he smiled with the same determined charm he had been using on Katherine of late. "Ah, Seigneur, 'tis nothing but a misunderstanding. You may use one of my lances. Now let us see who the real victor will be."

"You are most kind, Bartingham, most kind indeed." When Darbonnet cantered away, cursing his squire, who bowed profusely, taking the blame as well as a kick in the derriere, Stephen turned to Katherine.

"I owe you my eternal gratitude," he said.

She would not tell him his safety was sufficient repayment. Nor would she mention her wildly beating heart, nor how difficult it was to look into his handsome face without swooning. Rather, she said, "Then repay me by winning this final joust."

"Done." He spurred his horse to the far end of the lists,

reining his eager charger, who champed the bit and snorted impatiently.

For the last time, the herald waved a white staff and cried out, "Do battle!"

Off went the horses. Foam flew from their mouths. The earth rumbled. The jousters grunted. A spear cracked and echoed in the stands, and one knight howled in pain. Armor flew through the air as Seigneur Darbonnet landed on his back. Thrown from his horse, he lost the entire challenge. Stephen was the victor. The spectators roared.

Katherine smiled, blinking inexplicable tears of joy. She backed away into the cheering crowd, wondering why she felt as if she had won the match herself.

CHAPTER TEN

✠

That evening the Great Hall abounded with drunken knights and dancing. The French visitors enjoyed a great feast given in honor of Stephen and the other knights who had been victorious on the lists. Darbonnet's jongleur and minstrel jangled the air with music and noise. It was a night of festivity such as Katherine had never seen, and through it all she was the focus of three men's attention. Stephen cast her intimate looks during the meal, reminding her of the first time they had danced and kissed without fear or judgment. She blushed with pleasure at his repeated thanks for her keen observation during the joust. And, of course, Seigneur Darbonnet's defeat did little to dampen his spirit of lechery. He insisted on dancing with Katherine after the meal and much too close for her liking.

Then there was Marlow. He watched her with furtive eyes over the brim of his chalice as he swilled his mead. He stole glances in her direction even while he boasted and argued with the other knights. When he was dancing, it seemed his gaze always found its way back to Katherine. This unwanted attention made her gravitate to Stephen all the more. She prayed Marlow's sudden interest in her would come to naught.

After all had retired for the evening, and the castle was dark, the door to Katherine's chamber flew open. Rosemary, huddling beneath the covers, sprang from the bed in fear. Katherine sat up and drew a sheet to her breasts, straining to recognize the imposing figures who stood silhouetted against the candlelight from the corridor.

"Stephen? Is that you?" she whispered, hoping it was, but knowing from the arrogant stance of the intruders that it was not. "Rosemary, go fetch Europa."

The tiny young woman darted past the men. One started after her but, apparently deeming the task too inconsequential, returned.

"Come, milady. Lord Marlow would have audience with you," the man said in a gruff and disrespectful voice.

"At this hour? Surely you jest."

" 'Tis no jest," said the other. "When Lord Marlow has a whim, 'tis best to cooperate. He wants to see you in the Great Hall."

"What foolery is this?" Katherine wondered aloud. Marlow had had many opportunities at more appropriate times to request her presence. She blanched at the memory of his constant gaze cast in her direction during the feast. What trick was he pulling now?

"I will not go unless my Lord Stephen commands it." She added haughtily, "I will forgive you bursting into my chamber this time, but it is unseemly. Pray, do not let it happen again."

The first who had spoken, the tallest, stepped forward, and Katherine inched away from him across the bed.

"Stephen is not master here, lady. You'll find that out soon enough when the earl dies."

Was there eagerness in his words? Katherine thought so, and she wondered what evil schemes Stephen had contended with since his return. She was newly worried for him.

"Now, come along, milady, or I shall have to obey Lord Marlow's orders and carry you to the Great Hall."

He reached forward as if to make good his threat, but Katherine held out a firm hand, staying him. "Wait outside," she ordered.

The men hesitated, but then obeyed. She crawled out of bed naked, and in the darkness fumbled in her trunk for her robe. She hoped with bitterness that her appearance would suitably shame Marlow for his ridiculous request.

Pulling back her hair, letting it cascade in loose waves down her back, she opened the door. "I am ready now. May I follow, or do you still wish to carry me?"

She saw no reaction; it was too dark. The men turned abruptly and marched down the hall, one in front of her and the other behind.

Europa met them in the corridor on their way to the Great Hall. She ran to Katherine, muttering under her breath. Her gray hair, usually pulled back neatly, hung in disorder. Alarm made her pudgy features vibrant.

"By the gods, milady, I like not the sound of this. 'Tis not right that Marlow should call you in such a fashion. He's up to something. I've seen him in one of his moods, Katherine, and 'tis frightening."

"I'm sure he means no harm," Katherine said hollowly. She grasped Europa's hand but stared straight ahead with a show of false courage.

"I will go to Stephen once I've given Marlow a piece of my mind."

Europa cut her assurances short when they rounded the archway and entered the Great Hall. It might have been day for all of Marlow's posturing. He sat in an ornately carved chair in front of the hearth. Half-eaten food and a pitcher of mead crowded a small table next to him. A hound sat curled at his feet with a weary expression, oblivious to its master's ribald laughter. A young scullery maid sat propped on his lap as he explored the smooth expanse of her breasts with his heavily bejeweled fingers. Several knights stood nearby, lost in their own argument.

Katherine halted and backed away, but the man-at-arms who followed from behind became a wall which her small frame could not move.

"Katherine!" Marlow shouted. His garish voice broke into drunken laughter. "How good of you to visit me, though I did not think to have the pleasure of your company at this hour. What brings you here so late? Is Stephen not man enough for you?"

The others broke into hysterical guffaws, save for Europa
and the embarrassed kitchen girl, who slipped from Marlow's
lap and hurried from the room.

"Europa," Katherine whispered, "I can not bear this
humiliation. Where is Stephen? Does he not know of this?"

"Nay, but fear not, milady," Europa comforted her. The
old woman took a deep breath and marched forward. She
glared down at Marlow like the Crone of Death. "You lay a
hand to Katherine and I'll seek the King's sheriff myself
if I have to to see you punished properly."

Marlow looked up with disdain, gulped his mead, and
waved her away. "Who is this that has entered my
castle? Get you hence, fat little gnat, or I'll swat the life
out of you."

Katherine watched, barely breathing, while jovial Europa
turned purple with rage.

"By the love of Christ, I know not what bile you drank
as a child, Marlow. I always tried to be fair with you, I did,
but no more. You have no right to flaunt yer power so."

"Are those flapping lips of yours suited for anything but
expelling hot air?" Marlow quipped, winking at the others.
"Nay, but you are too old and wrinkled for my tastes. Go to
bed, Europa. You bother me."

"Come, milady," Europa said, her rage suppressed. "I will
return with you to yer chamber."

"No!" Marlow shouted, truly irritated now. He motioned
to the soldiers. "Bothwell, bring the lady to me. Cramer,
hold that harping magpie tightly. Put a hand over her mouth
if you have to."

"Stephen will hear of this, Marlow. As soon as he knows
you have dared to treat Katherine this way, he will have your
blood on his knife," Europa threatened, her words ending in
tears of frustration.

"At least we all know what Stephen is wont to do with his
sword," Marlow said smugly, standing as Katherine came
to a halt a few feet away. He motioned her to the chair
opposite him.

She sat, but remained rigid. At least the fire was warm; despite the nausea and dread that coursed through her, she was comforted by the warmth of the fire. The floor stones felt hot against her icy toes, and she let her feet fall flat, though her hands remained clenched in tight balls.

"What is it that you wish to say to me, Lord Marlow? I am young and naive to the whims of noblemen such as you, but I know enough to regret my presence here. It is unseemly. I pray that the countess does not hear of it. My virtue comes to Sir Stephen without blemish. I would keep it so and do not like to think the servants will soon be whispering about our midnight meeting."

Marlow clapped his hands together in a mocking, loud way. "Very well said, Katherine. I am most appropriately impressed with your indignation. And even more impressed by your hair."

He reached out in fascination, grasping a lock. His handsome face was lit with a moonstruck madness which Katherine assumed had been conjured by the mead. Even as she recoiled from his presence, she noticed his similarity to Stephen—the same intense blue eyes and the ruddy, high cheeks; but the inner workings, the character, were so vastly different. When he wasn't mocking, Stephen always carried an air of intense outrage barely contained beneath the surface. With Marlow it was some madness simmering beneath his veneer of nobility and poise.

"Such an unusual color of hair," he said softly, his fingers brushing her neck. "Pumpkin, wouldn't you say?"

"Keep yer hands off her, you villain!" Europa shouted until Cramer clasped a hand over her mouth.

"Do not touch me," Katherine whispered, staring at the floor.

"But of course I won't touch you," Marlow said, leaning back in his chair. He stretched his legs out and rested them on the beleaguered hound. "Leave us now, won't you?"

Several knights nodded their acquiescence and staggered from the room, singing some filthy song as they went.

"Now we have privacy," Marlow said.

When Katherine looked up uneasily at the men who had rousted her from bed, he added, "Bothwell and Cramer are like brothers to me. More so than Stephen. You needn't fear their ears or tongues. I have brought you here so I would not embarrass you in front of the countess and my brother."

Katherine looked up sharply, intrigued by the serious tone in his voice. "What do you mean?"

Marlow rubbed his hands together and smacked his lips, searching for words. "I am concerned about your background. Though Father chose you for Stephen, I will soon be the earl, and I must carefully approve anyone who would join our family."

Suddenly feeling her exhaustion, Katherine stood. She stared at him, boredom dulling her green eyes, and said, "Have you stirred me so late to discuss my lineage, Lord Marlow? I am but the daughter of a baron. I had hoped that was plain to all. I am not ashamed of my standing. Indeed, I am proud of it. I see that nobility comes naught with the title, but with the spirit."

Her implied insult did not go without recognition. Marlow remained silent and then smiled, but only with his lips. His eyes cut mirthlessly through the smoky air. "You have been listening to my brother's lofty philosophies, I see. We shall address that momentarily. But for now there is something more pressing on my mind."

He reached for the table and grasped a pouch that Katherine had not noticed before. His sloppy gesture sent his pewter tankard tumbling to the floor. Dangling the drawn, leather object from his fingers, he said, "Does this look familiar?"

He held the pouch of herbs she had given to Constance. She compressed her lips and sat down again, feeling the blow but not giving his victory away. Had Constance tattled on her so quickly? More than fear of what Marlow would do to her for meddling in his affairs, she felt betrayed. She had thought there was some connection, some small understanding with Constance, especially after her friendly overtures during the joust. It was clear now that Katherine had imagined it.

"Does your silence mean aye or nay?" he continued. "You see, witchcraft is a sin against God punishable by fire."

"Witchcraft?" she said with half a laugh, frowning incredulously.

"If these are herbs, they are ones that I have never tasted or smelled. I fear they have magical properties."

"Am I on trial here?" she challenged, detesting that tendency in some men to act as authority incarnate.

"God's Wounds, no." He sprawled lazily in his chair. "But witchcraft might be construed as heresy."

"The Inquisition has not ventured to our island, Lord Marlow," Katherine challenged. Her eyes glinted with loathing. "Or would you act as the Inquisition's representative?"

"No need for that, I think. The archbishop has been too wise to allow the Inquisition here. But he allows his bishops to conduct their own trials, and witchcraft is the worst offense a woman can enact in the bishops' minds."

"I am not a witch," Katherine said, incredulous over the turn of conversation. Never had she imagined she would have to defend herself against such a preposterous accusation. Indeed, the world had gone daft with the Pestilence.

"Then you deny you gave this witch's concoction to my wife?" He taunted her with cruelty gleaming in his eyes. "You are not yet married to my brother, Katherine. This will not sit well with our mother."

Katherine looked to Europa for some guidance, but there was little the older woman could do. Her mouth was still covered, but her eyes beamed intensely at Katherine, and she shook her head.

"If you have not done this, then it must have been Elizabeth," Marlow carried on in the silence, staring at the pouch as it dangled from his fingers. "I know you went to see her. It's long been said that Elizabeth is a witch."

His petulant words filled Katherine with foreboding.

"Bothwell, go to Downing-Cross and fetch Elizabeth. Then take her to the bishop and tell him she is to be tried for witchcraft, and leave a donation for the Church. A large one."

"No!" Katherine cried. Her shrill voice halted Bothwell. She looked wildly at Marlow. "It is not right. You will charge an innocent woman."

"There is no such thing as an innocent woman. Eve tempted Adam. Women brought the downfall of mankind. All are sinners at birth, and entirely expendable thereafter."

"You are the one who blackens the name of Bartingham, Marlow," Katherine uttered in a low, threatening voice, caring naught what vengeance he would wreak on her. "You haven't even a fraction of the honor your brother possesses. Fate has been overkind to make you earl. But then life is not always just. The Pestilence is proof of that."

Her words hit the mark, for his lips twitched with unuttered oaths.

"Marlow, what is this? What foolishness so late at night?"

Constance stood in the archway, looking askance at Europa and Cramer, suspiciously at Bothwell, and lastly in bewilderment at Katherine and Marlow. She shivered and huddled in a blanket. Her mousy brown hair hung straight down her back. Her bitter expression had transformed into one of pain, as if her sudden waking in the night had been too jarring for her to resume her habitual mask.

"What are you doing now, my husband?" She inched forward in dismay.

"Did you miss me in your bed, dear wife?" he queried with sarcasm. "I can not say I share the sentiment."

"Why is Stephen not here?" she persisted.

Katherine tried to catch her attention, to read her intent, but Constance's angry eyes fastened on Marlow.

"Stephen is not here because he sleeps. I did not wish to disturb him. I am merely trying to get Katherine to admit she gave you these enchanted herbs."

Constance's eyes alighted on the pouch, and her hand flew out. Snatching the leather sack, she pulled it to her breasts as if it were a child. "Where did you get this?" she hissed. "How dare you steal this from me. Did your henchmen rifle through my chamber?"

"So it was Katherine who gave you the pouch?"

"Nay," Constance said with dignity. She glanced calmly at Katherine and returned her gaze to Marlow. "She gave me nothing. She is but a self-centered little snippet."

Katherine would have been angry, but she was too enthralled by the magnificent performance of this woman about whom she had once thought so little.

"This pouch," Constance said, so much hidden in the even, untelling flow of her voice, "contains dried flowers, my husband. Not some witch's brew."

"Dried flowers?" Marlow sat up, disbelief and disappointment marring his features.

"Aye," Constance continued. "Every time you have given me a flower in the last fifteen years of our marriage, I have dried it and saved it in this pouch. As you can see, it is a very small pouch."

"It smells not of flowers to me," Marlow argued. He rose and confronted his wife. Her age showed in the flickering firelight, and something else Katherine had not seen before—dignity. "If you are lying to save this witch you will pay for it, my wife."

Constance lowered her eyes humbly. "I would never turn against you. I speak only the truth."

Marlow grew discontent with the turn of events. He flexed his hands and drew them into fists, strutting before the fire.

"I am bored with this interview." He turned to Katherine. "But I will not say good night until I warn you about the one you would marry."

Katherine tensed with wariness.

"Your eyes have hardened to my words. He has persuaded you of his noble character, has he?" Marlow rested his hands on the arms of Katherine's chair and leaned forward, speaking almost in a whisper. "Did he tell you how misunderstood he was by our mother, and that I am the favorite? And did you pity him as all the women before you have? Did he speak to you of honor and love? He is very facile with his words, Katherine."

Katherine grew numb. How did Marlow know the words Stephen had spoken to her?

Europa sensed the tiny crack in Katherine's armor and struggled anew, her shouts still muffled by Cramer's vise-like hand. Constance shifted nervously, staring intently at Katherine.

"Do you deny it then?" Marlow persisted, growing excited now that he had grazed her delicate skin with the sharp point of his words. "Do you deny it?"

She did not answer, but bit her lip and brushed at a small stain marring her robe.

"No, of course not," Marlow continued. "Do not be deceived by my brother's glorious philosophies. I have seen him protest his love to his ladies and then whore in France, taking two or three at a time."

"Steady, Katherine," Constance murmured with wide, griev-ing eyes. "Hold fast."

Marlow ignored his wife, so delighted was he to see the wilting of the rose. "He does not love you. You are a con-venience to him. My brother does not know how to love. He knows only the form and the words. The only difference between us is that I do not pretend to such misconceived notions as love and fidelity. I am more honest."

Seeing the wounded bird falter in the sky, he swept forward and pulled her into a tight embrace. Reeling with vertigo, Katherine pushed away in vain.

"Katherine," Constance hissed, her humiliation paling beneath a greater urgency, "remember—we are nothing without it."

Marlow glanced at Constance with irritation. He did not understand her subtle message. Oblivious to the wounds caused by his effrontery, he turned back to Katherine with lust painting his features.

"Do not be persuaded by my brother. He will be cast out from this castle soon enough. He is a rogue, Katherine, and never to be trusted."

His mouth descended on hers. His tongue slithered between her lips, plundering their moisture.

Katherine pounded on his chest, but he would not stop. When she could breath no more, when she could think of no other recourse, when she could see him taking her without a thought to her honor and virtue, without a thought to his wife's dignity, she bit him, tasting blood as her teeth gripped his wet, chafing flesh.

"You she-devil!" he bellowed, reeling back and clutching his mouth. "You bit me. I don't even take that from a French whore."

He reached out with an easy sweep and pulled her to his chest. "I may desire you, wench, but I will not take your disrespect. Soon you will know who is master of this castle, and you will come crawling to my feet for favors."

He pushed her to the ground. Constance knelt beside her, pulling her close.

"Lord Marlow!" Ramsey stood in the archway, dread etched on his face. His hand flew to the hilt of his sword, and several guards stood fully armed behind him. "What is this? Your father is dying in his room, and you would disgrace him in this way!"

Marlow stepped back, distancing himself from Katherine. As he did, Stephen ran into the Hall and halted abruptly. He was but half-clad, his chest bare, a gipon hastily thrown over one shoulder. He stared in disbelief at the scene before him. Instant rage tightened every muscle, and he bolted forward with huge strides, but a clamor behind Ramsey stopped him again.

"Milords!" shouted Giles. Running from the solar, he stopped beside Ramsey. " 'Tis the earl, milord, he has stirred. He is asking for Sir Stephen."

Stephen looked at Katherine still huddled on the floor. He waved to Ramsey. "Block the door and send your men quickly."

Ramsey and his men-at-arms hurried to the solar while Marlow motioned to Cramer and Bothwell.

"This is my castle, Ramsey. If anyone is barred from my father's side it will be Stephen." Marlow hurried after his men while Constance ran from the room in tears.

"Katherine!" Stephen strode forward and pulled her into his arms while Europa wept and begged his forgiveness. "Katherine, are you well?"

She drew back, a flower arching in the wind, and searched his eyes, an anguished sky blue. "I thought you would never come," she said. *I thought you had abandoned me.* "Go to your father, Stephen. Europa will take care of me."

"Wait for me here. If my father has revived, I want you at my side." At the sound of clashing swords, Stephen started for the solar. "I will come for you soon."

Katherine rose in the silence that followed. She wiped at her sullied lips and fought tears of humiliation. Marlow had despoiled her in the quietest of ways. Not so much with his kiss, but with the doubt he had tried to implant. Stephen had warned her not to listen. Marlow had warned her also. Whom was she to believe?

CHAPTER ELEVEN

✠

Stephen ran to the solar, pulling on his clothing as he went. Silver gleamed as weapons clashed—five men fought on either side, including Ramsey and Marlow. Stephen joined the foray when Giles threw him a sword. With three quick motions Stephen parried Marlow's blows and flung his brother's blade clattering to the floor. Stephen lunged forward and steadied the tip of his sword at Marlow's chest.

"If you ever entertain Katherine in your presence alone again, my dear brother," he seethed, "I will cut out your heart."

The others ceased their melee, turning to the conquering Stephen. Giles went into the solar and came out quickly.

"Milord, Earl James calls your name."

Stephen turned and nodded. "I am coming. Ramsey, guard the door."

"You may speak with him," Marlow said, panting for breath, perspiration beading on his brow. "But it will all be over soon enough. When I am earl, I will cast you out."

Stephen gave him a lopsided, bitter grin. "I know that, Marlow." He turned and retrieved Katherine from the Great Hall while the others dispersed in tense silence.

After leading Katherine by the hand into the solar, Stephen closed the door behind them. He drew in a thick, malodorous breath that smelled faintly of death—heavy, reeking of the body, as if the physical form of his father cried out to the senses, making its presence known with strange odors and sounds just before the spirit left for a more lasting dwelling place. He glanced at Katherine's pale visage, tight and drawn, and gripped her hand reassuringly.

"Do you wish to be here?" he whispered. "I know we've been at odds. But this may be the last chance you have to know my father. I want you by my side."

Katherine blinked slowly and regarded him with an open expression he had not seen in so long.

"I want to be here, but do not worry about me. You must speak with your father."

Nodding, Stephen took in a deep breath and turned to the deathbed. Near it, several tapers burned, exposing the bent figure of the priest and the swaying form of the old physician.

"Stephen?" His father's frail voice rasped in the darkness. The earl motioned the other two figures away, and they slipped past Stephen with weary faces. "Come hither, my son."

"Dear Father." Stephen went to the earl's left side. Katherine sat in a chair to the earl's right.

Stephen knelt by the bed, taking the older man's hand in his. It was so limp, the skin so smooth. A fever made his flesh soft and warm, like the translucent skin of a featherless baby bird. Birth and death were so similar, Stephen thought. One was of this world and one . . .

"What . . . what is it, Stephen?" The earl frowned up at his son.

"I was just wondering about the preciousness of life." *Of your life,* he added silently. Had he ever known how much he loved his father until now? Now, when the absence of him would come like an expected but unwelcome frost? More than ever, Stephen knew that what his own existence depended upon, the thing that made his toil and sorrow worth the living, was this intangible thing called love, this exchange of energy between father and son, lover and lover, God and self. To look into his father's eyes and see the light in them, dimming though it was—this was life everlasting. He glanced at Katherine. She was an elegant statue, watching him with gentle patience.

"What is it, my son?" the earl prodded again.

Stephen blinked and smiled richly at the older man. "I am so honored to be your son, Father, to live this life with you. I have been truly blessed."

The earl began to weep. Stephen pulled him into his arms and held him fast like a child. Though it hurt to switch roles, for Stephen to be the parent, to be that much closer to death himself, it was the next inevitable step. He would be strong and usher his father from this world with stoic arms just as his children would usher him when his own beacon dimmed in the night.

"To say I have loved you, my son, is inadequate," James whispered with surprising lucidity. It was as if he had merely been sleeping, not unconscious with an unexplained malady. Lying back down against his perspiration-damp pillow, he said, "You were the star brightening the dark heavens. Do not be sad that I am leaving soon. Be proud that my blood flows through your veins."

Stephen's nostrils flared as he struggled with so many feelings. "Are you proud, Father?"

James drew in a breath. "Oh, yes, yes. Stephen. I saw your goodness the moment you'd sprung raging from the womb. I am sorry my foolish pride came between us in later years. I should have . . . have tolerated your youthful stubbornness. I know you abandoned Blackmoor because of your brother."

"I am no Black Prince, Father. Try as I may, my coat of arms will never glisten as brightly as that of Edward's cherished son."

The earl shook his head. "To me you are. The devil take the others. Resting at death's gate, I see how unimportant the opinions of others are. You were wiser than I in that way."

Silence filled the room until a falcon shrieked from the mews. Stephen frowned, wondering if a moment could last an eternity if one did not jangle the silence. He and Katherine exchanged a smile, and he was grateful to share the moment with her.

"I am making you heir to Blackmoor, Stephen," his father whispered at last. "You will be the next Earl of Blackmoor."

Stephen squinted in the low light, searching his father's face. Katherine stirred in her chair.

"I do not understand."

"You are my only son, Stephen. Marlow is a bastard."

Stephen's heart thudded in his chest, pounding like a battering ram against the castle walls. The implications were enormous.

"Your mother was unfaithful to me long ago," the earl continued in a resigned voice. "Your Uncle Robert is Marlow's true father."

Robert's name cut Stephen's entrails like a stone-sharpened dagger. He could not speak at first, and then he muttered, "Lord Roby . . ."

"Aye, Stephen, I know. Lord Roby called Rosalind a harlot. He spoke the truth, and you killed him for it. But you did not know. God will not judge you for it."

"Katherine," Stephen muttered, looking at her with imploring eyes. "I did not know. You must believe me, I did not know Roby spoke the truth. Dear God, I took a man's life in vain, and my soul will burn for it."

For the first time, the earl noticed Katherine. He squinted in the flickering candlelight. "Stephen?"

" 'Tis Katherine Gilbert, Father. The woman you have chosen as my wife."

"Ah, Gilbert's girl," the earl said contentedly. "She is beautiful. Do you judge Stephen, girl, because he killed a man?"

Stephen shot a glance across the bed. Compelled to defend her, he said, "Katherine has a keen sense of chivalry, Father. I've violated that code."

"Nonsense," the old man said, waving a trembling hand through the air. "You've much to learn about life, girl."

Katherine's cheeks grew hot, and she shut her eyes, feeling petty. She could not possibly explain herself to these men who did not understand her conscience. The Bartingham men were a different breed. "I do not know what I think anymore, my lord earl. Stephen has me questioning everything I've ever believed in."

"I should have known," Stephen said, angry with himself. "I always wondered about Mother and Robert." He fell silent and shook his head. "I wanted the countess to love me. That was all I ever really wanted."

James took his son's hand and squeezed it lovingly. "The heart of a woman can be fickle. Though it burns a man like fire, there's nothing to be done."

Stephen's head pounded as if a lance had struck him blind. What a strange twist of fate that he should inherit all of Blackmoor. He had never wanted it so dearly as Marlow had, and yet none of this was truly a surprise. On some unspoken level, he had known.

"How did you find out, Father?"

The earl looked away, his vision turning inward. His lips curled in an ironic smile. "Marlow told me. Can you fathom that? I grew angry with him one day. He was beating a serf, and I told him he acted like a changeling, for no son of mine would stoop to beat a rustic." James pawed at his throat, and Stephen tipped a chalice of water to his lips. Then the earl continued. "Marlow turned to me with so much . . . hatred, and cried that he was indeed a bastard, no son of mine. It sounded as if he boasted. I don't know what he thought to gain by that, but he wasn't thinking at the time, I suppose. I had always suspected as much, but was unwilling to face the truth."

Stephen shook his head in wonder. "Poor Marlow, the one truly honest moment of his life, and he lost his inheritance for it."

"Do not pity him," James instructed. "I cast him out because his greed has grown uncontrollable, not only because he is a bastard."

"He is my brother," Stephen uttered with frustration, pressing rigid fingers to his temples. "I damn him, but I love him still. Some part of me grieves for Marlow."

The earl chuckled ruefully. "Such is the way of the heart, my son. I still love your mother, but love was not meant to be simple, I fear. 'Twould be too boring for the Creator to watch us spinning our webs if the strands lay straight for even a fool to dance along. Finally we are crowned with all our titles. Not only earl and cuckold, but now a wittol, too."

Stephen smiled with a glimmer of sarcasm. "Humbleness is a virtue, they say."

"Then we shall both be seated at the right hand of the Father for all our virtue." The earl blinked quickly with a tremor of pain. "I babble as though I've another score to live. There is much to do. And I will not let it wait another moment. Get the priest to betroth you and Katherine tomorrow. Fetch a scribe now. I want a missive sent to the King tonight. Nothing must get in the way. Call Ramsey to witness the deed."

Stephen went to the door and gave orders to the steward. Soon a sleepy scribe entered with parchment and quill. In hushed amazement, the lad transcribed the earl's words informing King Edward that Marlow was to be disavowed his inheritance, and that Stephen was the earl's only son. When the ink dried, Stephen took the parchment in trembling hands. Ramsey and Katherine stood apart in respectful silence. When the scribe melted the sealing wax, he turned expectantly to the earl for his insignia.

"My ring!" James said, touching his bare finger. "My insignia has been taken from me."

Stephen turned sharply, regarding the earl's hand with foreboding. He had never seen his father without that ring.

"Ramsey, tell Giles to question the physician and priest. We must find the ring," Stephen ordered.

The earl waved his hand with resignation. "It is Marlow who has taken it. Can you think it was any other? We will make do without it. Take my medallion."

Stephen bent down and gently removed a small dragon crest that hung from a chain around his father's neck. It had been a gift to him from the King, for the earl's bravery at Crécy.

"Send the medallion with the missive. Then Edward will know beyond doubt that it is my will that this transaction should come to pass."

The parchment and medallion were entrusted to Ramsey, who rushed from the chamber, heading for the Great Hall to arrange the journey. Stephen turned back to his father.

"Shall I tell Marlow?"

The old man shook his head. "Wait until I announce it to the others. I think he will know. He may already. For all his faults, he is perceptive in his own calloused way."

Stephen embraced his father and sent for the priest and the physician. When he turned to Katherine, he smiled with appreciation for the strength and dignity she'd displayed throughout the night. If he was shaken, he marveled at how she must feel. They left James under the watch of Giles and his men, but only after Giles reassured Stephen their vigil would be constant.

When Stephen and Katherine left the solar, the world quickly pressed around them. His mother and her lover, Uncle Robert, waited fretfully in the corridor. The peace Stephen had felt in his father's presence vanished.

"Hello, Katherine." Rosalind gave her a clipped nod and turned to her son with tortured eyes.

"He is just recovering, Mother. You may see him, but do not say anything to hurt him. He still loves you."

Rosalind looked at him strangely. Was she feeling guilt? She pulled her hand from Robert's, as if she didn't want Stephen to see their affection. She knew. She knew that Stephen was now aware of her treachery. It was all unraveling.

"Let me in, my son. I must see my husband."

He let her pass but blocked Robert's entrance. Thrusting his chest against Robert's, he grabbed the older man and flung him up against the stone wall.

"You are not to see my father," he said through clenched teeth. "Not now, or ever. If you go against this order, I will kill you."

Robert's handsome face, usually gay and charming, wrinkled with fear.

"No matter what you think, nephew, I do not deserve this treatment," he choked indignantly.

Stephen laughed at his pathetic charade. "Get you from my sight."

Robert obeyed. Tugging at the folds of the hood hanging about his neck, he shrugged off the indignity Stephen had thrust on him. He strutted away, joking shrilly with a knight who waited in the shadows. Robert was so much like Marlow. How blind had Stephen been all these years. He waited until Robert left, and then he escorted Katherine to her chamber.

"I will return later," he said outside her door. He brushed a lock of hair from her forehead, longing to drink from her lips, to draw some understanding, understanding he was not sure would be there for him. Never had he felt so alone as he felt standing before the woman who had the power to accept or reject him as no other person had before.

"Stephen . . ."

"Say nothing, Katherine." For once, he could not read her. Her placid features were indefinable. Fear as he had never known reared up and taunted him. "Say nothing. I'm not sure I could bear it."

He turned and left her in stung silence, standing in the doorway. Moments later, he joined Ramsey in the Great Hall.

Ramsey ordered his own son, Cornelius, and two others to relieve Giles at the earl's door. Cornelius was a strong lad, a full head taller than his father and as loyal as any man. Stephen knew that if anyone could protect the earl, it was Cornelius.

With Ramsey at his side, Stephen hurried toward the stables. It was agreed, as they trudged through the haze of a blue moon, that Giles should bear the message to the King.

John and Elizabeth had raised an honorable young man. Not only was Giles the chief messenger, he was trustworthy and unafraid to travel through the night. Accompanied by Sir MacCormack, another vassal loyal to Stephen, Giles and the missive would arrive safely. They had to. Without the backing of the King, it would be difficult for Stephen to claim his due. Marlow would surely put up a fight.

Arriving at the stable, Stephen was disconcerted to see the torches already burning low and four empty stalls. Two horses would carry his men. But the others?

"Who has gone out at this late hour?" Ramsey barked to the bowing stable hands.

"We just saddled up two of our best geldings on orders of Sir Bothwell, milords. Two men I do not know rode out on Lord Marlow's command."

"Where did they go?" Stephen queried, suspicion growing.

"They'd not say, milord, but they were in a hurry, by the devil."

While Giles and MacCormack mounted their prancing roans, Stephen pulled Ramsey aside. "Marlow may have divined our mission, Ramsey, though I do not know how. He might have guessed Father's intentions. Make sure Giles and MacCormack are well armed. They might meet those wretches on the road tonight."

"Aye, milord," Ramsey replied.

Stephen watched quietly while Giles and MacCormack received their instructions from the steward. They shook hands with Stephen, who added one last word about the importance of their mission, and then they galloped through the portcullis and dashed into the darkness.

Katherine sat in bed, propped up on pillows, watching though not seeing the play of flames on the crumbling embers in the fireplace. Rosemary lay curled at her side, and Europa dozed in a nearby chair. Though it was well past midnight, several tapers glowed in the chamber. Katherine could not sleep, waiting for Stephen's return.

She weighed the evening's horrible events, playing the scenes over and over in her mind. Marlow claimed Stephen did not love her, would not love her, but merely use her. But to what end? Surely if Stephen cared nothing for her, he would not have asked her to join him at his father's side.

Though that visit had been an honor, she had never seen more clearly than at the earl's deathbed how much she was a pawn in this family drama. Stephen needed her to beget a child quickly, to further weaken Marlow's anticipated fight for the estate. Though she understood the cold calculation with which noble marriages were arranged, the very thought that she was being used by Stephen made her ill. Her chest ached with a searing pain. She felt so vulnerable. Damn her foolish notions, but she wanted Stephen to love her. Even without having to give of herself. It was a selfish and flawed expectation, dooming their relationship to sadness, but that was how she felt. Give to me, she longed to cry out. Tell me you love me and maybe, just maybe I'll show you the love that dwells within, I'll share my bed, I'll sacrifice my vow, and burn in Hell for you, but 'twill be worth it, for then I'll see Heaven as long as I'm in your arms.

Over and over she combed the red-gold hair that veiled her breasts. Lost in thought, she tried to solve the conundrum. Georgie was right. Stephen had killed a man in a fit of passion. How ironic! Before, she would have welcomed this excuse to repel Stephen. But it was too late for that. Somehow he had wheedled his way into her heart. Rather than blame him, she felt as if she shared Stephen's guilt. She cared for this man.

She . . . loved . . . him.

The words were slow to form in her mind. Oh, God, that was it. That was why her insides were ripping apart with grief and fear and ecstasy. She adored this man. She knew him, knew his soul, knew his pain. In the silence, her heart mingled with his. Without words, she had already joined him. His guilt was her guilt. His future was her future. She could run, deny it, curse him, beat him, but if she ran to the ends of the earth, her spirit would linger with Stephen's.

"No," she whispered with a groan, clutching her face in both hands. "It can't be."

She bolted upright and clutched the bed with white-knuckled fingers. He could never know. She would never tell him how she felt, for he might ruin her with this knowledge! She could not trust him with her heart. *Oh, Lord, protect me from him.* He was not an evil man; he was a good man, but he did not love her. Of course he wanted to make love to her, but how could a man possibly know and return the kind of love that had thrown her into this morass? It was not possible. Men were brutes when you stripped away the veneer of chivalry.

"Katherine," Stephen called from behind the door, and then came a gentle rap.

Dread pierced her from head to toe. Goose bumps rose on her arms.

Europa sprang from her chair as if she'd never closed her eyes, and Rosemary stirred sluggishly from her dreams, rubbing her innocent face and looking up at Katherine with affection and concern.

Katherine nudged the girl from the bed while Europa opened the door.

Stephen entered and motioned for them to leave. When he swung the door shut and pivoted on his leather-bound heels, he riveted her attention. All other thoughts and sounds faded from Katherine's perceptions. Her heart trilled with excitement and dread, beating swiftly like a rabbit's. He was so exciting to behold. She was losing her ability to deny it. Had her secret admission of love enhanced his dashing features? Had his cobalt-blue eyes always been so enigmatic and alluring? Had his cheekbones always been so chiseled and rugged?

His sensual lips curled up on one side with a bittersweet smile, cracking a stony facade carved in somber relief. With a solicitous look, he came forward and sat by her on the bed. He stroked her cheek, and she shuddered, for his hand was cool and soothing. He cupped her face in his hands and forced her eyes to meet his.

"God help me, but if Marlow hurt you, I will never forgive myself."

Katherine squeezed her eyes shut, staying a flood of tears born of relief and joy. He did care. But it would not be enough if he did not love her also. *Be careful, Katherine, steel your heart.*

"Nay, milord, fear not. Marlow did not wound me. I am not so fragile as that."

"Methinks you are."

She blinked open her eyes and found him staring at her in the most knowing way. Her mother had once told her that eyes were the windows to the soul. She jerked her gaze to the moonlight filtering through the embrasure. *Protect yourself.*

"Marlow did try to tell me that you would never love me. He said you were using me."

Stephen's spine stiffened. "Then he knows. He already knows why Father brought you here. Oh, a bloody fight awaits us indeed."

A heavy silence fell between them as Katherine waited in vain for reassurance. Finally, she turned to him with a cool expression. "So you are to be the next earl."

"And you will be countess. What say you, Kate? Are you ready for such a task?"

" 'Tis the least of my worries."

Stephen frowned, his eyes hard like a chisel that would chip away at her porcelain mask. "I am sorry, my dear lady, that this new duty was thrust on you so quickly. I had no idea. S'Blood! I had no desire for the title. I brooked no thought of ownership until now, but by God, I like it not that my uncle's spawn should take the legacy of my dear father. We will take this castle, you and I."

His voice echoed the promise of victory, of bloodshed, chaos, the unknown. Katherine shivered, wondering if she had the strength to greet the future.

"You have gone away," he said, surprising her with his simple truth. There was infinite sadness hovering about his cheeks, deepening the crow's-feet at the corners of his eyes. It was a gaunt man who studied her dispassionately and accurately. "You've left me, Kate. I can see it in your eyes."

"Nay, milord," she said uncomfortably.

"Aye, you have. And I know why."

She swallowed the lump in her throat, and replied in a croak that eked from her dry mouth. "Why?"

Grim irony shadowed his eyes like smudges of charcoal. "Because my soul is black. I killed a man for no good reason. You are right to hate me, Kate."

Her mouth dropped open, and she shook her head. He had it all wrong. "Nay, milord—"

She reached out to stroke the sorrow from his forehead, but he firmly brushed her hand aside.

"Don't say it," he whispered harshly. "I can't bear it now, Kate. Tomorrow, perhaps, but not now."

He sucked in a long breath; his nostrils flared in the firelight. He stood up and turned to go, walking in a new and awkward gait, but then paused and turned back, his features dead save for an implacable look of determination.

"I'll expect you at the church at dawn, Kate. You'll join me for the wedding banns?"

To say no would shatter the very heart of this bold knight, she was sure of it, but they were none the closer for this realization. She nodded stiffly, a door in her heart slamming as he eased shut the door to her chamber.

CHAPTER TWELVE

✠

An hour before dawn, Marlow awoke with a start. He thought he heard a wolf's cry, but straining in the oppressive darkness he realized it was the wind whistling through the castle's loopholes. Constance slept soundly as far from him as she could huddle in the sagging feather bed.

It must have been a dream, he thought, and a flush of color returned to his wan face. For weeks he had dreamt of a wolf ravaging his throat, tearing him to pieces, leaving his tattered corpse lying in the blood-soaked snow, a frozen scrap for vultures' tenacious beaks. He rubbed his neck and gulped as the last terrifying images of the dream vanished like a morning mist.

In the cold, dark chamber, the once blazing fire now smoldered—white and red embers. As he dressed, Marlow felt no remorse for what he was about to do. When an action becomes inevitable, no feeling is required. Merely clarity. And he was very clear when he picked up Stephen's dagger, running one bejeweled finger along the blade. Sucking in his soft belly, he tucked the ruby-studded weapon into his belt, next to his own sheathed dagger, and tiptoed from the room.

Stealthily, he passed Katherine's chamber, and then Stephen's, and lastly his mother's, where an unexpected qualm made him pause. He stilled his heavy breathing and listened. To what? he wondered. Was his father, Robert, taking Rosalind in the early morning darkness? Did their passion still rule them as it had on that adulterous night when he was conceived thirty-three years ago? If he had learned nothing else from Rosalind, through all his bitter education, he knew that passion reigned ultimately. Even now, Rosalind believed herself innocent of sin. She loved the earl, Marlow knew this without question. But she had failed her husband. She had succumbed to the hollow charms of her husband's brother, and Marlow was the sin grown up. He shrank from the doorway, disgusted with himself. Robert wouldn't be sleeping with Rosalind now. That would be too foolish. Besides, he didn't care what his father did. Marlow only used him to achieve his own ambitions.

When he reached the solar, two men slouched at the door to Earl James's chamber, while Ramsey's son, Cornelius, kept watch. The guards dozed, but Cornelius stood alert, seeing Marlow as soon as he rounded the corner.

"You have done well, lad," Marlow said, stopping in front of the younger man. Cornelius's face, though hard to read, showed a glimmer of disdain. "I'm sure the earl sleeps soundly within. The sun will be up soon, so you may put your vigil to rest."

The guards stirred, and seeing Marlow, their forms bolted from careless heaps on the floor to erectness, blinking away their sleepy haze as best they could.

Cornelius cast them a withering glare. Turning to Marlow, he said, "Unlike these do-littles who slept through their watch, I am content to stay, milord, as Sir Stephen instructed. 'Tis no hardship. 'Tis an honor to guard the earl."

Cornelius spoke with formality, avoiding Marlow's eyes save for one last glare that expressed his distrust. Marlow squelched an urge to strike the bloody whelp across his golden face. No better than his father, that traitor Ramsey.

Instead, he motioned for the guards to leave. They exchanged a worried look and then shifted uncertainly where they stood.

"I said go! If I have need of you I will call," Marlow barked. His eyes sparked with impatience.

"Sir Stephen bade us stay, milord," one of the men offered.

"Stephen is not master here, boy," Marlow said with uncharitable disdain. "If you wish to stay after the earl's death, you will obey me, not my brother. Serve your master well, and you will be well served in turn."

They turned to leave, giving one last furtive look to Cornelius, who faced Marlow with greater courage than Marlow had ever suspected he possessed.

"I will not be ordered away, milord," Cornelius said, squaring off in front of the doorway. "I know not Sir Stephen's reasons, but he wants no one to enter this chamber until he returns. He is noble, and I trust him. I will not be leaving now."

Marlow smiled wryly. "You love Stephen well, then?"

"Aye, Lord Marlow."

"Do you love all of him?" Marlow pressed.

"All that a man might know of him, aye. He's a good man."

"Then know this," Marlow whispered. Whipping out Stephen's dagger, he thrust it into Cornelius's heart before the latter could even see a flash of silver. A look of startled betrayal crossed the younger man's features, followed by disbelief, and then the glassy stare that comes when the soul has flown. Cornelius crumbled to the floor, blood pouring from the wound in his chest. Marlow glanced with fleeting fascination at the steam that rose when the hot blood hit the icy stone floor. His attention moved on quickly to his next task. He withdrew the dagger, wiped it clean on Cornelius's tunic, and turned to the solar door.

There was no need to put the dagger away yet.

Stephen and Katherine swept from the candlelit chapel, followed by Ramsey, Europa, and Countess Rosalind. Everyone stopped at the front steps, stunned by the glory of the sunrise.

Rosalind and her handmaiden then hurried from the church to the Great Hall while Ramsey headed for the stables. Europa discreetly made for the kitchen, leaving the newly betrothed couple to their wonderment.

Stephen could not tear his eyes away from the horizon. It looked as if streaks of blood spattered across bursts of daffodils, all crimson and gold against the azure sky. He stood behind Katherine and pulled her to him, wrapping his arms around her.

"Look at that, Kate. When I see such beauty, such color, I feel as if I'll live a thousand years," he whispered.

"It looks as if God has been crying blood," she replied. "I pray it is not some omen on this, our morning of betrothal."

After a moment of silence, he bent down to nuzzle her cheek with his lips, satin brushing silk. "Thank you. Thank you for doing this. I know in your heart you do not want to marry me. I'll try to make it up to you somehow."

"Nay," Katherine said. She turned to face him and took hold of his hands. "Hush, Stephen. You owe me nothing."

Her hands tingled with the heat of his body, and she could see nothing but his lips. They were full and inviting, lost in a maelstrom of fog as his breath billowed and crystallized in the cold air. How she had longed to touch him since last night, to comfort him. Though she was afraid to let him get too close, she felt terror at the prospect of losing him. Sweet, miserable love.

"How does it feel, Kate, betrothed to a murderous rogue?"

"Perhaps you should look at it another way. Betrothed to the next Earl of Blackmoor."

His eyes glimmered with a familiarity she interpreted as an unspoken truce.

"I will send word to your parents immediately. As soon as they can get here, we will be married."

She nodded. "Go to your father. I will make arrangements for my parents' arrival with Europa. I don't think I can count on your mother's help. She looked distraught when she arrived at the church so early this morning. I think she likes me but little."

"It is not you, Katherine. She fears her games are crumbling about her. She knows I've spoken to Father, and she fears the worst. It has nothing to do with you."

Stephen leaned forward again, not kissing her, but inhaling the sweetness of her breath. After a moment, he bade her farewell and made his way toward the Great Hall.

He hurried through the Hall with long strides, passing over the muted purple-and-red reflections cast from the ornate stained-glass windows high above. With each step, his pace quickened, for the Hall was strangely silent. He began to wonder if, as Katherine had mused, the vibrant sunrise were indeed an omen. Crossing through the grand arch and turning the corner to the solar, he saw that in fact it had been. Cornelius's lifeless body swam in a pool of blood.

Stephen raced to his side. He knelt by the young man and gently lifted his head. With stinging regret, Stephen stroked the lad's cold and clammy cheeks. *Poor Ramsey,* he thought with remorse. The steward would go mad with grief. His only son had danced from the Scythe of the Reaper during all the Pestilence's reign, only to take the blade in a moment of stillness long after the music had died.

The moments that followed—the lowering of Cornelius's head, the brushing shut of his eyelids, Stephen's slow rise, the boom of his riotous heartbeat, the turn to his father's chamber with dread—all took place in some timeless sphere, as things do when one knows with certainty that after the next moment is confronted nothing will be the same again.

The solar door was ajar. Entering, Stephen paused as his eyes caught sight of the physician slumped by the fire. The doddering old man might have been dozing, as he often did, but for the puddle of blood that had coursed over one knee to the floor. Stephen's eyes swept across the room to his father's bed. The falcon had struck; the dove lay crushed in red snow.

Later, Stephen recalled with excruciating vividness every inconsequential detail of this moment—the salmon-pink light of dawn filtering through the arched window; the hissing of the dying fire; the putrid smell of bile that rushes from every orifice of the dead; a young, black crow tapping its beak senselessly against the windowpane. But at this moment he was aware of nothing but the irreversibility of death. He marched forward on stiff legs and stood over the still form of Earl James sprawled on the bed, a savage tear where a dagger had been thrust and churned.

When his eyes had fully absorbed the sight, Stephen knew with growing certainty who had done the deed, the only one capable of such wickedness—Marlow. A tumult of rage and grief rose from his intestines, and Stephen cried out. Numbly, he pulled his father into his arms, cradling his lifeless form, and wept.

"A stoic man does not cry but for love and death," the earl had once told him. "He'll cry once at love found and then at love lost, with all its shattered innocence. And then he'll cry for death. Any death."

And so Stephen wept now.

"Dear God, no!" he heard someone cry in the hallway. Then came a flurry of running feet, a chorus of murmurs, cries, Ramsey's voice breaking in grief, and a whoosh of air as the door to the solar flung open at the hand of Countess Rosalind. Katherine rushed in behind her, and both stopped abruptly, their faces registering shock, horror, confusion.

"Stephen!" the countess cried out, pointing to him accusingly. Her eyes landed conclusively on his bloody hands and clothes. "What have you done?"

"Stephen!" Katherine uttered.

He strained to read her mind in that one desperate word. Did she accuse him? Condemn him? Love him? Love—Lord, no, they were past that. No matter. Her voice stilled his shaking grief. Even without her love and devotion, he needed her. God help him but he needed her. At last he let go of his father, laying him down on the bloody sheets. Now Stephen was bathed in the sticky stuff, marked damningly for all who would suppose the worst.

"You murderer," the countess croaked in a shaking voice. "You murderer. What have you done to my husband?"

Stephen rose as if from the dead, stiff and unfeeling. He walked numbly forward, and Katherine met him. She did not turn him away but embraced him. God pity him, but he would take her charity. She smelled so sweet, like honeysuckle. He craved her warmth, for his heart felt so cold.

"I am so sorry, Stephen," she murmured, pulling him close, heedless of the blood that marred her white gown. She brushed the tears from his cheeks. "I am so sorry."

Stephen grasped her close, and in the comfort of her neck he held himself still, then pulled away, his sorrow shifting to anger. He went to his mother, who stood shaking with astonishment. He grabbed her arm and roughly pulled her to the bed, pushing her down beside the corpse of her husband.

"Get into the bed where you belong, Mother," he said bitterly. "Lie with the coldness you gave my father for so long."

Rosalind began to weep, uncertain whether to embrace her husband or recoil. Shaking with anger, she stood and slapped Stephen across the face. It was a mighty blow for such a petite woman, and Stephen's head rocked back from the force of it.

"Take him to the tower," Marlow said, appearing at the door with Bothwell and Cramer.

"You bloody bastard," Stephen bellowed and lurched toward his brother, reaching for his throat. Four guards rushed forward and overcame him after a fierce struggle.

"Put this murderer away before he kills anyone else in our household," Marlow said.

"No!" Katherine cried. Her eyes locked with Stephen's until the guards hauled him away. Katherine looked pleadingly to Countess Rosalind. "You know he did not do it. He is innocent."

When no response came from the dazed countess, Katherine turned and hurried after Stephen.

As Ramsey still grieved over the corpse of his son, Stephen passed, and they exchanged a look of understanding. Then Ramsey caught sight of Marlow and attacked.

"Bastard son of the devil!" Ramsey shrieked. He choked Marlow's mail-covered neck. "God will be avenged for this slaughter of innocence."

"Take him also," Marlow grunted to the guards, pushing Ramsey away with a blunt shove. "Put them both in the north tower."

Katherine ran after them. "Stephen!" she cried, but Bothwell's elbow slammed into her cheek. The brute blocked her path. Europa appeared and tugged at her arm.

"Milady, let them go. There's nothing to do now. If you make trouble, you'll end up in the tower yerself."

"Let me go," Katherine said. She flung Europa's arms from her shoulders. "I want to be with him."

"You will do more good here, milady. Marlow won't keep him for long."

Katherine stared at Europa in disbelief. She was now convinced that there was nothing Marlow wouldn't do. What would keep him from murdering Stephen? But she was no match for Marlow's henchmen.

Katherine hurried back to her chamber and ordered Rosemary to retrieve her mantle. Despite Europa's pleading to remain calm and safe in the privacy of her room, Katherine could not sit still. She would not rest until she saw Stephen again, free from Marlow's men and command. There must be a way. If she could only think! She had to get away.

She slipped past the others as tumult overtook the castle. She strode single-mindedly, determined not to pause as Countess Rosalind's deep lamentations rose in a piercing shriek. The morning air whipped Katherine's eyes as she hurried through the frost-covered bailey. Images of Stephen cradling his father's bloody corpse haunted her, and she sobbed, caring naught that her voice echoed through the castle yards.

She arrived at the church, and her feet skimmed across the slick steps. The priest was gone—she'd seen him lurching across the courtyard, stumbling in his frantic effort to reach the bloody spectacle. Inside the chapel, the candles still burned. A shimmering, faint smoke filtered through the air, mingled with incense, giving a mystical quality to the statues of the Virgin Mary and Christ, who hung dejectedly from his wooden cross. He looked to the heavens with a pleading gaze.

Katherine knelt in a pew, numb with disbelief and despair.
The one person who had finally touched her as deeply as
Georgie had was gone. She had wanted the prerogative to
push Stephen away, for he threatened her fragile tranquillity,
but she had never wanted him stolen from her, particularly
not by one so evil as Marlow. When the numbness faded, a
deeply felt anger forced her from her position of supplication.
She strode to the altar, growing angrier with each step. Why
did God allow so much evil? First the Pestilence and all its
wretched misery, and now this injustice against her betrothed.
He would likely hang for a deed he had not committed.

"Why?" she shouted. Her voice bounced back from the
marble altar and surprised her with its vehemence. "Dear
God in Heaven, why did you allow Marlow to take him?
Why must he be blamed?"

She knelt at the wooden railing that separated sinners from
priests.

"Why!" she shouted, her face contorting with emotion, and
when that simple question seemed so utterly inadequate, she
burst into tears. Was this vile deed God's revenge for her
broken vow? It had been so very long since she'd prayed
for Georgie.

The image of Georgie was replaced with a haunting portrait of Marlow, and her tears halted abruptly. Something
new replaced her sorrow and remorse. She had no name for
it. It was deeper than hatred. Marlow threatened her very
future. He tore asunder everything that was good. She still
remembered his plundering kiss and wiped her mouth again
as if it had just happened.

"You will not kill him, Marlow," she said slowly, her eyes
clouding over as if she were in a trance. "By God, I will not
let you lay a hand on Stephen."

She pushed herself up, staggering until she caught her
balance. She looked up at the figure of Christ.

"By my oath to God, Marlow, you will not take his life.
And this oath I will fulfill or die," she whispered savagely.

For too long she had watched nature wreak death across the land. About that she could do nothing, but one man, one evil man, could be stopped.

"You will not die for this, Stephen," she whispered, closing her eyes with her solemn promise. "Somehow I will clear your name of this horror."

Doubt descended on her as soon as the promise was made. How could she save Stephen? He was locked in a tower. No one would care what she said about him. His family wanted to believe him the murderer, and so they would.

She pressed her hands to her face. How weak she was! How easily discouraged!

Help me, Georgie, she prayed desperately. He would have to forgive her long enough to help her. Feeling release from a burden she had unconsciously borne, she saw a ray of hope.

She wiped her tearstained cheeks and ran her sleeve beneath her sniffling nose in a most unladylike fashion. Turning on her heels, Katherine Gilbert pulled back her shoulders and marched out of the chapel as if to war.

CHAPTER THIRTEEN

✠

Stephen spat a curse to the guards who escorted him and flung open the door to his mother's chamber. Splattered blood had caked on his chin, in his hair, down his tunic. Grief and anger had battled for control of his emotions all day. Weary from the struggle, he was now merely numb. Even so, he felt a sickening disdain for the triumvirate who greeted him.

Robert stood poised at the fire, refusing to look Stephen in the eyes, his mother sat in her chair, and Marlow smiled up with cool triumph.

"Thank you for joining us," Marlow said, motioning to a chair.

"I had little choice," Stephen replied, turning back to Bothwell and Cramer, who had roughly dragged him from the tower. Stephen kicked the door shut in their faces. "Why this little audience? Are we to grieve together as a family? Is that what Father would have wanted?"

"It matters naught," Marlow whispered through tight lips. "Father is dead."

"My father is dead," Stephen said. "Your father is alive and well and wants nothing more than to paw the nearest scullion girl."

Marlow started forward, but Robert leapt in front of him.

"You are both grief-stricken," Robert said. "Do take caution, Marlow."

Marlow shrugged and poured himself a tankard of mead. "Well, brother—"

190

"You mean half brother." Stephen sat in the chair proffered earlier and kicked out his heels.

"It matters naught what I call you, for soon you will be dead," Marlow parried.

"If I am put to death, the people of Blackmoor will rise up against you."

Marlow shook his head. "You overestimate your power here. You may have been the earl's favorite, but he was blinded with a father's love. Just as Robert is blinded to my weaknesses," he added sarcastically.

"Why did you bring me here?" Stephen queried. "You killed James. We all know it."

Marlow raised his hand so his brother could see the flash of silver in the firelight. "Your dagger, Stephen. It is bloody. I found it after you left the solar."

Stephen's lips thinned momentarily, and then he shrugged. "I would have expected nothing less from you, Marlow. You are a thorough man. But the countess . . ."

He turned to his mother with undisguised loathing. Heretofore, she had been listening in silence, clearly pained by Stephen's presence, her eyes still luminous with shock.

"Did you know about this ahead of time, Mother? Did you plot your husband's murder with your bastard child?"

She began to shake, neither denying nor agreeing with his accusations.

"And when I am dead and buried," Stephen continued, "what will become of Rosalind, Countess of Blackmoor? The world is not charitable to an old whore."

Rosalind gasped, and her eyes fluttered. She fell back in a faint, and Robert rushed to her side, carrying her to the bed.

"Such insults do not become you," Marlow said.

Stephen chuckled deep in his throat. "What does it matter? I am but a dead man if you have your way. My only hope is that there is some justice in this world. Then you will be the one to pay for your own murders."

Marlow smiled victoriously. "But there is no justice. It is only a matter of weeks before you die for my deeds. I called you here so that you might clearly know my intentions. I am sending you to the King, who will surely execute you for your heinous crime."

"The King will learn the truth."

Marlow smiled without mirth. "This is the only truth Edward will know."

He held up a scrolled parchment, and for a moment Stephen's heart leapt. It looked much like the one signed by the earl, but this one bore the earl's insignia. Stephen's eyes shifted to Marlow's hands, and there, in the dim light, glinted the missing insignia ring.

"These are the earl's last wishes," Marlow said ironically, waving the as yet unopened parchment. "I know what it contains because I wrote it. You will be disowned for your treachery and your blackened name. Reason enough to murder an ailing earl, wouldn't you say?"

"And the real document?" Stephen asked, his hopes fading, only to be stayed by a brief look of uneasiness that crossed Marlow's eyes.

"It won't reach the King, I can assure you."

"You do not have it, do you?" Stephen pressed, leaning forward.

Marlow waved him off, his face still shadowed with discontentment. "What does it matter to you? Your messengers are dead. They never made it across the river."

Stephen's eyes flickered shut. John and Elizabeth would be racked with grief. They had trusted Stephen to look after their only boy, but he'd been felled like so many pawns in Marlow's bloody game.

"Did you not think to spare them?" Stephen whispered savagely, focusing at last on his brother.

"They are nothing in the scheme of it all."

"Just as I am nothing?" Stephen countered, searching his brother for something familiar, some old feeling. "Will you feel nothing when they behead me for your deeds?"

"Now, that is an interesting question," Marlow responded. Shutting his eyes, he paced a moment. "Damnation! Aye, I shall feel something, I think. There is some small part of me that loves you still. Can you fathom that?"

Stephen nodded.

"I always wanted to hate you because James loved you best. Mother confided in me as a child that I was a bastard." Marlow lowered his voice to within earshot only of his brother; he glanced back at Robert, who sat on Rosalind's bed, stroking her forehead. "I held no love for my true father, and so I ingratiated myself to yours. But he'd have none of it."

Stephen pitied Marlow; he spoke now as a child. And in his handsome, hollow features Stephen could see a spark of the freckle-faced boy who had then been so ardent in his enthusiasm and his love for the earl.

"But how could I hate you, the one with so much wit and charm? One for whom life came easily while I guarded my place, mistakenly gotten. I could not hate you, Stephen. Just as James could not, even though you shamed him."

"What happened then?" Stephen said. "We were happy once as a family. I looked up to you. Why did you let it come to this?"

Marlow spun around to face him with quivering rage. "We were never happy. Never!" Spittle flew in the cold air. "You speak of fleeting moments of feelings. They are nothing when you are born a bastard. I did not belong in the place I would one day inherit. Do you know what a burden that is? To know you do not deserve the title? I tried to prove myself in every way. Eventually I gave up trying. I would never gain James's approval. Outwardly, yes, but what I wanted was not an outward reward. That I had already coming to me. I wanted his love, damn it! Do you know what that is like to want?"

Stephen paused. "And all these years he suspected you were not his own, but he never said a word."

"Nor would he have if I had not confronted him with the truth not long ago. Seems foolish of me, does it not?"

Stephen stared blankly.

"Perhaps I wanted to confess. Before he died, I wanted him to know I did not deserve what he was about to give me."

"And so you murdered him for it in the end," Stephen concluded.

"The thought of losing this land," Marlow said with fervency, "this castle . . . Oh, God, it was intolerable. After he learned the truth, I lived in abject terror of what I knew must surely come to pass—his disinheriting me. It was only then that I realized how important this all was to me. It had become the focus of my life. Without it, I felt as if I were nothing."

Stephen stared in wonder at his brother. "Why are you telling me this now? When it is too late for me to do anything to save you? You have never confided in me before. Why now?"

Marlow smiled. "Because you are about to die. I wanted you to know the truth."

Katherine threw open the oak door to the tapestry room. She paused beneath the door frame, looking like a wild Irish faerie. Hair hung in a tangled spray over her shoulders. She wore a fresh cote-hardie, but the hem was torn. She had tripped earlier during an unsuccessful attempt to reach Stephen in the tower.

She caught her breath in short snatches and bit her chafed lips. The women stitching at the tapestry looked up, aghast, afraid to speak. Constance turned from the window and dabbed tears from her eyes.

"Katherine," she whispered, too distraught to be bitter. Ever since Marlow had accosted Katherine in the night, the two women had shared a silent bond. "Katherine, whatever can I do to help?" she whispered. Waving her attendants from the room, she said, "Leave us."

They scurried away, and Katherine shut the door after them.

"You must help me," Katherine whispered, her voice harsh with emotion. She had debated coming to Constance for assistance. She knew the dangers but had decided to take the risk. "You must help me. I have to save Stephen. I do not know where to begin. Your husband—"

Constance grabbed her hands and squeezed them. "God will be avenged on my husband, dear Katherine. I promise you. He is a beast. I have given up on him, but I have not given up hope this child will survive." She caressed her belly. "I drink the teas daily."

In spite of her grief, Katherine saw the light of hope shining in Constance's once destitute eyes. That in itself was a miracle.

"How can you stand to bear his child? The babe will bind you to him forever." Katherine shuddered at the thought.

"I have no choice." Constance smiled sadly. "He is all I have ever known. He is an evil man, but somehow I still . . . I still care."

Katherine nodded her understanding. "I now know that love is not simple. Sometimes it's even incomprehensible."

"Aye, gentle girl, you speak the truth. Now let me help you if I can." Constance turned her focus to Katherine with intrigue. "I will do all I can to thwart my husband's wicked ways."

Katherine's mind began to reel with hope. "Can I trust you?"

The older woman sighed with impatience. "You know the answer to that. For you I stood up to Marlow. For the first time in my life."

Katherine nodded. "I need to see Stephen. If I do not help him escape, Marlow will kill him. It was Marlow who tried to replace Seigneur Darbonnet's blunted lance with one of steel, wasn't it, Constance?"

Marlow's wife crossed her arms and heaved a sigh. "Aye, it was. I overheard Marlow. You are correct on all accounts."

Constance knelt and retrieved a piece of red silk thread that one of the ladies had cast aside while stitching. She wrapped it round and round her index finger as she paced the room. At last she stopped. As she came to a conclusion, her inscrutable gaze returned to Katherine.

"Very well, I will help you in the only way I know how. 'Twill be a risk for me, but worth it, I think. However, you must trust me. Completely. Can you do that?"

Katherine nodded. "Yes."

Constance cast the thread to the stone floor. "Then you must fetch some sort of disguise for Stephen and the steward. Steal the priest's vestments if you have to. Meet me at the base of the north tower at midnight, and make sure those loyal to Stephen are ready to escape as well."

When Constance whirled about and started for the door, Katherine ran after her and grasped her arm. "What will you do, Constance?"

"Whatever it takes, my dear, to help you."

At nine o'clock, marbled clouds swept in from the west and cloaked a bright, round moon. At ten, raindrops the size of shillings splattered the castle walls. By eleven, a torrential rain beat the stables where Stephen's loyal knights bound and gagged the stable hands, then saddled their mounts for the escape. By midnight, Katherine huddled in the tower's doorway, waiting for Constance. The rain began to freeze, and a treacherous crystal sheen hardened on the grass in the bailey. She shivered and clutched two monk's robes to her breasts. Stealing from a church! She and God would have much to talk about before the night was over.

Constance hurried across the bailey in a dark cloak. When she spied Katherine's bundle, she said, "Well done. I'm going to the top of the tower. The guard should be asleep. One of my ladies-in-waiting delivered a tankard of ale to him an hour ago, pretending her real mission was to flirt. The ale was heavily spiced with a sleeping potion given to me by the physician during a spell of restless slumber. If it worked, and the guard is unconscious, I will free Stephen and Ramsey. Wait five minutes. If I have not returned by then, join me upstairs."

Katherine tried to swallow her heart, which seemed to be pounding in her throat. "Very well."

*   *   *

Stephen immediately heard Constance's shuffling steps. The prisoner jumped from his cot to the door. His hands, rigid with frustration, gripped the bars that crisscrossed a window in the door.

"Constance," he rasped.

"Shhhh . . ." She pressed a forefinger to her lips and stepped from the stairwell into the guard's quarters adjacent to the prison. To her right, a snoring sack of bones slept in a crumpled heap on the floor, an empty tankard in the guard's slack fingers.

Constance fumbled at his belt for the keys, and rushed to unlock the prison door. By now Ramsey had risen, too, and both men watched her in silent anticipation.

Stephen flung open the door as soon as it was unlocked, and pulled Constance into a tight hug. It was the first time they had ever embraced. He pulled back and studied her at arm's length. "Constance, you have put yourself in great danger. Why? There was never any love lost between us."

Footsteps, growing louder, rose from the stairwell. When Katherine stepped into the room, Constance tilted her head over her shoulder and said, "I did it for her."

At the sight of his betrothed, Stephen's heart tugged in his chest. The tendons in his neck flexed as he struggled to hold back untamed emotions. She was so beautiful, stunningly so. Her eyes glittered like rare stones, reflecting wisdom and strength.

"This was Katherine's idea," Constance added, smiling at his obvious adoration.

"It was my idea, but you have taken the greatest risk," Katherine said. "If I'd known you planned to put yourself in this danger, I would never have agreed."

Constance blinked slowly. "Oh, yes, you would have. Besides, 'tis the least I can do for you. I've just entered the fifth month of my pregnancy. 'Tis a miracle. I think perhaps your independent notions may have played a part. Whatever the reason, you've given me strength. This was a risk I had to take."

The creak and thud of the drawbridge jolted Stephen to attention. "We must fly."

Katherine handed them their disguises; the men pulled the cowled hoods over their heads until their faces were shadowed, then they made a dash to the stable with Katherine in tow.

In the stable, a dozen men waited, mounted on their horses. Five of Marlow's loyalists were bound and gagged in a hay pile. When Stephen saw Katherine's mare saddled and ready for the journey, with saddle pouches stuffed full, he turned and grabbed her arms with iron fingers. The others slipped quietly from the stable, one by one, riding torchless over the drawbridge with only moonlight to guide their way.

"Katherine, you can not go. I will not let you."

Inwardly, she winced at his rejection. Outwardly, her face hardened with disdain. "You have no say in the matter."

"The hell I don't."

"The hell you do! If it weren't for me, you would never have escaped."

"And I am grateful," he shouted sotto voce. "All the more reason I will not let your name be ruined. Now you are a baron's daughter. Come with me tonight and you will be a murderer's whore."

Katherine recoiled at the epithet. "I don't want to hear your cruel words."

Stephen growled. "I only tell you what others will say."

Katherine turned and furiously adjusted her stirrups, yanking on them with determination. "I see now how you have used me. You plied me with tender words to get me to back your cause. And now that I have saved your life, you would cast me aside like a trifling whim. Well, you won't be rid of me so easily," came her whispered shout. Her raging eyes glittered in the torchlight. "You've taken me too far along your wretched journey, Sir Stephen. You are stuck with me now."

Stephen's stark features flushed red, and he clawed a hand through his hair as if to tear it out. For a moment she thought he would strike her, and she flinched.

"God! Women!" he bellowed. He looked out into the bailey. It was still empty, but not for long. They could waste no more time. "Your parents are on their way for our wedding. When they arrive, go back with them to Shelby Manor. I will come for you when I've proven my innocence."

He leapt astride his mount and gathered the reins.

When she realized he would dash into the night without so much as a good-bye, she pulled herself up into her saddle, crawling and clutching at leather. Once she was astride the animal, her thick wool mantle parted to expose men's breeches.

"What the bloody hell?" Stephen muttered. He took in the rugged sight of her—she had tied her hair back in a knot, her legs gripped the saddle as any man's would have, and she wore a mean scowl. Despite his anger, he could not hold back a snort of laughter.

She ignored him. Tucking her feet into the stirrups, she kicked her mare, but Stephen reached out with a sweeping gesture and pulled the graceful beast up short.

"Have you thought of your honor?" he shouted through clenched teeth. "You will be ruined if you run away with me now."

"Damn honor to hell," she said, lips quivering. Anger sent a flood of tears down her cheeks. How she hated to cry in front of men! They never understood tears. So she dug her heels deep into the flanks of her mount and bolted into the night, where he could not possibly see or mock her feelings.

Stephen followed, cursing all the way.

CHAPTER FOURTEEN

✠

Katherine did not sleep at all that night, and fear of Stephen's wrath had little to do with it. The ride to Downing-Cross had been miserable, cold, and treacherous. Shortly after they escaped from Blackmoor, the rain had turned into hail. By the time they reached their destination, the onslaught had ceased, and a strange calm enveloped the country manor. Blinking beneath frozen eyebrows and lashes, Katherine marveled at Mother Nature's merciless April whims.

To make matters worse, there was no fire to greet them at Downing-Cross. Nary a torch nor a candle lit the darkened stone house.

A shivering Katherine waited on her mount while Stephen and Ramsey leapt from their steeds to look for John and Elizabeth. Several other knights staked out a fortress at the fief's entrance while others stalked about the yard like ghosts, blue and stiff in the cold moonlight. The curious knights explored land they would soon have to defend if Marlow besieged them as expected. Their arrival excited the geese that ran loose behind the manor, honking imperiously. Pigeons in the dovecote whirred in desperation at the cacophony, and a single wolf howled from its cage.

At this, Katherine stiffened in her saddle, waiting to hear a chorus of the plaintive cries, but she waited in vain. Only one of John's "children," as Stephen called them, remained at Downing-Cross. What had happened to the other wolves? What had happened to their master? she wondered.

"The house is abandoned," Stephen announced, stepping from the manor and joining Katherine. "You've not frozen to death, I pray."

Though his voice was wary, still flecked with anger, he reached up and gave her hands a squeeze. She felt woozy, warmed by his touch, but still angry herself. Tempted though she was to wearily fall from the saddle into his comforting arms, she straightened her spine with the dignity she thought he expected. "You needn't worry for me, Stephen, but what of John and Elizabeth?"

"I fear the worst. Marlow may have sent his men to kill them after they cut down Giles." He reached up and grasped her waist. With an easy tug, he lifted her from her saddle and lowered her to within a foot of his agile frame.

"Perhaps they escaped," Katherine offered, and she would have placed her cold fingers on his warm chest, but he turned away.

"I hope you are right." Stephen surveyed the group of men who had gathered around, all remarking on the eerie silence.

"Start a fire in every hearth, in the kitchen as well," Stephen ordered the men. "Embers still glow in the Great Hall, so our friends' departure was recent. I did not see any sign of blood or struggle. I hope they are in hiding. We will search later, but for now we must heat the manor or we will never thaw out."

Stephen started away, calling out more orders. The other men, beginning to recover from the arduous journey, jumped into action, leaving Katherine alone and forlorn in front of the manor. She did not expect to be treated like a queen, but neither did she want to be ignored as useless baggage.

"Stephen!" she called, and ran forward when he did not pause. She caught up with him just as he reached the stable.

"Milord," she said through chattering teeth, forcing him to stop with a tug on his arm. "I did the right thing by coming tonight. When you've given it some more thought, I'm sure you'll change your mind on the matter."

"And you'll change your mind, I'm confident, on your long journey back to Shelby Manor when the sun rises."

"You'll have to take me dragging and screaming."

"I'll take you any way I can, milady." Stephen smiled like the devil himself. "You name the place."

He gave her a curt bow and strolled away with a low chuckle.

"Damn you," she muttered with frustration, knowing, as he rounded a stall and vanished from sight, that she had been thoroughly charmed.

It was dawn before the manor was warm enough for comfort. Until then, they shivered and waited for the fires to penetrate the deep chill that clutched the stone fortress. Even without sleep, Katherine managed to survive the next day, running on energy inspired by fear, excitement, suspense, and doubt—all the feelings that flooded her alternately as they awaited Marlow's next step.

Katherine started the morning meal at sunrise, with Sir Markham at her side. He was a good-natured soldier, a few years younger than Stephen, and a better cook than Katherine. After an hour of improvisation over the spit, they served up a hearty breakfast of grains and cheese. When Stephen stomped into the kitchen after a brisk ride through the fief, Katherine made herself scarce. She was too tired for confrontations, even friendly ones, and she didn't fancy a long ride back to her parents' home as soon as he remembered last night's threat. Katherine pulled on her mantle and stepped out into the crisp morning air. Despite the unseasonable cold, she could see the work of spring. Buds glistened on every tree, awaiting their chance.

She smiled at the welcome sight, rounded the dovecote, and then halted. In the distance, a wolf howled near its empty cage, a beautiful gray creature with thick fur that blended into the pastel sunrise. The wolf turned to Katherine with a forlorn look.

"Greetings," Katherine called out. Compelled to befriend the lonely animal, she continued forward with cautious steps, inwardly chastising herself for forgetting an offering of raw meat.

The wolf shifted its hindquarters to better observe the stranger's approach. A faint mist hovered over the ground. Katherine progressed through the gray pillows of air. The wolf blinked like a doe in the forest, eyes patient, sad, and innocent. In that instant, Katherine knew she had found a friend.

"Hello, beauty," she whispered, halting a stone's throw away. Behind her, Stephen's men clamored and shouted as they started their day's work, preparing their defenses. The wolf glanced at the men uneasily.

"Easy, girl," Katherine coaxed, close enough to discern the creature's gender. "They will not hurt you."

Katherine continued her slow progress, taking tiny steps. The wolf cautiously shimmied back a few paces, but her tongue lolled casually over her teeth as she panted, no fangs bared. It was a good beginning.

"Do you have a name?" Katherine knelt an arm's length away. It was only then she realized that the wolf had been injured. Blood streaked her flanks. A gash had left a trail of dark, dry blood on her forehead. The markings were clean and looked suspiciously like the work of a whip. Katherine used all the more caution as she held out her hand, palm upward. "Who did this to you, little one? Where are your brothers and sisters? Where did they go? And where is John?"

The wolf's ears pricked up at this, and Katherine smiled. "Yes, little she-wolf. I am a friend of your master's. What did he call you?"

The wolf took three steps forward and one step back.

"I'll call you Lupa. Here, Lupa. Come here, girl."

It seemed to take forever, but eventually Lupa responded. She ambled over, head low to the ground, and tipped her snout under Katherine's hand. Very slowly, Katherine turned her palm downward and stroked the velvet hair on the creature's forehead, taking care not to touch the wound.

"Katherine!" Markham bounded over the hill with a wave and a shout. That was more than the wolf could take. Every muscle in Lupa's body went rigid. She bared her teeth and bolted away, leaping through a field.

Katherine sighed, envying Lupa her ability to run free at will with no consequences, no judgments.

"What is it, Markham?" she said to the knight as he trotted forward.

"Sir Stephen would have a word with you."

To her relief, Stephen did not meet with Katherine alone. When she joined him in the Great Hall, he was already fully engaged in a debate with his men. Katherine sat on the hearth next to a blazing fire while the others argued at a huge round table.

"Attack I say!" said one rotund knight. "There's twelve of us, and all more loyal than those who fight on Marlow's side."

"Marlow has twenty men serving fealty to him now," Markham argued. "With all the defenses of the castle at their disposal, we don't stand a chance."

"Fifteen of those men will be gone in a fortnight when they've fulfilled their forty days of service. Our chances will be better then," Stephen offered. He leaned back in his chair and kicked his spurred heels up on the table.

"Aye, but Marlow has his hands on the purse strings now, milord, and when those knights return to their own fiefs, Marlow will buy the help of mercenaries."

It was Markham who spoke again, and Katherine noted how carefully Stephen listened to him. The slender knight seemed to be a voice of reason.

"Why not rely on the truth?" Geoffrey offered. When all but Stephen turned to the squire with scornful skepticism, he hurried on. "Let us find the will and medallion and prove Sir Stephen's innocence. Then the King will be on our side. Marlow can not beat that."

Katherine nodded, eager to hear Stephen's reaction. But it was the big-bellied knight, the one the others called Seeley, who responded with a loud gust of air.

"S'Blood! Horse droppings on that idea, I say. Marlow wouldn't be so stupid as to let us get our hands on the evidence."

"But we should try," Katherine interrupted in a voice that rang out with clarity. The men turned in her direction. Some gave her a patronizing smile; others waved her off.

Stephen waited for more. "Go on, Katherine."

His voice was deep and gentle, and she felt newly confident. "Unless my lord Stephen wishes to continue his brother's legacy of bloodshed and treachery, he must at some point prove his innocence. If not to his family, then to the vassals he will one day rule."

Stephen squinted at her from afar, a strange glow emanating from his eyes. She turned her focus to him, expecting to find anger. She was pleasantly suprised to find respect instead.

"You must keep searching for the will, milord," she continued with greater urgency. "I don't know why, but I believe you will find it if you try. Certainly take other measures to win back the castle. But do not give up on proof of your innocence. You are innocent, after all."

"How do you know we will find the evidence?" Stephen queried in a soft voice.

Katherine stood and held Stephen's gaze. "Instinct, milord. I just have this . . . instinctual feeling."

Stephen sat in utter stillness, his eyes never leaving her. Slowly, his lips parted in approval. Her heart flip-flopped in her chest, and her breath grew short. Even after the others resumed their debate, he watched her until she had to turn away. She fumbled with a poker, stabbing aimlessly at the fire.

The masculine voices blurred until they were a hum. Katherine no longer heard them. Something about this place set her free, and she felt as Lupa must have felt earlier, racing off to the horizon.

"Then this is it," Stephen said in conclusion. "Markham, it will be your task to search the countryside for the will and medallion the earl tried to send to the King. Geoffrey, you will take word back to Blackmoor that they can expect a siege in a week if Marlow doesn't surrender the castle. We'll see if we can bluff our way through for now. Let Marlow think he's in greater danger than he is. Sir Seeley, travel west toward Shirewood in search of the honorable Seigneur Etienne Darbonnet. It's time for me to collect my prize from our joust—the service of two of his most skilled warriors. We'll need all the men we can muster. They can't have traveled far in two days' time. Gerald," he said to a flaxen-haired knight who had listened intently throughout, "I'll leave it to you to contact the King. Find out where he is and get word to him directly. I'll advise you on that myself. Ramsey, what say you? Anything you want to add?"

The steward slumped next to Stephen, his eyes distant and red. "Nay," came his hoarse reply. "I have nothing to add, milord. If Cornelius were here . . ."

Stephen gripped his friend's shoulder. The steward had tried a dozen times to speak about his son, but the wound was still too fresh.

"There, there, Ramsey, 'twill be all right." Stephen spoke gently. He leaned forward, and his eyes glinted with passion. "Think about justice, old friend. That will get you through the night. We must see justice done."

"Aye! Here, here!" the others joined in.

"What about her?" Seeley jerked a chubby thumb in Katherine's direction. "What do we do with her?"

"*You* don't do anything with her." Annoyance flared in Stephen's gruff voice, and the impertinent knight covered his embarrassment by swilling his mead.

Stephen looked at Katherine with a curious mixture of sugar and spice. "Leave Katherine to me."

At the end of the day, when she was about to undress for bed, Katherine wondered what he had meant by that. Would he at last scold her for her disobedience? Would he ravish her against her will? To her chagrin, her mind was all too willing to imagine that prospect, readily warming to the image of his rugged body encompassing hers. She cast off those fancies as not only sinful, but improbable. Stephen had proven himself honorable. He wouldn't take her to his bed without her permission. *Would he?* she wondered with a childlike frown.

Katherine smoothed her hand over the bed that now graced the women's bower. It was as if Elizabeth had expected her return. The once empty room looked quite homey with a huge bed pushed against the wall across from the hearth. Four bedposts rose one at each corner, draped with burgundy wool. It was easy to picture Stephen's naked body prone on the burgundy down bed cover. So easy that she moved her fingers inches above the bedding as if she caressed the long, iron-tight sinews of his legs. Her hands smoothed down the length of his golden calves, and up, up over his thighs, and . . .

She halted, her hand shaking in midair. What was she doing? Pretending to caress Stephen as he lay naked on the bed? She was so shocked by her effortless fantasy that for a moment she couldn't breath. She smoothed her surcoat against her hips and turned in a quandary to the fire. This was not good. Not good at all. Indeed, Stephen wouldn't have to ravish her if she pandered to these shameful fantasies.

"You shouldn't be here."

Katherine twisted around to find Stephen in the doorway.

"The least you could do is knock, Stephen," she said in a voice made strident by her embarrassment. She prayed he hadn't been watching her from the shadows of the corridor. "You nearly took my breath away."

He leaned against the door frame as if reluctant to join her. With great concentration, he poured from a pitcher into one of two tankards he held in his left hand. "Care for some mead?"

"Mead might just take the edge off my nerves. Has it been heated?" she queried hopefully.

"Aye, just for you."

"Then, yes." she walked toward Stephen, modestly fastening the top button on her gown, which she had loosened on the way upstairs.

Still clutching her low collar with one hand, Katherine reached out with the other and eagerly took the steaming liquid. "Smells delightful."

"Just . . . like . . . you."

She looked up at Stephen, his nose and cheeks reddened from the mead, and an indulgent grin sneaked up her cheeks. He was drunk! She could hear it in his voice—the methodical rhythm, the faint slur.

"How much have you been drinking, Guy?"

"Guy?" He grinned sardonically at his tankard. "I'd thought you'd forgotten that little term of endearment." He started to sway in her direction, but she took a quick step to the side.

When he regained his foothold, he turned to her with an intense frown. "Now, what was it you wanted to know?"

"How much you've been drinking."

"Not enough."

"It seems to me that you've had more than enough."

Stephen waved his hand, batting at the air as if her objection had taken flight.

"Nay, I may be feeling no pain, Katherine, but I am far from drunk. For if I had overindulged, then my mind would not be plagued with thoughts of you. Dangerous thoughts," he added morosely.

Sitting on the end of the bed, Katherine froze in place, the tankard poised at the edge of her lips. Something in his quavering voice, in his drunken, dark humor alerted her to possible danger. She was utterly alone with him, and she realized for the first time that perhaps *that* was the greatest reason he had not wanted her to join him at Downing-Cross. Here, there was nothing to stand between them save for their own resolutions. Perhaps she expected too much self-control from him.

He plunked down next to her and regarded her with a blank expression. He was so close she could feel his breath against her cheek.

"Katherine, my brother isn't the only one who lusts . . . and craves beauty. Did you not think of that when you so . . . so . . . im . . . impetuously followed me here?"

She faced him, just to prove she wasn't in the least bit frightened by his nearness. In the depths of his oceanic eyes, she saw molten desire.

"Milord," she whispered, "I trust you completely. And I am sorry you feel compelled to drink away your thoughts of me. I would have hoped thinking about me would not be such an odious task."

"It wouldn't be," he replied, drawing a long, gulping draft, "except that you're such a damned tease."

She winced. "That is unfair, milord. How can you possibly say I've encouraged you in any way? You constantly berate me for spurning this noble love you foresee for us."

"This noble love," Stephen mocked, cocking his wrist and tossing a hand daintily to one side. "I say, milady, 'tis a brutish lot, these men, with nothing else on their minds but planting figs in their ladies' gardens."

Stephen let out a cynical snicker.

"Oh, Stephen, must you spoil every moment by reducing it to the basest of male urges?"

"Male urges? Is that all we're talking about? By the Mass, I suppose so . . . if . . . if you feel nothing in return, then they can be so described." He abruptly stood, balancing himself once again, and then he began to pace the room, scratching the stubble of a beard that shadowed his chin. "Male urges. Perhaps you are right."

"Perhaps, indeed." Katherine drank deeply from her tankard. The mead was sweet and hot and delicious. A sticky trail lingered on her lips. "Oh, what is to become of us? Here we are without home, without benefit of matrimony, without even a truce between us."

"You should have thought of that before you dashed away in the night. More to the point," he said emphatically, much louder than he would have if sober, "what's to become of *you?* If you do not return home tomorrow morning, then all

hope is lost of ever restoring your honor. I will not allow
that. You must return to Shelby Manor. You might pass off
a day or two of absence with some tale about being lost in
the woods. But if you spend much more time here, you will
be branded a murderer's tart for life."

Katherine smiled sweetly. "Don't I have to make love to
you before I earn that title?"

"Do you think any man here at Downing-Cross believes
you haven't already?"

He hiccuped loudly, and had his question not been so sad,
she would have laughed at the comedy of it. She went to
the window and stared through the frosted glass at stars that
twinkled and glittered. "It does not matter what others think,"
she said.

"Oh, you are naive."

"It only matters what God thinks."

Patience snapping through his drunken haze, Stephen turned
on her suddenly. "And what will God do for you when you
are left alone after I am taken away and hung like a common
criminal?"

"Then I will live here at Downing-Cross," she replied,
flippantly pushing her own fear aside. "You said it was mine
if anything should happen to you."

"And here you will live," Stephen continued with a theat-
rical sweep of his arm, "until Marlow and your father force
another husband on you."

She turned slowly. Their eyes locked. He spoke the truth,
but a flicker of compassion in his eyes told her the words left
a bitter taste. Sensing his empathy, her eyes stung with tears,
and she angrily blinked them into oblivion. She would not
show the embarrassment and rage she felt at being a pawn
in her father's foolish schemes.

Stephen took another drink. His eyes grew hard and distant. "Your beloved father will no doubt be all too happy
to go along with the powerful Earl of Blackmoor. Perhaps
Marlow will reward one of his henchmen with your hand

in marriage. Perhaps Cramer will take you as his wife and bed you . . . with far less consideration of your feelings than I have shown, I might add."

"Does it always come down to that?" Katherine said, not even trying to hide the disappointment and impatience that resonated in her voice.

"Nay," he fairly snarled, wiping perspiration from his forehead. "If bedding you were my sole consideration, lady, you would surely be blossoming with my seed by now."

"You are a coarse man," she whispered sadly.

"You are a coldhearted wench." Stephen threw his tankard against the far wall. It bounced off a stone and clattered to the floor. Muttering a curse, he began to swill from the pitcher.

"Nay, milord, do not numb your senses any more." Katherine turned to him with resignation. "You will regret it in the morning."

Stephen merely shook his head, as if words were too much effort during his journey toward unconsciousness.

Katherine returned to the hearth, resigned at last on how to end their discord. She would give him what he wanted, but on her terms, before it could be taken, as it surely would be. She would surrender, at least her body. There, before the leaping flames, she began to disrobe. She shrugged her shoulders from the loose constraints of her surcoat and placed the flowing gown neatly on a chair. Continuing her task, she caught Stephen's astonished gaze. He stared, slack-jawed, mesmerized by her ritual.

"What are you doing?" he barely whispered.

"What does it look like I'm doing?" came her bitter reply.

"You're undressing."

"Oh, well done, milord. You should have been a scholar. You waste your keen ability to reason on the ignorant masses, a group that sadly I must account myself a part of."

A pained expression twisted his mouth, and he whispered another curse as he swilled from the pitcher.

"Now, now, milord," she admonished as she unbuttoned the front of her kirtle. "If you drink too much, you will hardly be able to do your duty. At least that is what I used to overhear Georgie discussing with his boyhood friends."

Georgie's name fell like a boulder between them. She halted her hands at the third button and swallowed a lump in her throat.

"You don't want to do this," he said, his words a jumbled slur.

She turned to him with a savage glare in her eyes. "What I want has little to do with it, you witless brute! Haven't you figured out that much by now?"

Stephen bolted to a stand and staggered until he towered above her. Grasping her wrists, he pulled her to him. His lips covered hers, tentatively at first, and she was surprised at the sensuality and tenderness he was able to muster in his inebriated state. Without thinking, she parted her lips. He drank from her, stealing the velvet softness, snatching her breath away.

Urged onward, he groaned and pulled her hips to his groin. White heat spread around them, erasing all barriers, and just when she thought she might give herself to him completely, he pulled away, so quickly a breeze fanned her cheeks.

"No," he muttered, blinking rapidly in the firelight. Sweat glistened at his temples. " 'Tis not right. Not this way, Kate. I want to be . . . to be perfectly clear . . . when we . . . when we . . ."

He staggered back, waving her off, and made his way for the bed. "Where's my bloody pitcher?" he complained, and found it sitting precariously on the bed where he had left it.

"Maybe I'll get lucky and pass out," he said. Taking one last swallow, he tossed the empty pitcher to the floor. "This isn't right. We shouldn't . . . shouldn't consummate . . . in this fashion."

Katherine sighed wearily. "Oh, you are such a prude, I must say. At this rate I'll never lose my virginity. How can I proudly bear the title of murderer's whore if I've never had the pleasure of your sword sheathed between my legs?"

Stephen scowled instantly, his face red and mottled. "You'll not talk like that to me, Kate."

"Why not?" she callously returned, unclasping the last button. Her breasts, swollen and ripe, bulged from the confines of her gown. "You'd think nothing of such language from the tart whose favor you accepted the other day."

"That is different." His angry gaze turned soft when his eyes fell to her breasts.

"Why?" she asked innocently. The passion of a seductress lent a smoky haze to her slow-blinking eyes. She shrank from the confines of her gown, and the soft linen crumpled to the floor, leaving her naked and exposed and pale in the flickering light.

"My God . . . ," he muttered and clutched his chest. "You are stunning."

A tiny smile tugged at the corners of her mouth. She wanted him to find her beautiful. She inched forward, overcoming the voice inside her that screamed a warning to stop before it was too late.

Stephen's mouth hung open in amazement, and he inched away when he realized she was approaching him in all her glorious nakedness.

"Nay, Kate, you can't do this now. Your oath."

She nearly stumbled over his words and halted to regain her balance. "Do not speak to me about my oath."

"Why not, Kate?"

"Because it doesn't matter anymore," she said through clenched teeth.

"It matters to you."

"Nay." She shook her head slowly. "You were correct about one thing. I have no rights. If not you, then someone else will take my womanhood, my name, my property. No one cares a whit about my oath. Not even my father. Let us just do the bloody act and get it over with."

The closer she drew, the farther Stephen inched back onto the bed. The mead rendered him less than debonair, and he

tumbled down into the pillows when a tenuous elbow gave
way under his own weight. Katherine took advantage and
crawled atop him, naked and sleek and seductive.

"Go away, Kate. Leave me alone," he pleaded.

But his words were false. He wanted her to stay. She could
tell by the stiffness that pressed against her thighs.

"Hush, milord," she whispered and placed moist lips on
his mouth. She slid her tongue over his taut lips and teased
them. Soon his resistance melted, and she kissed him fully.
Committed to action, she frantically unlaced the leather ties
that closed his shirt. Hungry hands dipped through the opening and caressed his bronzed nipples. Stephen groaned and
writhed like the contented victim he was.

Katherine forced the tunic up and kissed his firm belly,
her tongue wrapping around the hard muscles that went rigid
beneath her caress.

Her breath rasped in her throat, caught in a tangled web
of desire and determination. Oh, how she wanted to end their
battle. If she gave him what he so craved, then he could never
take it from her. It was a way to control her destiny. A small
but significant way. He wouldn't be the victor if she gave
him the last thing she had to give—her body, her promise.

And it was determination more than desire that forced her
hands to tug frantically at his breeches. With great effort,
and no help from Stephen, she pulled the wool pants down
from his hips. She grunted as she tugged, yanking the tight
material over his thighs, his calves. When she finally pulled
his shoes off and tugged his breeches over his feet, she turned
back to Stephen and mewled a bleak sound.

"Oh," came her tiny gasp.

His manhood was flaccid. Gone was his pressing need.

"Stephen," she groaned with a pout and flung herself to
his side. But he did not hear her. He was asleep. A tiny snore
blustered through his mellow lips.

She kissed them anyway. And since she knew he wouldn't
remember anything she did from this point onward, she let a
single tear fall to his cheek. She drank it with a kiss, so salty

on her tongue. She let her lips linger, sniffing in his scent, loving him. Yes, loving him. Never wanting to let go.

"I love you," she whispered, knowing he could not hear her, wondering why she felt this way, unable to change it. "Oh, my dear lord, how I love you."

CHAPTER FIFTEEN

✠

Katherine slept as if *she* were the one who had consumed a pitcher of mead. Throughout the night, she did not stir except to nestle closer in the crook of Stephen's arm. Hearing his heartbeat, the easy draw of his breath, and the howl of the wind outside, she felt a sense of exquisite contentment. Georgie must not have known how wonderful it felt to sleep in someone's arms when he asked her to swear against such pleasures.

When she finally awoke the next morning, she reached for Stephen, only to discover with a pang of disappointment that he was gone. She sat up in the soft gold light of dawn and looked around with a yawn and a stretch. A newly stoked fire crackled at the hearth, and a steaming bowl of porridge awaited her on the stand next to her bed. Though she suspected Markham was the cook, it had to have been Stephen who'd brought the food to her side. He would never have sent his squire to wait on his naked betrothed.

She smiled her pleasure at his thoughtfulness and gulped down the tasty grains. Feeling very much like a lady of leisure, she hugged herself beneath the covers and contemplated her day's activities. There was much work to do. The neglected animals needed tending, and she wanted to search the house for any clues John and Elizabeth might have left behind.

But first, she wanted to nurture a budding friendship. She dressed in the kirtle and surcoat Europa had packed, and tugged on sturdy leather shoes she found in a trunk in a storage chamber. Pulling on gloves and her mantle, Katherine slipped down the stairs, through the Great Hall, and out the kitchen unnoticed by all but Ramsey. The grief-stricken steward glanced at her with hollow, unseeing eyes.

"Good morning, Sir Ramsey," she said brightly, but she moved on when he did not respond.

Katherine snatched a chunk of dried beef from the kitchen and stepped into the brisk morning air. Lupa howled in the distance, and Katherine smiled with a sudden burst of joy and a sense of purpose.

"Morning, Geoffrey," she said to Stephen's squire as he backed out of the dovecote with a shovel full of droppings.

"Aye, good morrow, milady, you're looking chipper today," he replied, his nose wrinkling at his smelly task.

"I slept well," she said with a gracious smile, "and it is such a lovely day."

Katherine found Lupa outside the cage again, and she paused at a distance, struck with pity for the lonely creature.

"Poor baby," she murmured. "You just can't accept that your family isn't coming back, can you?"

Katherine continued with confidence toward the cage. When Lupa spotted her, the wolf's ears fell back, and she lowered her head in a gesture of submission.

"Here, girl. I have a treat." Katherine knelt and gave Lupa the beef. The wolf gobbled it in a second and sank down at Katherine's side.

Katherine knelt and gave her a hug, petting her over and over. "I won't abandon you," she whispered in the wolf's ear. "You are safe with me."

"You have a new friend," Stephen said.

Katherine looked up and found Stephen's magnificent figure leaning casually against the end of the cage. His body blocked the sun, and the juxtaposition between light and darkness made him a giant black shadow with a flaming gold halo. Katherine blinked at the contrast and held a hand over her brow, squinting up at him.

"I am no longer afraid."

"Indeed," he said and nodded proudly. "You are a brave woman."

He took a step forward, and Lupa growled, baring fangs, hair bristling down her spine.

"Hush, Lupa," Katherine scolded the animal. "I think she doesn't like men. She ran yesterday when Markham approached."

"No doubt it was a man who gave her those scars with a whip. Poor creature." Stephen stepped from the cage and knelt down a few paces from the wolf. He held out both hands and coaxed the animal in a low murmur. "Here, Lupa. Come here, girl. You are safe. Come to me, Lupa."

Katherine knew that she would come if Stephen called her so gently. His voice was soothing and rich. She remembered her silly attempt to seduce him last night and turned her head away with chagrin.

"There, there. Good girl."

When Katherine turned back, the wolf was crawling to Stephen as meek as a rabbit.

"You traitor!" Katherine laughingly accused the creature.

Stephen smiled as he patted Lupa's back. "Don't worry. She knows who her master is." His eyes twinkled up at her. "The one who feeds her, and you are the only one who had the kindness to do that."

Katherine rose and brushed her fingertips together. "Stephen, last night . . ."

"Katherine, I owe you an apology." He, too, stood, his mantle billowing in a sudden breeze. He ignored the long brown locks of hair that curled around his rugged cheeks. "I should never have indulged in so much mead, at least not in your presence. I said things I shouldn't have."

"I *did* things I shouldn't have," she responded with a nervous gesture.

He narrowed the distance between them and wrapped his arms around her in a strong embrace. "Nothing you did was wrong if you were true to your heart. You lashed out at me as I deserved. At least you have finally commanded my touch, even if I wasn't up to a command performance."

Katherine's heart swooned with love at his easy self-deprecation. Responding to her gushing affection, he tilted her head back and kissed her with aching tenderness. It was a healing kiss, and Katherine felt the last remnants of her embarrassment fade. When she moved away, drawing in a much needed breath of air, her head spinning, she stepped on a patch of ice. Her feet flew out, and she fell with a yelp.

Stephen grasped her arm and cushioned the fall. He knelt at her side, laughing with unchivalrous glee at her distress. "As I said the last time we were at Downing-Cross, I think you had better find a new dancing partner. 'Tis a dangerous occupation."

Katherine sat up with a groan of pain, and then realizing the absurdity of the moment, she sank back into the brittle grass and laughed herself. "I can not blame you for your concern, milord. But I do wonder how you always manage to arrange for my downfall when you think we're alone."

Stephen glanced toward the manor. Several men were working the horses in a small corral. "We might as well be alone. They'll never see us," he said with a grin. "Perhaps now is the time to ravish you, now that you have as much as begged for me."

Stephen fell atop her and kissed her with loving passion. Katherine wrapped her arms around him, wondering with irony if after all their squabbles it would be in a melting patch of ice that they finally made love.

She warmed to his touch, opened moist lips to accept his kiss, his hot tongue. She arched toward him when his hand found a breast and gently squeezed. And then she burst out in new laughter when she felt another tongue—Lupa's. The wolf licked happily at Katherine's forehead and then proceeded to lap up the sweet taste of Stephen's neck.

"Blasted animal!" Stephen yelled, gently pushing Lupa

away. The wolf stepped back, only to return when Stephen resumed his passionate kiss.

At last Stephen gave up. He leaned on one elbow and cast both lover and beast an exasperated grimace. "Very well. You ladies win. I'll not ravish Lord Gilbert's daughter here in the light of day."

"Stephen, you can not think I arranged this interference." Katherine giggled at his consternation.

His eyes narrowed, and he grinned. "I don't know what to think. Except, maybe, that my luck with women has run out. Perhaps we'll try again tonight. Inside. Where it's warm. When I'm sober."

"Perhaps" was her tantalizing reply.

That evening, spring roared and clamored at the door to Downing-Cross Manor. The angels of new life beat their wings against the gales of winter. A warm wind from the south whirled and battled for dominance, shooing the cold, making way for a thaw that would free the crab apple buds and daffodil shoots from their hibernation.

"Spring is here," Katherine said as she hugged herself and shivered in the doorway. The others finished their evening meal behind her at a trestle table in the Great Hall. "It's been here for weeks. We just did not know it because of the ice storm."

"S'Blood!" Geoffrey shouted when a loose window burst open for the hundredth time, it seemed. "Milady, must you admire nature now? That open door creates a maelstrom."

Wiping crumbs from his mouth, the squire bustled over to the window and fought with the shutters.

Katherine merely smiled, her hair billowing around her shoulders. "I like the breeze. It smells of the sea. It brings the hint of faraway lands. Perhaps flowers are in full blossom somewhere we've never even been to, and their scent sweetens this breeze. The sun sinks slower these days, have you noticed? The sun doesn't want to rest at night. It wants to shine until everything blooms."

"If all women have an imagination like that," Geoffrey grumbled, blowing on his hands to warm them as he climbed back onto the bench where the others ate intently, "then I swear I'll never marry. 'Tis not practical. Think how many logs it will take to bring the heat back into this Hall."

"With that attitude, you'd make a good lady of the castle yourself, Geoffrey, counting every log and rush used at your lord's expense." Ramsey's sarcastic comment astonished the others. They fell silent, realizing that this was the first jest he had made since the death of his son. One, and then another, began to laugh, until all the men shook the table with their booming voices.

Even Geoffrey was so relieved to see a spark of life in the steward that he burst out with laughter at his own expense. "By heaven, 'tis a good one, Sir Ramsey."

"Someone is coming." Katherine's simple statement stopped the revelry cold.

Stephen was the first to rise. Straightening the plain tunic that hung to his thighs, he joined her at the door. He placed his hands on Katherine's shoulders, that simple gesture melting some of the goose bumps that had risen on her arms.

"A single rider on a horse," she said. The orange sun had just touched the horizon; everything else was a charcoal silhouette. The horse slowed down the closer it drew and finally stopped when the rider met the men guarding the entrance.

Stephen squinted. His fingers tightened around her arms. "By my troth, 'tis a woman. I can tell by the way she rides."

Katherine gave him a puzzled frown. "Could it be Europa? Perhaps with some warning?"

Stephen shrugged. "We'll find out."

Hand in hand, they walked down the front path. The south wind that had snuck in during the afternoon had already done its part to melt a lingering crust of ice and snow. Water seeped into their leather shoes.

They met the hooded rider halfway up the manor road.

When she drew in her reins, she toppled from her horse into Stephen's arms. Stephen clutched her legs, which were tangled in a foot mantle. His other arm gripped her shoulders. Her head bobbed against his chest. Katherine pulled back the black hood that shadowed her face and gasped.

"Constance!" Katherine exclaimed. "Jesu! Stephen, look! She's been beaten."

Black-and-blue marks shadowed the pale woman's face. She clutched her abdomen and groaned.

Stephen's body went rigid with anger. " 'Twas Marlow."

Katherine gave him a sober nod. "Let us take her to the fire."

Stephen's men hauled the trestle table away from the fireplace and brought down a bed frame, a mattress, and blankets from upstairs. While Stephen still held her in his arms, Katherine gently removed Constance's shoes and cape. They tucked her into the bed in her gown.

"She'll need all the warmth she can get," Katherine said, tucking her in. But moments later, the unconscious woman was hot to the touch, and Katherine feared she might be suffering from a fever. Whatever the malady, she needed nourishment. "Geoffrey, warm some milk in the kitchen."

Constance's eyes fluttered open, and she gave her new friend a tremulous smile. "Katherine! I am so glad I made it. The road was so long . . . so cold."

Katherine gripped her hand and stroked her high forehead. "You are safe now, Constance. Just rest. You really shouldn't have come. 'Tis not good to ride with a babe in your womb."

"My baby . . ." Constance squeezed her eyes shut, and her lips trembled. She grasped her abdomen. " 'Twas for my babe that I left. He . . . he beat me . . ."

"Marlow?" Stephen had been pacing by the window, but he stalked forward at the mention of his brother's name. "Just tell me it was my brother, and I'll kill him once and for all."

Constance glared fearfully at Stephen after this unexpected

outburst and nodded. Tears fell to the pillow. "He found out that I . . . I helped you escape."

"You knew he would, sister," Stephen said in a choked voice. He began to pace again, pounding a fist into his other hand. "I wish now you had never taken that risk."

Constance blinked a desolate look across her smooth face. "He was going to kill me."

Geoffrey tiptoed to the end of the bed and proffered a chalice of steaming milk. Katherine thanked him and lifted Constance in her arms. "Drink this, friend. It will be good for you and your little one."

Constance did as she was told, clutching the chalice in two bony hands. When the cup was empty, Katherine wiped a milky trail from Constance's lips and lowered her onto the pillow.

"I never thought I would have to fear for my life as long as I was pregnant," Constance said mournfully. "But I know if I did not leave tonight I would have . . . *fallen* . . . from one of the towers. Marlow went into a fit of madness over my betrayal."

"And what of these?" Katherine gently stroked each bruise that marred Constance's features. She suffered from a blackened eye, a red welt on her right cheek, and a broken tooth.

"He beat me and then put me in the stocks."

"In the stocks!" Katherine drew back and pressed a hand to her thumping heart. "In the dungeon?"

"Nay, outside. For hours at a time. And for all to see." The older woman turned the side of her face into the pillow to hide her embarrassment, unwilling to meet Katherine's look of horror.

"That bastard!" Katherine pressed a clinched fist to her mouth. She looked for Stephen in the shadows of the room and found him staring at her with rage that exceeded her own. They were of one mind on this matter. It was comfort enough to help her relax. More anger and hatred was the last thing Constance needed now. "How did you escape?"

Constance managed a faint smile. " 'Twas Cramer. He

arranged for a horse and let me slip away when the others were preoccupied. Of course, I swore I would never tell Marlow."

"Cramer?" Stephen sat at the end of the bed and frowned in disbelief. "That weasel? I would never have thought it possible. Are you sure he wasn't setting you up in one of Marlow's traps?"

Constance shook her head ruefully. "I am certain. Cramer *pitied* me," she replied. The word gurgled with bitterness. "Who would not? Except, of course, for my husband."

For a moment, Constance looked like the dour, haunted woman Katherine had first met, but her hard expression melted. Exhaustion mellowed her.

"If Cramer sided with you, then that's the first defection in Marlow's troops." Stephen played the tactician, eyeing Katherine speculatively. "Hopefully, there will be more."

"Let us not worry about the future now," Katherine gently admonished him. "Our first order of business is to bring this fair lady back to health. You are warm to the touch, Constance. Did you catch a fever?"

"I've been cold and then hot throughout the day. But that is not what worries me the most." Her mouth began to quiver again.

"What is it?" Katherine coaxed.

"Pains. Here." Constance rubbed her abdomen.

Katherine blanched. She had avoided making too much of that unconscious gesture when Constance first arrived. But now the danger of a miscarriage could not be ignored. She rose and forced a bright smile. "Well then, we'll just have to get you a good meal and restore your strength. There will be nothing but bed rest for you tonight. I plan to see to that."

Katherine exchanged a worried look with Stephen and went to the kitchen to gather a meal.

She stayed by Constance's side throughout the evening. When Ramsey suggested a private chamber, Katherine refused. The Great Hall was the best heated room in the manor, and she didn't want to risk Constance catching a deathly chill.

Though it seemed spring had arrived, the warmer breeze that blew in from the south was no match for the drop in temperature that came with nightfall. Katherine had never been so grateful for shelter before. It wasn't just the chill that settled in her bones. It was the ominous sense that Constance was in greater danger than Katherine had at first assumed. She was glad for Stephen's presence. He seemed so strong, so fearless. She knew he regretted a lost chance to be alone with her, but he never said a word, his concern for Constance evident in his unfailing presence.

Katherine wrapped herself in a wool blanket and dozed in a chair at the bedside, lulled to sleep by the rattle of the shutters.

"Dear friend," Constance said to Katherine a half hour later, as if she had never slept at all.

Katherine's head bobbed up. She rubbed her stiff neck and looked down in surprise at her patient, whose eyes were at last entirely lucid, though her cheeks were still bright pink with a fever.

"How are you feeling?" Katherine leaned forward and gave her a loving smile. Stephen did not stir. He slept upright, his back against the fireplace, his legs sprawled out on the floor.

"I had a dream," Constance said. "A dream that I was traveling to a place I've never been before. A lovely place that was warm and filled with loving people. My mother was there, waiting for me with open arms. 'Tis a funny thing. I haven't seen my mother in ten years, not since she died."

"Dreams can be odd," Katherine said softly.

Constance gripped her hand suddenly, squeezing it tight.

"Hold me, Katherine, please hold me," she pleaded.

Katherine swept forward and sat on the bed, pulling her into her arms. "What is it, Constance?" She pressed her cheek to the older woman's hot temple and stroked her hair.

"I . . . I just had the coldest feeling sweep through me.

As if the Crone of Death were tapping on my shoulder. Sometimes I am so cold. I just want someone to hold."

"I'm here, Constance. I'll warm you. Just hold tight."

They remained entwined, rocking back and forth in the amber glow of the fire until Constance fell asleep again.

Stephen stirred and brought from the men's bower a mattress and another blanket for Katherine. He cast them beside Constance's bed.

"I must check on the others. Can you spare me here awhile?"

Katherine nodded. She brought the palm of his hand to her mouth and kissed it with gratitude. "I will call if I need anything."

Without another word, he kissed her forehead and went upstairs.

Settling on the makeshift bed, Katherine fully expected a peaceful sleep. The meal seemed to have done Constance good. But she awoke an hour later to a shriek of pain.

Katherine bolted upright and scrambled to her side.

"What is it? What is happening?"

Constance tossed her head from side to side, her face a twisted mask of grief and pain. "My womb. It is casting out the babe. I know it. I know it."

"Perhaps not," Katherine reasoned futilely. "Perhaps 'twas the meal I fed you."

"Nay, it has happened a dozen times before. I'm losing my baby." She groaned again and doubled over in pain.

Katherine stood rigidly, fists clutched at her side, unaware that her nails plunged into the palms of her hands. She licked her lips and fought the vertigo that came so quickly, just as it had when she had watched so many loved ones succumb to the Pestilence. Knowing of nothing else to do, she threw back the covers from the bed, praying she could then dispute Constance's fear of miscarriage.

"Oh dear God," she whispered, her eyes narrowing in on a patch of blood that stained the bed beneath her friend's hips. A wide circle of red marked the tragedy—Constance was indeed having a miscarriage.

"We must stanch the flow," Katherine said without the vaguest idea how that could be done. Savage determination took shape in her eyes like emeralds transforming beneath the harsh cleaves of a jeweler.

Looking about wildly, Katherine spotted and then seized a dagger lodged upright in the surface of a trestle table. She retrieved it and ripped Constance's gowns from top to bottom. Gently, she freed the pained woman from her soiled garments. Constance was left naked, but it was better than chafing in a bloody, stiff gown.

"You are bleeding, friend," Katherine whispered in her ear, feeling inadequate.

Constance merely nodded her head. What could Katherine tell her about pain and loss that she had not already experienced?

"Tell me what to do, and I'll do it. I'll do anything."

Constance did not even bother to answer. She drew in ragged breaths of air through flaring nostrils and gripped her womb. But then her eyes blinked open, a tiny ray of hope shooting in the darkness. "The herbs . . . I cursed myself for leaving them behind. But they came from Downing-Cross . . ."

Katherine rose quickly, a faint smile softening the tense muscles in her cheeks. "They are upstairs. I know exactly where they are. Oh, please, Constance, please hold onto that babe as long as you can. I'll be back . . . soon."

She pivoted and ran right into Stephen, nearly knocking the wind out of herself. "Oh, Stephen, Constance is very ill. You must send for a midwife from Blackmoor."

He gripped her arms and frowned in shock. "A midwife? But she is only—"

"Yes, 'tis much too soon. But there is nothing I can do. I fear the baby . . ." For the first time, tears burned behind her eyes, and her lower lip quivered.

Stephen nodded his understanding. "I'll send Seeley right away."

Katherine gave him a grateful nod and allowed him to wipe a tear from her cheek before he dashed off on his mission. She lit a taper in the fire and bolted up the stairs to the drying room.

Katherine flung open the door and shielded the candle when a gust of cool, herb-scented air blew against her hot face. A vacuum in the corridor sucked the medicinal chamber air like a dying man gasping for one last breath.

Katherine held the flickering flame high and stepped hesitantly into the collection of herbal mysteries. "Where are you?" she whispered to the yarrow and lady's mantle. Using her memory, she searched for and found the wooden casks Elizabeth had used before. Katherine rushed forward and grabbed the herbs she needed, throwing fistfuls into the folds of her surcoat, clutching the material to her breasts. Just before she ran from Elizabeth's sacred room, she turned back and took in the numinous silence.

"Dear Goddess," she prayed as Elizabeth had, "may your gifts grant good progeny."

And then, to pay for her blasphemy, she made the sign of the cross and shut the door.

By the time she returned to the kitchen, Ramsey and Geoffrey had stirred and stood by, ready to be of assistance. Katherine ordered them to boil water and steep the herbs. Stephen told her that it would be hours before Seeley returned with the midwife, and that was contingent on Marlow giving permission for the old woman to leave the castle.

Katherine's shoulders slumped, and she frowned against despair. "I don't know how to help her. It brings back so many memories, Guy. With Georgie and Agnes, I tried potions, poultices, anything I could think of. Everything failed."

"You can always pray."

She looked up in surprise at his suggestion, wondering how strong his faith was. Then her surprise melted to sadness. "Prayer did not work then, either."

With trudging steps, she returned to the Hall and swallowed the suffocating dread that rose within her.

"You're back," Constance said, clutching Katherine's hand as a beggar would a scrap of food. Her terrified eyes were big brown pools suspended in the depths of her pale complexion.

"Aye, I've returned. The herbs will be ready soon."

"How wrong I was to judge you when you first arrived at the castle. How did you ever look past my bitterness? No one else wanted to be my friend but you. And I thought you were horrid."

Katherine smiled with irony. "Likewise. I thought you some weak-willed creature. I was equally in error."

The pale woman's face shuddered with pleasure at the compliment. "Friendships can be forged in unexpected places."

"I need a friend." Katherine knelt at her side and stroked her forehead. "Be strong and get better. I don't want to lose the only friend I have right now."

Constance gave her a wan smile. "You have the best friend you'll ever need standing over there."

Katherine followed her gaze to Stephen, who had entered silently, like a guardian angel. He stood by the window, ready to provide aid, if needed.

"But will he always be there for me?" she whispered.

"You shouldn't be afraid. You really shouldn't."

Katherine sighed, a little surrender, as one more chunk of the wall standing between her and Stephen crumbled.

They waited in silence until Geoffrey brought in a cup of the herbal mixture. Constance drank it with gratitude, her faith in the herb's ability to help her obvious as she gulped the liquid. A quarter of an hour later, when Stephen had withdrawn to the kitchen with the others, Katherine silently drew back the covers to see if Elizabeth's brew had helped.

She gasped at what she saw. The bloody pool had only widened, so much so that a puddle of blood sat atop the sheets, unable to sink into the wide circle that saturated the mattress.

Katherine replaced the covers and rushed to the kitchen. She could barely hear herself speak as her head pounded.

"Sheets . . . I need sheets. Cloth, any kind of cloth. Now!"

The men's casual concern snapped into fear at the urgency of her demand. Geoffrey and Ramsey scrambled to do her bidding. Stephen raced with her into the Great Hall.

Katherine squatted next to the bed and reached under the mattress, touching the boards that supported the thin feather bed. When she pulled her hand back, it was covered in blood.

Stephen grimaced and caught her gaze, holding it with compassion. He knew. He knew how frightened she was. Thank God someone knew.

Barely seeing the shadow that approached, she felt him pull her up. Her tearstained cheek smashed against his soft tunic. She inhaled the musky scent of him. His heartbeat echoed in her ear. Life, sweet life! He was strong and alive; gripping her to him, squeezing her, cooing some reassurance she could not hear, though she could feel the words vibrate in his chest. She longed to feel the vibration more deeply and nestled her ear against the opening in his tunic, against the mat of hair, the cushion of muscles.

"Don't die, Constance," she muttered in a whimpering voice. "Don't die. Don't die. Don't die, Stephen. Don't leave me."

"I won't," he murmured.

When Ramsey returned, she pulled away in a daze, her hair a tangled mess, and took the clean rags he proffered. With an angry gesture, she wiped the blood from her hand. Most of it had dried, and a sticky bronze layer clung to her fingers, infiltrating her pores, staining the lifeline in the palm of her hand. And then she turned to her ward, who had by now fallen into a state of unconsciousness.

"Please leave us a moment," Katherine requested, and the men obeyed.

She sopped up the blood that oozed from the bed. When more replaced it, she went to the source and pressed the sheets against Constance's body, between her legs. She pushed and pushed the white strips of cloth against her womanhood, but

they came away red and sticky. And all the while a tiny red
river flowed from Constance's body.

"Oh, dear God," Katherine whispered. Terror lit her eyes
greater than the fire ever could. Her lips were white and
thinned. She began to shake.

"Georgie," she whispered. She saw him again—gaunt, desperate, tinged with black circles. Why him and not Katherine?
Why Constance and not Marlow? What sense did any of it
make? What power did she have to stop the sorrow? None.
None at all.

Realizing the futility of her task, Katherine threw her
soaked rags to the floor in defeat. Her efforts were useless.

Constance stirred with a little moan. Her eyes shot open
when she let out a cry of pain. She emitted another cry,
a soundless gurgle, eyes bulging, and grasped Katherine's
hand.

"Here 'tis," the older woman whispered desperately. "My
babe has come. Save him if you can. Save him, Katherine."

"Constance, it is only five months. Five months . . . Nothing can be done. Nothing."

"Try . . ."

Katherine's gaze lowered with dread over the swell of the
pregnant woman's belly, to the apex of her thighs. There
between Constance's legs lay a child, half formed.

Katherine sobbed and hung her head, silently weeping until
Constance's fingers tugged at her gown.

"What is it? Tell me, Katherine. You must tell me."

Katherine gasped for breath and wiped at her soaked cheeks.
" 'Tis a boy" came her choked reply.

"A son," Constance whispered, her eyes burning like pyres.
Sorrow and anger pulled her mouth down to her chin in a
dreadful moan. "A son. Marlow would have been so proud.
So proud. He would not have beaten me if he'd known 'twas
a boy."

Katherine looked at her in horror. "He is a murderer,"
she rasped. "He murdered your son. Don't you dare make
excuses for him."

Constance sobered at Katherine's admonition. "Of course, you are right." Her eyes widened with sudden fear. Heart-stopping fear. "Am I going to die, too? I don't want to die. Katherine, I don't want to die. Help me. Help me . . ."

"Oh, Constance, Constance," Katherine cried out. She collapsed onto the bed and pulled her friend into a full embrace. Desperately she clutched at Constance's hair. They pressed their cheeks together, tears mingling, bodies racked with sobs. But no matter how hard they hugged, they could not assuage the shattering desperation they shared. This was a moment of friendship so poignant it took Katherine's breath away.

"Dear Constance! Don't go. Please don't go."

Together they wept until the sorrow of the moment faded. If passion or determination could have willed death away, it would have been long gone for all their keening. But Katherine knew the limits of her power. When she could not cry another drop, she gently pulled from Constance's embrace. Their gazes locked in a final reflection. Constance's eyes were on fire, the last flare of dying embers.

With a hiccuping sob, she fell asleep.

Katherine waited, wide-eyed, barely breathing. She watched the rise and fall of her friend's naked chest. Once. Twice. A thrice and final time. And then came stillness.

CHAPTER SIXTEEN

✠

Katherine accepted no help as she swathed mother and child in tight sheets for their journey back to Blackmoor. It was midnight by the time she finished. Markham and Sir Gerald carried the bed and the corpses to the solar at the end of the Hall, while Geoffrey cleaned the floor.

Ramsey forced Katherine into the kitchen and kept guard at the door while she gratefully washed herself in a tub of hot water he'd prepared for her. The soothing bath washed away evidence of the evening's tragic events, though not the memory. Warmed by the steaming water, Katherine dried herself and donned nothing more than a velvet mantle and her woolen stockings. She wearily climbed the stairs to the bower. When she entered the oblong room, Stephen was waiting for her. Rather than banking the fire, he threw another log on it. Weary from sorrow, riddled with anger and frustration, he was not prepared to sleep any more than she was.

Katherine stared numbly at the fire. Her face was swollen from crying. She had spent her anger in tears. Her breasts rose and fell in deep undulations as her breath slowly returned to an easy pattern, punctuated only by little spasms. Faced with such loss, she had no more vows to swear, no more excuses to make for a God who let so many of His good children die miserably.

Kneeling by the fire, Stephen held both hands before the yellow flames, heat so intense it stung his palms. The pain felt good. It diminished the aching in his heart. He looked at

233

Katherine—her wild hair framing a cynical, sad expression,
her arms crossed beneath the heavy folds of an elegant mantle—and wished there was some way to relieve her sadness.
It was an excruciating dilemma, a frustration greater than any
he'd felt during the Pestilence. For then, he had had only
himself to console. Now there was another. Someone whose
feelings he wanted to put before his own. But he could not
spare her, and he felt a sense of failure—to see the mystery of
life and death so close at hand and yet be helpless to change
the outcome. Another death. Another grain of sand flowing
to the ocean, chipping away at the beach, testing Katherine's
faith. God, he would have done anything to spare her that.

And, in an odd way, he realized that sorrow was a knife
shredding the last barriers between them, the final illusions.
Without even touching her, he knew what she was thinking.
His mind was her mind, their sadness one. Confident in that
oneness, he rose and stood behind her, nestling his chin in
the twisted skein of her silken hair. She smelled of fresh rose
water and smoke, a soothing blend that made her so real, so
womanly. Wherever her body touched his—along his chest,
his groin, his legs, his arms—he melted, unable to maintain
his stoic pose.

They didn't speak for a long time. Lupa gave a faint-
hearted cry. She had begun her dirge almost from the moment
Constance's soul passed over. Like Stephen and Katherine,
the wolf had grown weary and settled for a plaintive whimper,
just loud enough to pierce the silence.

"Are you all right?" Stephen whispered.

When she didn't respond, he hugged her tighter, feeling
her answer, letting his compassion pour from his arms into
hers. He pressed his shadowed whiskers against her temple
and gave her a smile she couldn't see, his sensual lips curled
with wise irony. "Why are we still here? That is what you
want to know. Why us? Why are we left behind to ponder
fate's riddles when other good souls flee this earth?"

Katherine shrank even farther into the haven of his arms.
Huge, stinging tears pounded at the back of her eyes,

demanding outlet. She blinked hard. She was willing to cry for Constance, unashamed of those tears, but she could not bear to weep for her own sense of loss and confusion, not in Stephen's presence. A small tremble worked from her stomach through her heart and up her throat to her pounding head. *Please do not cry,* she pleaded inwardly with a self she couldn't control. She *did* wonder why, as Stephen had so simply put it. If he knew her doubts, if he saw her rail at God's injustices, if he knew how angry she was at the Creator, would he laugh at all her pious pretenses? Would he finally know what a hypocrite she was, clinging to her vow to Georgie when her very faith was in question? And would he spurn her?

"I . . . I . . . don't wonder about anything," she said in a halting, breathy voice, "because I . . . I don't . . . *feel* . . . anything."

When she had said the lie, tears made an honest woman of her. They flowed in big dollops down her rosy cheeks, one after another, without demanding so much as a whimper or sob.

Stephen nudged her shoulders around to face him, but her gaze never left the fire. The profile of her rigid frown pulsed in the shadows. "That is not true, Kate, and you know it. You feel. You feel too much."

"How much is too much?" she hissed, her head whipping in his direction. Here it came, his condemnation, his lack of understanding, which would prove him once and for all to be as shallow as a man could be. "How much is too much, Stephen?"

His eyelids fluttered, registering the blow. "We must be strong, Katherine. We must go on, just as we did after the Death. We are still alive. We can't let sorrow drown us."

"It is too late for that," she answered bitterly. "The water is already above my head."

She shook with a shiver and inhaled a faltering breath as if it were her last before the undertow swept her away.

He leapt in after her and wrapped his arms around her supple back. As if her life depended on it, he pressed his

lips to hers even as water flooded his own eyes. He had
never wanted to kiss a woman and cry at the same time,
but he would cry if he lost her now. He forced her mouth
open with a tongue spurred not so much by passion as by
a desperate desire to give life. He breathed into her, forcing
his own sweet breath into her body. He sucked the essence
of her into his lungs, taking the cynical vapors from a woman
possessed by sadness and despair. He felt like a god, like
an immortal from legends past, for he was certain only he
could lift this pall from the princess and save her life, thereby
saving his own.

"Forget the sadness," he whispered against her mouth. His
lips pecked along the exquisite heart formed by her red lips—
he licked and nipped and tugged and slid his mouth over hers.
Her eyes fluttered with life, and then with fear or anger, he
could not tell which. She pressed her fists against his chest
in protest, but moments later those feline hands clawed his
tunic, pulling him closer. Push and pull, fear and desire. She
whimpered tiny chirps like the song of an injured bird.

It was spring in his soul. Perspiration burst out on his
forehead. He was hot and wanting, no longer the savior but
the seducer. Having saved her life, he would transform her
from a maiden into a woman. The time had come.

"I've wanted you for so long," he whispered.

His moist breath seeped into her ear, and she shivered
with desire. "Yes," she muttered, melting against the heat
their bodies exchanged.

Stephen's hands skimmed over her protective mantle, following the curves of her body. He boldly slid one hand
through the cape's opening. Skin touched skin. His hand
slid down her abdomen and found her womanhood, cupping
it firmly, claiming her for his own. Katherine quivered and
groaned. She was blazing and wet, ready for him. Long
past ready.

Every bit of her attention focused on the gentle kneading
of his hand in that most secret place. Confused and dazed, she
responded to his kiss as an afterthought. Belatedly her mouth

molded to his. Without design, her tongue stroked his. But the combination of his vigorous kiss and his smooth caresses of her velvet softness built to an explosion within. She arched and quivered like a butterfly in his hand. And soon her thoughts flew into the darkness. Her senses took flight.

She flew above ordinary life, far away from sad things like death and tears. Sensing a chance at immortality, she longed for a greater closeness with this strong, loving man. She ripped at the bow that bound her mantle to her pulsing neck. The heavy velvet slid unaided to the floor. She slipped off her stockings. And all the while he gripped her gently at the apex of her being.

"Ohhhhh," she groaned at the intimacy.

Distracted by new enticements, he removed his fingers from her darkness and smoothed both hands up her sculpted abdomen. His fingers crawled up the velvet terrain. Stephen knelt and admired her naked form, blue eyes sparkling. He cupped his hands around the full mounds of her breasts. His fingers tugged and gently kneaded her nipples.

She drew a hissing breath and flung her head to one side, a thatch of hair flying a moment later.

The heat of her body flowed out in loving waves, and he pressed his cheek to her belly, her womb. Overcome with a sense of infinity, with a sense of women's creative power, he reveled in her softness. When he wrapped his arms around her, he embraced the world. And then he rose, lifting her high in the air. She did not protest when he lowered her to the bed. She watched in hungry silence as he disrobed, his hard body gleaming like a beautiful sculpture in the golden glow of the room.

Loving what she saw, craving that masculinity, she smiled and brushed her fingertips through the hair flowing languorously from her temples.

"Ah, Kate," he whispered and turned to face her fully. His manhood was enormous and erect.

Katherine gasped and stared in wonder at a fullness she had only imagined until now.

Stephen chuckled. His eyes twinkled and soothed her. "Do not fear, maiden. I will be gentle."

Stephen's strong legs bent and knelt upon the mattress. He covered her body with his own—his skin hot and smooth and taut over what seemed like acres of hard muscle.

She felt him long and firm between her thighs, and she parted her legs. It would be such an easy entry, she thought, if she just shifted her hips a little lower. If she just wriggled the right way, he would slide through her moist passage, ending her longing. But he would not satisfy her panting needs so quickly. He would only kiss her. And so he did, while his hands clutched her wrists, holding them high above her head against the pillow.

An eternity passed this way it seemed, hands clutching, mouths drinking, until she drew back breathlessly. A touch of fear glimmered in her eyes.

"Stay with me. Always stay with me. Never leave me."

He answered her with another kiss. He drank deeply of her love, knowing that this was right. He would claim her finally.

Impatient to see as well as feel her, he drew back and studied her baby-soft skin. He knelt between her thighs, forcing her legs apart even farther, exposing her fuchsia flower.

Feeling nasty and wanton, exposed at last, she groaned beneath his gaze.

He smoothed a hand up her thigh, over her hip, and around her alabaster breast. Her breasts were flawless, punctuated only by two pink buds, round and tumescent, another image he would etch onto the canvas of his mind.

Stephen lowered his head to her breasts, like a druid bowing to kiss the earth. She ran her fingers through his tousled mane and clutched his temples when his lips consumed the tip of one full mound.

"Oh, milord," Katherine said with a shuddering breath. A quiver bolted through her as his tongue swirled in an achingly sweet dance over the crest of her taut nipple, and she arched against him. "Oh, dear lord, you are so tender to me."

And so they rode the sea of desire in a long ship, riding the crest of each wave, sails billowing with the force of love, though Katherine could not have named it so as she keeled and swooned with delight.

Rolling her over into his arms, he parted her legs, and in the dark stillness of her being he wove a tapestry of unbridled passion. When she could but gasp and moan for mercy, he filled her completely. A moment of discomfort gave way to an overwhelming sense of oneness. Completely entwined, they stared into each other's eyes in the hazy firelight, both startled, aching with love, sensing a higher power, a connection with something immortal. For if ever time had stood still, it was at this moment, in an act as old as time itself.

Unearthly thoughts were cast aside by the searing heat that grew between them. He was hot fire forging the depths of her soul, and the gentle motion that rocked them with increasing urgency soon shattered her faint grip on reality. From some distant land she heard her own cries of abandon, like the piercing cry of a falcon. Then came Stephen's bellow of ecstasy, not so much heard, in her dreamy state, as felt. A deep vibration that echoed their oneness.

Stillness followed. A gentle wind rattled the shutters.

Had she lived before now? she wondered as consciousness returned. Gasping for breath in unison with this beloved man, she realized a whole new world had been born this night. A world where the trappings of the mind were frail and useless, where the essence of her womanhood, where humanity, ruled.

She had drunk from the chalice of love this night. And though that silver cup might tarnish on the morrow, she would never forget the sweetness of its contents. Until fingers of light drew back the night, she would clutch the silver rim to her lips.

With loving hands, she raised Stephen's head, from where it nestled against her breasts, and kissed him again.

* * *

Katherine was the first to awaken the next morning. A fresh, warm breeze whirled over their naked bodies, the night's chill long forgotten. She nestled against Stephen's chest, blinking with the slow realization that her life had been utterly transformed. She felt complete contentment in a way she had never conceived possible. It was as if someone had ripped away a dark hood, exposing blinding light so brilliant it made retreating to the shadows impossible. Even if she wanted to forget their lovemaking and confess her sins to a priest, her heart and body would never forget.

Katherine drew in a rich, deep breath of air. The lingering scent of sex tickled her nose. This was so real—lying in his arms, the gentle ache in her groin—all new, all exquisite sensations.

And yet even in the afterglow, her sense of duty raised its stern head. She could love Stephen and relish his affection, but she could not turn away from a friend. Duty called.

Katherine sat up in bed. A whoosh of air swirled around her. Her exposed nipples hardened and goose bumps rose on her arms. Constance. Constance was dead. No amount of ecstasy could erase that fact. A dull ache built in her chest until she put it to rest with a resolution. She would take Constance back to Blackmoor and see to it that she received a Christian burial. She trusted no one else to be stubborn enough with that mission, for if she were any judge of character, she knew that Marlow would try to rob his wife of even that honor.

With regret, she slipped from the haven of Stephen's arms and quietly prepared for her departure. Ramsey greeted her in the kitchen, chattering away in remarkably good spirits. Katherine asked him to saddle horses for her and an escort.

She did not relish a confrontation with Stephen over her plans, and so she let him sleep long after she was prepared to depart. She played with Lupa, delaying the inevitable farewell as long as possible. The wolf was waiting for her and eagerly snapped up her offering of dried beef. Katherine gave her a big hug and scratched behind her ears.

"Would you like to come with me, Lupa? I think I may need your protection where I'm going."

"And where is that?" Stephen said.

Katherine twisted around and found him staring down at her with a stern expression, arms akimbo. He bore only his breeches, leggings, and shoes. His massive chest was bare. He had obviously dressed hastily.

"Milord, you startled me."

"I expected to awaken with you in my arms," he replied irritably.

"I had that pleasure. Forgive me for denying you the same." She stood and faltered, suddenly light-headed. She braced her legs and cleared a lump that had congealed in her throat.

"I must go back to Blackmoor, Stephen." At his quick frown, she hastened to explain. "Do not take issue, milord. My decision has nothing to do with us . . . or with the beautiful thing that happened between us last night."

Stephen blinked in surprise at her ability to speak openly about their shared passion. "Last night was exquisite." But still her leave-taking rankled. "Why? Why must you go so quickly?"

"Constance deserves an escort. It is the least I can do."

Stephen winced and rubbed his brow. "I should have known you would try to do this. But you can not. Send her back with another escort. What difference does it make who takes Constance to Blackmoor? Why must it be you? I fear for your safety."

"I must make sure she is properly honored, that she receives a Christian burial." She frowned and cast a guilt-ridden gaze to the sunrise. After the ultimate betrayal of her vow last night, she was probably the last person who should be concerned about religious rites. "I've asked Ramsey to have a litter hitched to my mount. With the roads melting, it should be an easy enough journey."

Stephen relaxed his angry stance and pulled her into his

arms. Her silky hair was soft and tender against his chest. He wanted never to let her go. If she left now, he feared he would never see her again.

"Last night you begged me," he said and choked softly, "you begged me never to leave you. And now—"

"I'm not leaving you," she whispered, hugging him tightly. "Not in my heart. I swear I will return."

"I won't let you." He pulled her away and held her at arm's length. Fury and fear shadowed his eyes. "I will not allow you to leave. Do you hear me?"

But even as he issued the edict, he knew with a sinking feeling that she had already left. He could not force Katherine to ignore her sense of duty. If he were to deny her that, he would change the very heart of her. Though it maddened him like the fires of hell, it was her sense of duty that, in part, made her such a unique and treasured person.

" 'Twas only yesterday you threatened to send me packing," she said, not for a minute bowing to his bluster.

"But to Shelby Manor. You saw what Marlow did to Constance. I will not let him lay a hand on you."

"I've spoken with Ramsey," she said. "Sir Seeley returned from Blackmoor but an hour ago. It seems Marlow could not spare the midwife to help save the life of his wife and son. The bastard! But Seeley did return with news from the porter. My parents have arrived at the castle. As long as they are there, I will be safe. I'll tell them what has happened and arrange for Constance's burial, and then I'll return to Downing-Cross."

Stephen snorted a skeptical chuckle and knelt down to stroke the wolf, who sat on her haunches, patiently waiting for attention. "What makes you think they'll let you leave? Your father will never approve of your alliance with me now . . . now that I'm an accused murderer."

Katherine turned to him with a blank expression. "I doubt they'll want anything to do with me, Stephen. You were right. My honor is ruined. I'll probably be disowned. Then

I will be free to do as I wish."

Stephen blinked hard and looked away. He spotted a pebble in a puddle of water and cast it far out into a bed of nettles and bracken. Several sparrows took flight with worried chirps.

"Stephen, do not take heed what others think of my character. I knew this would happen when I left Blackmoor in your company. I no longer care what others say about me."

Stephen rose and folded his arms in an impatient gesture. "It is more serious than that, Kate. If something should happen to me, you will be without a name, a home, cast out from this world of men."

"This world of men be damned," she said with gentle strength. She cajoled him, tugging at his arms until his hard stance melted. "Don't you remember your prophecy? The night we first met, you promised I would want you without any title other than peasant or rogue. And you were right. It seems to me that should work both ways."

He allowed her to swing his arms back and forth as she clutched his hands in each of her own. She was a winsome filly, playful at the oddest times. He gave her a grudging smile.

"This makes me all the more determined to prove my innocence. One day everyone will call you Countess of Blackmoor. I swear it."

Katherine smiled and gave him a shrug. "I don't care what they call me. I just want to sleep in your arms again."

She nestled into his embrace, shutting out all the doubts, all the guilt. She had lived too long for others—for Georgie, for her parents. When she returned from Blackmoor, she would start pleasing herself.

"I will return," she said confidently, casting him a casual smile. "I promise."

"I will send Markham with you. He will wait in the village and escort you back. You are to stay no more than twenty-four hours. That will give you time to speak with your parents. If you don't return, I will come after you."

Katherine shook her head. "Nay, that is too dangerous. You don't have enough men."

"I will come after you," he repeated with an implacable glare.

CHAPTER SEVENTEEN

✠

A week churned by and Katherine still had not returned to Downing-Cross as promised. She had become a virtual prisoner in Blackmoor Castle. Just as Stephen had predicted, her parents were bent on ending their betrothal. Along with Countess Rosalind, Lord Gilbert and Lady Eleanor acted as if Katherine's honor were still intact. They pretended she had been lost in the woods after escaping the clutches of the murderous Sir Stephen. No matter how strongly Katherine railed against their pretense, she could not convince her parents that Marlow was the real murderer.

She pleaded for release, but her father and Marlow had become quite close in a short time, the blustering baron ever eager to please the new earl. Both decided it was in Katherine's best interests to stay within the bailey's confines until Stephen was captured, except for her daily walks with Lupa, and then she was closely watched by men-at-arms atop the battlements. She had been wise to bring her pet wolf. The creature made everyone cower, including Marlow.

The bastard had had the audacity to wear black following the return of his dead wife and son. Determined to play the aggrieved husband, he gave Katherine no argument in her preparations for a proper burial. After that mission was accomplished, Katherine spent hours at her chamber window, looking for any sign of Stephen. She knew he would be half-mad with worry after Markham returned to Downing-Cross without her. She just hoped Stephen would not attempt a premature siege. He didn't have the manpower to succeed.

Riddled with anxiety, she was strung as taut as a crossbow when her parents called her to their guest chamber for another family conference.

"Europa tells me you've spent most of your time in your chamber, Katherine," Lady Eleanor said. She motioned her daughter to join them at a table arrayed with a delicious spread of fish, cheese, fruit, and bread. Eleanor's purple cote-hardie flowed and shifted in concert with her stately gestures. She looked as regal as ever, her gray hair swept up beneath a delicate veil and wimple. "The rest has done you good. You don't look quite so pale."

" 'Tis outrage that stains my cheeks their robust hue," Katherine said with rancor. She reluctantly sat and stared in dismay at her father's gluttony. How could he wolf down a meal when she was still so miserable?

"All you needed was a little time to recover from recent events," Eleanor continued. "Does she not look well, Seymour?"

Lord Gilbert grunted as he chewed and looked up at his daughter. His eyes flowed with wary love. The frown wrinkling his bald head softened as he swallowed, and in a gruff voice that made his jowls wiggle, he said, "Of course. Hopefully you've also come to your senses."

"You know this is a mockery of justice," Katherine replied. "Stephen is innocent. I will not be silent on this matter until his honor is restored. Let me go to him. I beg of you."

The baron choked on a piece of manchet when the bread lodged deep in his throat. His cheeks billowed with each hacking cough. He pushed his trencher away and pounded his chest while his face turned red. Lady Eleanor slapped his back, but Katherine, knowing his penchant for dramatics, waited serenely until he had recovered.

"Justice has been done!" he shouted at last. "You were betrothed to a man who murdered his father. He should have been beheaded, not allowed to escape in the night. I should have known you would rally to his side. You have always backed impossible causes. Just to spite me!"

"This is more than defiance!" she shouted in return. "I am no longer a child, but a woman, and I have a mind of my own, Father. You know not what goes on in this castle. But I do. I know that Marlow murdered the earl."

Her parents fell ominously silent. Lady Eleanor nervously twisted her hands together while the baron chewed his protruding lower lip. Katherine blinked in confusion, and finally dread forced her to speak.

"You didn't summon me here to argue about Stephen, did you?" she whispered. She walked to the window and savored a breeze that billowed her veil. "Why have you sent for me?"

"We have found a more suitable mate for you," her father said with the confidence of one who has the final say. "You are to be betrothed. This time it will be legitimate."

Katherine turned and stared at them bitterly. "Nay, say it is not so. Tell me you have called me for any reason but that."

Lady Eleanor rose quickly and turned to the fire, covering her face with her hands.

"You are to marry someone of nobler station and character than Sir Stephen. Someone much more powerful," the baron said quietly.

"Who?"

"You will marry his brother, Marlow, the Earl of Blackmoor."

"What?" She gasped as if pummeled in the stomach and swooned, gripping a bedpost. The dreadful silence that followed was quickly filled with a hideous pounding in her head. "Oh, churl! You can not mean this."

"I am utterly resolved in this matter, my dear."

"How can you condone this match less than a week after Marlow buried his wife?" Katherine cried out.

"Marlow and I agree that it is best for him to beget an heir quickly, and so a traditional mourning period is impossible. If you bear him a son, Marlow's legacy will be secure even if his brother does him harm."

"He might have had an heir had he not beaten the unborn child's mother. And having cruelly dispensed with her, he now takes another to his loathsome bed. Only this time he takes his brother's wife."

"Wife," her father said. "You are not Stephen's wife, and a betrothal to such a scoundrel can not be considered valid. Unless . . ."

He turned to her with bulging eyes. "You did not . . . You have not given him your honor?"

"Aye," she spat out, twirling to face him defiantly. "I have given him my honor."

"S'Blood!" the baron cried, circling around the table. "I will beat you for your shame."

"Seymour, no!" cried Lady Eleanor.

"Fie on you," Katherine said with such force her father was stilled in his tracks. "You do not know the meaning of honor. You thrust me upon Stephen without thought of his reputation because of your own greed."

"I was greedy for you if greed it was," he protested.

"And now that I have fulfilled my duty to him, promising him my life, you would have me break my word because you have found one even more powerful and rich."

" 'Tis dishonor to wed a rogue," the baron argued.

"Honor be damned!" Katherine proclaimed. She pounded her chest. "The honor I hold in my heart is untouchable."

"Did you or did you not bed him, you impish little tart?" her father bellowed threateningly.

Dare she confirm the truth? It would put an end to her father's misbegotten scheme. But it would also put Stephen in even greater danger. Given the chance, her father would kill him.

"Nay," she whispered, turning frosty eyes on the aging baron. "My honor is intact."

After a moment of doubt, the baron nodded with satisfaction. "Good then. I have given my word to Lord Marlow that this marriage will come to pass."

"Your word?" Katherine laughed. "And where is your

word to me? God, how many more women will be impaled on the rusty words of their men? I have been bought and sold. You are no longer my father but my master."

"Lord Marlow will make a good husband. In time you will see that. I will encourage him to delay before the actual wedding takes place. Your mother and I will return in a month for the formal betrothal. We don't want to appear too hasty."

"He is a murderer and a bastard," Katherine whispered harshly, squeezing her eyes shut against the nausea that welled within.

"One day you will be able to admit Stephen committed a heinous deed. And then you will thank me for this."

Katherine staggered toward the door. The baron reached out for an embrace. She struck his arms aside and shot him a look of loathing, too numb to feel sorrow for the breach between them. What had happened? How had fate taken such a deplorable turn? she wondered, returning to her chamber in a complete daze.

Several days after her parents departed from Blackmoor Castle, Katherine combed her hair and gazed dejectedly out her chamber window. In the distance, she spied three young women beyond the castle battlements. They had thrust a tall pole into the ground. Wrapping it in garlands of lilies, they danced around the festive pole in full daylight, swinging their heads in a fashion more primal than prim. It struck a chord deep in Katherine, and she caught her breath, mesmerized by their pulsing moves.

"Those girls," she whispered, "they dance so strangely."

Rosemary came to her side and craned her neck for a glimpse. "Why, of course, milady. They dance around the Maypole."

"Maypole?" Katherine repeated as if she'd never heard the term.

Rosemary laughed at her. "Of course, milady, 'tis the eve of May."

"May Day!" Katherine exclaimed. "How could I have forgotten?"

"Aye, milady. Tomorrow we will all dance around the Maypole and ask the blessings of the tree-spirit. But tonight we will light the fires, for you know the witches will be a flyin'."

One of the girls danced with a limp, but her face was extraordinarily alive. Her joy transformed all physical limitations. She might have been the Goddess Brigid dancing in the woods for all her grace and ease. Katherine envied the girl her freedom.

"We'll all be a dancin' a fair bit wilder than that around the fires tonight, milady," Rosemary said, smiling at Katherine as she stared out the window with fascination. "Lord Marlow, he takes us up to the hill beyond on Beltaine . . . er, rather on the eve of May."

Rosemary nodded an apology for using the pagan name. But she did not shock Katherine, who knew many villeins still clung to the old pagan celebrations.

"Do you go to the woods and dance around the Beltaine fires with the others, Rosemary?"

"Aye . . . I went last season. I am now thirteen," she added, justifying her libidinous actions.

"Does everyone go?" Katherine could hardly believe that Earl James and Rosalind condoned pagan mating rights.

Rosemary shook her head. "Oh no, milady, ye know now the priests do not, nor the elders. 'Tis only for those who do not fear the witches."

"And you, Rosemary? You do not fear the witches will take your soul on such a night?"

"Never seen a witch, milady, but I have seen some lads to feast my eyes on." Rosemary blushed and giggled.

Katherine sighed, wondering what mischief the night would bring. Lupa howled in the distance with a fervency that should have warned her. The wolf seemed to sense the quiet rumblings of the earth, quickening into fertility.

When the sun sank and purple twilight descended, Marlow

demanded Katherine's presence in the bailey. Though she flatly refused in a most uncompromising fashion, Cramer and Bothwell appeared at her door. Swearing vengeance on them both, she dressed as modestly as she could for what would no doubt be a night of debauchery. Donning a wimple, which hid the evocative folds of her hair, she looked as austere as a nun.

"Lady," Marlow said when she mounted her horse, "you have not dressed properly for the evening's festivities. Tonight is for freedom, the kind of freedom found in the old ways."

"I am free to observe this strange custom of joining the commoners for pagan rites," she replied tartly. "That is the only freedom I shall need."

Marlow ignored her venomous tone and led the way through the portcullis. Though Katherine held her own reins, she could not even consider turning away from the procession. Fifteen other castle dwellers followed on horseback. Escape was impossible.

As they rode down the winding road, Marlow took in a deep breath.

"See how the fires glow," he shouted in the whipping wind, pointing to the village below. There was youthful glee in his voice, and he turned in his saddle to see if the others shared his eagerness. "Fertile seeds shall be planted tonight, I daresay."

Katherine was torn between her desire to forestall any misunderstanding, any belief on Marlow's part that she would take part in this wayward celebration, and her fascination with the festivities already in progress. Fires glittered and danced at the edge of the village, but the greatest fire of all, a bonfire on a nearby hill, leapt up toward the darkening heavens.

As they approached the inferno, Katherine inhaled the scent of burning clothes. Several revelers recklessly leapt through the blaze. When their tunics caught fire, others gathered to stamp out the flames. Marlow laughed, and Katherine gasped.

"Why such foolishness?" she inquired, frowning in curious horror. "Are they hoping they will burn to death?"

Marlow laughed again. "Nay, 'tis but a ritual. They pretend they are the ancient god of the pagans, Bel, who must burn for his love of the queen of the magic woods."

"Bel?" Katherine replied. "You mean Beelzebub? The devil?"

"Beltaine, Katherine," Marlow answered. "One man's devil is another man's savior. Do not be so prudish. These are just old customs. The villeins will not give them up entirely. I watched them with fascination when I was a boy. Nobility rarely knows such wild abandon. 'Twill do you good."

Katherine laughed bitterly. "And you accused Elizabeth of witchcraft."

Marlow shrugged. "It suited me then. What good is the power of the Church if you cannot jerk its rabid dogs with your own leash?"

They reined in their horses at the edge of an oak grove. Several dancers skipped into the trees to consummate their fervent dance. Katherine saw the passion in their eyes, glazed and wild. In the sweet wind that billowed about them, she sensed the lust, the desire to implant the seed, to thrust the Maypole into the fertile earth.

To Katherine's surprise, Marlow dismounted without even attending to her. It was just as well. With the help of a page, she slid off her horse and huddled in its shadow while Marlow sauntered over to the fire. Did she dare run now when no one would notice? But where would she go? And what would Marlow do in his rage when he learned she'd thwarted him? Better to hide in the crowd, she concluded.

Many of the revelers around her wore masks, but Katherine thought she recognized some of the kitchen serfs. In this strange ceremony, all were equal. Some danced openly, their eyes blurry with exultation. She stared in amazement, feeling like a child who had wandered where she did not belong. Even Katherine wasn't immune to the pulsing of the night, for something drew her toward the fire.

Marlow had already circled around to the other side of the blazing flames. He drank from a gourd, throwing back his head and sucking deeply. When he had quenched his thirst, he looked up with glazed eyes, and Katherine realized that the drink was drugged. No wonder the others danced with such freedom. Marlow started swaying to the primal voices of the crowd, flirting with a girl who could not have been more than fourteen.

It was an odd mixture of people—some of the village's richest merchants, knights from the castle, and the poorest churls all melded together without thought of status.

"Have you ever seen such a sight? By my troth, I'd wager not at Shelby Manor." The familiar voice rustled against the nape of her neck like a warm summer breeze.

"Stephen," she whispered, low enough that no one else might hear. She nearly fainted with relief and desire, for his hot breath against her neck snapped her back into the memory of their lovemaking.

"Do not turn around. My face is covered. Marlow will not suspect me."

A drunk man stumbled at Katherine's feet. To avoid him, she took a step back into Stephen's arms. She waited for the figure to rise, but instead he began rubbing his groin in ever quickening strokes, his organ shockingly exposed to the night air.

Katherine stared in disbelief, reeling with embarrassment and forbidden arousal. Stephen's hard body set her skin ablaze; her head swooned with a tumult of carnal images. At last, clarity returned when the drunk man grunted his satisfaction.

Katherine turned away, overwhelmed, stumbling a few steps toward the grove. Stephen followed close behind. She gasped when she turned, for he was cloaked in a brown hood and cape. His eyes peered from behind a mask that curled up into antlers carved out of wood. He depicted the mythological stag, Actaeon, consort mate of the moon goddess, Brigid. He was breathtakingly handsome.

"Queen of the woods," he said, "I am your servant, your stag. I have come to protect you from this mad scene of debauchery. 'Tis not fitting for a woman bound for the nunnery."

She gave him an ironic smile. "I am afraid our own night of debauching circumvented that destination."

He stepped to within inches of her moonlit profile. His lips hovered near hers. "Do you regret it?"

Katherine moaned and inhaled his sweet breath. "How can I regret the greatest moment of peace and contentment I've ever known? Except, of course, for the fact that now my soul may burn in Hell an eternity."

In an instant, Stephen realized the ambivalence she had lived with since their night of lovemaking. There was no going back, no forgetting the passion, no hope for a chaste life. And every subsequent kiss was a tiny sin, a small breach of her oath to Georgie. Yet even as he understood her lingering turmoil, he longed to sin again. And again. And again.

"Kiss me," he whispered.

She obliged. Skin melted against skin, flesh scorched, tongues soothed.

At last he withdrew. Knowing there was much to do before he fulfilled his mission, the more practical side of Stephen Bartingham took charge.

"Stay at the castle a few more days, Kate."

"Nay, Stephen," she whispered desperately, tugging at his arms. "My parents say I must marry Marlow. I tried to escape. If you only knew how impossible it was. Believe me."

"Hush. Shhhh," he said, smoothing the frown from her forehead. "I understand. I know what you were up against. I do not blame you, Katherine. I admire you for your courage. I know about Marlow's plans, and I have one of my own that should solve everything."

She looked at him with a mixture of love and skepticism.

"And are you also an alchemist with the ability to turn base metal into gold?"

"I think it best if you are ignorant of my scheme. Just trust me. You will be watched at all times. I swear he will not hurt you."

"Please tell me your plans," she whispered urgently.

"Nay, you must trust me."

With a sigh of exasperation, she crossed her arms and tilted her head to one side. "Have I ever remarked on your stubborn streak, Sir Guy? 'Tis as deep as an ocean."

"While you, of course, are as malleable as clay."

Friendly sarcasm rang in his voice, but she ignored it. "If I can escape, I will search for the will and medallion myself."

His reply was swift and emphatic. "Nay, you will not. I forbid it, Kate. 'Twould be too dangerous for you. My men continue to search. If the evidence is there, they will find it."

Doubt glared in her dubious frown.

"Come hither, milady." He inched closer until he loomed over her. In the moonlight, the blue shadow of his horns fell larger than life against the surrounding trees. He pulled off her wimple, unbound her hair, and kissed her alabaster neck. "One last kiss before I dash into the night."

When his lips descended, she shivered. With a groan she succumbed to the sensuous swirl of his tongue. He wove his fingers through the silky skein of spun gold that fell down her back. Tightening his grip, he gently pulled her head back, exposing her neck to the moonlight. He licked and kissed his way up to her lips. His insistent tongue darted into her mouth, and with her last shred of resistance, so ingrained she did not even know what she was doing, she pounded his chest with a feeble blow, but her lips never left his.

She hated him for making her want him beyond all reason. But it wasn't hate that compelled her to wrap her arms around his neck. He knew nothing about the courage it took to open her heart to him. Surely she would pay for her broken vow. And yet . . .

Stephen clutched her soft bottom and pulled her to his groin, his hips twisting around and around, leading her in a slow dance. They gasped as their need built—a desire for sexual union provocatively forbidden by the clothes that separated them.

"Your body is tense," he whispered as she pressed her cheek to his. "You were afraid. You did not trust that I would be near. I told you I would come after you."

Katherine groaned. " 'Tis not distrust, but fear of . . . of losing . . . losing . . . oh . . ."

She arched against him as a spasm of pleasure bolted through her. The moon throbbed with a blue glow. The earth smelled of fecundity—black, rich earth bursting with probing shoots, all the earth's regeneration working on their senses.

"Katherine!" Marlow shouted. He was barely ten feet away, judging by the sound of his voice. "Damn it, where are you?"

Katherine recoiled from Stephen's arms and rubbed her swollen lips.

"Marlow," she whispered and watched with agony as Stephen slipped into the darkness with an enigmatic smile. Twigs snapped beneath his retreating footsteps. Giddy laughter swelled in the distance. Katherine's mouth went dry, and smoke from the fire burned her eyes. Touching up her hair, she turned to greet Marlow's wrath.

"Katherine," Marlow said churlishly, "what are you doing out here?"

By the sound of his slurred speech, she knew he was still drugged. "I . . . I wanted to get away from the noise, Lord Marlow. This fete is not to my liking."

He stepped forward, and Katherine veered back, retreating from his foul breath.

He raised a hand as if to argue, but then his face lost all expression. He belched loudly, and then collapsed to the ground, unconscious.

Katherine stared in astonishment. Watching him warily, she held her breath, waiting for his resurrection. When it was clear Marlow had passed out, she shuddered and laughed in disbelief. Escaping to the other side of the grove, Katherine waited, hoping for Stephen's return. But when he did not come back, she reluctantly returned to the castle with several other weary revelers.

Stephen had not abandoned her as she had once feared he might. She was not alone. He had a plan, and for the first time since she'd left Downing-Cross, she was filled with hope for their future.

And yet Marlow wasn't the only one standing in the way of her happiness with Stephen. There was another. The ghost of a man. Georgie. Somehow Katherine had to bury him once and for all.

CHAPTER EIGHTEEN

✠

Two days after the bizarre Beltaine celebration, while dining in the Great Hall, Marlow pulled Katherine into his arms and kissed her in front of guests. Katherine was so stunned she did nothing but stare at him with trembling disbelief. Then she wiped her lips as if she'd been kissed by a serpent and quietly exited the Hall, seeking refuge in her chambers. Her reaction angered Marlow, but she cared naught. From that moment, she feared anew for her safety.

Adding to her sense of foreboding, Lupa had been missing for several days. Katherine couldn't overcome a sinister hunch that her wolf was in danger.

The next afternoon, determined to search for her pet, she ordered her mare saddled. When the porter refused to let her pass over the drawbridge, she argued with him, but finally agreed to an escort. She and two guards had just mounted and started away when Marlow and his hunting party pranced through the portcullis. His cheeks had been burned by the spring sun; a quiver full of bloody arrows hung across his back.

"Are you going riding, my beloved?" he called out and halted near her. His horse snorted and pawed the ground.

"Aye, Marlow," Katherine said coldly, fussing with her reins. "I have not seen Lupa in two or three days, and so I thought I would go fetch her. It is a beautiful day for a ride anyway."

"Lupa," Marlow said with a scowl. "That wretched beast. I shall go with you."

"Nay!" Katherine fairly shouted. She cast her eyes downward. "Rather, it is not necessary. I will be well guarded."

"Oh, but you are not a prisoner, dear lady. No need for guards. Let me escort you. I believe I saw a silver creature loping through the far fields while we were returning from our hunt. I will lead you there. The way is not familiar to you, I'm sure."

He did not wait for her response, but waved the others away, shouting a few orders to his falconer. Katherine hesitated, then heeled her horse, taking the lead until Marlow caught up.

Indeed, Marlow led her on a path through unfamiliar territory she would have had difficulty remembering. They passed through a meadow filled with heather. The sun beat down on Katherine's cheeks, and she was soon lulled by the sound of horse hooves swishing through sprigs of grass as birds chirped and fluttered from tree to tree.

They exchanged no words. In the silence she could almost pretend she was alone, her aversion to Marlow temporarily forgotten. But then his deep voice shattered her sense of peace.

"I could love you, I do believe."

The words came to her as if in a fog. She thought perhaps she had imagined them, for his tone was uncharacteristically warm and earnest. She glanced sideways, taking in the sight of the nobleman, and it was clear his intent was straightforward.

"You think ill of me," he continued, looking more like Stephen in the sunlight than he deserved.

"You disgust me," Katherine said, looking away from Marlow.

"I am not so terrible, really. With a lady of your quality, your beauty, I might find love to soften my rough nature."

Katherine's every muscle tensed. She clutched the reins until her knuckles turned white. She could more easily tolerate Marlow when he was cruel. It was embarrassing seeing this false man humble himself for an emotion of which he knew so little.

"I am but the daughter of a minor baron. Therefore, I am hardly a lady of much quality," she said.

Marlow shrugged. "Your physical beauty far outweighs your standing, my dear. Do you think you could find it in your heart to love me?"

"Nay, I could not. It is impossible," she answered without pause.

Silence fell between them. They rode beneath a cluster of beech trees, young leaves rustling against the gray bark. They ducked low to avoid being thrown from their mounts by low-hanging branches. Soon they were again in a vast stretch of heather fields.

"I do not believe you," he pressed. "Why can you not learn to love me?"

Katherine stared at him, then cleared her throat, struggling for words. "You are an evil man, Marlow. I account you responsible for Constance's death, and that of your son, who would have lived had you not beaten his mother. You murdered your father. And you have taken from me the only man I could love. Do you wish me to find more reasons than that?"

She did not speak bitterly, rather plainly, as the truth is often spoken.

They came to the pinnacle of a sloping mound and simultaneously reined in their horses, both struck by the beauty of the endless purple and green hills that stretched out before them. Katherine breathed deeply the sharp, fresh air. Her circlet and veil whipped away from her head, and she let them fly into the wind. She could almost imagine she was free in a place such as this.

"The wind blows with a chill," Marlow remarked, nearly shouting to be heard against the whipping gales of air. "Always a chill, come summer, winter, or spring. My bones ache with it now, Katherine. I thought the Pestilence would take me. I thought it was some divine retribution. But it left me here knowing that God has no plan, no justice, which spurred me on with my quest to grasp all that should not have been mine. I even have you now, but it seems like not such a sweet prize unless you want me in kind."

"I will never want you," she shouted. Locks of hair flew into her eyes, her mouth. Pulling them away, she added, "Never. I spurn you. Let me go. Let me have Stephen."

He acted as if he hadn't heard, but his open mood vanished. "I will take you to see Lupa now."

She didn't understand his change in temperament, his suddenly rutted brow, but she followed as he cantered down the hill. Then it became clear. Lupa lay dead in the grass, an arrow sticking up from her heart. Blood stained her silver coat.

"Churl!" Katherine cried. It was a ghastly sight, and she drew her hand to her heart. "Slain!"

"With my arrow." He watched her with sick humor winking in his eyes, a smile slashed across his face. "After the Beltaine celebration, I tried to visit you in your chamber. That damned wolf growled outside your door like a jealous lover. I couldn't get in. She won't protect you anymore, Katherine. Nothing will protect you now."

She felt as if her very soul had been felled. This animal represented all that was wild, free, untamed, instinctual. A savage beast tamed by love.

"I should never have brought her to this castle of death." Katherine spoke in a daze; a stream of tears streaked her dusty cheeks. But then her sorrow turned to rage.

"Heathen!" she cried. She struck out at him and pounded his arm with her fist. "You devil. Must you kill all that you touch?"

Marlow winced and then laughed hollowly. "So you may curse me on our wedding night, which will be tomorrow."

Katherine gasped and halted. "Tomorrow?"

"Aye, I have been too patient, agreeing to your mother's entreaties to be gentle. No more. You are mine. Let no one doubt it. Least of all you."

"Tomorrow?" Katherine turned her back to Lupa and whimpered softly. "Oh, dear Lupa."

Marlow fetched her reins and led her away. As they retreated, Katherine twisted around in her saddle. She watched as the stiff creature became smaller and smaller.

Europa prayed that no one would notice as she slipped out the postern. The castle guards attended some arrival at the main gate, and so she hurried with waddling steps toward the village. Even if she were caught, she was certain no one would question the items she had taken from the kitchen, bundled in a cloth sack, clutched to her breasts like a precious baby: flour, berries, and wool from the storage room. Surely these would not be missed. Not to worry, she thought, if she could just get beyond sight of the castle.

By the time she reached the village, she was bathed in perspiration; her cheeks flushed scarlet in the hot afternoon sun. Now, where was he waiting? She wiped her brow with the edge of the sack. The village stable, that was what the messenger had said.

Europa lost herself in the shadows of the village stalls and bustling shops. She nodded to those she knew and slipped nonchalantly into the stable. Unlike the castle's, this structure was tall, with an open entrance, a row of stalls, and in the back a workroom with a high plaster ceiling, where the farrier shod horses.

Hugh, the owner, noticed Europa when she entered, but he did not greet her. A fixed expression veiled his emotions, and he waved toward the back room.

Europa understood. He could not acknowledge his complicity, but he would direct her to her destination. She passed the neighing horses. The smell of leather and manure filled her with a comfortable feeling. When she reached the back room, she squinted, for it was poorly lit, save for a shaft of light that filtered from the roof above. Then Stephen stepped into that light, and Europa's heart leapt with joy.

"Sir Guy!" She dropped the sack and threw herself into his open arms.

"Europa, I knew you'd not fail me."

She pulled away and laughed a snorting guffaw. "Nay, I'd never fail you, milord. I have everything you asked for."

"Good." Stephen smiled down with affection and hope. "How is Katherine?"

"She holds steady, Sir Guy. But Marlow threatens a wedding . . . tomorrow!"

Stephen nodded and flushed a deeper bronze. "So I have heard. That is why I called you. Let us get to work."

Stephen retrieved a stool and sat squarely in the beam of light.

"We'll work on the face first, milord," Europa said, humming as she bustled, sorting through the items in her sack. "The berries first, me thinks."

She pulled out a handful of dried blueberries and mashed them in one hand until they crumbled. She mixed them with water in a tin cup. "Tilt your head back, Sir Guy."

Stephen did as he was told, feeling like a child once again at the hands of his old nursemaid.

"Hold steady, milord," she snapped at him when he moved his head. "Hold steady."

Silently, Stephen obeyed. Europa dipped two pudgy fingers in the purple mixture and made several swipes under each eye. "You'll want to look haggard now, milord. Like the blood has been sucked out of you from all yer hard work."

The air quickly dried the berry juice, staining Stephen with dark circles beneath his eyes.

Europa drew back to admire her work. "By Beelzebub, you look a fright already!"

"If the artist took time to praise every brush stroke, Europa, he'd not finish before his subject died. Hurry on, you old tart."

Europa laughed loudly and boxed him on the ear. "Watch yer mouth, my boy, or I'll put you in the stocks."

Next she withdrew a bowl filled with flour and salt. She fetched water from a bucket and stirred the mixture. When it was pasty, she pulled out a vial of saffron and sprinkled a bit of the orange powder. Then came the rest of the berries. When folded together, the mixture became a hideous color, purple and yellow, the shade of a wicked bruise, or a scar that would not heal.

"Lean back, Sir Guy," Europa instructed and plastered a healthy portion on his clean-shaven face. She painted the thick substance up to one ear and down the cheek to his chin. Then she folded a wad of wool. "Stuff this in yer mouth."

Stephen did as he was told, the wool distorting his cheek and speech.

Next came his clothing. Stephen had brought one of the priest's brown robes stolen the night he escaped. Now died black, it would disguise him yet again. Europa lifted the long gown over his head. She tossed him an eye patch she had sewn, and then she stuffed a large ball of wool under his gown at one shoulder. A perfect hunchback. Quickly, she sewed it in place.

By the time they finished, the sun had sunk past the window. After straining to admire her creation, Europa fetched a torch. When she returned, she stopped abruptly.

With his hood drawn over his forehead, Stephen had risen. What little of his face she could see in the shadows of the hood was a frightening sight—bruised and scarred skin, gaunt shadows beneath his eyes. His naturally tall stature had been transformed into a stooped, crippled figure.

"*Bonjour, madame,*" he mumbled, his cheek confined by the plaster scar. "*Mon Dieu,* but you looked frightened."

Europa exhaled at the perfection of his French accent. His many years in Brittany had served him yet again.

"Who are you, now? Why have you come to Blackmoor Castle?" Europa prodded.

Stephen chuckled a bitter sound. "Long ago I was a Cathar, a deacon in that holy sect the Church now calls heretical. I was a holy man. I believed that there were two gods—one who created the soul, and the other the devil, who created the body and all its evils. And I believed in reincarnation. That was a blessing for me, for I was not a happy man. I had been poor and angry with the Catholic Church."

Stephen limped forward, slowly transforming himself into his character. The anger he felt for Marlow spurred his imagination for the angry character he had to portray convincingly.

"Then the Inquisition in France purged our religious community. Burned, hundreds of them. Because we did not believe in the Roman Church."

Stephen pointed to his shoulder. "I was torn on the rack. My face was dipped in boiling water. My legs were stretched until they snapped. And then I confessed. I confessed my heresy, and I paid my penance—a pilgrimage to the holy lands. When I returned, a useless, broken body, the Dominicans had mercy on me and made me one of their own."

Stephen smiled a wicked, obsequious smirk. "Now I am a believer. LaMort is my name. I am the inquisitor, come from France to sniff out all heresies. I have come to make others suffer as I have suffered."

Stephen shivered with these, his final words. Europa stared at him, dumbfounded, while he limped away.

At dusk, Stephen road slowly through the village of Blackmoor, winding his way past timber and plaster houses and market stalls, following the familiar stone road that led up to Blackmoor Castle.

Lingering rays of light painted thatched roofs with burnished orange. The clink of shod hooves from his horse and that of his two French companions echoed from house to stall. Dirty children laughed in the street; old women bustled them indoors, stopping to look with fear at Stephen as he passed. He recognized many of their faces, but they did not recognize him. The villagers, who had known Stephen as the good Sir Guy of Blackmoor, only saw an ominous representative of the Inquisition, though they could not have

named him such. Soon they would call him the dark man of
the cross, come to stir trouble, come to torture in the name
of God.

Stephen carried the official Tribunal crest, hastily painted
on a banner he held in one hand. His two attendants carried
crosses of gold as well as the French flag. The Inquisition had
never invaded the domain of the Church in England. It had
ruled most cruelly on the Continent. But now it had arrived,
or so Stephen would have them all believe. He would have
preferred to have Ramsey and Geoffrey at his side, but it
was best they wait at Downing-Cross. Their presence would
have raised suspicion. Darbonnet's French warriors would
suffice.

When Stephen and his men reached the moat at Blackmoor
Castle, he called out to the guards, first in French and then
in broken English, performing his best French accent. After
a series of mumbles and shouts, guards lowered the drawbridge, and they entered the bailey.

The first test of his disguise came when Piers Townley,
Marlow's steward, came to greet them.

"What, ho!" Townley called out, barking like a rabid dog.
He was a stocky man who would sooner run a man through
with his broadsword than greet him with good cheer. "Who
comes to see the earl?"

Townley stopped short when he spied Stephen's hideous
scars. He grimaced and made the sign of the cross.

"Monsieur," Stephen replied, sneering at the steward, "I
am an official sent by the French Inquisitor. LaMort is my
name."

Stephen dismounted and limped toward Townley.

"I have been sent upon command of the most pious Pope
Clement IV himself, ruler of the Holy Empire in Avignon,
to inquire into heresy and sorcery on this dark island of
Britain."

The steward was speechless and regarded Stephen suspiciously. Stephen knew not whether it was doubt in Townley's
eyes, recognition, or merely hatred for the Church.

"I have heard nothing about the Inquisition on this island," Townley said at last, mustering false courage in the presence of the hideous LaMort. "The archbishop reigns supreme here."

"No longer!" Stephen shouted, pushing the gruff man aside and surveying the castle as if he would soon claim it as his own. "There have been reports of heresy here, pagan worship, and I have been given the authority to imprison the guilty. Those convicted will be handed over to the secular courts to be burned. Now, take me to your master."

Townley hesitated, this time with genuine fear, and then motioned reluctantly for LaMort to follow.

Stephen barely concealed a whoop of joy over his success. He still doubted the wisdom of his charade, for the greatest test was yet to come, when he confronted his family. Stephen's only qualm in this moment of exhilaration came from the fervency with which he had assumed his role. Was there darkness lurking beside the goodness in his soul? A good as well as an evil creator within, as the Cathars believed? Or perhaps a bit of the blackness he so condemned in Marlow? He shook off these thoughts and proceeded to the interview with his brother.

He was taken directly to the solar, where Marlow sat with Cramer.

"Earl Marlow," Townley said, bowing low, "the French Inquisition has sent a representative to preside here. His name is LaMort."

Stephen nodded, struggling not to smile as Marlow rose in obvious confusion and disbelief. Marlow's cheeks twitched as he tried to hide his revulsion at LaMort's disfigurement.

"The Inquisition?" Marlow said, waving away Cramer and the steward. He turned back to the fire. "By the Mass, this is unheard of. The Inquisition has not set foot in our country."

"Until now," Stephen replied, helping himself to a goblet of mead. "Heresy is a cancerous blight that is spreading to every corner of the world. You should get down on your knees and thank us for coming to save you from such corruption."

"Indeed," Marlow said evenly, weighing his responses to this disturbing turn of events.

"*Mais oui*," Stephen continued. "Unless, of course, you have some sin to hide."

"Sin?"

Stephen gave him a disfigured smile. "Some little heresy? Of course, the greatest heresy of all is to deny the supremacy of the Inquisition. Even the Pope's legates would burn for that, I'm afraid. You see, my lord earl, I have suffered every indignity you might imagine in my lifetime, and I'll have no more of it. You won't turn me away, or I'll invent tortures for the people here not even imagined by the Tribunal in France."

Marlow stared blankly, and then he nodded. "I understand, LaMort. I've seen the work of the Inquisition in France, and it chills my blood. You are welcome at Blackmoor tonight. My guards will happily escort you to Canterbury in the morning."

"But I have reached my destination," Stephen pronounced, laughing in triumph. His voice quieted to a purr. "At least for the moment. I wish to inquire into the religious devotion of you and your vassals. You need fear nothing if you have been true to the Church."

"I am master here, LaMort," Marlow said in a low voice. "I like it not that you enter my castle in this way."

"Many of the condemned heretics are women, Blackmoor," Stephen rasped through his twisted mouth. "Condemned of witchcraft. But many are also men such as yourself, noble in every way except for fidelity to the Church. I myself have ordered the torture of French noblemen who denied their heresies, and then charged them for the food they ate in prison. When they refused to confess their evil deeds—"

"Perhaps they were innocent!"

"—then they were put to death by fire. Their lands were forfeited to the Church. Precedent has been set many times over. You have worked hard to maintain your position in these troublesome times, *n'est-ce pas?*"

Marlow said nothing.

"Do not throw it away so easily now, Earl Marlow. All I demand is your full cooperation."

"For the moment." Marlow grudgingly acquiesced. "But I will invite the Archbishop of Canterbury to join us immediately. We will see what he has to say about the Inquisition's intrusion in England."

Even though he was consumed by his character, Stephen realized the implications of Marlow's astute move. Even if the archbishop believed Stephen's charade, he would condemn the Inquisition's arrival. How much time would Stephen have before word reached Canterbury? At least a fortnight.

Stephen nodded confidently. "Call on the archbishop. I'm sure he will acknowledge my supremacy. Meanwhile, my men will search the castle for any unusual signs and occurrences. I expect no intervention."

He stared hard at Marlow with his one patchless eye, and when no final argument came, he left the solar, breathing a sigh of relief. But he knew he must work fast. His time was precious.

CHAPTER NINETEEN

✠

That evening, Stephen limped into the Great Hall, unnoticed at first. He instructed his French companions to sup with the other knights feasting at trestle tables. His warriors were loyal and strong, and Stephen was glad to have them on his side. If his gambit failed, they would not recoil from the cold hilt of their swords.

"*Ne parlez pas avec les autres. Regardez* Marlow. Do not venture far from me," Stephen ordered.

He scanned the room and realized how much had changed since his father's death. Laughter enlivened the air, but it rang hollow. Though Marlow sat at the center of the head table, with Katherine reluctantly at his side, his seat might have been empty for all the dignity he brought to it.

Katherine barely ate from her trencher and did not smile when the others broke into laughter. Stephen felt for her and blamed himself for her present misery. At least she would be safe now that he had returned.

He entered with a flourish, limping and nodding imperiously to the dozens who looked up in awe. Marlow motioned the minstrel to cease his gentle strumming, and an awkward silence filled the Hall.

"*Bonsoir,* Earl Blackmoor," Stephen said, bowing low. "Is there a place for me at your table this evening?"

Marlow rose slowly. "LaMort, I would not think of offending a member of the Inquisition."

A chorus of whispers swept through the room like wind. Everyone strained for a better look at Stephen, eyeing him with hostility and suspicion. Katherine looked up sharply in blatant disapproval.

"As I promised, I have sent an inquiry to the Archbishop of Canterbury regarding your arrival. Meanwhile, you may join us at our table."

Stephen stared intently at Katherine but she did not recognize him. Yet he caught her curiously observing him throughout the meal.

Stephen sat by his mother and Robert. As the older couple shared a bowl of broth, Stephen watched Rosalind closely. Her hair was now almost entirely gray. That manic quality she had once had, controlling and conniving, was gone. There was a pall in her faded blue eyes, an ennui with life.

"LaMort," Rosalind said, turning her head in his direction, "you come at a propitious time."

Stephen cocked one eyebrow. His mother drank heavily. She quaffed from her pewter goblet and motioned for refills faster than her dinner guests.

"The carcass of nobility is rotting, and the stench overcomes me," Rosalind said.

No doubt it was the wine that spoke, but Stephen was taken aback. He had not heard his mother speak so openly in years. Perhaps it was because she thought him a stranger.

"What sickness has killed the beast, madame?"

"Greed . . . lust . . ." She blinked slowly, her eyes focusing on Robert. She took a drink of mead and nearly missed the table when she set her goblet down. A splash of scarlet alcohol spilled on the table. "How often that which we crave we want not when we have it."

"Madame, it sounds as though remorse has loosed your tongue."

Her eyes shot toward him, carefully scrutinizing his features, and momentarily Stephen thought he had gone too far.

"What do you know of remorse, LaMort?" she said at last, laughing cynically. "Everyone has heard tales of the Inquisition. You are merciless in your hunt for heresy and witchcraft. Do you not regret even one single condemnation?"

Stephen looked up from his trencher and caught a glimpse of Katherine sitting at the far end of the table. She watched him, not with recognition, but with intense curiosity. He tried to say something to her with a subtle look, but it was impossible—she was too far, too many gawkers still watched him, and subtleties were lost beneath his disguise. He turned back to his mother.

"Madame, regrets will eat at your heart and soul. You must confess whatever sins you may have committed."

Rosalind blinked back tears and sipped from her goblet. Placing the chalice on the table, she smiled with great vulnerability. "God already knows my sins, LaMort. And I will burn in Hell for them. I do not need to confess them."

"*Dieu de Dieu!* But that in itself is heresy!" Stephen turned to her with forced indignation. "You must acknowledge that the vicars of the Church are the only ones who can speak directly to God. You must confess your sins through the priest. In France, people have been burned at the stake for lesser blasphemies than that, I must tell you."

"Burned at the stake?" Rosalind replied. "That might be a welcome reprieve to the burning embers of regret that singe my entrails."

She meant it, Stephen knew, and he felt a pang of deep empathy. After Katherine left Downing-Cross, Stephen had spent many hours contemplating recent tragic events. At first he was filled with bitterness, even hatred, for the evils his mother had condoned. But presently he saw her in a different light. Nothing lasts forever—no sin, no thought, no hatred—and now she was changed. How many years had she held the image of Robert in her heart, subtly turning away her own noble husband? Now that he was dead, she saw the tarnish in Robert's armor; she felt the chink in his mail. This new knowledge tore asunder all that she had lived for—lust, want, greed for a shimmering dream that vanished on the waking. Stephen pitied her, for he was sure only death would expunge her sins in her own mind.

"Madame, we must not impale ourselves on our own sharp judgments. Leave condemnation to our Lord in Heaven. 'Tis not ours to judge," Stephen said softly, placing his hand over hers. He turned away from her look of astonished gratitude, hoping that no one had heard his words of consolation.

By now the others were leaving the Great Hall. The meal had ended. Stephen watched with longing as Katherine made her graceful exit, looking back at him only once. Then Marlow pulled him aside.

"LaMort," he said, "I have my doubts that the archbishop will condone your arrival in England."

"It is not his to condone," Stephen interjected. "The Inquisition has a higher power than that of the archbishop."

Marlow smiled. "Time will tell that, my friend. Since you are here, however, I think you should know of something suspicious I found in Countess Rosalind's chamber."

Stephen frowned, for he knew in an instant that his brother was up to some betrayal. "Countess Rosalind? You mean your mother? I have not once heard you refer to her thus."

Marlow shrugged his shoulders. "Does the Inquisition care what I call the woman who gave me birth?"

"I must be aware of all things, my lord earl," Stephen answered. He had broached too personal a topic. Shifting his weight, he recovered. "It is in small things that great sins are found."

"Rosalind is my mother, LaMort, but she is also an embittered, powerful woman . . ."

" . . . who interferes with your absolute control of this earldom?" Stephen offered, giving him a conspiratorial smile.

Marlow was too shrewd to respond. Instead, he pulled out a small figurine of a woman covered with many breasts. At her feet lay a crescent moon.

"I found this pagan idol in her chamber," Marlow continued. "At Beltaine, I believe she went into the village and participated in pagan rights some of the churls and minions still cling to."

Stephen turned sharply, laying a hand upon a cold pillar. He could not believe his brother's treachery against the woman who had adored him for so long. He frowned against the shadows on the floor and then faced Marlow.

"This is a grave accusation," he said, hoping to frighten Marlow out of the falsehood.

Marlow shook his head sadly. "I am as shocked as you. But I am a pious Christian and do not wish to tolerate any heresies or idolatries in this castle."

Stephen nodded. "There is no time to waste. We will begin a trial immediately. In the meantime, I must investigate this charge. I want to question every servant and vassal in this earldom regarding Countess Rosalind."

Marlow's eyes narrowed and his skin blanched. "Is that necessary? In France, you charge a man on someone else's word, and then you torture until that man confesses. Is there need for an investigation?"

"Our entrance to this land must be gentler. I would like others also to condemn her before burning."

"Burning?" Marlow whispered. A look of regret quickly flashed across his face and then was gone.

"It is the law, Lord Marlow. The Pope has stipulated that no blood should be shed at the hands of the inquisitors, and therefore burning at the stake is the only method of execution allowed. Then no blood is spilled. And burn she must if she will not confess her heresy. If others see her sin, they will concur with the punishment. An investigation only confirms your charge. Unless there is something you are hiding also?"

"Nay," Marlow said slowly. "Nay, I have nothing to hide. You question whomever you wish. There may be others you'll want to investigate as well. We've a flock of sinful women in the village."

"Make a list for the investigation. Then have your steward announce Lady Rosalind's trial. We'll begin in the morning." Stephen bowed crisply and limped away, inwardly rejoicing. Now he would have access to every member of the household. It would be natural to ask about Earl James, even the will, as he investigated charges against the countess.

By the time he reached his guest chamber, Stephen's steps were slow and his head pounded. He felt the exhaustion of a suspenseful day. But, more than that, his heart was heavy. He forced the reluctant door to his chamber and, once inside, leaned wearily against the door frame. What had come over him so suddenly? Perhaps it was sadness over Marlow's cruel turnabout. To accuse the countess of idolatry. What treachery! He knew Katherine would be equally appalled.

How noble and dignified she looked tonight, he thought with pride as he paced in aimless circles. And then he halted, overwhelmed by a profound realization. He loved her. When they had made love, they truly became one in a way Stephen had only heard about in romances sung by daft minstrels. Seeing her at a distance tonight, he had enough perspective to recognize the depth of feelings only faintly glimpsed until now. His heart ached with the sweetest love. So why was he melancholy? Wasn't love what he had been searching for?

Stephen tugged irritably at the mantle choking his neck. He would have given anything to rip off his constraining costume, but he had to wait until servants brought in his bath. Europa was overseeing the task in the kitchen. It wouldn't be long before the tub arrived. He brushed back his hood and removed his eye patch. Sitting in a chair, he kicked up his heels on the stone hearth, finally recognizing the reason for his discontentment.

He had caused Katherine so much turmoil, so much grief. For her, the very act of loving him required sacrifice. When all was said and done—when the castle was reclaimed, when he was recognized as earl, when they were finally married— would it have been worthwhile for her? Would he look in her eyes and see happiness, or longing for a choice she was never allowed to make? He had determinedly ignored her desire to fulfill her deathbed vow. Now he wondered if he'd been fair.

If he loved her, he would let her choose her own fate. Like the peregrine he had impetuously loosed from the jesses as a lad, before the bird was properly tamed. It earned him a whipping from the falconer, but he would never forget the poignant screech the falcon made when flying through the trees to freedom. It had been worth the beating.

Tears and laughter came to him at once. He leaned forward and rested his arms on his knees, staring at a misshapen stone glowing on the hearth. He bit his lip until blood mingled with his salty tears.

"A stoic man does not cry but for love and death," his father had said. "He'll cry once at love found and then at love lost, with all its shattered innocence . . ."

"Oh, Katherine, I love you so," he whispered to the shadows.

"Milord," Europa called from the corridor.

Stephen wiped the trail of tears from his cheeks with callused fingers and replaced his hood and eye patch.

"Come in!" he barked.

Europa threw open the door, making way for a line of servants carrying his bath.

Two men who tended the kitchen fires hauled in a wooden tub not quite large enough for Stephen to stretch out his legs in, and placed it before the fire. A half dozen scullions followed with huge pots of steaming water. They emptied their loads into the tub, and moments later another string of servants from the kitchen entered with even more hot water.

Stephen chuckled to himself. Europa had made sure the castle staff treated him as though he were a visiting king. Marlow would be furious when he learned more water had to be heated for his bath.

"Guard the door, will you?" he asked her after the others filed out.

The nursemaid gave him a wink and a nod as she exited. "As you wish, LaMort."

At last he could undress. It felt wonderful to cast off his suffocating disguise. He tossed the eye patch to the ground and crumbled the plaster molding his cheek, flinging the remnants into the fire. When he was naked, he turned to the wooden tub and sank into the warm haven.

Outside his chamber, Katherine crept softly to the door. She hugged Europa and motioned for silence, pressing a forefinger to her lips. The old woman nodded, agreeing to secrecy, and raised the door latch, entering alone.

"Europa?" Stephen queried tensely.

"Aye, milord, 'tis just me. Go about your bath."

Stephen looked over his shoulder at the bustling nursemaid. "Did you bring me a sponge and soap?"

"Of course, milord. They're on the chair. I'll fetch them."

When Stephen turned back toward the fire, humming quietly to himself, Europa motioned for Katherine to enter. The younger woman grabbed the requested items and placed them in Stephen's outstretched hand.

Europa, grinning broadly, ducked out of the room without a sound. Katherine unbuttoned and rolled up her sleeves.

"I need to speak with Katherine as soon as possible," Stephen said, gazing thoughtfully at the sponge as he rubbed it briskly over his right forearm. "Do what you can to arrange a rendezvous, Europa. I know it is dangerous, but I must speak with her."

Katherine coughed a response, fearing anything more intelligible would give away her identity.

"It should be easy enough for you to arrange," Stephen added. "By now, I've come to the conclusion you could move the moon and the stars if you thought it necessary."

Wishing Europa could have heard the compliment, Katherine sank to her knees behind him and encircled his chest with her arms.

Stephen gave a start, but relaxed when her hands smoothed over his wet chest, dipping below the still surface of the water.

"Europa, you've changed," he murmured, running his hands up and down the length of her slender arms.

Katherine laughed softly. "Is that bad, milord?"

"Nay, 'tis good. Very good. So you recognized me."

"Nay. Though there was something familiar about you, I would not have known were it not for Europa."

He twisted around, sloshing water, and kissed her soundly. His chiseled lips were warm and wet. She clutched his cheeks, wishing she could devour him, for so much strength was given in that one kiss.

Withdrawing, he glanced over the edge of the tub and pouted grandly. "You're completely dressed. 'Tis a pity."

"That can easily be rectified." She rose and stepped nearer the fire. Shrugging from her surcoat, she placed it neatly on Stephen's bed. When she began to unbutton her kirtle, he cleared his throat and scowled at the shadows hovering near the hearth.

"Kate, come hither."

He held out an open hand and she grasped it, her heart beating madly. Why was he suddenly so serious and sad? "What is it, Guy?" she queried with a frown, settling on the smooth rim of the tub.

"I fear I may have been selfish, and there's something I have to ask you. When we made love so passionately at Downing-Cross, did you . . . did you welcome me to your bed by choice?"

Her frown melted, and she smiled incredulously. "Milord, you know I did."

"But your vow, Kate. I made it impossible for you to keep your vow."

"Nay," she said emphatically. "*We* made it impossible. It was my choice. I do not regret it, Stephen."

He blinked thoughtfully several times. The shadows of twilight lingered in his eyes.

"Stephen, I will admit that I have not made my peace with the memory of brother. And that must be done. But don't you see? That is *my* task. I *want* to be with you."

Katherine was determined to reassure him. He had to see what joy he brought to her. She would make him see.

Once again, her hands went to the buttons constraining her gown. They popped readily beneath her lithe fingers. She stared at him all the while, at his wonderfully masculine body. He was like a sculpture of a Greek god, a lesser god who'd spent most of his time on earth, tempting mortals. She rose and disrobed. Completely naked, she stood in silence, waiting for him to look up. When he did, the hunger was immediate.

"Dear God, you're beautiful," he whispered, pleasure gleaming in his eyes so intensely it looked like a flicker of pain.

Katherine knelt by the tub and kissed his face, over and over—his damp forehead, his furrowed brows, his scarred cheek, his lips. Grasping the sponge, she wiped at the traces of purple still lingering under his eyes, the stains that gave him a haggard look. Then she rubbed more soap on the sponge and pressed it sensuously against his chest, molding the rough ball against his nipples.

Stephen sucked in a hissing breath and scowled. "Katherine, be sure this is what you want."

She did not answer. Words would not suffice. She would show him exactly what she wanted. Round and round her hand went, over the muscles cording in his chest, down his firm belly. Lower and lower, down the thin line of hair leading to his groin. When she touched an impediment, stiff and unyielding, she halted.

"I see your torch still burns bright for me," she said in a husky voice.

Casting off his sadness, Stephen gave her a wicked smile. "Aye, and you started the fire. Now only you can quench it."

The teasing glint in his smoky eyes gave way to astonishment when she boldly gripped his manhood. Already firm, it turned to steel in the warmth of her fingers.

"Oh, God!" he bellowed, and then he groaned in ecstasy. "What are you doing to me? Lady, you play with fire."

"Is that what you call it?" she replied, all innocence. "Then we must dampen the flames."

He did not argue when her hand started to massage him. Minutes later, her fingers withdrew, leaving him panting and craving. He watched helplessly as she stepped into the bath. He had never wanted a woman more in his life, but he would not take her. It had to be her choice. Willing his hands into obedience, he gripped the edge of the tub as she straddled him.

"Mmmmmm," she cooed. "The water is just the right temperature for making love."

Stephen's gaze climbed slowly up her lily-white thighs to the golden nest between her legs. "You are so beautiful," he whispered.

She squatted down, the nest rustling against the surface of the still waters. Golden curls rippled and lengthened in the silver pool. She painted her flesh with droplets, splashing a handful against her face. The rush of water curved down her neck to the narrow valley between her breasts. Unable to stop himself, he leaned forward and drank the trickling drops.

Katherine sank even farther, and he slid into her effortlessly. Interlocked, they stared at each other, carnal light and tender love shooting back and forth betwixt their eyes in a light show to rival the stars.

He began to laugh, slowly at first, delighted, and then helplessly, his manhood throbbing in the utter stillness of her. "You are wicked. So wicked. It makes me very happy. And very hard."

Then thunder cracked in his chest and lightning bolted through his groin. His lingering smile turned into a fierce grimace. He wanted to touch her heart, from inside. He began to thrust. Upward. Into her. Farther in. Nothing would stop him.

Katherine's eyes flew open in shock, and then she quivered as if he'd kissed the tenderest part of her, as if a secret key had opened a vast well of seething desire within her. She jerked against his thrusting motions, taking him in, farther and farther.

"I want you . . . forever!" she gasped between jarring thrusts, a violent proclamation, uttered in exquisite frustration, for no matter how grand their movements, they could not get close enough. But it was delightful trying.

And then she exploded. Crying out, she arched against him.

Her satisfaction fulfilled, he cut loose like an animal, thrusting into her, filling her, filling himself.

Afterward, when even the lapping water had calmed to but a ripple, Katherine found herself staring down at the man she loved, her vision slowly coming into focus. She was spent. Completely. Yet she knew her hunger for Stephen would never be satisfied. Never. Her wanting was eternal.

Sinking to his chest, she wondered just how long she could make eternity last.

CHAPTER TWENTY

✠

With a flourish, Stephen entered the Great Hall early the next day, to begin Rosalind's trial. Success in this gambit was critical. He could not dwell on last night's exquisite interlude with Katherine—the involuntary smile such thoughts provoked would be contrary to LaMort's vicious nature. He focused instead on all that was at stake.

His French soldiers had arranged benches in a semicircle around a table with two large tapers and a crucifix from the church. Barons sat on the benches while merchants and knights stood behind them, filling the Hall in anticipation of the spectacle. Robert, Marlow, and Rosalind took their places of honor in chairs.

In France, inquisitions were conducted without audience, but Stephen needed a public forum to expose his brother's calumny. He addressed the crowd first in French, followed by Latin, pretending to read from an inquisitor's handbook. When everyone in the Hall seemed appropriately awed by the mystery of the ceremony, he shut the book and placed it on the table.

"These are solemn proceedings which will be undertaken today," he began, drawing out each word with drama and eloquence. "There is a charge of pagan idolatry against Lady Rosalind, Countess of Blackmoor. If she is found guilty, she will be burned at the stake."

A low rumble of discontentment, even outrage, rippled through the crowd. All eyes looked to Marlow for action, but he sat contentedly giving obeisance to LaMort.

"Who has charged her?" One neighboring baron spoke out at last.

Stephen smiled, for the man who dared to ask the question was Lord Stewart Durham, a man well loved by his father. "She has been charged, sir, by the Earl of Blackmoor, Lord Marlow."

Everyone turned in shock and horror to Marlow, who then regarded LaMort with a look of betrayal. Stephen waited until the room quieted again, the expression on their faces changing from outrage to dismay.

"The Inquisition reigns supreme on the Continent. Only to this isolated land is it new. You must accept my verdict as final in all matters. I represent the Inquisition, which represents God."

Angry murmurs rippled through the room.

"Countess Rosalind, come hither," Stephen said.

Rosalind rose with trepidation and sat in the chair indicated by LaMort.

"Do you worship the Christian God who created Heaven and earth?"

"I did," she replied, staring at Marlow.

"Madame, I did not hear you clearly. You did, or you do?"

She paused. "I do."

"And do you recognize that there is one true Church and that salvation comes only through that divine Church?"

Rosalind nodded.

"Do you worship with the pagans, with those debauchers who still say the Goddess made the world?"

She frowned. "Of course not."

"Then what is this, and how did it come into your possession?" Stephen produced the statuette and handed it to his mother. "What is this figurine?"

"Obviously, it is the Goddess of fertility, the Earth Mother," Rosalind answered wearily.

"It is yours then?"

"Nay, it is not. If my son has said that it is, then I suggest you ask him where he found it. Ask him how he celebrated Beltaine."

"Interesting, Lady Rosalind, that you call that festival Beltaine and not the eve of May as Christians commonly call it. Countess Rosalind, we are just beginning this trial. I beg of you to confess your sins. If you will not, we will find your guilt. Do you have anything to say to me before we proceed?"

Rosalind looked up with a bitter glare. "If the pagan beliefs were true, that it was a woman who created earth, then women gave birth to good and evil. Every babe from the womb is not of goodness made or born. Let you all remember that, lest you love your issue without discernment. For myself, I wish I were not a woman at all, for then I would not have born such sorrow into the world."

Marlow shifted uncomfortably in his chair, avoiding Rosalind's burning look. The crowd broke into a murmur.

So it continued for several hours. Katherine watched from the shadows of the Hall. But soon she grew weary of the proceedings. A parade of accused, mostly women, were brought before Stephen after he had questioned his mother. Some were accused of witchcraft merely because they bore a birthmark.

Katherine knew that Stephen heard these accusations only because he needed more time. In truth, he needed much more than time. When Marlow realized who LaMort was, Stephen would die, not by formal execution, but by a dagger from his enraged brother. She had to find the will and the medallion herself, even if it meant risking her life. Their destinies were now entwined. Stephen would not see it that way, would not want her to risk herself. She could only hope that one day he would recognize the wisdom in her decision. But she could not stand by idly, awaiting the worst. She would start at the beginning. Return to Downing-Cross. If there had been any way to do so before his death, Giles would have entrusted the will and the medallion to his parents. She had to find them.

Stephen always acted on instinct and faith. If she did as well, perhaps she would succeed where others had failed.

Eight hours later, when the afternoon sun had begun its slow descent, Katherine and Markham hesitated at the edge of Ravens Wood. She glanced nervously over her shoulder, wondering if the thug they had avoided had caught up with them. Her mare snorted a weary breath, and Markham wiped perspiration from the flanks of his steed. She paused not only to catch her breath, but to ponder the spooky turn of events that had led them to this giant wood.

Earlier that day she had slipped away from Blackmoor without fanfare. Marlow's guards were so intrigued with the Inquisition that they were making bets over Rosalind's fate when they should have been watching the postern. To Katherine's surprise and delight, Markham greeted her as she passed through the village. He had been keeping watch for Stephen and insisted on escorting her after she explained the purpose of her journey. His presence was reassuring until Katherine realized that Bothwell was following them, no doubt spying for his master. They quickened their pace, and eventually lost him.

At last they reached Downing-Cross, where Katherine's instincts were vindicated. After muttering a quick prayer for guidance, she found an old gypsy wandering the fields behind the manor. The mysterious crone sadly informed Katherine that Elizabeth had died of grief after the death of Giles, and John had sought refuge in the caves of Ravens Wood. Grateful for the old woman's information, Katherine went to her horse to fetch a coin, but when she returned with the reward, the crone had disappeared. Strange though the encounter was, Katherine wasted no time speculating on the woman's inexplicable appearance at that crucial moment. She set out for Ravens Wood, with Markham reluctantly leading the way.

" 'Tis right to give pause, milady," he argued when they finally arrived two hours later. " 'Tis a giant wood. Thousands of trees ramble on for endless miles. People wander into Ravens Wood and are never seen again. When I was a child, I found my way to the caves, but the path is surely overgrown now."

"But there was a path, you say?"

"Aye, from what I remember."

"How much sunlight is left, Markham?"

"Only two hours at best."

Katherine nodded, squinting at the sky. Her assessment matched Markham's. "How long on horseback to the caves?"

Markham shrugged. "If we do not get lost, an hour. Mayhap a little more."

Katherine brushed a nagging fly from the weeping eyes of her mare. "Then we could get there and back before sundown."

"Just," Markham said doubtfully. "If we do not get lost. If we get what we want with no struggle. If—"

She waved him silent. "No more, Markham. You are right to doubt the wisdom of this journey. Though I have no choice, I will not make you risk your life for the earl's will."

She nudged her horse forward, but Markham halted her with a desperate plea.

"Katherine! You do not know the way to the caves."

She smiled over her shoulder. "Fear not. The wolves will act as my guide. I can not help but think that meeting the old crone was providence. Why else would she appear now, just when we needed a clue the most? I simply must proceed."

The dark-haired knight shook his head and slapped his thigh with frustration. "Blast it! That does it. I will go with you. You will never make it alone."

He started forward and passed her without a smile or a word of approval. She wanted to tell him it was not necessary, but in her heart she knew that Markham might be her only chance for success.

When they dodged beneath the first low branches barring entrance to the forest, cool air fanned Katherine's burning cheeks with welcome moisture. Little sun filtered through the canopy of trees. An owl hooted overhead, branches rustled in the wind, twigs snapped beneath their horses' hooves—but otherwise silence reigned in the dark, primeval forest.

They followed a narrow path that led them deeper into the still woods, and soon Katherine lost all sense of time.

Her anxiety grew the deeper they went, and then hope sprung anew when she heard the faint sound of a waterfall. They urged their skittish horses forward, but then Markham stopped abruptly.

"What is it? Did you see something?" A spider dropped in front of Katherine, on a silver strand from a branch overhead. She slapped at the hairy-limbed creature and grimaced. "Pray tell, why did you stop?"

Markham turned in his saddle, his face creased with concern. "Milady, we are lost."

"Lost?" She frowned and waited for him to rebut the statement.

"Aye. The path we were on has ended. Now two paths shoot out before us. I know not which to take."

Katherine pulled beside him and studied the forked trail, wishing the old crone would reappear to give her guidance.

"We will travel on separate paths," she concluded, sounding much more decisive than she felt. "Pass two hundred trees and then return here. If you see any sign of the caves, call out and I will join you."

Markham nodded, too weary to argue. He seemed resolved to whatever fate she chose for them.

Katherine nudged her mare forward, heading toward the sound of the waterfall. Her decision to travel on alone was frightening but also exhilarating. Whenever she made a decision, she at least felt that fate was still in her own hands. But her courage faltered when a vulture's cry pierced the silence. In the distance, a shadow fell across her path. Was it Bothwell? She nervously drew back her reins. Several paces away, a mouse scurried across a bed of needles, and her horse whinnied and stepped aside in fear. And then, blessedly, she heard the howl of a wolf—distant, yet distinct.

Quelling her fears, she urged her mare to trot and swiped at sticky cobwebs that stretched across the trail. After rounding a bend, she finally spied a wolf poised on top of a boulder in the distance.

"Vixen?" Katherine called out, praying it was John's wolf.

"Who is it?" an incredulous voice replied.

Katherine jerked her reins short and twisted in her saddle. When John stepped forward, smiling within the depths of his shaggy gray beard, she gasped with joy. He was just as Katherine remembered him, save for a haunted look that saddened his eyes.

After exchanging astonished greetings, John said, "Be you hungry, milady?"

Katherine let out a peal of laughter. "That is the most welcome question I've heard in a fortnight. Aye, I'm hungry. Will you take me to your cave?"

The old man bobbed his head on his strapping shoulders. She wanted to ask him about the will immediately, but something held her back. Until now, it had never occurred to her that John would not help her if he could, but his countenance had changed. A meal would do much to restore her strength and their friendship.

Together they found Markham and journeyed on to the caves. A waterfall roared next to the hollow dome John called home. They ducked low to enter the lichen-covered cave. John had staked out his lair with a crackling fire.

"Hello, Wild One," he muttered to a wolf curled against the wall. The silver beast looked up with the greatest disinterest and curled back up into a ball.

John urged them to sit while he bustled about. He produced a wooden bowl of water, in which they washed their hands.

"You will stay here tonight," he said, not a question but a command. Markham looked tentatively at Katherine, as if he expected her to argue, but she did not.

"Aye, John, and I thank you for the respite. We would never make it out before nightfall. 'Twas foolish to think otherwise."

After laying out a meal of venison stew and unleavened bread, John joined them at the fire. They sat on furs and ate from gourds, talking like old friends. They were bonded by the silence and the solitude, for little sound could pierce the cool, protective stone engulfing them.

Katherine sipped the last drops of stew and dusted her hands. "That was as good as any meal I've eaten at Blackmoor. Nay, better."

" 'Tis no wonder. You traveled long and hard for this food."

Katherine remembered the loving hospitality shown her at Downing-Cross. "I'm so sorry about Elizabeth and Giles."

The old man's eyes hardened like pebbles. "Only now can I even think of it without blind rage. 'Twas Marlow, all Marlow's doing."

"I know." Katherine momentarily shared his bitter reflection. "He has done much to hurt innocent people. That is why I have come. To stop Marlow."

He looked up with doubt. "How can you do that, milady? How can anyone? With Sir Guy in prison . . ."

"Stephen escaped." She whispered the news as if she were presenting a precious jewel and his reaction didn't disappoint her.

"By the Mass," he whispered, hope kindling beneath his wrinkled eyelids. "Has he now? By the Mass! 'Tis wondrous news."

Two wolves howled outside. Night had fallen. The only light in the deep, dark forest came from the fire that seethed before them.

"He wants to take Blackmoor, but he needs the will and the medallion. They alone can prove that Stephen is his father's true heir, and that he's innocent."

John looked at her with a fearful gaze, then stood abruptly. Clearing the bowls away, he shook his head. "I can not give you the will. If Sir Stephen is free, tell him to come to me."

John nodded to Markham for emphasis, but he would not look into Katherine's eyes.

She reached out and grasped his hand. "Stephen can not come to you now, John. He is at Blackmoor in disguise. If he does anything suspicious, he will be found out and killed. Give me the will. It is our only hope."

Removing his callused hand from hers, John ambled to a small trunk. Pulling out a bent parchment, he paused, staring hard at it, struggling with some inward battle. After a long moment, he proffered his treasure with trembling fingers.

Katherine clutched the parchment to her chest with gratitude. Gently, she said, "And the medallion?"

He shook his head with a touch of panic. "Surely, 'tis not necessary, milady. Is the will not enough? It has the earl's signature."

"Only the medallion can verify that signature. Marlow has already produced a false document that was sealed with the earl's insignia."

Tears welled in John's eyes. His face was creased with pain. At last, he sighed with resignation. "Well then, milady, let me show you where you can find your treasure."

Katherine exchanged a puzzled look with Markham.

"Ready yerself for a ride." John grabbed a giant stick wrapped in a fat-dipped cloth. He touched it to the fire, and the stick was transformed into a torch.

Where could John possibly be taking them to? Katherine wondered nervously, but her ardent desire to complete her mission overrode all doubts. She mounted behind Markham, while John led the way on her horse. When they exited the forest, Katherine inhaled a breath of fresh air. They rode a few more paces, until they reached the bottom of a hill.

She scanned the grassy knoll, and her heart began to race. Blood pounded in her temples, and she scowled at her guide in disbelief.

"This is a graveyard," she whispered hoarsely.

"Aye," John replied. "The medallion is buried with my boy."

CHAPTER TWENTY-ONE

✠

After tethering their mounts to a tree, Katherine and Markham followed the old man through the graveyard, their path lit by the torch and the round, white moon.

As they ascended a sloping hill, Katherine grew faint and paused. She leaned for support against a headstone. John and Markham proceeded to the top of the hill, where a giant oak tree etched the moonlit sky.

"Oh, dear God, is this your revenge?" Katherine whispered heavenward. She flexed her fingers and brushed them together as she had the night she buried Georgie. The dirt had stained her fingers for days.

"Oh, Georgie," she whispered harshly.

Stephen, she thought, Stephen needs the medallion. She lurched up the hill, snatching air in short breaths. She could almost smell the stench of rotting corpses that had assailed her from the mass graves during the Pestilence. Wiping a hand across her face, she tried to dispel the image. By the time she joined the men beneath the oak tree, Katherine was in a stupor.

John thrust the torch into the ground near two mounds of earth. The dirt had been churned only weeks ago, and grass still struggled to take hold.

"There lies Elizabeth," he said forlornly, pointing to the smaller grave. "And there lies Giles." A burst of wind swept over the top of the hill, pushing him forward as if to make the old man embrace his family. He quickly regained his balance and continued.

"On the night Giles and MacCormack were sent to the King, a young boy from the village came to my door and said that Giles was dead. Aye, that sad thing he said to me, and asked me to come for his body." Tears fell down John's wizened cheeks and disappeared in his beard. "I went to my son, not far from Blackmoor Castle. He lay by the side of the road near MacCormack. Felled by a great gash across his chest, he was, his precious blood spilled hither and thither on the road. I reached down to embrace my boy, but already his strong body had grown cold. I lifted him up in my arms like I had when he was just a babe, and I laid him over my horse. I knew he must have been transporting something precious, or he wouldn't have been killed. The lad who fetched me said he was on some mission for Sir Guy. So I searched my boy, but found nothing. I searched MacCormack, too. But then I spied another body thirty paces away. I figured it to be one of them that killed Giles. Did he have Giles's precious cargo? That I wondered, but found nothing again. And then far beyond that wretch I found another man. The bloody coward had not gotten far before he bled to death from his wounds. Served him right. He had the will and the medallion. He had almost made it back to Marlow, but the whelp died. I took the will and medallion back with my son and waited for some word from Sir Stephen. When they said Stephen was imprisoned, I decided all was lost."

Katherine and Markham listened in respectful silence. A wolf howled at the moon.

"I buried the medallion with my son, milady," the old man said at last. "I thought he deserved that honor. How oft had I seen that shiny treasure around the neck of Earl James. I wanted my boy to bear it on his cold journey back to earth."

Katherine nodded compassionately while she attempted to overcome her growing dread. If the medallion was buried with Giles, she would have to dig it up.

"You may have it, milady," John said. "Retrieve it if you will. But I can not . . . I can not bear to see my son the way he will be."

John stumbled away. Markham looked at Katherine with horror.

"Milady," he whispered. "You can not stir a grave. 'Tis a mortal sin. You will burn in Hell forever. If the Church finds out, you will be excommunicated!"

"Is it a sin to seek justice, Markham?" she said, racked with her own fear, angry that he could muster no more courage than she.

"Whatever your reasons, Katherine, there can be no cause great enough to rob a grave."

"It is not robbery if I take it for Stephen. That medallion is his."

Markham paused at her logic but then looked up with tormented eyes. "Still, it is a sin. You will go to Hell."

"Get you hence," she shouted, waving him away, her eyes riveted all the while on the mound of earth.

Markham stepped back as if he'd been dealt a blow. He left Katherine alone with her desperate need and equally desperate fear. By now, Giles would be . . .

She could not even think of it. She began to shake and gag. How would Georgie look now after so many months in his earthly prison? Rotten and cold and so alone. Ah, sweet Georgie, beautiful Georgie.

Pray for me, Katherine, or I will burn in Hell.

How long could she run from her vow? She had promised Georgie she would not go to Stephen, that she would spend her days in a convent, but she had failed at both assurances. And now she would defy the Church, disturb the dead, and for what? To help Stephen. Did he deserve such an act? No matter how much she loved him, was he really worth bringing down the revenge of God Himself?

Katherine dropped to her knees and touched the mound of death. Could she tear away the soil, fumble with the bones to retrieve that which she so desperately needed?

"Do not sully your hands, little love," Georgie had once said to her when she was burying a pet bird. She was eight years old then, but she still remembered the look of loving disapproval on her brother's face, that beautiful face framed with golden hair and a dazzling smile. "You are an angel from Heaven," Georgie said. "Brush the earth from your perfect little fingers, Kate."

Katherine pulled her hands away from the mound and rubbed the grit from her fingertips.

"Forgive me, Stephen," she whispered, "but I can not do it."

Stephen stared out his chamber window like one of the walking dead. He was numb from the absurdity of his own pretense, his muscles weary from his affected limp.

From this window, he could see down below to the village. All night, a slow stream of villeins had marched up to the edge of the moat. They carried torches, shouted in defiance, and threw stones at the curtain protecting the bailey. Presently, fifty churls and burghers stood just beyond the moat chanting, "Kill the inquisitor!" They had had enough of his trial. They feared that LaMort would soon condemn to death one of their own, and so they had united in protest.

Stephen had never expected such a reaction. It was testimony to the success of his disguise. It also bespoke the courage of these villagers.

Lost in thought, he stroked his chin over and over. He was far from certain of success, and yet the trial had gone well thus far. His audacious questions had stirred up powerful anger in the burghers and castle dwellers that could serve him if redirected at his brother.

Yet all these considerations paled when his mind returned, as it had dozens of times already, to Katherine's absence. She was gone! Without telling him. Most certainly she had ventured in search of the will and medallion. That's what she had said she wanted to do at the Beltaine celebration.

"Damnation," he muttered, rubbing his forehead with frustration. Curse the woman, but he had warned her not to go. Why would she defy him? But it wasn't the defiance that tore him apart, though that stuck in his throat like bitter fruit.

It was concern for her. Where was she? Why had she not returned?

Stephen turned from the window with an oath of self–condemnation. For judge her though he did, he still prayed she would be successful. Standing before the fire, lost in the pulsing flames, he realized he needed her help.

"God, do not let her be hurt," he whispered.

Stephen felt a rush of cold air. The door to his chamber flew open and banged back on its hinges. He thought he had locked it. He grasped his dagger, for whoever entered would die before exposing LaMort's true identity.

Turning quickly, he whipped out his blade. Two hooded figures waited in the doorway. Bothwell and Cramer? he wondered until they pulled back their hoods.

"Ramsey! Geoffrey!" Stephen cried out. He rushed forward and took them both in an embrace. Geoffrey pulled away and shut the door behind them.

"I expected to see an inquisitor," Ramsey said with disappointment. "But 'tis just you, Sir Guy."

Stephen laughed and rubbed his face where the skin had been chafed by the plasters. He regarded his dusty, road-weary friends with affection. "The disguise has worked better than I could have hoped. The villeins are ready to hang me outside the castle walls."

"We saw them," Geoffrey said, coming to his master's side. "Luckily, they were there to distract the guards or we never would have gained entrance."

"I am glad to see you both, but why did you leave Downing-Cross? Have you found the will?"

"Nay, we have not," Ramsey replied. "We left Downing-Cross yesterday after giving up hope of finding it. We've been hiding in the village."

"Did you see Katherine? She has ventured off on her own."

Ramsey grimaced. "Gods, nay, we did not."

Disheartened, Stephen pinched the bridge of his nose. "Did you receive some word from the King?"

"Nay," Ramsey answered soberly, pouring himself a tankard of ale. "Sir Gerald was unable to reach the King. It seems many of your supporters in Edward's court died during the Pestilence. Nay, we do not come with good news. The prior of Rievaulx Abbey and his men are on their way. Marlow did not want to wait for the archbishop's arrival, so he asked the abbot of Rievaulx to send a representative. Geoffrey overheard as much when the delegation stopped to let their urine on the side of the road."

Geoffrey shrugged with a sheepish grin. "A spy must take any opportunity . . ."

Stephen articulated a low curse. "The prior speaks with enough authority to expose my travesty, to be sure. And so soon! How close are they?"

"The last we saw them they were pulling into Shirewood Abbey," Ramsey replied. "That is a day's ride hence. As I suspected, the delegation is taking a day or two to empty a few barrels of the abbey's famous mead. The prior looked to be a gout-infested beefy sort with a taste for the good life."

"Indeed." Stephen paced with stiff strides. "In any event, they'll arrive too soon. We need an army!"

"We're all brave sorts, milord," Geoffrey offered. "We might take Marlow on."

Stephen shook his head. "There are twelve of us. Even with Darbonnet's men, it will not be enough."

"If the prior doesn't fall for your trickery, it will be enough to hold off Marlow's men while you make your escape," Ramsey countered.

"I do not want to escape," Stephen uttered impatiently. "Blast it, I must find that will before the abbot's delegation arrives."

Katherine. Stephen shut his eyes and inwardly called out to her. Had she by some miracle succeeded? Right now she was his only hope. He opened his eyes to find his friends staring at him with curiosity.

"I have one last ploy, Ramsey. I must play it out to its conclusion. And then I must find Katherine."

"Katherine is not in as much danger as you, Sir Guy."

"Oh, yes, she is," Stephen said intensely. "You see, she has given me her heart, and I dare not take it with me to my grave. She deserves better. I never before realized how important words are. But there is something I must tell her, and I can not die before I do."

He shook off his morose demeanor and turned to Ramsey with a wicked grin. Snatching the older man's tankard from his hands, Stephen took a quick swill of ale. "Besides, I mean to turn her over my knee and blister her bottom for disobeying my orders."

"A whipping won't be enough to break that spirited filly."

"You speak the truth, Ramsey. Now, off you go. You'd best leave, too, Geoffrey. If anyone finds you here, they will kill you."

"We'll hide in the village, milord," Ramsey said. Bowing, they slipped out the door, raising their hoods as they went.

Katherine knelt at the grave, trembling and shaking. It seemed an eternity since Markham had left her side. A balmy wind did nothing to dry the perspiration that drenched her body. She licked her numb, salty lips, wishing to the depths of her soul that she could walk away from this grave without hating herself. She was not one to turn her back on that which was required of her, and if she did so now, she would loathe herself.

"I am not a coward," she whispered. "I must help Stephen."

Still, she could not move. One of John's wolves howled incessantly in the distance, and she thought of Lupa. She whimpered with longing for her wild friend, her wolf. Anger at Marlow stirred her briefly from paralysis. He had killed Lupa, just as he would destroy Katherine's future. But the anger faded, leaving her again with overwhelming fear. It would take more than rage to overcome the challenge that confronted her. She would have to be moved by something greater and more positive than hatred. If only someone would hold her now as her brother used to.

But there was no one, and so she threw herself on the mound of earth, crying for so much death, for her past, for the death of the girl she once was. She wept for Constance's untimely end, for the frailty of life, for the love Katherine had embraced, which was so vulnerable. Vulnerable because the object of her love, Stephen, was a man and therefore mortal, just like Georgie. And finally she cried because she was a woman now and had to do so much more than cry. When her sobbing receded to a gentle moan, her head resting on her arms, a thought formed oh so quietly in the back of her mind.

Yes, she loved Georgie, and the love she felt had continued after her brother's death. Love's shining light had not paled when he died. So, too, would her love for Stephen survive. The love that had moved her through exquisite torture these few months passing was greater than herself. It came from a source more powerful than any single person she had ever loved. It was eternal, it was a gift from God, it would survive. It would survive. She would survive.

Katherine rose from the grave, her spirit resurrected by a powerful insight. If love lived on after death, did she not commune with her brother daily, indeed every second? Was love not a form of prayer?

"Oh, Georgie, I will love you evermore," she fervently whispered. "That is my gift to you, brother. Now give me your blessing in return. Let me love the living, dear sweet brother, and trust me to love the man who is best for me."

The wolf ceased its howl; silhouetted by the moonlight, the creature turned to Katherine and then loped off into the night. John, huddling by a gravestone, stirred in the silence, and Markham ambled to Katherine's side, shovel in hand. For the first time since the Pestilence, Katherine felt an inner peace. As if she had awakened from a trance, she blinked several times and brushed the dirt from her cheeks.

"You will need some help," Markham said.

"Nay, give me the shovel."

Markham hesitated. "I am here to do your bidding. I'll not let a lady work like a churl."

"And I'll not have you lose your soul for me."

"Nay, milady . . ."

"I'll not have it any other way," she said, her words clipped with fierce determination, and Markham acquiesced. Katherine pierced the ground with a mighty thrust. Scooping a load, she flung the dirt aside. "This task is mine to do. I can not . . . ask . . . another to do it for me."

Her words came in grunting gasps, coordinated with each heave of the shovel. Soon Katherine's hands blistered and bled, but it mattered naught. She would obtain her prize. The realization made her exultant and stronger with each stroke.

At last her shovel found the wooden coffin. The jolt shot through her bones and made her shiver. Her intense efforts were no longer needed, and in the stillness that followed, Katherine broke out in a cold sweat.

"I have found him," she whispered.

"Step back, milady," Markham commanded. "You will never get the lid off. Surely it is nailed shut. I've never seen a blasted woman work so hard as you."

He muttered as he pried the coffin lid with the shovel blade; he grunted with each jerking motion. Katherine hovered over his shoulder. The sudden hoot of an owl sent goose bumps rippling down her arms.

With one final jerk, the lid gave way and flew open. With it came a rush of stench. Markham bellowed and rolled back, gagging.

"God's Wounds!" he shouted, choking and eventually vomiting in the grass.

Katherine, too, reeled back from the putrified odor. Death. She had smelled it a hundred times before. Her eyes fluttered at the memory.

Holding her breath and gritting her teeth, she pulled back the coffin lid until she could see Giles. It might have been any man, for the skin was drawn and black, stretched across the skull. Bugs crawled from his mouth. A fly was soon buzzing in the casket. The clothes were still intact, and the medallion . . .

Her hand went out involuntarily, like a greedy robber, but the closer she drew, the more hideous the figure appeared.

" 'Tis only Giles," she whispered, sorry for this violation, this disrespect to the dead. He deserved the medal, he truly did. "Just take it, Katherine," she admonished herself.

At last, her hand clutched the medallion. She pulled at it, trying to free the dragon crest from the chain. But nothing would give. Dropping the medallion back onto the chest of the decaying corpse, she panted for air but nearly gagged with each breath. There was no choice but to pull the chain up around Giles's head.

"Dear God be with me," she muttered, clutching his tunic with one hand and the medallion with other. Tugging on the material, she pulled the figure up and, groaning all the while, lifted the chain over his head. A spider crawled up her arm, and she flung it away in a frantic effort to cast off the scurrying creature. She staggered away from the grave and clutched the medallion in the moonlight.

As she panted and groaned in revulsion, her panic ebbed with the realization that she had captured her prize. She alone had done it, with determination and faith. Her life would never be the same.

CHAPTER TWENTY-TWO

✠

Stephen rose before dawn to a quiet castle. He savored a few moments in peace. This would be his final act, his final bit of trickery against his brother before the abbot's men arrived. Whether he succeeded or failed, he was prepared.

He knew that he had lived his life well, as honorably as he could. There was a weariness in his bones from living, from struggling. Yet there was a certain bliss he felt knowing his next steps would lead him to the crowning victory of his life, or to its end. Either way, he had loved in his time. And love was the great redeemer.

Europa bustled into his chamber before light broke and administered his disguise. They were solemn and preoccupied. His very future rode on the next few hours. He was not a praying man, but he did cross himself as he left his chamber.

When he swept into the Great Hall at sunrise, throngs of spectators awaited him. Everyone had heard that LaMort might render his verdict today. Marlow looked downright gleeful.

"Lady Rosalind, I call you before the inquisitor!" Stephen bellowed his command.

Rosalind rose tremulously, and the others murmured when she took her seat next to LaMort.

"Madame, you are aware that the Inquisition has final say in all matters of heresy. There is no reprieve or second trial for those who refuse to admit their sins. Again, for those who do confess their sins, the Inquisition is lenient. Will you now proclaim your guilt?"

Stephen leaned forward in a dramatic pose. Countess Rosalind would not meet his gaze but smiled bitterly. "Nay, LaMort. Take me to your burning stake. I weary of this world."

The chorus of onlookers gasped in amazement.

"*Très bien,*" Stephen replied. "Madame, as official representative of the Inquisition, the Tribunal, and Pope Clement VI himself, I pronounce you innocent of all heresies."

"Innocent!" Marlow jumped out of his chair, confounded by the unexpected.

The audience broke into applause and cheers; Rosalind turned slowly to Stephen and pulled him close by the sleeve. "Who are you?" she whispered.

Stephen pressed a forefinger to his lips. "Later, madame." He turned to quiet the crowd.

"Silence," he hissed. "Though I have suffered the pain of the rack, I still have my wits about me. Not everyone who is charged will be guilty, and not everyone who has gone unnoticed is innocent."

The onlookers quieted, sensing some new turn in the drama. Stephen paused for effect. "In the course of my investigation of the countess I found another who is guilty. One who was not charged by his peers but who will be charged by me, the inquisitor himself."

"Who?" a nervous voice called from the back of the room. "Who is it, LaMort?"

"The one who has brought sorrow, hatred, and ruin to this castle. Lord Marlow, Earl of Blackmoor," Stephen answered, his gaze falling at last on his brother.

"On what charge?" Marlow said defiantly. His eyes darted back and forth between LaMort and his mother.

Stephen smiled. "You are charged with the murder of your father, James."

"This is outrageous!" Marlow bellowed. "What evidence do you have?"

Stephen motioned to one of his men, who handed over a scrolled parchment. "This is the true will of Earl James. In it, he disinherits you, Lord Marlow, for you are his bastard son. He names Stephen, your condemned brother, as his sole heir."

"That is a forgery," Marlow yelled, turning to the others for allegiance. "I have the earl's true will."

They both were liars. Stephen's will was as false as his brother's, but no one had to know that now.

He turned to Marlow and pointed an accusing finger. "The only will you have is the one which you yourself wrote, sealing it with the insignia ring you stole from the earl."

Marlow quickly grasped his ring finger. "How do you know about the ring?"

Stephen turned away, and Marlow took a step closer. "That will is a fake," he persisted. "No one has the will of which you speak. It is gone, destroyed."

"This session is over," Stephen said, gathering his papers. "I leave this will for the local barons to peruse." He handed it to Lord Durham. "We will resume this session this afternoon."

Stephen hurried from the room. Marlow unwittingly allowed him more time for escape by shouting his denials to the barons. Stephen headed directly for the stables. His only hope now was that Marlow's peers would see the truth in the document Stephen had forged and take the matter up themselves. He had to get out before Marlow sent his men. He had to find Katherine.

He quickly mounted a saddled horse; a stable boy handed him a sword. "You'll be needing this, milord," the young boy said.

"Thank you, lad," Stephen said, no longer feigning his character. "I'll not forget your help."

Stephen urged his stallion forward. By some miracle, the drawbridge creaked and clanked in a downward motion. Perhaps Ramsey was awaiting him on the other side.

"LaMort!" Marlow stood with his sword drawn in the middle of the bailey. He was a madman now. He ran forward toward Stephen. "Dismount, you coward! You will answer to this sword for blackening my name in my own castle."

"Your name was blackened long before it touched my lips, Marlow," Stephen answered, not as LaMort but as himself. Gone was the French accent, returned was the implacable loathing of two brothers at war.

Marlow shifted in the morning light, lifting a hand over his brow to get a better look. "You are not a Frenchman."

Stephen dismounted and faced his brother. Marlow reached forward and tore back Stephen's hood, clawing at the disguise until the plaster scar had crumbled and the eye patch lay on the ground.

"Lying, black-hearted knave," Marlow shouted so loudly the words echoed off the castle walls. "Die, you son of the devil!"

Sword met sword, silver glinted against silver. Years, lifetimes, of rage, jealousy, and betrayal sung with each clash of their blades. They were perfectly matched—two strong sons of the same strong woman. The fight would be to the death, of that Stephen was sure. Clashing and grunting, he did not pause to think of whose lifeless body the carrion birds would soon circle over.

He had to live, he had to speak with Katherine one more time, to tell her. Her sun-kissed face flashed in his mind. *Katherine!* he called inwardly, and in that moment of beseeching, Stephen stumbled onto his back, his sword cast aside. Marlow was on him in a second, his blade poised at Stephen's throat.

"You're a coward," Stephen shouted, spittle flying in the early morning light. "You're a bloody coward."

Marlow trembled as he held his sword, so much rage filling him that he choked back a sob. "I hate you, Stephen," he cried out. "I hate you."

"Then kill me while you have the chance."

Marlow raised his elbow in preparation for his downward thrust.

"Milords!"

Marlow halted in mid-thrust. Neither he nor Stephen had noticed the arrival of visitors during their fight. Marlow turned, stepping away from his brother. The banner of Rievaulx Abbey flapped in the breeze. Five men dressed in robes of the Church stared down at them in dismay.

"Milords," the prior said. "We come by command of the abbot, who speaks on behalf of the Archbishop of Canterbury. Who is the Earl of Blackmoor?"

"I am," Stephen and Marlow answered in unison.

Katherine whipped her horse anew when she saw Blackmoor's four towers looming in the hazy afternoon mist. The medallion rested safely in a pouch strung from her wrist. Dried earth streaked her flushed cheeks, her hair was matted and tangled, and fierce glory shot with determination from the depths of her eyes.

"Faster, Markham," she urged her escort, who lagged behind. "We are almost there."

She treasured the prospect of Marlow's dismay when she finally exposed him as the earl's murderer, but more than that, she eagerly awaited Stephen's reaction. She had a gift for him that would complete the cycle, conclude the macabre drama that had torn his family apart.

She laughed in the wind, hunched over her galloping horse. Success was a brilliant, delicious state of being. She knew that this moment would live long in her heart, and for once in her life, she was utterly certain that she had done exactly the right thing at the right moment. Now she could return Stephen's love with a certainty that had eluded her before. She was free from the past.

A rider pulled onto the road in the distance; Katherine and Markham slowed their pace. It was Ramsey. The steward greeted them with a broad grin as he balanced on his prancing steed.

"Ramsey, I had not expected your return to Blackmoor," she said, panting for breath.

"Sir Stephen needed my help, milady, and I thought you might, too. Do you have it?"

She smiled, relishing the moment, and then satisfied his curiosity. "Aye, I have the will."

"Saints above!" Ramsey shouted with laughter. "You are an amazing woman, Katherine."

She humbly nodded in acknowledgment of his high praise and spurred her horse.

"What ho! Follow me!" Ramsey shouted to his men, who waited along the road, hidden by the hedges. They came out on thundering horses, so gruff and bedraggled they looked like Vikings of old. There was heavily built Seeley, the faithful Geoffrey, fair-haired Sir Gerald, and the others. And so Katherine and Markham entered the gatehouse at Blackmoor Castle with an unexpected entourage.

They rode into the bailey unchecked, as if all the men-at-arms had fallen fast asleep on their watch. Marlow's closest advisors darted to and from the Great Hall, heedless of their arrival.

"What is amiss?" Katherine asked Ramsey, instantly worried for Stephen. "What has happened?"

"The Church's delegation arrived today."

Katherine dismounted. "Then I've returned just in time."

Ramsey jumped down from his horse. "You must present your evidence immediately. I will send for the local barons to bear witness."

Katherine nodded and headed toward the Great Hall. Stephen's men boldly staked out their positions in the bailey while Ramsey and Geoffrey carried on. Europa waddled out of the Hall and pulled Katherine into her arms.

"Milady, you're alive! Blessed, blessed day."

Katherine hugged the old woman fervently. "Where is he, Europa?"

"With Marlow. They're arguing their sides before the prior."

Europa led Katherine to the Great Hall. She entered unannounced, but halted her determined stride when all eyes turned to her in astonishment. Only then did she glance down, remembering her unkempt appearance. Her breeches were mud-encrusted, her hair a jumbled skein.

"Milords, I pray you, overlook my appearance." She started to curtsey, but her knees locked when she spied Stephen. He stared at her with soulful eyes, a hint of a smile twisting his lips. An overwhelming sense of love engulfed her. Everything she had done, she had done for him.

"Father Prior," Stephen said, breaking the awkward silence. "This is my betrothed, Katherine Gilbert."

My betrothed. Like her, he had not forsaken that vow. Her heart clamored against her ribs, and she grew short of breath, enjoying a wonderful sense of giddiness.

"His betrothed who will soon be my wife," Marlow shouted.

The prior waved his pudgy hands and shook his head. "Enough!" he pleaded. "You both tell me you are the earl, you both tell me your brother killed your father, and now you both tell me you will marry the same maiden."

"Except she is no maiden," Marlow sneered. "She is as tarnished as a harlot. She spent days alone with my brother at Downing-Cross."

Katherine blushed, but Marlow could do little to mar her sense of triumph. What mattered now was Stephen's inheritance.

The prior and his four monks leaned together and mumbled their exchanges. At last they parted, and the old man regarded her with curiosity.

"Katherine Gilbert, perhaps you can shed some light on the matter."

She joined Stephen and grasped his hand. "This is the man whom I will marry. Lord Stephen, the true Earl of Blackmoor. That is if he will deign to have me," she added with a tart smile meant only for him.

Stephen pulled both her hands to his lips and kissed her blistered fingers. "What have you been through for me, my love?"

His concern was the sweetest balm. "I will marry Stephen. He is the man to whom I am betrothed. And since he is a man of great honor, he will fulfill that vow."

Stephen nodded his agreement. She then turned to Marlow with eyes that bespoke her loathing.

"Furthermore," she continued, "I have evidence that Marlow killed Earl James."

"She lies," Marlow said. "No such evidence exists."

Katherine withdrew the medallion from the pouch and pulled the will from her mud-spattered shirt. "Here is the earl's will and his medallion. Proof enough, methinks."

"Father Prior," Stephen said, "just before my father was murdered, he made a will in my presence, making me his successor and disinheriting Marlow, who is my mother's bastard son. His insignia ring had been stolen from him—you see it on Marlow's finger—and so he sent this medallion as proof of his intent. It was a gift to my father from the King."

The prior nodded, eyeing the medallion closely. "I recognize the craftsmanship of Edward's guildsmen. Lord Marlow, do you have anything to say?"

Marlow did not answer. He merely stared at the medallion, hollow eyes blinking. He turned and left the Hall. Ramsey quickly followed.

"This has been a most unusual visit, Sir Stephen," the prior said. "I will take this evidence and present it to the abbot. In the meantime, I think we can ignore the arrival of the French Inquisition," he added, his displeasure laced with a smile. The paunchy graybeard's eyes twinkled with something akin to admiration.

"If you are agreeable, we will stay a day or so to recuperate from our journey."

Stephen bowed. "My castle is open to you, Father Prior."

As the others departed, Stephen turned his full attention to Katherine. They were alone at last.

Flushed with contentment, she wrapped her arms around his waist. Here was the comfort she had been craving at the graveside, and all she had to do to claim it was overcome the past, a task that seemed inconsequential in the shadow of its reward.

Stephen, handsome and radiant, leaned forward and nestled his lips against hers. With one tender kiss so much was said.

But it was not enough. He had to say the words. "I love you," he whispered.

"I know."

Stephen shuddered, exhaling a harsh breath of pain and relief. "I love you," he whispered again in her ear. "God, I should have shouted it from here to Cornwall long ago. But I was afraid."

She smiled as tears of happiness poured freely down her cheeks. "I love you, too, Stephen. I think I've loved you from the moment I first saw you."

As close as two people can be, they strolled arm in arm across the Great Hall.

"Why did you succeed where I had failed, Kate? How were you able to find the will and the medallion?"

How could she answer him when she did not know the truth? "An old hag appeared to me, Stephen. An old crone."

"The Crone of Death?" He grew solemn. "Surely not. There has been too much death."

Katherine laughed softly. How could so valiant a man be superstitious? "Nay, Stephen, she was just an old woman."

She paused and looked back at the Great Hall, her new home, thinking of all that had taken place here since her arrival. She thought of Constance and their brief, poignant friendship. Katherine was happy to know that, in the end, it was a woman who had shown her the way.

"Old woman be damned." Stephen pulled her close. "You did the deed, Kate, and do not think otherwise. You had the courage and the determination. Will you be so stalwart in marriage?"

Katherine grinned broadly. "I swear it."

She thought he would kiss her again, but instead he scooped her into his arms.

"Then swear it before a priest, my love." He headed for the church. "I'm marrying you now."

"Stephen!" She struggled in his arms. "I am dressed in a most inappropriate manner."

He chuckled and eyed her seductively. "You'll be naked before the eyes of God. That suits me well enough."

She exhaled a groan of resignation, sinking into the strength of his arms. Soon she would be naked before the eyes of Stephen, too.

CHAPTER TWENTY-THREE

✠

The next morning, Katherine awoke to the sound of birds singing. She had dreamt of Lupa and at first thought the sound was the bittersweet howl of a wolf. But when fully awake, blinking in the peachy haze of morning, she could not mistake the song of a lark floating through the window above their bed.

She nestled against Stephen's chest, marveling at how natural it felt to awaken in his embrace. His skin was smooth and warm; he smelled like her—sultry and musky—for their scents still mingled after making love through the night. How she loved him! God, that was sweet. She loved him and no longer had to deny it. She lifted her hand into the pinkish morning light to admire the ring adorning her finger, symbolizing their bond.

At last, Stephen stirred. She leaned on one elbow and kissed him. His lips intoxicated her, erased all barriers between them. They were one, and the passion started to rise.

Stephen pulled back. "I could take you again and again."

"Do," she said with a throaty laugh. "Oh yes, milord, I pray you do."

Stephen frowned and sank back onto his pillow. "First I must speak with you, Kate. I must decide Marlow's fate."

Katherine stiffened and drew back an arm's length. "What is there to discuss? You must send him to the King for punishment."

"That punishment will be death."

"And so he deserves. What other choice is there?"

"Banishment."

"Nay, Stephen, he will not stay away from the castle under banishment any longer than you did after your escape."

Stephen raised himself on one elbow and stared intently into her eyes. "Marlow could have executed me, but he did not. He could have sent an army after me the moment I escaped, but he did not. Does he not deserve the same mercy?"

"Nay," she said with a hard edge to her voice. "He would have executed you if you had given him half a chance. He is a murderer, Stephen."

"He is my brother, Kate."

Stephen rose, and in the void a cool rush of air skimmed over Katherine's naked body. She shivered and stared sullenly at his distant figure, so strikingly illuminated by the light from the farthest window—broad shoulders glimmered in a jonquil hue; ribs etched peaks and valleys in an otherwise flat torso; legs set wide made clear his rigid stance. She could hardly believe this gorgeous man was her husband, whom she loved, whom she was free to love at last. And yet marriage did not erase all barriers. He was still just as stubborn as she was. He would not hear her arguments now, and so she kept them to herself. She would broach the subject another time, when he would listen. If he would listen.

She turned to the window overhead, and realized the larks had grown silent.

Shortly before noon, Stephen and Katherine sat side by side in high-back chairs in the solar. It was a particularly warm day, even inside the castle, and no fire burned at the hearth. A breeze carried the scent of rain after a light shower. The wind billowed in gusts, and Katherine rose to partially close the windows. Her veil rippled through her hair, which hung down her back. Without the simple gold band that rested on her forehead, the gale would have sent the silk veil floating to the rush-strewn floor.

She turned with compassion to Stephen, who waited in tense anticipation for Marlow's and Rosalind's arrival. This would be the last family meeting for the Bartinghams, and though Katherine offered to leave them in privacy, Stephen insisted on having her at his side.

When Marlow entered, delivered by two tower guards, he looked haggard and distant, humbled by his fall from grace. A moment later, Rosalind arrived with the aid of a cane. She smiled weakly at Stephen and Katherine, and then frowned at Marlow, so many conflicting emotions warring in the depth of her eyes.

"Mother," Marlow croaked.

"You do not look well, my son," she said. Reaching out to caress him, she thought better of it and pulled back her bejeweled hand.

"Please sit," Stephen said in greeting. "Sit if you wish."

They did as instructed, all gathering in a circle. So much had come to pass between them all, so much sadness.

"You are looking well, Rosalind," Katherine said, breaking the silence.

The older woman smiled in gratitude. "I've been through the fires, Katherine, and still I live. 'Tis an undeserved miracle."

"Where is Robert?" Stephen asked.

Rosalind smiled again, this time with a hint of bittersweet. "I know not. He left the day you declared me innocent of all heresies."

"I see," Stephen said, thinking it ironic that the man she'd given up her reputation for should abandon her at the moment of her reprieve.

"He'd taken a fancy to a woman whose visage has not worn like a broken-in saddle," Rosalind concluded. "I do not think we'll see any more of Robert."

"Not until he goes hungry," Stephen warned.

"He stole some of my finest jewels," Rosalind said with a wave of her hand, a ruby ring jumping in the light. "I left

them out where he could take them. I knew he was anxious
to go and needed money."

"What do you wish to do now, Mother?" Stephen said.

Katherine took his hand. "You are welcome here,
Rosalind. Stay at Blackmoor if you like. We all have
much to forgive and to forget. Already the wounds heal,
I think."

"Thank you, daughter," Rosalind replied. "But I will go to
Shirewood Abbey. There I will live out my days in enough
solitude to ponder all that has come to pass."

"And as for you," Stephen said, turning to Marlow, "I
must decide your fate now, brother, for the abbot will surely
find in my favor and recommend to the King a harsh sen-
tence for you."

Marlow stared with a wild look out the window. He turned
a blank gaze to Stephen. "You were right, brother. I am a
coward. I would have turned my blade upon myself, but I
just could not do it."

"A dagger should never be turned inward, Marlow. I have
a better solution. You will be banished to the Continent,
never to return."

Katherine turned to Stephen with a sharp look, and he
responded immediately, turning to her with great love in
his eyes.

"My beloved wife would send you to your death, and I
know she is wiser than I." He turned to his brother with
an agonized look. "But you are my brother. That means
something. For that reason alone, I will ask the King's mercy
on your behalf, and I will ask the abbot to recommend the
same, though I may live to regret it."

Marlow stared at him, new clarity forming in his blood-
shot eyes. "Do what you will, but first joust with me, brother. It's been a while since we've tested our strengths, eh? If
ever you loved me, grant me this one final wish."

Stephen sat still for several minutes. Memories flashed
through his mind. Memories of gaming with Marlow when
they were young. Once, they had been innocent. Marlow

would deny that, but Stephen knew it to be true.

"Very well, Marlow. One last competition. It won't matter whether I win or lose. In all that matters, I have what I want." He smiled at Katherine and squeezed her hand, smoothing away her frown of concern with a kiss on her forehead.

"Let us go to it, then," Marlow said, a certain madness in his smile.

They wasted no time. Stephen gave orders to Geoffrey to set out the best jousting lances and armor. They would use the earthen strip just south of the castle where the knights played their war games and practiced with the quintain. The ground there was better dampened than the lists used for formal jousts.

As soon as word went out that Stephen and Marlow would compete, the castle was abuzz with speculation. Even the villeins came up from the village in droves, laying aside their work to see the match of a lifetime. Soon a crowd gathered on benches, waiting for the challenge.

In her chamber, Katherine dressed for the occasion in a red wimple, Stephen's color, though it would not be necessary to give him a favor. He knew her loyalty. Submitting to Rosemary's ministrations, she did not talk about the foolishness of the upcoming match, or her fears that Marlow would finally injure Stephen as she knew he had always hoped to. She held her tongue, though her face, knitted with concern, clearly expressed her displeasure. Europa stitched by the fire, humming a melancholy song.

When Stephen entered, the women looked up, taken aback by his imposing demeanor. A metal shell encased his chest. He tucked his helm under one arm. As he stood there encumbered in his armor and mail, his temples gleamed with perspiration. Like a wild man of the woods, his hair clung in disorder to his forehead. He was so much a man. So much the earl.

The hint of a proud smile cracked the corners of Katherine's mouth despite her anger.

"I'd have the countess on the sidelines," he said as he came to a stand but a few feet away.

Beholding his beauty, she remembered her love. "I do not know if I can watch you fight your brother."

"It is the final bout, Kate. The final healing."

Katherine twisted in her chair to regard him fully. "How can you say healing? You will fight him not one last time but one more time. He will go, and then he will return. Maybe not soon. But one day, when our sons will have to deal with him. Don't you see, Stephen? The enmity goes on and on."

Stephen waved the women away, nodding toward the door. When they left, he beheld his bride with an impatient look.

"Why must you be so stubborn?" His voice fairly boomed against the walls. "Is it not possible that I know my brother better than you? This is an important match, Kate. Even if I sent him to the King, he would still haunt our lives were it not for this final bout."

"If you sent him to the King, he would die. Then he would be out of our lives forever."

"Nay," Stephen said, shaking his head. "He will be in our hearts, gnawing away at us. We must even the score, he and I, and then it will be finished."

"A fight for honor, is that it? Men's foolish, damnable honor," she snapped at him.

Stephen blinked slowly. " 'Tis not honor. 'Tis compassion. Would you take that from me, Kate?"

She shook her head and squeezed her eyes shut.

"I will joust with my brother, Katherine, and as my wife you must accept that."

"S'Blood!" she cursed, covering her face with her hands. "You sound like my father. As your wife! As your wife must I stand by while you let yourself be killed? While you foolishly leave yourself open in the name of some misbegotten sense of fairness?"

Stephen did not answer at first. His eyes widened with sudden understanding. He came forward and gently placed his hands on her shoulders. "Are you still so afraid I will abandon you?"

She nodded her head. Tears streaked a salty path down her pale cheeks.

"You still do not know the half of me, my wife," he said, his voice low and loving. "Trust me this once. I will not be hurt. I will not leave you."

She smiled at his reassurances and wiped her tears. "I do trust you, my husband. I am learning to. I just do not want to lose you."

He leaned forward and kissed her intensely. "I love you," he whispered against her lips. "I love you, my lady love, with all my heart and soul."

"Oh, Stephen," she whispered. She pressed her wet cheeks against his hands. "I love you, too."

Of course she did, he thought with the confidence of one who is loved. Of course she loved him. He stood abruptly and cast her a mischievous smile.

"I may be around longer than you've bargained for." He started for the door, then turned and pointed a finger at her. "We will start soon, but not before I see you in the crowd."

With his hand on the door latch, he paused. "You will be there?"

She heard the need in his voice, and she smiled. "Of course, milord. Till death do us part."

Stephen exited, leaving her alone to pray her words were not an omen of early demise.

Stephen's mount clawed the earth with impatience. His destrier had borne him in many jousts. The animal knew his signals almost before they were given. For that reason, in part, this would be an easy match. But more so because Stephen had always been the better gamesman.

Pennons atop a hastily raised tent flapped in the hot breeze. Katherine stood on the sidelines, pacing nervously. Stephen waited patiently at one end while Marlow rode to the other.

Cramer and Bothwell presented his lance and shield.

This would be their last confrontation. How appropriate it should be a joust, Stephen thought, as the past and present blurred in his mind. He had always beaten Marlow at this game, and it galled his brother. Marlow was older, in many ways stronger, but he lacked the finesse Stephen possessed.

A glance to the sidelines assured Stephen Katherine was in place. All was well. He could charge Marlow one last time, giving his brother a chance to even the score, and then it would be finished. Marlow would know his life at Blackmoor had ended.

Briefly, Stephen considered the danger to himself. Only once had he been hurt falling badly after a blow. The concern flickered through his mind and melted in the noon sun.

Ramsey called the match. His voice pierced the air. Marlow and Stephen raised their lances.

Stephen lowered his armored visor. It protected his eyes, but also limited his vision, which reduced Marlow to a distant object, barely visible through the slit. No one to hate or pity, merely an opponent to cast off a horse. So often Stephen had longed for such a dispassionate bond between them. For a few moments, he could have it.

He leaned forward, gripping his horse with muscled legs, and aimed his lance at his opponent. Ramsey swung his baton downward and gave a shout. Stephen's spurs dug into his horse's flesh. Rider and beast lurched forward.

Stephen grunted with sudden determination. He would win this match. Though he wanted to give his brother some victory to assuage Marlow's wounds, Stephen knew he had to hold fast. He was the better jouster, and this object—this man approaching on a horse—was only an opponent who would soon know the strength of his blow.

That was Stephen's last clear thought. The following moments jumbled together. The gleaming sun momentarily blinded him. He lost sight of his mark. He shifted his head, avoiding the glare, but by the time he could see Marlow again, it was too late. His brother had thrown away his shield, and just as they were about to make contact, Marlow pulled off his helmet, casting aside a crucial defense. Through the narrow slit in his helmet, Stephen could see the flash of a resigned smile. Marlow lifted up his arms as if to embrace the blow.

"No!" Stephen shouted, pulling his lance away, but it was too late. Already Marlow was tangled around the pole. Stephen heard the gut wrenching sound of the lance's wooden coronal thudding against his brother's skull.

Stephen dismounted and flung his shield to the ground. Running in his cumbersome armor, he fell at his brother's side, stunned by the sight of Marlow lying in a twisted position. His hands trembled and clutched at the air. One eye was already swollen shut where the blow had landed, and blood formed a widening pool beneath his head. He was dying.

Spectators rushed forward but kept their distance. Cramer and Bothwell knelt at Marlow's feet.

"I did not want to be your murderer," Stephen whispered savagely, bending close so Marlow could hear. "I was determined not to be like you, a murderer, and now you have made me in your likeness. In the end you have the final victory."

Marlow turned his head and blinked his open eye at the sun, searching for Stephen. When he found him, he smiled. "In the end, we are all the same, Stephen. Murderer or innocent, wise man or fool. In the end we all go back to the earth, back to the worms."

"Nay, I shall not. I shall go to Heaven," Stephen persisted beyond doubt.

"Are you sure?" Marlow whispered, his voice growing weak. "Are you sure you will go to Heaven? You have killed, too."

"Not like you, Marlow. Not for the same reasons."

Marlow chuckled. "Do you think He cares what the reason is?" Marlow pointed to the sky.

Katherine moved through the crowd and knelt by Stephen. He was grateful for her presence. In her eyes, he could see Heaven regardless of what Marlow said. And with that touch of love, he was a man again, no more the frustrated younger brother.

"This is all yours now," Marlow said, eyeing them both. "I could never have given it up. This was the only way. You are free now as I never could have been. You are free."

These last words were said with such vehemence, Stephen could feel the old love between them struggling forth, gasping for air. He could feel it cut his entrails with grief he had not allowed himself to experience, even after his father's death. Sadness nearly overcame him. He could not hold back the tears that fell silently down his dusty cheeks, falling on his brother's armor.

"I loved you once," Stephen said with a croaking sound.

"I hate you," Marlow whispered. "I hate you and I love you."

Stephen nodded, their last agreement, their last understanding, and then the breath went out of Marlow. His last breath. Not a sigh, but a shudder.

No one held his hand. In the end there was no one to carry Marlow's torch into the night. And so Stephen entwined his brother's fingers with his own before they could grow cold.

EPILOGUE

✠

A week later, after Marlow was buried and Rosalind departed for the convent, after the abbot's delegation left them to start their new life at Blackmoor, Katherine and Stephen went riding alone.

They rode over the hills surrounding the castle, cherishing each other's company, treasuring the beauty of all that was theirs, all that had been won by their love.

Now and then, they glanced at each other, amazed to be together at last, in peace.

It was a dream come true, not by wishes, but by hard work, courage, risk, and tears. It was a bond forged in the hottest fires, and both rested content that theirs was a union that would last until death. Nay, beyond death.

When they reached the pinnacle of a steep hill, Stephen helped her down from her mare. Taking her hand, he led her to the highest point, from where they could see the green and gray land of England stretching for miles and miles in all its subtle glory.

Katherine breathed in the fresh, moist air. Strands of hair, whipped by the wind, covered her face, and she brushed them aside. Stephen wrapped his arms around her while they admired God's creation.

"All this is yours now, Countess," he said. His hand swept across the horizon. "Father's gift to us."

"His gift to you," Katherine said. "To you, his only son. It is what you deserve, Guy. It is what you have always deserved."

He sighed deeply. "I have thought so many times of Marlow this week passing. In the end, his death was a blessing for him. Though I resented his staining my hands with his blood, I know it is a burden I can bear. He is at peace now. And, after all, his blood is not only on my hands, it runs through my veins. We are all connected, we are all one. At least on this earthly plain. I know not what the afterlife brings."

Katherine turned to him with great compassion and wonder burning in the depths of her jade-green eyes. "You are extra-ordinary. Nor do I know what I shall see in the afterworld, save for you, my shining light."

"My shining light," he repeated, stroking her cheek.

"I am with child," she whispered.

Stephen thought it was the wind that had spoken. "What, Kate?"

"I am bearing your child." She laughed and took both his cheeks in her small hands. "Through all this darkness, a seed was planted that shall live on. It shall bear witness to our love, on and on into eternity. I am going to have our baby, Stephen."

He encompassed her with his strong arms. Burying his tearstained cheeks in the warmth of her neck, he lost himself in love. His life was complete now. It had all come full circle. From death to birth, from loneliness to love, from darkness to light.

It all was worth the living.

"I love you, Kate. There will never be a time of not loving you."

"I know," she whispered. The knowing was of faith and something greater. It sprang from love, and that was the greatest power of all.

FREE ✦

Romance

(a $4.50 value)

Send in the Coupon Below

To get your FREE historical romance and start saving, fill out the coupon below and mail it today. As soon as we receive it we'll send you your FREE Book along with your first month's selections.

Mail To: **True Value Home Subscription Services, Inc.** P.O. Box 5235
120 Brighton Road, Clifton, New Jersey 07015-5235

YES! I want to start previewing the very best historical romances being published today. Send me my FREE book along with the first month's selections. I understand that I may look them over FREE for 10 days. If I'm not absolutely delighted I may return them and owe nothing. Otherwise I will pay the low price of just $4.00 each: a total $16.00 (at *least* an $18.00 value) and save at least $2.00. Then each month I will receive four brand new novels to preview as soon as they are published for the same low price. I can always return a shipment and I may cancel this subscription at any time with no obligation to buy even a single book. In any event the FREE book is mine to keep regardless.

Name _____

Street Address _____ Apt. No. _____

City _____ State _____ Zip Code _____

Telephone _____

Signature _____
(if under 18 parent or guardian must sign)

Terms and prices subject to change. Orders subject
to acceptance by True Value Home Subscription
Services Inc.

0015-8